Under the Weeping Willow

Sheltering Trees: Book Two

Jenny Knipfer

Jenny Knipfer © 2021

JENNY'S OTHER BOOKS

BY THE LIGHT OF THE MOON SERIES:
Ruby Moon
Blue Moon
Silver Moon
Harvest Moon

SHELTERING TREES SERIES:
In a Grove of Maples

For Dad, who passed from Alzheimer's in 2010,
and for all those who have suffered from depression.

Praise for the
By the Light of the Moon series

"Readers who love being trapped in a character's mind should relish this finely written, gripping series. A must read for fans of historical fiction." The Prairies Book Review

Ruby Moon

"This novel is filled with drama and a writing style that is insightful. From the beginning, the author creates a sense of mystery, capturing sensations in a style that defies perception." Readers' Favorite, five-star review

"Knipfer's characterization is stellar in this novel, and she skillfully ties in the themes of faith, forgiveness, and trust." Wisconsin Writers Association

"Ruby Moon is the type of book that hooks you from page one... and has you quickly turning the pages to discover more." Ya It's Lit Blog

"The prose is just beautiful with a lyricism that ebbs and flows perfectly. I love a story that sounds to me like a song." Jypsy Lynn

"Jenny is a talented wordsmith who knows how to be creative and brazen with her thoughts and think outside of the box. I adore how Jenny took risks with Ruby Moon and decided to put a twist on a much-loved genre..." The Red Headed Book Lover

"It does not always happen but when it does it feels miraculous. I'm talking about when you read a book and you are immersed in it. I started to read the first page… and when I got to the last page, I closed the book and held it to my heart." Linda McCutcheon, book blogger and reviewer

Blue Moon

"Knipfer creates a strong sense of place, and she draws on her own experience with MS to depict the course of Valerie's illness with great sensitivity." Wisconsin Writers Association

"Blue Moon continues a well-written and highly engaging saga of family ties, betrayals, and heartaches. A must-read for historical drama fans everywhere." Readers' Favorite, five-star review

"In Blue Moon, the author tells a breathtaking story of twins Vanessa and Valerie. Page after page, the author masterfully weaves other exciting characters into the story…" Ksenia Sein, author of Agape & Ares

"Knipfer continues to welcome her readers into Webaashi Bay… back into the town and characters we fell in love with… For in this book, Knipfer has woven an entrancing tale we all need to hear." Amazon reviewer

Silver Moon

"Silver Moon is a highly recommended read for fans of historical wartime fiction, powerful emotive drama, and excellent atmospheric writing." Readers' Favorite, five-star review

"I am stunned by the amount of detail the author gave in this single story. On one hand, we have powerful characters... and on the other, we have a plot that demands all our attention. Jenny Knipfer pulls no punches and holds nothing back." Readers' Favorite, five-star review

"This story felt comfortable for a first-time reader to the author, more like being welcomed by new friends. The setting, a time of need, camaraderie and survival, brings the large cast and reader together. Ultimately, Silver Moon *is a story of forgiveness, second chances, prayer and patience."* Wisconsin Writers Association

"Silver Moon is very highly recommended for readers who want a compelling inspection of love, duty, and battle based on historical fact, but flavored with the struggles of very different characters intent on not just surviving but creating a better future for themselves." D. Donovan, Midwest Book Review

"Taking an original angle on a tumultuous time in history, Silver Moon *by Jenny Knipfer is a sparkling slice of historical fiction. Rather than focusing solely on the violence of this tragic conflict, Knipfer fleshes out the complexity of wartime... a thought-provoking and surprising work of historical escapism."* Self-Publishing Review

"Not a light-hearted read, this book will engulf your senses, evoking the deepest and highest of emotions as you cheer and cry for the survival of dearly loved characters." Kathryn V. Goodreads review

Harvest Moon

"As in her prior books, Jenny Knipfer does an outstanding job of cementing place, time, and culture against the backdrop of evolving relationships. These approaches lend a solid feel of authenticity and attraction to her plot to keep readers both educated and engrossed, as spiritual and social matters evolve." D. Donovan, Midwest Book Review

"Wielding descriptive language and unexpected imagery, this narrative transports a reader with ease. Harvest Moon is a moving, authentic, and original work of historical fiction, while this series is a testament to Knipfer's skilled and versatile storytelling." Self-Publishing Review

"Harvest Moon by Jenny Knipfer is one of the best books I have read in 2020. In fact, it is probably one of the best historical fiction novels I have ever read. I have come away deep in thought, feeling somewhat like I've had a mystical experience and one I will never forget." Viga Boland, Readers' Favorite, five-star review

"The author created the perfect atmosphere for her story to truly bloom and progress. I would highly recommend this historical fiction novel to anyone who loves reading stories with intricate plots and powerful characters." Rabina Tanveer, Readers' Favorite, five-star review

"Knipfer creates her characters with so much emotion and physical presence that they become almost real in the imagination. A captivating and evocative novel of the importance of family, faith, and forgiveness and how, together, those things help heal a broken heart." Gloria Bartel, Wisconsin Writers Association

"It is also a powerful story of strength and survival and of love and forgiveness. A memorable read." *New York Times* Bestselling Author Lorena McCourtney

"Harvest Moon is a gripping story told through flashbacks and a split timeline. Knipfer is quite skilled at creating lively characters that drew me right in." Regina Walker, author of *We Go On* and *Still With Us*

Praise for the *Sheltering Trees* series

In a Grove of Maples

"… a heartfelt tale of the struggles of married life on a nineteenth-century farm. Edward and Beryl are both relatable and sympathetic. Knipfer expertly captures the emotion and stress of their lives and relationship. It's a touching and realistic portrayal of love, loss, and friendship." Heather Stockard, Readers' Favorite, five-star review

"Dramatic character development and lavish descriptive language make Knipfer's prose shine and carry this emotionally stirring plot from start to finish. The storytelling is casual but unmistakably

aged, and the research into this particular time period is remarkable, while the variation in narrative format keeps the story engaging throughout." Self-Publishing Review

"Readers of women's fiction and Christian historical romance will find In a Grove of Maples an engrossing story of 19th century rural life that examines matters of heart, ethics, morality, and belief as Beryl faces a new world with few resources other than her faith and love. It concludes with an unexpected twist that comes full circle to leave the door open for more." D. Donavon, Midwest Book Review

Under the Weeping Willow

"A heart-rending, emotionally packed love story between a mother and daughter, Under the Weeping Willow is a journey of loss and brokenness coupled with forgiveness and healing. This time-split novel captured my heart and didn't release it until the final page. Beautiful and haunting, Robin and Enid's story swept me to another era. These characters lived, and I loved watching them find their way to each other. Keep the tissues handy. You don't want to miss this story!" Candace West, Selah award finalist and author of the Valley Creek Redemption series

Weeping may endure for a night,
But joy comes in the morning.
Psalm 30:5b

Isn't that all that we are—memories?

CHAPTER ONE

Enid
June 1983

I rub my hand over my mother's words. My throat clenches, and I hiccup, forcing back a sob. A tear lands on the lined page of the diary with a splat. The word "willow" starts to bleed with the moisture. I read through the entry once more.

April 10th, 1977
Dear Diary,
I put the silverware in the breadbox today. I don't know why. I went to pull a loaf of bread out of the red, tin box to make a sandwich, and instead I pulled out a fork. I haven't found the bread yet.

Yesterday, I couldn't recall my phone number, when asked to give it over the phone to the clinic scheduler. Nothing appeared in my mind when I tried to imagine it. I could pull no number out of my magical memory hat. I had to read the number off the label under the receiver cradle. After about an hour, the number suddenly came to me, like I'd been hit with it. Did my memory go on vacation for an hour?

I have been noticing these strange things recently. It frightens me. It's as if someone else has done these things. I don't remember moving the bread at all. I try, but only a black hole appears in my mind when I do. That emptiness slowly sucks at me, like a vacuum. One day I fear there may be nothing left to remember.

Maybe I'm going crazy, but I swore I'd never go there again. I see the edge of the pond and feel the dangling willow branches tangle in my hair as if it were yesterday. The water pulls at me like Velcro, clinging, drawing me in. Why can I remember that from so many years ago and not where I put the bread today? I know one thing: They will not put me in an asylum for the mentally deranged. Not again.

I lift my eyes from the diary and look out the window in the sitting room. The willow tree still stands watching over the pond despite having battled several storms and suffering lost limbs. I whiled away many a summer day under its canopy of hanging branches. Mom didn't like me playing by the willow, and she hated the pond. She was always after Uncle Hal to drain it. I never knew why.

The ink smudges as I swipe at the damp spot on the page of Mom's diary, and I try to comprehend the words. *Crazy... asylum?* What could she possibly mean?

I swallow the lump in my throat and try not to be overburdened by guilt.

This was Mom's first full week in the Dunn County Nursing Health Care Center, a glorified name for a nursing home. I hate that I had to admit her, but she'll be safe. They won't treat her like a crazy person. Will they? No, dementia is different. Well, Alzheimer's the doctor called it. The staff are professionals and can care for her better.

I groan and swipe at my eyes. I can tell myself any number of things to justify my mother being tucked away like an old rag doll, but at the bottom of the justification lies the fact that I am the one who brought her there.

I sigh and close the diary, placing it back by her wingback recliner. We can't have a repeat of this last winter. The neighbor had caught her bewildered and walking down the road in the middle of January with no coat on. She could have died.

"Enie! Where are you?"

"In here!" I shout at my husband, Clive.

I hear his footsteps and in seconds he rounds the corner of the old farmhouse kitchen and stands in the large opening to the sitting room. I sit up straighter in Mom's gold, velvet, upholstered recliner. Too bad there wasn't room for her chair at the nursing home.

"Thought I'd stop by and see if you need some help."

His solid, brown eyes hold sympathy. He leans against the wood trim accenting the doorway. His slouchy shirt and Levi's give him a relaxed appearance. A smile warms his face. He knows how hard it's been for me, moving Mom. I smile the best I can in return, studying his familiar, unconventionally handsome face.

Clive's eyes are evenly spaced under contained brows of the same shade, but his face is rather full. I suppose some would call him pudgy, but I like that he's not skin and bones. He's stocky and thick. Reliable.

"No. Just collecting a few trinkets to add to Mom's room to make it feel homey."

I hide the journal in the cleft of the chair cushion. I don't want to talk to Clive about what I've found. Not yet anyway. I shouldn't even be reading her private diaries, but I can't help it. I would have found and read them one day, after she passed. Why is now so different? She's as good as gone. Her memories have flown away, and isn't that all that we are—memories?

"All right then." He steps closer and leans down, kissing me on the cheek. The stubble shading his jawline scratches me. "Hey." His eyes sparkle at me. He hovers inches from my face. "How 'bout we hit the A&W tonight in Menomonie. We could take our food to the park and eat. Just you and me."

He kisses the tip of my nose.

I push my brown, owl-like glasses farther up my nose and gently push him back so I can stand. "Weren't the kids supposed to come over tonight?"

"Na, Kelly called the shop and canceled. Said the twins are sick."

"Sick? Well, why didn't he call me?"

I wonder what has my thirteen-year-old twin grandchildren, Penny and Pamela, under the weather.

Clive stands up straight and digs in the pocket of his jeans. "Well, you were here, Enid. The phone's been shut off. Remember?"

I sigh. "Oh, right."

He dangles a set of keys at me. "Take the truck. I'll grab your car and do an oil change today before I come home. Then we'll go grab some food."

I take the keys. "It's a date."

Clive kisses me again and starts to head out. "Keys in the Buick?"

"Yep."

"See ya later."

He whistles as he leaves. I hear the screen door slam and

soon the car starts. The Skylark has a whine, which has been getting noticeably louder the last few days. Whatever it is, Clive will fix it. It's his job. He worked at his dad's garage before he set up his own, shortly after we married in 1945. He didn't fight in the war due to the hearing loss in his right ear.

I watch out the window as he leaves. I can hardly believe we are in our sixth decade. It seems like yesterday we were kids, but now we have grandkids. Where does the time go?

I head back to Mom's chair and dig out the diary. I replace it next to the stack of others in her rolltop desk. I'll save them for another time. I've read all I can handle at the moment. I grab the tote of newspaper-wrapped knickknacks and head out, locking the door behind me.

An idea settles in my brain as I hop in Clive's black '67 Dodge with red and white pinstripes along the side. The engine rattles in a good way as it comes to life. On Monday I'm going to head to the library and look up where there would have been a sanitarium or mental hospital around here. I don't remember one, and I certainly don't remember Mom being in one, so it had to be before I was born or when I was too young to remember. Places like that must keep records.

I expect my heart to lighten with a goal in mind, but the ache in my chest is as heavy and cloudy as the dust trail from the gravel driveway that I'm kicking up behind the Dodge. I cough and roll up the windows and turn onto county highway E to head into town.

Near the edge of the pond stood the grandest tree
Robin had ever seen...

CHAPTER TWO

Robin
April 1917
Sixty-six years prior
Rural Colfax in Dunn County, Wisconsin

Robin ran her hand through the willow's weeping boughs. It felt like running her hand through a curtain of beads. She had done that once at the county fair back home. A gypsy fortune teller had come and set up a tent with a curtain of dark beads for a door.

Her mother had almost skinned her hide for wasting a nickel on "such foolishness," but Robin had not cared.

That was the day she had met Willis Holcombe—tall, handsome, and well-mannered. Just as the gypsy had predicted. Oh, Robin knew the old crone had probably said those words to every young lady who entered her tent on that steamy July night, but for Robin it had come true.

"Making a friend?"

Robin sucked in a breath and almost choked. "Crimminy, Willis—you scared me!" She widened her eyes at her husband

and shook her head. "Yes, I suppose. You know how I like trees. Maybe growing up with so many trees around me has grown that fondness in me."

"I didn't mean to frighten you." Willis shrugged his broad shoulders and looked innocent. His deep-set, brown eyes twinkled at her in amusement. "Didn't you hear me?"

"Lost in thought, I guess." Robin leaned against the thick base of the willow's trunk and gazed out over the serene pond. "I'm remembering how we met, if you must know."

She aimed a sideways glint in his direction.

"You mean how you spilled your soda down the front of my shirt?"

Willis leaned against the tree with one hand and hovered over her. The smell of his aftershave, spicy and deep, made Robin's heart beat faster.

Robin met his warm, brown eyes and melted into their depths. "There was that. But what was a girl to do?" She grinned coyly up at him. "I had to get your attention somehow." She puckered her lips.

"You succeeded."

Willis placed a kiss on Robin's waiting lips. He brought his arms around her waist and pulled her to him. Robin relished the kisses her husband gave her. His soft, warm lips on hers sent her head spinning. He caught her lips between his in teasing, slow, and easy kisses, which tasted of something more.

Only one month ago, they had married. Robin would never have thought she would move so far from home—across the state of Wisconsin from Maple Grove to Colfax—but she had. She had exchanged one rural community for another. Robin had gone where Willis had led.

They had lived with Willis's folks for several weeks after the wedding, but then a letter had come for Willis from his uncle, Halifax Holcomb (his dad's brother), asking if Willis would be interested in learning farming. Apparently, Halifax and his wife, Marge, only had two daughters, and neither of them had married men who wanted to delve into the rural life. The years had advanced, and Halifax had looked for a successor, and Willis had taken the offer.

Willis let Robin breathe. "Still glad we came?"

A smooth, serious expression accompanied his question. His eyes searched hers. Robin reached her fingers up to his jawline and traced his clean-shaven, chiseled, muscular face.

"Of course. I love your aunt and uncle, and the farm is beautiful." Robin turned to look off to the north. The rambling, white farmhouse and red barn sat nestled in the shadow of hills covered with deciduous trees starting to leaf out. Greening pastures off to the left and right of the house were dotted with Holsteins. A ring of yellow and red tulips brightened the brown flowerbeds skirting the house. In front of the house, a long drive led to the county highway. In between the house and the road lay an expanse of lawn and a large pond. A clutch of chickens clucked and pecked in the spring-green grass. Near the edge of the pond stood the grandest tree Robin had ever seen, the large weeping willow she leaned against. Its branches hung over the water like a woman hanging her long hair over a washbasin. All together, the scene painted a perfect image of country living.

Just then, a clanking sound echoed.

Willis turned his head toward the house. "Must be Aunt Marge calling us in for dinner." He let Robin go and took her hand. "Come on, wife of mine."

He helped her up the slightly banked edge of the pond and

dropped her hand, giving her a wink.

"Race you!" he shouted, and he took off like a shot with a whoop and holler, his long, lean legs putting some distance between them.

Robin hesitated but a second before sprinting after him. Her Mary-Jane-style heels dug into the grass.

"Willis Holcomb, you're gonna eat my dust!" she shouted back.

They ran like children back to the house. Willis probably would have beaten her, but he tripped over a stone. He fell, and to Robin, it looked like he grubbed up the knees of his pants on the gravel driveway. He recovered quickly, and she reached the side doorstep a few seconds before he did. Marge had watched the race.

She looked up at them from her short but plump frame. "Still kids at heart, I see."

She smiled, and her wrinkles smiled with her as she spread her petite mouth wide. Her graying brown hair was gathered in a bun on the top of her head. Blue eyes, a little too close together and the color of blueberries, centered her oval face, along with a narrow nose with a slight bulge at the end. Skin the color of toasted almonds covered her features.

"Always," Willis claimed. He bent over, taking a deep breath. "You're faster than you look. Have pity and don't rub it in."

"I wouldn't dream of proclaiming that—*I won*." Robin said the words in a loud voice. She tipped her chin up and peered down her nose at her husband, but then she burst out laughing. "Your sad puppy-dog face. Oh…" She kissed him on the cheek and whispered in his ear for the sake of his pride. "You would have won, if you hadn't stumbled over your two left feet."

"Why you…"

He reached out, but she slipped away from his grasp and ran laughing into the house.

"You might have your hands full with that one," Marge commented in her dry, even tone before Robin let the screen door slam behind her.

"That's what I'm hoping," Willis answered.

Robin smiled to herself as she rounded a corner into the kitchen. *And I'll give you plenty to hang on to.* She determined to always be one step ahead of her husband. Oh, she didn't need to win or be first in every effort, but she knew Willis was the kind of man who needed something to chase. Robin wanted it to be her.

Later that day

Willis leaned his head against the large, spotted, black and white, dairy cow and looked deep in thought. Robin liked to think they had acclimated to the farming life well. It sat right with her. She knew Willis enjoyed the hard work and being outdoors. Uncle Hal met each day with an easy-going spirit. She found him to be a kind man, not unlike her father and Willis's. Robin gazed at her husband cramped up against the cow's side and wondered if he missed his father, but the shop life had never appealed to Willis: dealing with customers, keeping track of inventory, and tallying accounts. He had not cared for any of it.

His folks had been disappointed when he'd agreed to his Uncle Hal's proposition but not angry. It had seemed his folks wanted them to be content, so Mr. and Mrs. Holcomb had not stood in their way.

Willis finished milking and patted the cow on her bony hip. "Good girl."

She uttered a low "Moo" in response. He stood up and straightened, stiffly.

Probably has kinks in his back, Robin thought.

He lifted the bucket of milk up by the handle. The frothy, white liquid sloshed slightly as he carried it to the end of the row of cows where one of the large, hip-high, ten-gallon, metal cans stood. He removed the cover and poured the milk in slowly through a strainer. He set the empty bucket down and capped the can again.

They had finished the late-afternoon milking, so he and Robin each took a handle on either side of the can and brought it to the milkhouse, where it would be kept on ice until they could deliver it to the creamery after the next morning's milking.

Halifax stood in the milkhouse, peering at the store of cans. "Thank you, Son."

He had taken to calling Willis "Son," and Willis didn't appear to mind the term of endearment.

Hal tipped his hat at Robin. "And you too, Missy."

She smiled.

"That's what I'm here for." Willis gave a nod to the older man and winked at Robin. "Well, we."

Halifax—though in his fifties—cut a strong, manly figure. His biceps were as large as Willis's and his middle as lean. Steel-blue eyes behind horn-rimmed glasses would have made for the most prominent feature on his face, if it wasn't for his broken nose. His long nose had a bump in the middle and tweaked slightly off to his left. Boot-black hair peppered with gray peeked out from underneath his striped engineer's hat. Robin had hardly ever seen Willis's uncle without his hat, but when she had, she'd spied the large comb-over Hal had on the top of his head. Underneath, a shiny bald spot had begun to form.

Halifax pulled up the shoulder strap on his overalls "Almost time for supper, I reckon."

He yanked his hankie out of his pocket, cleared his throat, and blew his nose into the piece of blue fabric, as if blowing on a horn.

"I'll scrub up and meet you in the house," Willis offered.

"I've left Marge doing all the work," Robin said.

She groaned inwardly. She liked sharing the milking with the men, but she loved being in the kitchen with Marge. It reminded her of cooking with her mom.

"Oh, she can manage," Hal said to Robin. He stuffed his hankie back where it had been and turned to leave the barn, but he paused. "It's right good to have you here, Willis, and you, too, Robin."

He turned enough as he said it to look Willis in the eye.

"Right good to be here," Willis acknowledged.

Halifax turned and resumed his lazy, loped stride. Willis and Robin scrubbed the buckets and their hands, saw to it all the cows had feed, and shut up the barn doors. Robin walked with her husband back to the house.

"Smells like Marge has made your favorite," Robin told him when they got nearer.

She smiled at him. She tucked a few stray hairs into her rolled, light brown hair, nestled around the base of her head. Frizzy, wavy strands had curled loosely around her face while she had milked.

Willis touched her face and looked her over. "Your jaw is like your father's. It's the only piece of you inside or out that has a sharpness to it." He touched a frizzy hair she'd missed. "I love you, Robin Holcomb. Is Aunt Marge serving up a plate of you this evening?"

She rolled her eyes. "No, silly. Smells like apple pie."

Willis took a big sniff and helped Robin up. "Sure enough."

He placed a quick kiss on her lips before they headed in.

Robin's heart felt content. She had a handsome husband, who showed himself to be content with farming, a peaceful setting in which to live, and kind people who cared about them as family. *What more could we possibly want?* It would be fine with Robin if life rolled along just as it was. She could picture it: a couple of children, maybe a dog, their own house.

Willis placed one arm tightly around her as they stepped into the farmhouse. From somewhere, the smell of plum blossoms wafted to Robin's nose and perfumed the air.

Early May 1917

Robin had hoped it would happen, but not this soon. She was pregnant. At least, she thought so. She had skipped her monthly and had always been regular. *A baby!* The coming of a child gave her deep joy and rounded out their life on the farm.

Every week that she and Willis had been with Hal and Marge, Robin had grown fonder of them. They were kind, even of temper, and large-hearted.

Robin's stomach fluttered as she thought about the Holcombs' daughters, whom she would meet today. Marge had invited them and their husbands for Sunday dinner: roast chicken, mashed potatoes, and canned corn. One daughter, Lynette, had a little girl and another baby on the way. Susan, the youngest and closer to Robin's age, was married but had no children yet. *Will they be as nice as their folks?* Robin had to think something of Hal and Marge must have been passed down to their girls.

Robin tied a heather-blue scarf, which matched her dress,

around her head and tucked the tails along the bottom of her roll of hair. Surveying herself in the mirror, she wondered what short hair would be like. She turned her head from side to side. A jaw-length bob might suit her. Her mother would most likely be scandalized if Robin chopped her hair off, but her mother lived miles away now. *As a married woman, I ought to be able to make changes, if I like.* But the risk of disappointing her mother, Beryl Massart, still bit at her conscience. Pleasing people was important to Robin.

The bedroom door opened.

Willis placed a light kiss on her cheek and wrapped his arms around her middle from behind. "All set? What's taking so long? Marge wants your help setting out the food. The family just rolled in."

"I'm finished."

They smiled at each other in the mirror. Willis squeezed her tight, then let her go.

He stepped back and gestured with his arm. "After you."

Robin giggled; she liked his theatrical antics. "I thank you."

She rolled the words off her tongue in a regal fashion and walked down the hall to the steps. Willis stayed close on her heels and tickled her sides as she was about to go down them.

The narrow stairwell trapped Robin, and she writhed under his fingers. "Ahhh!"

She squeaked, wiggled, and broke free, dashing down the stairs.

"Excuse me!"

A thin, pointy-nosed, young woman with brown, curly hair tucked in a low coil narrowed her eyes and righted herself after Robin slammed into her.

Robin had not seen her. "Oh, my gosh. I'm so sorry."

She sobered. *Great! So much for first impressions.*

Marge poked her head around the corner of the kitchen. "Oh, good. I see you two have met."

She held a covered dish of something in her hands.

"Well, actually, no." Robin held out her hand to the woman. "I'm Robin and," she turned and touched Willis's chest, "this is Willis."

The woman held herself stiff and straight. "So I gathered."

"Come now, Susan. Say hello to our boarders and fellow laborers." Marge shook her head from side to side in an exasperated way. With the wooden floor creaking, she walked to the dining table and set the dish down in the middle of the flowered tablecloth covering the table. "Don't mind Susan. She can be as stiff as new shoe leather."

Susan rolled her eyes. "Thanks, Mom." To Robin and Willis, she said, "Hello."

"Howdy do," Willis replied in his friendly manner.

Susan looked at Willis in acknowledgment for a second with a straight face and nodded before walking into the kitchen.

Willis and Robin looked at each other and silently shrugged their shoulders in tandem. Robin heard more people coming in behind them and turned to see who. Two men and a pregnant woman stepped into the house, talking to each other. One of the men, tall and blond, held an adorable little girl around two years of age in his arms, her blue eyes big and round as marbles. Robin wouldn't have called him handsome, but his face appealed to her. His forehead sloped in too broad a way, and he wore a line of small, round scars along one side of his jawline. But his eyes were kind. When he smiled, slight wrinkles formed around the edges.

The shorter, dark-haired man spoke. "I don't think that's the way it's going to be."

Robin would have called him swarthy. *Maybe he's Italian?* He definitely looked like he hailed from somewhere in the Mediterranean.

"America will be just around the corner. You wait and see."

Their conversation stopped when they saw Robin and Willis. The woman stepped forward with a hand on her back, apparently in some discomfort. The bulge of her middle pushed out the dotted pattern of her green dress.

"You must be Robin and Willis," she said. "Dad has been telling us so much about you."

Her eyes focused on Robin. *The same color as her dress.*

Willis curled his arm around Robin's shoulder. "Yes, that's us."

"I'm Lynette." She smiled, reflecting her mother's features. "This is my husband, Derek." She pointed to the tall blond. "And Susan's husband, Thomas. We all call him Tom."

The short, dark-haired man sent a toothy smile Robin's way.

"Pleased to meet you," both men uttered.

The men continued talking of the war and Willis joined in while Robin and Lynette went to the kitchen. Susan placed a blue, enamel pot of coffee on the table and sat down next to Hal.

Marge stuck a serving spoon in the massive bowl of mashed potatoes on the table then sat down on the other side of Hal. "Sit down where you like."

She patted at her brow with her red-checked apron. Tom sat next to his wife, and Lynette and Derek next to them. Their daughter—whose name Marge had told Robin was Cassandra—sat on a chair stacked with several books. Derek loosely tied a flour sack dishcloth around her middle and through the slats of the chair. Cassandra didn't protest.

"Say grace," Marge prompted Hal, with a squeeze of his hand.

He nodded and bowed his head. Everyone else did likewise.

"Our Father make us truly grateful for your provision. We thank you for this food and the company. Amen."

His words were simple but sincere. After the passing of food, the conversation started.

"How are you finding Dunn County compared to home?" Lynette asked in between bites. She ate like a hungry farmhand.

Willis caught Robin's eye and squeezed her hand. "We're happy here. It's beautiful with the rolling hills. Out home the land is fairly flat. Robin's family lives on top of the only hill for miles around."

"Does your family farm, Robin?" Derek asked.

He fed small portions of food to Cassandra. It warmed Robin's heart to see how tender he was with his daughter. She hoped Willis would be the same way. She ventured a look at him. *When should I tell him?* It should be special. She'd have to think of just the right thing.

Finally, she answered Derek. "Yes. They came from Quebec in the late '90s. The farm was only forty acres of tilled land when they bought it, but now Dad's cleared another forty."

"From what you've told me, he's a good farmer and a good man," Hal commented.

Behind his glasses, Hal's sharp, blue eyes spoke the truth of his conviction. He forked in a chunk of chicken.

"Yes," Robin agreed.

She loved her father. He worked hard and had expected her and her siblings to as well. He could be ornery at times, but she loved him all the same. She would call him steady, faithful, caring, but not magnanimous in his affection. He showed his care rather than spoke it. The time he had fixed Robin's doll with the broken arm had told her of his love for her, as did countless other little things.

Cassandra spoke through a full mouth and pointed to the plate of sliced bread. "Mama, some?"

"Yes, I'll butter you a piece." Lynette obliged her daughter. "Any jam to put on this, Mom?"

"Why, yes. I don't know why I didn't think of that."

Marge started to get up, but Susan stood and stopped her.

She sent a faint smile her mother's way, and her pinched look evened out. "I'll get it."

A daughter who is kind to her mother can't be all bad, Robin determined.

"The pantry?" Susan asked.

"Yes. Got one jar of strawberry rhubarb yet." Marge smiled widely. "Thank you, dear."

Susan went to find the jam.

Tom leveled his deep brown eyes at Halifax over the rim of his coffee cup. "They are getting hit hard over there. Think there will be a draft, Hal?"

His face hinted at a five o'clock shadow of dark hair, but it was only noon.

"Well. Can't say as I reckon one way or t'other. Seems like we'd be sticking our noses where we don't belong. But then again, we have to answer the plea for help. What kinda folks would it make us if we didn't?"

That was about as long a response as Robin had ever heard from Hal.

"We certainly can't let one country take over the world. And the way they are fighting. It's criminal." Willis laid his fork down. A deep furrow lined his forehead. "With the gas and all."

The men shook their heads in what looked like agreeing silence. The thought of Willis overseas fighting in a bombed and gas-ridden country pained Robin, especially now with the thought of a baby coming.

Susan arrived back with the jam and handed the diamond-patterned jelly jar to her sister.

"Thanks. You're a gem," Lynette responded warmly, but Susan only reciprocated with a nod.

Her stare bounced to Robin, who dropped her gaze to her plate and focused on her food. Robin had guessed that Susan might be prone to a naturally stiff demeanor—from Marge's previous comment—but she couldn't miss the glare in Susan's eyes, like she held some personal vendetta against Robin. Robin couldn't figure out what it would be; after all, she had just met the woman.

Robin listened with one ear while the men talked about war. With the other, she listened to Marge and her daughters discussing old family recipes, the way Cassandra was growing out of her clothes, and the latest women's auxiliary meeting.

"Now, Robin. You will have to attend with us next month," Lynette said.

She laid down her fork and took a large drink of milk. When she pulled the glass away from her mouth, a thin, frothy, white line clung to her modest upper lip.

"Moose-tash," Cassandra muttered.

She giggled and pointed at her mother's white, milk mustache.

Derek grinned at his wife from across the table. "We might need to get you a mustache mug."

Lynette rolled her eyes before wiping off the milk with her napkin. "Ha, ha. Very funny."

Tom looked Derek's way and tipped his head with a chuckle. "She had a fuller mustache than you can grow."

Robin studied Derek's face; no hint of facial hair showed.

Derek shrugged his shoulders and gave a sideways smirk. "Must be the Indian side of me coming through."

Robin inspected his features again. His coloring certainly wasn't native, with his pale hair, skin tone, and eyes. The shape of his face, however…

Yes, the high cheekbones and long, broad nose. She could see it.

"And I wouldn't have it any other way." Lynette leaned over and kissed her husband on the cheek. "Now, about the women's meetings."

Robin listened to Lynette and Marge talking about the local women's group, while trying to keep tabs on what the men discussed. They had all finished with the meal and lingered over cups of coffee and bread pudding.

"Mighty fine, Margie," Hal said before feeding his mouth a large spoonful of pudding with caramel sauce.

"Same as always," Marge commented. "Didn't do anything special. But I do know you're partial to it."

Marge turned her hazel eyes on her husband with a look of love: warm, knowing, and real. It made Robin desire that kind of bond with Willis.

"I 'spect you know what I like by now after…" Hal twisted his mouth up and appeared to be inwardly calculating, "oh, forty some years."

"Forty-two," Marge clarified.

Lynette took a drink of coffee and eyed her sister. "For your forty-fifth, Sue and I will have to throw you two an anniversary party."

"A party?" Sue's eyes widened. "That's about the time Dad will be retired. Right, Dad? We could celebrate both events."

She turned to Hal with one serious, raised eyebrow.

"Well...I haven't decided anything as of yet." Hal gave a noncommittal shrug and gobbled down his last bit of pudding.

Tom grinned. "Ha, they'll have to pry your hands off the stanchions."

Robin thought Tom fit the role of the joker in the group. He smiled and laughed about as much as his wife frowned.

"What will happen to the farm when you do retire?" Susan said in a clear voice.

Robin noticed how she narrowed her eyes at Willis before focusing on her father once more.

Marge scooted her chair back and stood up, starting to collect the dirty dishes. "Now that's something best discussed at another time."

Lynette got up too. "I'll help. I'll get the wash water ready. But just so you know," she placed a hand on her belly, "we're having a party for you. No if, ands, or buts."

Hal stood and paused to kiss Marge on the cheek before he stepped toward the sitting room. "I think I hear my chair calling my name."

Derek freed Cassandra from her chair. The little girl toddled after her grandfather. Derek followed. Tom helped Marge carry some dishes to the sink. That left Robin and Susan at the table alone.

Robin wanted desperately to ask the woman outright what she held against them, but she didn't dare. They stared at one another. Finally, Robin turned away and made to get up.

"No. Don't concern yourself. You're a *guest*." Susan stood and walked quickly away toward Lynette at the sink.

The warm family atmosphere had turned stale. Robin got up. Since Susan had dismissed her, she went to see what the men were up to in the sitting room. The clink of dishes and voices faded as she walked away. She tried not to let the sting of Susan's sharp words upset her, but they had made her feel unwelcome.

"What did Goldilocks do?" Cassandra asked Hal with eyes as big as saucers.

She sat in Hal's lap while he told her a story. It sounded like *The Three Bears*. Derek sat in another armchair, smiling at his daughter and father-in-law. Robin eased herself down on the settee.

She spoke quietly. "He has a way with little ones it seems."

"Yes. Lynette has fond memories of Hal telling her stories. Underneath the farmer's cap, a deep-hearted and thinking man resides."

Robin nodded in agreement. She had to ask, and Derek's soft words and kind smile gave her courage.

She leaned forward and practically whispered, "What will happen to the farm when Hal retires?"

Derek shook his head once and whispered back, "Don't know for sure, but I'm guessing they'll sell." He looked directly at her. "As much as Lynette loves her folks, neither of us wants to be tied to the farm. I don't think Sue and Tom would be interested either. To be frank, I thought that was why you and Willis came out here. Didn't Hal talk to you about taking over when he's done?"

Derek's light eyebrows scrunched down slightly.

"Well, yes. In a way. He wrote Willis's father asking for help with the farm. It was understood that it might be grooming for something more."

Derek nodded. "I see. You know…"

He didn't get to finish. Willis came and hooked his arms around Robin's neck from behind.

Robin's heart beat faster. "Oh. My, you scared me."

She placed her hands in his. He walked around her and sat down.

"Where were you?" she asked.

"Checking on a calf. Hal was concerned. The calf hasn't been eating well enough." Willis smiled at her then looked at Derek. "Discussing something interesting?"

Robin's gaze flicked to Derek's face. She pled silently with him to keep their conversation confidential.

"Oh, farming. How's the calf doing?" was all Derek said.

While Willis and Derek talked about farming and cattle, Robin thought about what it would be like to own Willow Farm. She certainly didn't want to usurp Susan and Lynette's inheritance, but it appeared like neither of them wanted the place. *Why cause a stink then?* Robin couldn't figure it out, but deep down she knew she'd find out from Susan at some point. It would undoubtedly be uncomfortable.

And so begins the pain of not being remembered.

CHAPTER THREE

Enid
August 1983

"How is she today?"

I direct my question to the CNA, who has stepped out of Mom's room. The nursing assistant looks tired. Sweat glistens on her brow, and her shoulders are slumped.

She smiles, wearily. "Well…" Rhonda—her name tag tells me—leaves her answer open-ended. The shoulders of her bright, butterfly-patterned uniform top hitch up for a second. "Every day is different." She looks back toward the room. "She's dressed and had her breakfast."

A call light flashes above the door down the nursing home hall. It beeps loudly with each flash.

"Excuse me." Rhonda ducks her head and hurries toward the room of the resident who needs attention.

I take a deep breath through my nose; the air smells faintly of reheated food and urine. I force my sneaker-covered feet into Mom's room. It's not that I don't want to see her; it's just that I know it will hurt.

She's on the edge of the bed looking out the window, which

faces a cluster of bird feeders amongst some hydrangea bushes. From the back she looks the same: composed. She wears a blue, floral blouse and polyester slacks; her small shoulders slope down. Mousy-gray hair styled in her usual short, jaw-length bob graces her head.

I walk closer and carefully touch her shoulder. "Mom?"

She turns her head and looks up at me. "Who are you?"

Her thin brows pucker. Her once pretty, oval face is shrouded in leathery wrinkles, a product of too many days in the sun. I look like her, except without the deep wrinkles, although my face is starting to show the passage of time.

And so begins the pain of not being remembered.

I lower myself onto a rust, vinyl-covered chair by the window. "It's Enid, Mom. Remember? Your daughter."

Her wrinkles deepen around her eyes, and she squints through her round glasses framed in pearl-pink plastic. "Who?"

"Never mind."

I pick up a photo of her and me from the bureau. We each smile widely in the picture with our heads touching. In the image she shows a nice set of teeth, while I hide my overbite. Water shimmers in the background. The silver frame has begun to tarnish. I rub at a blackening spot with my thumb.

I hold the frame out to her. "This is us. We're out by Lake Michigan at the county park in Oconto for a Massart family reunion, remember?" I give her a moment while she studies the picture. I gently remind her, "You're my mom, and I'm your daughter."

I watch her eyes. A faint glimmer of recognition registers and then passes.

"Oh," is all she says.

I put the frame back down, deflated as usual, and change the subject. "I bet it's nice to watch the birds."

"Yes, except those rotten blue jays are always scaring the songbirds away."

I laugh. "Is that so? Remember how you used to take the BB gun after the ones at home?"

"They were never my favorite bird." She looks down at her top. "But I do like blue." She looks up with a twinkle in her hazel eyes. "Willis always liked me in blue. The blue-checked dress was his favorite."

"I remember you telling me about that dress. I think there's a picture in the old photo album of you and Dad, and you're wearing it. You're posing by the willow tree, if I remember right."

"I hate that pond," she growls, but in another breath whispers with glee, "I'll have to put the blue dress on when we go dancing tonight. Do you want to come with us?"

Her eyes look myopic and large through the smudged glasses.

"No. No, not tonight." My heart falls. Mom thinks the past is the present again. "Maybe another time. Here." I reach out. "Can I clean your glasses for you?"

She doesn't protest as I slowly slide the glasses off her face and walk to the sink to wash them with soap and water. I dry them on the nearby hand towel and replace them on her face.

"Why don't you sit in the chair?" I help her get up and position her in the spot I vacated. I wonder what to talk about. I look over the books on her side table and spy a favorite book of poetry. "Should I read to you?"

She nods her head like an eager child awaiting a bedtime story.

"Okay then."

I sit on her bed and free the book from the sandwiched stash of Mom's classic collection of literature. I'm not sure why we brought the books from home. She can't focus on them anymore. I haven't seen her pick up a book to read in months. I begin to read through a few poems by Tennyson and Browning until I hear a slight, waffling snore.

Mom has fallen asleep. Her head bends down at an uncomfortable angle and gives her a double chin, but I don't disturb her. I tug her small, crocheted, granny-square Afghan off the end of her bed and cover her chest and legs. I touch her liver-spotted, wrinkled hand before I leave. I'll stop by again tomorrow. I exit the nursing home, waving to a few staff members as I go.

I'll go see if Clive's free for lunch. After, I'll head back to the farm and do some more organizing. Mom became a clutter bug these last few years. Kelly said he'd help me this weekend.

I love my son, but weeks can go by before we talk to one another. I suppose he's got his life, and we've got ours. He and Clive have lunch together frequently, but their workplaces are conveniently close to one another.

The Dodge starts up with a chug and a whirl. I pop it into gear and travel the short distance to Clive's automotive shop. Traffic in town is heavier than usual. College kids coming back, probably.

Pulling in, I notice the string of parked vehicles in the "to be worked on" area. "Yikes. A heavy load today."

I park the Dodge, hop out, and walk to the shop. Its bright blue siding sticks out like a hitch-hiker's thumb. A bell jingles as I open the glass door.

"Yep. Yours 'ill be coming up next…Ya. Sure. Okay. Ah-huh." Clive stands behind a counter with a phone receiver in his hands. His navy-blue uniform shirt has a rip near the pocket, just below his name patch. I'll have to mend it for him. He lifts his eyes and looks at me, shaking his head. He must be talking to a customer. "All right, then. Yep. Goodbye." He finally hangs up and blows out a "Whew!"

I grin at him. "Someone's long-winded."

"You don't know the half of it. This fella wants…"

But he doesn't get to finish. Roddy, one of the three mechanics Clive employs, barges into the customer service and waiting area, which smells of rubber tires, the same base of scent as Fleet Farm.

He rubs a greasy, red rag between his hands. "Clive, where's them gaskets you ordered last week?"

Clive moves toward him, and they discuss parts. My hearing shuts down. It's like they speak a foreign language. Two more customers walk in. This is not going to be a great day for Clive and me to have lunch. Matt, another mechanic, walks in from the back.

I get his attention with a finger in the air. "Hey, Matt."

"Enid, what can I do for you?" he asks.

I look to where Clive and Roddy are arguing over something. "Could you tell Clive that I just stopped to say hi, and that I'll see him later?"

I pick my keys out of my pocket and tap one against the counter.

"Ah, sure. Sure thing."

He nods and smiles before rifling through the shelves under the counter.

"Thanks. See you."

Matt doesn't answer. Clive still has his back turned to me, so I just leave. I think I'll skip lunch and head straight to the farm. I bring the Dodge to life and head northeast out of

Menomonie toward home, about fifteen miles. It's a nice drive, and I roll down the window and crank up the classic country radio station. Johnny Cash is playing *I Walk the Line*.

Soon I'm parked by the farmhouse, which needs a fresh coat of paint. The white is thin in some spots, chipped in others. I leave the Dodge, bang the screen door, and unlock the interior door into the laundry room and the kitchen. The house has a stale smell to it, like flat beer.

I don't know where to start. The bedrooms need cleaning out, and the entire kitchen needs to get packed up. Clive and I talked about renting the house, but we haven't decided yet. Kelly has no interest in it; neither does Cassie's family.

I stand in the living room, trying to decide where to start, but an unexpected wave of tiredness—or nostalgia—washes over me. *Mom's diary.* I pick it up from the stack of books I left it on last time and sit down in the recliner.

I thumb through the pages and find the pink ribbon marker where I left off. Mom's handwriting slants hard to the right. I have trouble deciphering a few words as I read…

April 20th, 1977
Dear Diary,
I can see how Enid looks at me—like I've lost my mind. I was supposed to meet her for coffee this morning and shopping, but I forgot. She said she called and reminded me last night, but to be honest I don't even remember her call.

Enid. What will she do with me? Will she have to babysit me? Heaven forbid. How the tables turn in life. I remember how new everything was as a young mother, all those years ago in 1918. It seems like a whole other lifetime. A whole other me.

I remember the good and precious moments of cuddles and

smiles, but I also remember the badlands I camped out in. That inward place pricked as dry as the desert and just as gouged out— a literal depression.

But no one outside of family knew that I spent two months at an insane asylum. Marge called it a sanitarium, but I knew better than that. Looking back, she and Hal probably deemed it necessary, and maybe it was. Things might have been different if Willis had been at home.

I remember that day by the willow. It had all felt so right at the time, but later I could see how dark a place I had been to. I don't know why I did it. None of the doctors gave me a definitive cause. They forced what they called "preventative" measures on me to help get rid of my feminine nerves. And the stupid, silly woman that I was let them do it.

I did not tell Enid the truth when she asked years later why she didn't have a brother or sister. I have had to shelter her from the grisly facts of my past. She doesn't need to know. What possible good could come from it? It's been done and over long ago, and that's that.

Time to go. I'm falling asleep. I hope I dream of Willis tonight. I always awake more clear-headed the next day if I do.

I close the diary slowly with an ache in my gut at what my mother might be referring to. What can she mean? I have a lot of digging to do.

Remember we are part of one heart now.
Nothing can separate us.

CHAPTER FOUR

Robin
May 1917

Robin smiled at Willis. "I tucked in all your favorites: ham sandwiches with watermelon pickles, potato salad, and ginger snaps."

Willis leaned toward Robin and used a pointer finger to dent in a corner of her mouth. "You know, your smile looks as if it's wearing an indented coma at each end."

"You goof."

Robin tried to straighten out her face, but she could not lose the smile. Any moment she would spill her secret to Willis.

"What are you grinning so intently about, anyway?" He narrowed his deep-umber eyes at her. Ignoring the spread Robin had laid out on a red-checked cloth, he teased her. "You know something I don't."

He pointed out and suddenly tipped her back on the grass, leaning over her with an arm hedging her in on either side. His mouth hovered above hers, and their breath mingled.

Should I tell him now or after we eat? Robin focused on his left eye and then the right. *I can't wait,* she decided. *But I'll toy with him first.*

She plucked at the collar of his blue, pinstriped shirt, which gaped at the neck; he had taken his matching tie off after church.

"I *do* have a secret."

Willis lowered himself until some of his body weight rested on her. He kissed her on the neck in the spot which sent shivers down her spine and a yearning in her lower abdomen. Over and over he kissed her until that's all Robin thought about.

She arched her back and reached her arms up behind his neck, playing with the hair at the back of his head.

He took a break and lay down next to her, drawing her close in his arms. "I'll get it out of you. One way or another."

"How can you be so sure?" Robin asked.

Willis took possession of her mouth then, and she fully let him. She enjoyed every second of their intimacy, but she had a secret to tell. Robin pushed back on his chest, giving herself some space from him.

Willis eyed her like a pirate eyeing his booty after a raid. "Are you ready to confess?"

"I am." She played along. "But first I think we should eat. I don't want our sandwiches to get soggy."

"As the mistress commands," Willis agreed. "My tummy's rumbling."

He sat up and pulled her up too.

Robin patted her hair back into place. Willis helped her unpack the picnic basket. She had planned the picnic lunch by the willow at the edge of the pond for just the two of them after church. It was the perfect spot to tell Willis that he would be a father soon.

Robin spooned some potato salad onto a milk-glass luncheon plate with a gold edge. She unwrapped the sandwiches from the tea towel she had enveloped them in and placed a sandwich on the plate too.

She handed the plate to Willis along with a teaspoon. "Eat up."

He took the plate. "Thanks, but when are you going to tell me?"

He took a giant bite of the ham sandwich.

"After we eat."

She winked at him and fixed a plate of food for herself. She set the cookies out on a napkin.

Willis groaned and rummaged in the basket. "What'd you bring to drink?"

He pulled out a bottle.

"I thought we could split a bottle of cider."

His face lightened. "Sounds good."

He uncapped the bottle and took a drink.

Robin started eating. She looked out over the pond. A few ducks floated on the surface on the opposite side. Tall marsh grass edged the sides of the pond, except in the spot where they picnicked. Here Uncle Hal had built a small dock that one could walk on and feed the fish from. The pond was pretty shallow at the edge but had a deep well. Hal had said maybe fifteen feet in the middle.

They both ate instead of talking.

When they finished their light lunch, Willis demanded his reward. "All right. Fess up."

He took a swig of cider and passed the bottle to Robin.

She took a big gulp before telling him bluntly, "I'm expecting."

She waited for his reaction.

He lowered one eyebrow. "Expecting what?"

Robin widened her eyes at him. "Think about it…"

His eyes mirrored hers. "You mean? Are you—?"

His gaze dropped to her midriff and returned to her face.

She grinned and laughed. "Yep."

He scooted closer and grabbed her hand, his face alight with happiness. "Well, when?"

"Late January." She turned serious and really studied his eyes. "You're happy?"

"Of course." He gave a whoop. "Me a dad?" He kissed her on the cheek. "And you a mom!"

Robin cuddled next to Willis as he draped one arm around her shoulders. "We'll be good parents, won't we?"

She looked to him to help her chase away the sudden worry which clouded her mind.

"Of course we will. We had good examples, didn't we?"

The question did comfort Robin. "We did." She thought of her folks. "I miss them."

"Maybe we could arrange to go home and visit at Christmas. We could save up for train tickets," Wills suggested.

The idea made Robin cry.

"Whoa…I didn't mean to make you cry."

Robin sniffed and wiped at her eyes with her sleeve. "No. It's not you." She smiled up at him. "That would be wonderful. I'm glad you suggested it."

She sniffed again and almost broke down in an outright sob. *What in the world is the matter with me?* Robin was no simpering female to cry at the drop of a bit of good news. She had a sturdy constitution, or so she'd always thought.

"Let's plan on it. Have you written your family yet about…our good news?"

She reached up and touched his face before placing short, intermittent kisses there—on his lips, cheeks, brow, and the tip of his nose. "No. I wanted you to be the first to know."

He reciprocated her tender affection along with the words, "I love you, Robin Holcomb."

"And I love you, Willis Holcomb."

Weeks later

"Never thought I'd read the likes of this."

Hal shook his head from side to side in a slow, mournful way. He pushed his glasses farther up his large nose with one finger, while his other hand held the newspaper. A damp breeze from the open window in the sitting room rustled the muslin curtains. The golden hour had passed, and the sun had nearly set; Robin could see little light outside.

"Read it again," Marge told Hal.

She knitted something with green yarn. The needles clicked furiously while she rocked.

Lynette and Derek sat on the couch, frowns on both their faces. Lynette had her hands folded over the top of her belly. Cassandra played with some blocks and her cloth doll on the floor, looking happily ignorant of the war which could take her father from her.

Tom and Susan were absent from the Holcomb family supper tonight. For what reason, Robin didn't know.

Robin sat on the floor next to a straight-backed chair, which Willis sat on. She leaned her head against his knee. His hand rested warmly on the side of her head. One finger brushed at her temple. Robin listened as Hal read the news again. The U.S. would be enforcing a draft of men to fight overseas. All men between the ages of twenty-one and thirty would be required to register with the selective service. Hal's voice shifted to the background of Robin's thoughts. *What will this mean for us, as a family? For Willis and me?*

She thought of her and Willis as being part of Marge and Hal's family. Lynette seemed like another sister to Robin, though Susan had yet to warm to them. The men all got along well. *What if all three of them are called away? Who will work the farm? How in the world will we manage?*

Questions bounced around in Robin's head. When Hal finished reading about the May 18th decree, they all sat stiff and quiet. Marge had even stopped rocking and knitting.

"Surely, the government won't require married men to...go. Will they?" Robin asked no one in particular.

The question hung heavy and unanswered in the room.

Willis stopped caressing Robin's head. "Where do we have to register?"

She sat up straight and serious, her gut feeling like she just swallowed a bag of marbles.

Hal crinkled the newspaper as he searched through the section he had read. "Says here on June 5th at the municipal building." He looked up. "Must fill out some paperwork, and I suppose if your number comes up, you'll get notified."

Marge had dropped her knitting in her lap, and her voice quivered as she spoke. "The Lord have mercy."

Hal folded the paper up and laid it on the end table near his chair. "It says that those who don't report will be held accountable."

Derek held out his hand, requesting the paper from Hal. "Can I see?"

Hal handed it to Derek without comment. A heaviness lurked in his eyes, which made him look well past retirement.

Derek unfolded the paper with a rustle of pages. "Well, like

Will said, there must be some way they'll select other than random. Did it say any more about who they will choose?"

Derek kept his voice steady, but Robin could tell by the way his eyebrows wedged down and his eyes crinkled at the corners that he was worried.

"Said single men first, then married with certain stipulations. Can't remember what those are," Hal said.

He swiped a hand down the side of his face. Robin noticed the tremor in his arm as he did.

Marge looked at the clock on the wall, reading 8:00. "Let it be. Don't read it again, Derek. We'll all have enough trouble getting those words out of our heads so we can get a decent night's sleep."

"We should be getting home," Lynette said. "Let's put these away, Cassie."

Lynette got down on her knees and helped her daughter put the blocks away in the basket they had come from. Derek folded up the paper and gave it back to Hal.

Willis stood and reached down for Robin's hand to pull her up beside him. "We better hit the hay. Guess after chores we'll have to head into town."

Robin's heart sank. She had planned to tell the family her good news after supper, but now she would have to wait. *How can we celebrate good news on the heels of this announcement? My announcement will keep.*

Robin tucked her hand into her husband's, and they went quietly toward the stairs. Robin ascended first; Willis came close behind her. When they got to the top, Robin turned and buried her head into the safety of his shoulder.

"What if you have to go?" she asked in a strangled half-whisper.

"I won't. It won't come to that. You'll see." He hugged her tighter. "Remember the locket I gave you when we started courting?"

She looked up at him. "Of course. I have it on now."

Robin felt for the gold locket she had slipped under her dress, so it wouldn't catch on anything while she helped Marge with supper. It was warm from lying against the skin of her chest. Robin pulled it out and opened it. Tiny pictures of her and Willis rested inside. Robin on one side, Willis on the other.

Willis touched her fingers and covered her hand and the locket with his. "Remember we are part of one heart now. Nothing can separate us."

Robin nodded and sniffed. She snapped the locket shut, holding it tightly. She wanted Willis's words to be true, but a drumming started in her head, which sounded like the drums of war. A war which could very well break their hearts apart.

Whatever unknown path is ahead,
I pray that you will walk it with me.

CHAPTER FIVE

Enid
Late August 1983

"What are we going to do with all this?"

Kelly gestures to the stockpile of dishes we've taken out of the china hutch and the kitchen cabinets in the farmhouse. Mom liked pretty dishes. She called them "usable art." I'd often hear her say, "*A painting just hangs on a wall, but a dish...a dish is practical too.*" Mom liked practical. She was practical. *Is.* I have to stop talking about her in the past tense, as if she's gone.

My gaze roves over the Homer Laughlin dinnerware set in the American Heritage pattern Mom received as a wedding gift from Dad's parents. Eating off those dishes served up a history lesson along with each meal. In the 40s and 50s, Mom started collecting Redwing pottery. She has several Redwing dinnerware sets. My eyes rest on a painted rose. I have good memories of eating off the Lexington Rose plates. The pattern boasts bold, thick-brushed roses in shades of rose and mauve. A distant memory rests in my mind of eating my favorite breakfast of cantaloupe, cottage cheese, and wheat toast with orange marmalade off those plates. And then there's the Fenton glassware. She's got tons of hobnailed glass in white and green. I run my hands over the bumpy texture of a compote dish.

"Mom? Hello?"

I look up. Kelly holds out his arms; his greenish-hazel eyes widen behind his metal-framed, aviator-style glasses, waiting for me to respond. His mustache twitches above his thin lips.

Every time I'm here I get stuck in memories.

"Ah. I'm not quite sure yet." My fingers scratch an itch on my head that isn't there. "I thought I'd let you and Doris pick what you like. Maybe the girls would like to have something." I shrug my shoulders. "Whatever you don't take, I'll probably give to the St. Vincent De Paul thrift store in Eau Claire. I've already set a few items aside that I know Cassie or her daughters might like."

"Gosh, I'm not sure what Doris would want. The girls aren't much interested in dishes. Boys, on the other hand…"

Kelly leaves his statement hanging with a sigh. There's no need for him to explain. Pam and Phoebe are teenage girls and thinking about teenage boys.

He continues, "But I suppose we could pack something away for them to keep. Why don't you pick a set for each of them, Mom?"

He smiles at me. His top teeth sit in a straight row. Years ago, Clive and I paid good money for those chompers to look so even.

"Okay." I smile back. "Well, Pammie likes flowers. How about the rose pattern for her?" I point to the cluster of dishes at the far end of the dining table. "Hmm, maybe the bobolink set for Phoebe, seeing as it's named for a bird and so is she."

Kelly looks around at the menagerie of goods, slight

exasperation in his tone. "Where's that one?"

It really does look like an antique store in here. We should have tapered down Mom's collections years ago, but I didn't have the heart to do it.

"The kitchen, I think. Over by the stove." I point in that direction.

"I'll get cracking and wrap those up." Kelly catches up a couple of empty boxes off the floor. He picks up a stack of newspapers from a dining chair and tucks them under his arm. "Doris might like that white stuff."

He tilts his head toward the middle of the table where the white hobnail glassware clusters together. He's dressed casually today in a green-and-white-striped polo shirt and jeans, with tennis shoes. Kelly's insurance job usually has him wearing a suit on a daily basis—the opposite of his father.

"Classic. Yes, I think you're right. Seems like her taste."

I respect my daughter-in-law. She's hard-working but manages to pull off a classy look. Every time I see Doris, she's put together perfectly. Not that I go about in rags, but my clothes and accessories don't always paint as cohesive a picture as her outfits. Plus, she's a good mom. Doris gives the girls freedom, but not too much.

Kelly nods and walks away to start wrapping in the kitchen.

I grip some newspaper. *Yuck.* I hate the feel of newsprint and the way it clings to my fingers. I pick up a pedestal piece of hobnail and wonder at its true purpose. It could be a candy dish or compode. I roll it in a sheet of paper and try not to dwell on the fact that I'm getting rid of Mom's things. She'd be furious. *Or would she?* She did like collecting stuff, but I never felt like she placed the importance of those things over me.

That thought pours guilt out on me again. It feels like salt on a wound. Maybe she should have moved in with Clive and me. No. I can't watch her 24-7. She's where she needs to be.

A loud sigh escapes my mouth, sounding like leaking air from a car tire. Kelly notices it over the crinkling of newspaper.

He peeks around the corner. "You all right in there?"

I tell him a partial truth. "Ya. Just thinking. Remembering."

"It's got to be hard for you to pack up Gram's stuff."

Kelly turns back and keeps talking while he works. I do the same. We can't quite see each other, but I can hear his efforts.

"Ya."

I roll another white piece of hobnail in paper. This one is a fluted bowl with a ruffled edge. I don't know how to tell him about my guilty conscience.

"It's not your fault, you know." His crinkling pauses. "This is what's best for Gram."

"That's what I tell myself," I admit and keep rolling.

"But it's not what you feel."

I hear more wrapping. Why is it easier to talk to my son when he's in another room?

"You got that right."

The crinkling stops again. He walks toward me and wraps his arms around me. My head fits under his chin.

"I'm sorry, Mom."

He holds me tight for a few seconds. I try not to cry. Changing the subject helps.

"Did you know Gram kept diaries?"

We release each other. I pick out a white vase and tuck it snuggly in a nest of newsprint.

He fingers another pedestal dish. "Really? About what?"

"Oh, about life. Little everyday things. Her thoughts. I just started reading them."

"Could I take a look when you're done?" He collects another box and heads back to the kitchen.

"Sure," I tell him, but I'm not so sure I want him to read them, at least not yet.

We work for the next hour and talk about the classes the girls will have this fall in their freshman year of high school and Doris's new job as a checkout lady in the Ben Franklin store. All of the dishes I had laid out are now packed up.

"You leave these boxes," Kelly says. "I'll take what we wrapped for Doris and the girls. Tomorrow I'll haul the rest to where they need to be. You don't need to do any more."

He eyes me with a "no-nonsense" expression. He's gotten my one-eyed stare down pretty good over the years. I must look as tired as I feel.

"Whatever you say," I concede.

I walk to the door and hold it open for him as he carries three boxes to his gray Oldsmobile sedan.

"You going back home? You should quit for the day and get some rest." He looks at his wristwatch. "If I didn't have to pick up the girls from piano lessons, I'd stay and help you finish the kitchen off. I assume you want to give it a good scrub before the realtor sees it."

"Yes. Gram wasn't as tidy these last few years." I swipe a chunk of my bobbed hair behind my ear. "You go. I'll sit for a while before I head home. Your dad won't be home yet anyway."

"Okay then. We'll see you Sunday for dinner."

He gets in his car, starts it up, and heads out with a wave.

I wave back and go back into the house. The space looks neater. I can't believe we got so much done in a couple of hours. My legs feel heavy; I need to sit down for a while. I head to the sitting room. Almost as if by reflex, I pluck the diary I've been reading off the desk and open to the page I've marked with a ribbon. Seating myself in Mom's gold rocker again, I begin to read.

May 12th, 1977
Today a general fog clings to my thinking. I feel sluggish. I tried to read for a while, but the words kept floating away. The volume was a book of my favorite poems by Shakespeare. A few of the old English words gave me trouble. I should have known what they meant, but for some reason—I didn't. No point of reference appeared in my mind when my eyes roved over them. I ended up looking them up in the dictionary but couldn't remember how to spell the darn things, so I had to keep checking in the poem book. Whilst and hitherto were two of the culprits.
After reading their meanings, they made sense again. But what worries me is why I forgot in the first place. This forgetting seems more than mere old age. Things that I've known for years sometimes disappear and leave a gaping hole where a memory should be.

Do I talk to Enie about this, or do I wait until she notices and talks to me? I'm afraid, by that time, I may forget something truly important. What if I forget who I am? Will I even be me then? Maybe I won't care.

I remember that dark time after Enid's birth. I forgot who I was, or I became someone else. Either way the end result was the same: I was not myself. Thank God I have never been that person again. I think His presence in my life has something to do with not retreating down such a rabbit hole. I wager some aspect of my physiology wasn't balanced, but whatever initiated it, He helped me through it.

As I tended my assigned section of the flower garden at the asylum, so he tended to my damaged mind.

Will he tend me again?

God, I am holding to the promise that You never leave or forsake us. Whatever unknown path is ahead, I pray that You will walk it with me.

I lower the diary to my lap. What did my mother go through all those years ago? I finger the corner of the diary, wanting to know more, but at the same time, I don't. Her thoughts are fairly clear here. This is '77. Six years ago. What has she written this year? I wonder if her dementia affected her ability to write down her thoughts. I get up and sort through the diaries in her desk—'78, '79...'83. I choose '83 and go sit in the recliner again.

The first pages are filled with phrases. They're not well-written. Her handwriting is sloppy, her words simple, and her sentences fragments. I leaf to the middle. I spy one page of the alphabet. Mom copied it out like a school lesson. I read over the letters. She forgot "m" and "f."

I turn more pages. Eventually I get to a spot which only has scribbles. Once in a while a legible letter peeks out of the messy penned lines. To me it appears a physical picture of her decline into Alzheimer's. A tear drops onto the page.

Mom was always so articulate and such a lovely writer. She had a number of pen pals around the world with whom she corresponded. There are boxes of postcards she collected underneath the TV stand. Maybe I should take a couple of them to her. One of them may jog her memory.

But is it my goal to get her to remember? If so, I'm fooling myself. That's a losing battle, at least from what Mom's doctor told me. On our last visit, Doctor Chang told me Mom's memory would slowly decline until practically nothing remained, if she lived that long.

Why does she have to slowly lose herself until there's nothing left? What cruel twist of fate handed Mom this? I imagine a large emery file in her brain, slowly grating away at her memories.

The words of Mom's written prayer in '77 come back to me, *"Whatever unknown path is ahead, I pray that you will walk it with me."* I wouldn't call Mom an overly religious person, but she brought me up to revere God. She grew up Catholic, but changed when she married Dad, who grew up Methodist. Seeing as there wasn't a Methodist church nearby the farm, we attended services where Hal and Marge went—St. Katherine's Lutheran, the local country church down the road. I recall plenty of the Sunday school lessons taught by Mom, who made the Old Testament stories of such characters as Moses, Daniel, and Elijah come alive. These last few years, she quit going to church. I think she got too confused and felt bad when she couldn't remember people's names.

The house is so quiet; I hear the electric clock next to Mom's chair flip over to 4:00PM. I need to get home.

After I raise myself from the chair and put the diaries back, I shut all the lights off, grab my purse, and lock the door. I stand on the cement stoop for a while and look over the yard. Dried blooms, which were once white, dot the large lilac by the clothesline. The aqua-machine shed sits off to the left, skirted in tall grass. The neighbor boy—whom I've hired to mow—must not be trimming close to the buildings. The barn looks mournful to me. The wooden doors show more space between the boards, and the red paint barely shows. It's been years since it had a fresh coat. The fieldstone foundation appears to crumble more than I remember. The whole farm has gotten old, not just Mom.

A melancholy mood leaves with me, as I hop in the Dodge and head for home.

What am I going to do with the old place? It needs some TLC, but Clive and I don't have the money to spend on renovating the buildings. I know we should put the farm up for sale and I've a scheduled meeting with a realtor next week, but if we sell, I'll feel like I'm losing my mother and my home at the same time. It's too much.

"Not yet," I tell myself.

I grip the Dodge's steering wheel tighter and press harder on the gas. I have a sudden need to see Clive. I need one of his larger-than-life hugs to help me squeeze this sadness back into submission.

She hoped and prayed that working the farm and having a child on the way would be enough to keep him on American soil.

CHAPTER SIX

Robin
June 1917

Robin took a breath. "I wanted to tell everyone the other night, but with the announcement about the selective service, I thought it could wait."

She squeezed Willis's hand under the kitchen table in the farmhouse. Willis, Robin, Hal, Marge, Tom, and Sue squeezed around the table over a supper of fried crappie that Tom caught on the river. Robin had just spilled the news of their expected little one. Hal and Marge looked wide-eyed at her. Susan wore her usual pinched look.

Tom was the one who spoke up. "Congratulations! Well, I'll be. The farm could use a little more life. Isn't that good news, Sue?"

Susan managed a smile. "Yes. Congratulations."

"Thanks," Robin said with sincerity.

She truly wanted there to be good feelings between Tom and Sue and herself and Willis.

Marge turned to Hal, who just grinned. "Well, when? Won't this be fun?"

"March sometime."

Robin picked up a piece of fish fried to a perfect crisp and took a bite. *Mmm, melt-in-your mouth delicious.* It was almost as good as the smelt from Oconto's shore her mother used to fry up in the spring.

Marge's plump, rosy cheeks spread wide with a smile. "We will have to rummage in the attic and find the bassinet the girls used. I have a tin of baby clothes too. Some belonged to the girls. Some were Cassandra's."

Willis looked at Robin. "Maybe we should get a baby buggy."

He shoveled a forkful of green salad into his mouth and crunched away at his food quickly. Robin had never heard anyone eat their food so fast. It was one thing about Willis which rather annoyed her.

"Think we got one of them too." Hal picked up his glass of milk and took a long drink. "Ah," he exclaimed when done. "Nothing like a cold glass of milk." He looked around at the kitchen counters. "Now, the only thing that would be better is a cookie to go with it." He looked questioningly at Marge.

"Always after some sweet or another." Marge pointed at Hal with disgust. "And you stay thin no matter how many you eat. It's not fair." Her finger dropped and her eyes rolled back. "Well, I'm sorry to disappoint, but there's no cookies in the jar today."

She resumed taking a dainty bite of pumpernickel toast and tipped her chin up. It was the first hint of annoyance Robin had seen from Marge.

"No one likes a scrawny turtledove," Hal said sweetly, reaching for Marge's hand.

She hesitated a moment before putting her hand in his.

Robin had heard Hal call Marge his little turtledove on a few occasions, but it still surprised her and almost brought a giggle to her lips.

"And it's a good thing too." Marge smiled and changed the subject off terms of endearment. "How's work going, Tom? Do have some shorter hours in the summer?"

"A little, but the dean likes to have the office staffed for answering correspondence, walk-in questions, and telephone calls." Tom finished the last of the fish. "Our enrollment will be up quite a bit from last year."

Hal looked at Tom. "How many years has the school been open?"

"Bowman Hall opened in '97, so 'bout twenty years." Tom wiped his mouth with his napkin. "Sure tasted good, Marge."

"Your wife and Robin helped too," Marge acknowledged.

Susan, unusually quiet through supper, spoke up. "Tom prefers your cooking to mine."

Tom shook his head and laughed. "I didn't say that."

Susan puckered her lips in a smirk. "Ah-huh. Sure. Think I'm deaf, too, in addition to being a bad cook?"

When not puckered up, Robin thought Susan had the most perfect set of lips on a woman she had ever seen. Her top lip came to matching points under her nostrils, while her bottom lip plumped out in a symmetrical curve. Susan could have been a lip rouge model. *But if Susan doesn't watch it, she'll wind up with a ring of wrinkles around those lovely lips.* All her pursing, puckering, and pinching might leave Susan with permanent damage. Robin couldn't tell for sure if Susan teased Tom or accused him.

"I only said Marge was a good cook." Tom held up his hands in surrender. "Is that a crime?"

Susan twisted her head and gave him a stare with one prominent eye. "It is when you don't say the same thing about your wife."

"I think it's time I took myself out of the battle zone." Hal got up and placed a kiss on Marge's cheek. "Thanks for supper."

Marge patted his cheek affectionately.

Tom got up too. "Think I'll join you."

"Smart man." Hal grinned. "He knows when to surrender. That'll take you far in a marriage."

"Hal Holcomb. Are you saying I'm contentious?" Marge squeaked out.

Hal simply shrugged his shoulders and walked toward the sitting room.

Robin couldn't hold it in any longer. A quiet giggle erupted from her and bubbled out.

"I'm sorry," she said between laughs. She covered her mouth with her hand.

Willis pushed back his chair. "Think I'll retire as well."

He touched Robin on the shoulder and followed the men.

Susan got up and helped her mom. "I am teasing, you know. Tom never complains."

She seemed to explain for Robin's benefit.

"Under his old farmer exterior, Hal's a bit of a joker too," Marge admitted good-naturedly. She started collecting the plates.

Robin helped Susan and Marge do the dishes. Marge washed, Robin dried, and Susan put them away. This kind of homey atmosphere and family working together made Robin miss her own family. She did hope to see them around Christmas as Willis had suggested.

But for now, this was her family, and the thought made Robin glad. She couldn't imagine one of them missing from the picture.

Days later

Robin held her dress up above her knees and dredged her legs slowly through about a foot and a half of water along the edge of the pond. *Lord have mercy, that feels good.* It was hot for June. The thermometer's mercury was pushing 95 degrees Fahrenheit.

Though Robin thought the pond far too green and murky to swim in, she enjoyed the cool of the water against her legs. Susan, prone to think the worst, warned her not to swim in it. She had called it "a breeding ground for Polio." But swimming and wading were two different things.

Robin waded to where a cluster of willow limbs hung out over the pond. She held onto the weeping boughs and closed her eyes, trying to imagine the cool she felt on her feet and legs on the top portion of her body. Envisioning a block of ice, Robin stood still. She did feel cooler.

Her eyes popped open when she heard the rattle of a car. Susan and Tom's black Model T Ford came into view through the leaves. It chugged to a stop near the pond.

Susan raised her voice in an authoritative way, meaning business. "Didn't I warn you!"

A car door slammed as if punctuating her words. Robin used the branches as a handhold and sloshed up the bank of the pond.

"I'm not swimming. I'm wading," Robin clarified.

She dropped the skirt of her dress down as she stepped closer to the car. Susan's sour face relaxed a little. Her brown hair was gathered in such a tight bun that it made Robin's temples ache looking at it.

"Close enough. You should stay out of there all together."

"What brings you and Tom out in the middle of the week?" Robin looked at Tom, waiting in the car.

He nodded at her. "Robin."

He barely turned the corners of his lips up, which Robin thought strange. Tom was a friendly, cheerful guy with a ready grin on most occasions.

Robin walked to the car and put a bare foot up on the running board. "Hey there, Tom. Off work today?"

Susan followed and got back on her side of the car, remaining quiet. *Strange.* She usually had some ready, tart remark to contribute to every discussion.

"Heard from the draft board this afternoon," Tom said.

He tipped the edge of his cocoa-brown fedora up and looked straight ahead, saying the words in a slow, dry tone—*so unlike him.*

"Really?" Robin asked and looked from Tom to Susan. They both remained silent and averted their eyes. "Well?"

Robin didn't have a very good feeling; her stomach tightened.

"I guess they wanted me bad enough," Tom said bluntly.

He faced Robin, looking older to her; slight bags hunched beneath his eyes. He looked like he hadn't slept. His usual five o'clock shadow looked deeper, and she could swear there were wrinkles splintering at the top of his cheekbones that weren't there a few days ago when she'd seen him last.

"But I thought they weren't going to take married men."

A pain like heartburn wedged in Robin's chest. Willis, Derek, and Tom had all gone on the fifth of June to register for the selective service as was required.

"I guess Uncle Sam changed his mind," Susan said drolly as she got back in the car.

"Do you think Willis will be—?" Robin couldn't finish. "Or…or Derek?"

"I doubt it. Not with a baby on the way and Willis working the farm." Tom offered her a deeper smile. "I'm guessing, first, they'll pull from the pool of men who are single or married but without children. Anyway," Tom removed his hat and toyed with the ribbon band, "thought we'd run by and give you all the news."

"I'm sorry, Tom."

Robin liked Marge and Hal's son-in-law; she would not care to see him put in harm's way.

"Need a ride back to the house?" he offered, jerking his head toward the farmhouse, a familiar smile back on his face.

Robin nodded. "Thanks."

Tom got out and pulled his seat forward, so she could get in the back.

They rattled down the gravel drive to the house. Marge stood outside unpinning clothes from the line. Robin had helped her with the wash a few hours ago. It had not taken long for their clothes to dry in the heat.

Marge folded up a pair of Hal's bibs and smiled in surprise. "Well, Sue. Tom. What are you doing here this time of day?" Extra skin hooded her eyes as she lowered her brows. "Is everything all right?"

"I wouldn't say that. Tom's been called up, Mom," Susan informed Marge.

"Oh dear." Marge rested her hand over her heart for a few seconds. "Well, let's sit on the porch, and you can tell us about it. Robin, will you fetch Hal and Willis? I think they're in the shed fixing a tine on the cultivator."

Robin nodded and walked toward the shed. She could hear the ring of metal being hammered.

In between clangs, she shouted, "Tom and Susan are here. Marge said to come."

Hal and Willis both looked her way. Hal held a hammer in mid-swing. Willis lay under the tiller with a giant splotch of grease on his cheek.

Hal lowered his hammer. "'Tain't supper time already, is it? Seems like we just had lunch."

Willis scooted out from under the tiller.

"Since when do you walk around in your bare feet?" he teased her.

"Since the temperature rose past ninety-five and made me feel like a blanched tomato." Robin widened her eyes at her husband and shook her head. "I've been wading in the pond."

Willis turned serious and wiped his hands off on a rag Hal handed him. "I don't like it when you go to the pond alone. You could slip or something."

Some irritation rose in Robin's tone. "I'm pregnant, not helpless."

Hal cut in, "What do Tom and Susan want?"

He tipped his blue-and-white-striped cap back, revealing a tan line on his forehead.

"Tom's been drafted," she stated crisply.

The men grimaced and followed Robin to the porch.

Robin grabbed Willis's hand and held fast as they walked. She gazed up at the lazy summer sky. Puffy clouds drifted by unperturbed by what folks were calling the Great War, now shoving its way into the Holcomb family. The profile of her husband made her tear up. Robin couldn't stand the thought of Willis getting called up. She hoped and prayed that working the farm and having a child on the way would be enough to keep him on American soil.

"Don't worry." Willis met her eyes. "I'll remain exempt, I'm sure."

He drew her close and kissed her cheek.

Robin nodded her head and agreed, "Yes. I'm sure of it."

She gazed up at the sky again, trying to keep her tears from falling, and noticed that a large cloud had passed in front of the sun.

Weeks later

Robin stood, ready to unload some more green beans in front of Susan. "Do you need more?"

Susan lifted up her apron and spoke dryly. "If you must."

Her tone sounded sarcastic to Robin, but she couldn't tell if Susan meant her words to be serious or a jab.

Susan sat on the porch swing snapping green beans from the garden, which Robin had picked that morning. She put the snapped beans into a large bowl and the ends in a bucket of scraps, which would later be poured out for the chickens to peck at.

Robin sat down near Susan on a wooden chair and heaved a pile of beans into her pink, flower-print apron. "I suppose you haven't heard from Tom yet."

"Got a postcard yesterday. He said everything went fine traveling to the training site at Camp Lee in Virginia, but you know Tom. He wouldn't mention if something had gone wrong."

"Always looks on the bright side, doesn't he?" Robin looked hard at Susan. "How…did you two meet?"

Susan caught Robin's questioning stare. "You mean to ask is: How did Tom end up with a crank like me?"

"No. I…well." Robin smiled shyly. "You do seem quite

different from each other."

Robin could hardly believe she was engaged in an actual conversation with Susan. Oh, Susan could spew out directions and utter the perfect comment in every situation, but Robin had not heard her talk about personal issues with any sort of candor.

"I work as a stenographer in the financial office at the Stout campus. Tom works as one of the heads there. After I marked up one of Tom's letters highlighting the editorial mistakes, he teased me. And for some strange reason, he asked me to accompany him to dinner. He said he needed someone who could tell him the truth. We fit together. Odd though we seem."

Susan smiled. Her usual tight expression softened, making her pretty, with her lips perfect.

"How nice." Robin determined to keep asking questions until Susan shut her down. "How long have you been married?"

"A while longer than you and Willis, although we got a bit of a late start. Tom and I are closer to thirty, whereas you and Willis can't be much over twenty. If that."

"Yes, you're about right. I'm eighteen, but Willis is a couple years older than me," Robin acknowledged.

Susan's lips pinched again, and her brows puckered. "I always thought I'd help Dad run the farm, but he had other plans."

Her hands stopped snapping, and she flicked her gaze to Robin.

Robin took her point but turned it back to Susan. "What about Tom? He didn't want to farm?"

Susan sighed and placed a large wad of snapped beans in a stoneware bowl. "No. He prefers the office to the barn." She looked toward the barn and turned her head to take in the view. "I miss being here, working with Mom and Dad every day. Don't get me wrong, I love Tom, but my heart will always be in the country."

"Why did you take a job in town then?" Robin asked.

"At the time, I thought I needed a change. In some ways I regret that decision now." Susan looked off toward the west at the fields of corn. "But I wouldn't have met Tom otherwise." She smiled and focused back on her work.

Robin needed to say it to clear the air between them. "I'm sorry that you can't be. I'm sorry if it seems like Willis and I took the place you wanted to have."

Susan smiled sadly. "Thanks. I admit I was angry when you first came, but…you're beginning to grow on me. And that takes some doing." She grinned.

Robin smiled back. "Hmm, I think Tom is rubbing off on you."

Marge stood behind the screen door, watching them. "No. She's just revealing the soft center of her heart beneath the hard shell that most people see, but I know different."

She opened the door and stepped through. The smell of baking bread wafted out with her. Robin sniffed deeply. *Is there any better smell in the world?* The smell of freshly baked bread reminded her of home. She missed her folks and siblings.

"Now, Mom. Don't be spreading rumors. People will think I have an actual heart."

Marge stepped forward and tweaked her daughter's cheek. "You never fooled me." She looked over their progress. "Almost done, I see. Good. We'll get this batch washed and packed in jars and in the pressure cooker." She picked up the overflowing bowl of cleaned beans. "You staying for supper, Sue?"

"I should get home. Romeo needs to be fed and walked."

"You and that dog. He's evidence enough of your soft center." Marge winked and went in the house.

"Romeo?"

Again, Robin had to ask. Susan had never spoken of a dog. Frankly, she didn't seem like an animal lover, but then appearances could be deceiving.

"Our Bassethound."

Robin just about laughed. If she could picture Susan having a dog, it would be a sad-looking hound. It fit her demeanor, but maybe not as well as she thought. Susan was proving herself to be different, more amiable, and that was a good thing. Given time, maybe they would become friends.

CHAPTER SEVEN

Enid
Early September 1983

"So, we have the kitchen packed up. Most of the bedroom stuff either given away or taken to a thrift store. What's next? The books?" Clive bites into a Mars candy bar with one hand, kicks back a drink of Dr Pepper with the other, and looks my way for direction.

I've saved the hardest for last. Packing away Mom's books will really make her departure from home real.

"Ya. I suppose," I half-heartedly say, as I allow my finger to brush down the row of book spines.

Classic titles rest on the shelves. *Little Women, Jane Eyre, The House of the Seven Gables,* and *A Tale of Two Cities* are mixed in with more contemporary literature: *To Kill a Mockingbird,* all three of Eugenia Price's *St. Simons Trilogy, Centennial* by James Michener, several titles by Irving Stone, and a slew of Agatha Christie novels. Mom had varied taste in novels.

"I'll get some boxes from the truck." Clive sets his snack down on the wide ledge of the craftsman-style woodwork framing the glass library doors and turns to walk out. He pauses and kisses me on the forehead. "It'll be all right, Enie. They're just books." He moves to go get the boxes.

Just books. I try to fortify myself for the weeding which must be done with those words.

A row of shelves six feet long and about the same height sit behind glass on either side of the wide doorway into the sitting room. The cabinets are original to the four-square farmhouse, which was built in the 1870s. Growing up, I recall thinking that something more important than books should be behind glass, but now I agree with Mom; books are worth treasuring.

Where to start? Maybe I should pick my favorites and set those aside and then pack everything else up to take to either the Colfax or Menomonie Library as a donation or to a thrift store. I scan through the titles again and select a few.

Clive comes back with the boxes. "You think the girls will want any of these? Are they into reading?"

"I think so, but maybe not this classic. I'll have to ask Kelly and Doris before we give them away." I point to Mom's recliner. "Why don't you sit and finish your snack while I decide which I want to keep for myself."

"Now, Enie, we don't have a lot of room at home for more books. You have stacks all over as it is."

Clive sighs and tilts his head to the side, which I know means he's annoyed. He eyes me briefly before picking up his half-eaten candy bar and soda and going to sit in Mom's recliner.

I grin at him. "That's just because someone needs to build me more shelving."

He shakes his head. "Will there ever be a thing as too many books with you?"

"Probably not."

"That's what I'm afraid of." He bites down the rest of his candy bar and crinkles up the wrapper, tucking it in his hip jean pocket.

"And yet, you love me anyway," I tell him.

I pick out one title and then another. After five it gets easier.

Clive snorts and guzzles his Dr Pepper. After, he belches out a quiet burp. *How polite of him.*

"Ahhh. I'm ready to work," he states.

I've hardly started. I look around for something to occupy his time while I get at least one box of books packed that I want to keep.

Behind Mom's chair a large stack of magazines catches my eye. "How about you get rid of those magazines for me? I think they're too old to donate. We should probably just burn them."

"You sure? There might be something worth saving."

Clive hates to throw anything out, even stuff that's not his.

I click my tongue. "And you're giving me a hard time over the books."

"Point taken." He rises from the recliner with an *oof*. "How'd your mom get out of this thing?"

It is rather sunk-in and low. He picks a box from the stack and proceeds to collect the magazines, most of which I know are *Good Housekeeping, Red Book, Family Circle, People*, and a few handi-craft publications.

"Wait. Check for any crochet magazines. I'll keep those."

Mom subscribed to several different ones. *Magic Crochet* is my favorite. Gosh, I haven't crocheted anything for a while, and the thought makes me want to dash home and dig through my stash of yarn.

"Gotcha."

Clive sorts through the stack, and reluctantly I focus back on my mission. I troll over the titles, selecting books by impulse rather than deliberation. It takes me less time than I think.

"What do you want done with these?" Clive has a full box of burn magazines and a small stack of keep ones. He stands by Mom's desk, holding a diary. "What are these anyway? Journals of some kind?"

"Mom kept diaries, it seems. I've been reading them. I'd like to keep them all."

He leafs through the one he's holding. Anxiety at his doing so makes me want to tell him to stop. Those are Mom's words, and I don't want anyone else reading them before I do, even if it is just Clive.

"You could box them up for me. I'm almost done here, and then we can pack these up too," I suggest to him.

"Alrighty, your wish is my command." Clive gets another box and starts packing up the diaries. "How many you think she has? One for every year?"

I add a few more books to my keep pile. "It looks like it."

"That's a lot of writing."

I laugh. "It doesn't look like she kept one every year. Otherwise, there'd be loads."

"My back thanks her that there isn't."

Clive quickly packs them up and moves to help me box up the books left on the shelves. As we pack, I wonder why there aren't more diaries. Mom has always enjoyed writing.

Clive hauls out several boxes to the Dodge while I tuck my keeper books in a small box. He makes one more trip, and I accompany him with a box that I can handle. Then we lock the door and prepare to head home. But first I dig in the diary box and locate the one I've been reading, tucking it under my arm.

We hop in the truck. Clive starts it with a chugging growl, and we're off.

He's quiet, so I ask, "Mind if I read on the way home?"

"Nope. That'll save me from having to pretend to listen to you." He winks at me, his full cheek rising up with the act.

I give him a playful swat on the arm. "Gee, thanks."

He drives and hums. I open up the diary and read.

July 12th, 1977

Dear Diary,

Something truly scary happened today—I forgot how to drive. Well, not entirely, but I had to take a detour because of some roadwork on 9th St., which is my usual route to get to the grocery store on the southeast side of Menomonie. I got confused and couldn't remember how to get to the store from the back way.

I felt myself getting flustered, and then I couldn't remember which pedal was the gas and which the brake. I mixed them up and nearly hit a car in front of me, and I forgot to signal when I turned. In consequence a car almost hit me. Let me tell you, my heart was racing.

Finally, I pulled over and parked. I sat for a while and tried to calm myself by praying. In a few minutes I felt better. I practiced touching the gas and brake pedals with my foot and saying their name with each tap. That helped. I pulled back onto the street but decided to go home instead of to the store.

All the way home I kept thinking about how I could have hurt someone. I need to get up enough gumption to talk about this with Enie, but I really don't want to. I feel like I am too young to be getting senile. Mom died seven years ago at ninety-three, and her mind had no trouble keeping track of details and memories. I'm only seventy-nine. Maybe it's more than old age.

Last week I watched a morning newscast on television about Alzheimer's, a kind of dementia. I wonder if I could have that. The thought scares me, but no more than what I went through today with driving. I pray the Lord will help me navigate this strange road.

I close the diary with a snap. We've barely made it out to county highway BB, but I'm crying again.

I don't want Clive to ask me why, so I sniff and say, "I've changed my mind. Think I'll read this later. It's too bouncy to focus on Mom's handwriting, which was never the best."

Clive nods. "You got that right."

He continues humming. He seems perfectly content.

I'm jealous of his peace. My heart has been in turmoil for years over Mom's decline into dementia, but reading her words and hearing first-hand how she struggled makes my heart ache for her. I wish I could have eased her fears, helped her more than I did. Mostly, at the beginning, before I knew what was going on, I was frustrated with her. Now I understand, and I'm crying for her. Not myself for a change.

CHAPTER EIGHT

Robin
September 1917

"Robin? Did you hear me?" Willis stood in front of Robin with a letter in his hand.

Robin had heard the words, but she couldn't make her mouth form the word yes, so she nodded. She turned heavy eyes up to her husband. He reached out and gently pulled her into an embrace.

Robin didn't hug him back. She leaned against him, as rigid as a freshly starched doily. She worked hard to focus on the words Willis whispered in her ear, but she kept hearing herself inwardly scream, *He'll never come back. He'll never come back!*

"Say something," Willis demanded in a careful tone, as he tipped Robin's head back.

He searched her eyes. She knew she should quiet her fear and try to be strong, but all she wanted to do was collapse and not process the heavy truth Willis had read to her—he had been called up and would be heading to training next week.

"I don't understand," Robin stuttered out. "I...I thought

because you were married, expecting a child, and working on a farm that you'd be safe." Robin dug her fingers into Willis's biceps, emphasizing her words. "It's not right! Not fair!"

"Most likely it will be over soon. With this last push of men, the end has to be in sight."

Robin could hear Willis trying to comfort her, but she wouldn't sit by and see this injustice come to be. "I'll protest. We'll make an appeal to the county draft board. Lynette told me that's possible. She heard it from a friend who's in the same predicament."

Robin had to try. She had to do all she could to keep the father of her baby on safe ground. She did not want to be a widow and a single mother. *Let Europe fight its own war.*

Willis detangled himself from Robin's hold. He shook his head and grimaced. "We can't do that."

"Yes, we can," Robin assured him.

"No, I mean, we can't go begging and embarrass the men whose difficult job it is to choose. This is the way it is now, and we will have to face it." Willis spoke the words steady and clear.

"I don't get it. HOW can you be so calm? Doesn't it devastate you that we might be separated for...ever? And what about our baby? The farm? Hal and Marge? They are counting on you."

Willis raised his voice and slapped the letter on his overall-clad thigh. "What do you want from me! To shirk my duty?"

Robin took a step back. She had not experienced feeling afraid of Willis before. At this moment, she was. But it passed, as he took a deep breath and visibly calmed.

"I'm sorry. I didn't mean to shout." He stepped toward her, but Robin backed up until she hit the wall of the bedroom. Willis held up his hands. "Fine." He turned, and the wrinkled letter floated from his hand as he strode out of the open door of their room. "I'm going to do the chores," he uttered as he left.

Robin pushed against the wall and slid down until her bottom met the floor. She kept her knees crunched to her chest and proceeded to sob. The fight had gone out of her, and now she gave in to the fear.

Just then, something her mother had said came to her.

"'Do not fear' is one of the most repeated phrases in the Bible. Do you know why?"

Robin had shaken her head and looked up at her mother with a question on her face. "Why?"

"Because He knew we would need to hear it. Above all, we mortals are prone to fear."

Robin dried her tears on her sleeve. She had no idea where her hankie was, and she didn't want to search for one. Her mother's words helped her dam up the flood of heartbreak.

She was afraid. Robin knew that. Who wouldn't be? But she had forgotten that God understood her fear and had compassion for her weakness. She would have to choose to place her trust in someone larger than her fear over Willis being killed.

"Help me, God," she prayed.

Robin bowed her head to her knees and poured out her fear to someone who could bear it for her.

The next week
They had all come to send Willis off. The depot in Menomonie was bustling with activity. A cluster of other families looked like they were doing the same thing. Here and there, men with luggage were engulfed in groups of family saying their farewells.

Robin's stomach flopped, and the baby rolled inside her. *Thank goodness for this little one.* Robin thanked God that a part of Willis would remain with her.

"'Spect you back shortly so's we can build that shed we talked about and get something to fill it with." Hal patted Willis on the shoulder in a gruff but endearing way. "Read about John Deer's Waterloo Boy in the farming journal."

Marge shook her head in reprimand. "Oh Hal, we can't afford such a thing."

"Now, my turtledove, don't get your feathers ruffled. I'm giving the boy an incentive to come back to us."

He reached out for Marge's hand, and she gave it to him, along with a slanted grin, which had a sad but loving look to it.

"What stands before you is enough incentive." Marge looked at Robin and reached for Willis with her free hand. She caressed his arm, as tears started to flood her eyes. "We are mighty thankful for you, Will. I'll be praying every day for your safe return."

Willis bent down and placed a kiss on Marge's cheek.

"Thanks," he said in a thick tone.

From Derek's arms, Cassandra reached out to Willis. "Unca Willie."

Derek moved closer, and Willis took her in his arms. "Cassie, my sweet."

Willis tickled under her chin, and she giggled. The scene warmed Robin's heart.

Lynette held her one-month-old, Reggie, with one arm and pulled a paper out of the bag on her arm with the other. "Cassie has something for you."

She held it out to Willis. A picture of an American flag was scribbled in waxed crayon and rendered pretty well for a two-year-old.

Willis took the offered paper and kissed Cassie on the cheek with a loud smack. "Thank you."

Cassie giggled again. He gave her back to Derek, folded up the paper, and tucked it in his chest pocket.

Derek spoke up, his blue eyes wide and warm, showing his regard for Will. "Godspeed, Brother."

Robin knew that in the short while they had been on the farm, Willis and Derek had bonded as family, like brothers. Derek didn't have a male sibling. He had been the only boy out of five sisters.

Willis simply nodded his head. He appeared too filled with emotion to respond.

Susan edged her way into the group. "If you see Thomas…"

She didn't continue. Fear etched lines on her face and hope turned her eyes into glossy marbles the color of slate.

"I'll tell him that you send your love," Willis finished for her.

She nodded and sniffed, holding a hankie to her thin, pointed nose. Robin realized Marge's words about her were true—Sue did have a tender heart under her pinched and aloof exterior.

Derek balanced Cassie with one arm and gathered his wife and baby close with his other. They moved back, and the others stepped away as if on cue to give Robin her chance to say farewell. Robin stepped close to her husband. Willis wrapped his arms around her. She was glad his previous anger had passed, and they could leave each other on good terms. She leaned her head against his shoulder, hoping to remember his scent of freshly mown hay, bay rum, and hard work. He caressed the back of her neck.

"It won't be long," he comforted her.

They were empty words, which didn't have a true, sure ring to them but sparked hope all the same.

"Take care of our little one," he whispered in her ear.

Robin took a deep breath, steeling herself to be strong. She tipped up her head. "I will."

Willis crushed a kiss to her lips. Robin didn't care what any of them thought. The train whistle blew, and Willis released her. A chill breeze blew over the platform and made Robin tug her indigo-blue, wool sweater tighter around her expanding middle.

Willis grabbed his suitcase and shouldered the bag Robin and Marge had packed for him with food and a canteen of water. He gave a final nod, turned, and walked briskly away to step on the train. He stopped and looked back, waving before he went into the car.

Robin could see him move down rows of occupied seats through the windows. She followed him along the side of the train as it pulled out. When Will reached an empty seat, he dropped the window, and their fingers briefly touched before the train chugged forward with another blow of the whistle and a shout of the last boarding call from the stationmaster. Robin kept her hand raised in a wave while the train took her husband away. Marge came to stand next to her and waved her hankie in the air too.

After the train rolled from sight, Marge tucked Robin's arm through hers. "Let's go home."

Robin nodded in agreement and allowed Marge to lead her back to the buggy.

"We'll see you soon, I'm sure," Lynette said kindly.

Derek and Lynette walked in the opposite way to Marge and Robin. They had walked from their home a few blocks away.

Robin waved; Lynette and Cassie waved back.

Marge raised her voice. "See you Sunday!"

When the little family had their backs to her, Robin looked around but couldn't see Hal in the throng of people leaving the depot platform.

"Where's Hal?" she asked Marge.

Marge wrapped her fingers tightly around Robin's arm. "He went to get the buggy ready. He's not one for goodbyes."

Robin wished that she had such a luxury, but the government had forced her into saying goodbye to Willis. She dutifully followed her surrogate mother to their buggy. Hal helped her in without comment, and he and Marge settled on the buggy seat on either side of her.

They hardly conversed all the way home, and Robin was glad. What was there to say in the face of sending her husband off to most likely get killed? *You can't think that.* Robin's conscience pricked her. In order to survive this separation from Willis, she would have to hold onto the hope of his return. Robin filled her head with images of Willis's return and the birth of their child. She thought about the baby and what the boy or girl would be like. For the moment it drove worry over Willis from her heart, replacing it with her hoped-for blessing on the way.

Robin wanted to be a good mother. *I'll pray for wisdom and do the best that I can until Willis returns.* She wouldn't say if.

October 1917

Robin looked around at the Holcomb clan, sitting around the dining table for their usual Sunday dinner together. Except this time two people were missing. She hated seeing those empty chairs.

Susan held out a steaming dish of mashed potatoes to Robin. "Robin? The potatoes."

"Oh, yes. Thanks." Robin took the dish and helped herself to a portion.

"What do you think?" Marge asked.

Marge looked at Robin waiting for something, but Robin didn't know what. Clearly, she hadn't been paying attention.

"I'm sorry. What were you talking about?" Robin asked.

All eyes at the table focused on her.

Hal spoke up. "Susan has offered to help us with the farm work. We have to get the corn in yet, and the cows are still producing well. Although, I think a couple will dry up shortly." He paused and looked pointedly at her with his light blue eyes. "We could use the help."

Marge's face was alight with happiness, no doubt with the idea of having one of her daughters under their roof again. "I've invited Sue and Romeo to use the spare room. That way they don't have to be bustling to and from town."

Hal tipped his head down a bit and peered at Marge over the top of his glasses. "We haven't settled on where that dog 'ill sleep yet."

"Now, you can make an exception, can't you?" Marge turned to Robin. "Hal's never let the girls have a pet in the house. His one mean-spirited point in my opinion." Marge gave Hal a snide look.

"There's no need for name-calling." Hal took a bite of food and chewed, appearing to be mulling a thought over. "Well...I suppose." He pointed his finger at Susan. "But at the first sign of fleas that varmint is boarding in the barn."

"Romeo does not have fleas, nor will he ever. Thomas and I have always kept him washed and well-groomed." Susan rolled out her words in a pointed fashion as if they came from the end of her peaked nose and not her perfectly formed lips.

Hal laughed. "Just you wait till he gets to chasing rabbits. They'll infest him, sure shootin'."

"Hmm." Susan sounded unconvinced.

"We've gotten off subject." Marge eyed Robin and spoke carefully. "We wanted to make sure Sue's move would be welcomed. She will have to stay in the room you intended to use as a nursery."

Everyone paused in their dining and waited for Robin to respond.

Robin thought about the arrangement. How could she say she objected? If this had happened months ago when they first arrived, she surely would have. Susan was nothing but a stiff stranger then, but Robin had a kind of fondness for Sue now. Even though Susan wasn't as sweet as Lynette, Robin wouldn't object to her moving in or helping out with the farm work. Robin had actually been worried how she would continue to manage to help Hal in her condition.

"Of course. It won't be a problem to keep the baby in my room. Now that…well, that there's more room." Robin looked down at her plate, feeling Willis's absence keenly.

"If Dad gets the extra bassinet down from the attic, we can scrub it up nicely for your little one," Lynette told Robin in her usual cheery tone. "I'm sure there's plenty of space in your room, if we rearrange the furniture a little for the bassinet and a little dresser of clothes." Her face fell as crying from the sitting room made her set her fork down. She sighed heavily. "Someone else is hungry too."

"You eat your food. I'll go get Reggie," Marge said.

She made to get up, but Lynette beat her mother, rising quickly.

"No. I'll feed him. He'll soon begin screaming if his belly doesn't get some milk."

"Bossy little mite," Hal commented to Lynette's back.

"Don't I know it." Lynette tossed the words over her shoulder as she walked to relieve her crying son.

Marge announced, "Let's dig into our dinner before the ham gets cold."

Derek looked around. "Thought I smelled something apple."

"Fresh apple pie for dessert. Made from Wolf Rivers from the tree down along the fence line," Marge explained.

Derek persisted in his pursuit of the pastry. "Where is it?"

"You'll get a slice of pie when we're done with the meal."

Marge sounded like a general but smiled like a schoolgirl. Robin had taken note that it pleased Marge greatly when her cooking was praised or craved.

While they ate, the family talked of the weather, the cows, the crops, and everything but the two missing people around the table.

Robin looked across at Susan. She never would have thought when they first met that they would share something in common at some point. *But then you never can tell about folks.* Robin had heard her father say those words a time or two as if he had experience in misjudging others. She supposed it showed wisdom—reserving one's opinion of people until you got to know them. It was surely the case with Susan, whom Robin could tell could be trusted despite appearances.

Susan caught Robin watching her and raised her thin eyebrows. She didn't smile but didn't frown either. That brief glance left Robin wondering how living with Susan would be.

I'm determined to celebrate the things she can still do
and no longer grieve so hard over what she can't.

CHAPTER NINE

Enid
Thanksgiving 1983

"Have some more turkey, Mom."

Mom looks up at me from her seat at the table, as if to question what turkey is. She doesn't object, and I put some small, cubed servings on her plate, which I previously dissected for her.

I give the platter of meat to Cassandra, my second cousin. "Pass this on down."

"Aye, aye, Captain," she teases, winking one of her bright blue eyes at me.

Her denim-colored eyeshadow and brown mascara highlight her baby-blues. Creases wrinkle along the corners of her eyes at her temples, showing her age.

Cassie's a few years older than me. We grew up together, and we're almost like siblings. She has a brother, Reggie, but they aren't close. He moved out west after school and has hardly been back to this area. I forget what Cassie said his current occupation is. If I remember right, it has something to do with Las Vegas. Why anyone would want to live in the desert is beyond me. Give me the greenery of Wisconsin any day over that.

I take my apron off and sit at the loaded table in our home in rural Menomonie. Kelly, Doris, and their girls cluster on one side of the table; Clive and I occupy the ends; Mom, Cassie, Sheldon, and Sheila fill the other side. It's a cozy picture. Out the dining room window, behind Cassie's family, runs the Red Cedar River, tranquil and smooth on this November day and almost frozen over. Current still runs in the middle, but the edges are solid and advancing toward the center every day.

Out here in the township of Tainter we are close to the other loves that I compete with in Clive's life: his mechanic shop and his favorite fishing spot. But I'm not jealous. I know where I rank—number one, of course.

I settle in my seat and pick up my fork.

"I took the liberty of filling your plate for you, seeing as you've been busy," Cassie informs me.

Her blonde hair shines as golden as ever, although some gray streaks show through.

I grin and spear a chunk of turkey. "Thanks."

I look over at Mom. She tries to pick up a slice of turkey with her spoon. It's not working, mainly because she has the concave side turned down.

"Use your fork, Mom," I tell her as I hold up mine to illustrate.

She squints her eyes at me in confusion. Cassie helps her out.

"Like this, Auntie Robin." Cassie stabs a chunk of turkey with Mom's fork. "See?" Cassie waits for a dawning recognition on Mom's face, but none comes. "Okay. We'll find another way."

Cassie pushes a piece of meat onto Mom's spoon and helps her hold it. Mom figures it out from there and puts the spoon in her mouth.

"There we are!" Cassie sounds tremendously pleased. "Tastes good, doesn't it?"

Mom chews and smiles but doesn't say anything. These last few months her speech has declined. Once in a while she'll come out with a phrase or an old memory. But I prefer this to the bursts of anger she's shown on and off, especially with the nurses taking care of her. Again, I taste the burden of guilt in the back of my throat like bile. It should have been me she hit and yelled at instead of those innocent nurses.

"Cranberries?"

Mom surprises me with the word, spoken like a question. I check her plate. I forgot to add cranberries, her favorite food at Thanksgiving. It brings a tear to my eye that she remembered.

"I'm sorry, Mom. I forgot the cranberries."

Pamela, who is sitting on my other side, passes the cut, leaded-glass dish of cranberries and sauce. "Here, Grammie."

She smiles wide at Mom, showing her row of braces on her top teeth.

I take the dish and spoon some cranberries onto Mom's plate. She succeeds in dishing some into her mouth.

"Mmm," she says with a smile.

My day has just gotten brighter. It should bother me—the fact that I must feed my mother like a toddler, but I'm determined to celebrate the things she can still do and no longer grieve so hard over what she can't. I don't care as much anymore if she can't remember who we are, or even who she is, as long as she's getting some enjoyment out of life. That's what matters. We can do the remembering for her.

Clive speaks loudly above the chatter. "You know, we forgot to say grace."

So we did.

"Let me remedy that," he says and tips his head down.

Everyone at the table grows quiet as he prays a prayer of thanks for family, friends, work, home, and provision. He ends it with a hearty "Amen."

Mom surprises me with an echoed "Amen."

Another tear squeezes from my eye, and Clive and I exchange smiles of thanks, love, and understanding across the table, while the others pick up their conversations where they left off.

One of the things Mom's journey with dementia has taught me is this: Life is in the small things, like the word "Amen"—a simple agreement, a yes to words prayed, and a statement claiming the promises of God.

I've cried and begged for Mom not to have to go through this valley of loss, but it has come regardless. Now my one plea is that—in all that she has or will lose—she will never lose the love of God and her family. That is a truth worth saying "Amen" to.

An hour later

We are all sated, lounging here and there around the house. Clive and Cassie play cribbage at the table, Pamela and Phoebe are working on making some paper snowflakes on cushions on the floor, Doris and Sheila are rocking and talking before the fireplace, and Sheldon is watching a football game on the couch. Mom snoozes in my stuffed reading chair in the corner of the living room with her feet up on the green, vinyl stool. Her chin rests on her chest and waffling snores escape her lips from time to time. Sheldon doesn't mind; he hovers on the edge of the couch, quietly rooting his team on.

That leaves me. The kitchen is cleaned up. I could join the girls or Doris and Sheila, but for some reason that I can't name, I want to be alone right now. I hang up my apron with the apple print on the hook in the kitchen and walk past my desk, grabbing one of Mom's diaries as I do. The rocking chair on the screened-in porch calls to me. I slip on my eggplant-colored parka, snow boots, and gray stocking cap and sneak out the back door. I settle myself in the wooden rocker and open the journal to where I left off a few days ago.

December 24th, 1977
Dear Diary
I still have not told Enid. Although she has mentioned my lapses in memory and judgement, she hasn't insisted that I see a doctor. Thank God I haven't had any more mishaps driving, except for hitting the neighbors' garbage cans and backing into the light pole at the grocery store. I'm sure Enie has noticed the back fender of my Mercury LTD, but she hasn't said anything. But that's how she is—not one to rock the boat.

My daughter has always hated confrontation. I remember the summer when she was five. I went to do the laundry one day and found green peas buried in the patch pockets of her dress with the Hollie Hobby print. Mashed peas were also tucked in the front pockets of her jeans. When I asked her about it, she cried and admitted that she hated peas. She could have told me earlier. I would not have been mad at her, but apparently, she didn't want to risk that. She avoided the situation by hiding the peas. Thankfully, Enie has grown out of the propensity to hide her preferences, but I believe that she still hides many of her true feelings.

In all fairness, I could say that we are two strands of the same yarn string in that regard. As a young woman, I often hid my true feelings from others. Mostly I had good intentions at heart, but for those few months after Enid's birth, I couldn't recognize what was true and what wasn't. I burned some of the diary entries from that year. Heaven forbid Enid read my ramblings after I die; I do not desire her to see how dark a hole I fell into.

I thank the good Lord that she has never experienced what I did. Granted, after Kelly's birth, a blue sadness shadowed her for several weeks, but after Enid's birth, I was past blue for far too long and dove into blackness. It's no wonder they put me in the asylum for the chronically insane in Menomonie.

Maybe our separation early on is why Enid and I hardly ever seem to understand one another. Rare moments sparkle like sunspots, and I can say, "She's my daughter." However, most of our interactions leave me wondering where she came from. I see plenty of Willis in her, but me? Now and then I catch a glimmer, but we are different people. I've come to terms with that over the years, but I'm not sure Enie has. I can tell I often disappoint her with our disparity in personality. I pray someday she'll understand that we don't have to be alike to truly love one another.

Reading back over what I've just written, I see my thinking is clear and bright today, as if Christmas itself has led the way back into my memories. The current issue at hand, however...

I don't know where I put the presents that I wrapped for Kelly's girls. I thought I had stashed all of the gifts for Christmas in the closet in the guest room, but obviously not. I crocheted blankets for them as a gift, one pink and one purple. I can't imagine where I would have put them. I suppose I should finish here and go take another look.

I wonder how my memory will be in the year to come.

"Oh, Mom…"

I swipe at the tears on my cheeks. Every time I read her diaries I cry. It saddens me to read her thoughts about my personality. I want to object, but deep down I know she's right. I'm thankful that, as we've gotten older, we've grown closer, but I still hate the idea of disappointing my mother.

I did see the change in her, but I guess I didn't think it very serious. I mean, I could overlook her forgetfulness, a bump in the car fender, and misplaced items. It was the day she didn't know who I was that woke me up to reality.

It didn't last long. Maybe twenty minutes. I had come to pick her up for a morning coffee and muffin at my place, but she was still in bed. When I woke her, she became distraught, wondering who I was and crying, saying she would call the police if I didn't leave the house.

I hated that day. Is there anything worse than not to be known for who you are? *Maybe not knowing who you are.*

"Hey. What ya doin' out here? You must be freezing."

Clive's voice startles me. I glance up. He stands in the porch doorway. I didn't even notice him opening the door. I missed the screen door's tell-tale squeak. I close the journal and tuck it under the chair cushion. *And there we are—I'm hiding my actions again.*

I pull it back out and stand up. "Just getting some fresh air and reading a little."

I smile at him and kiss him on the cheek, his whiskers tickling my lips. Every autumn, Clive gets a stint where he doesn't like to shave and he grows a beard. Inevitably, in the spring, it comes off.

"Well, come inside now. I think Cassie, Shel, and Sheila plan to head home."

"Sure." I walk through the doorway as he holds open the porch door.

"What you been finding in those diaries of your mom's?" Clive asks to my back.

"A lot of stuff I didn't really know about," I confess truthfully.

Clive helps me take off my coat. "Well, hope that's a good thing."

Is it?

"Ya, I think so," I agree.

He smiles at me and yanks off my boots when I offer him my feet one at a time. "I'll listen anytime you want to talk about it."

Yes. He will. He's a good man.

"I know. Thanks."

We kiss each other with more than a peck, and again gratefulness for the loving man who is my husband rises up in me. We share one last smooch before Clive puts his arm around me and we walk into the kitchen to prepare to say goodbye to our guests.

Having breaking points and cracks can be a good thing.

CHAPTER TEN

Robin
Thanksgiving 1917

The day had started out bright, but now a covering of clouds clustered over the farm. Robin looked out the barn door, watching a few lazy flakes of snow fall from the sky. She leaned against the red, wooden barn door and turned her back on the image of a straining cow giving birth. The sight of it sent a shot of worry straight to her gut, as if her anxious thoughts were a shot of whiskey. And she knew what a gulp of whiskey did. She had joined in a toast at the bar once with Willis, back in Oconto. She had not anticipated the burn which would accompany such a drink.

A loud, bovine groan made Robin turn her head. Hal had his arm halfway into the backside of the cow, who was lying down on her side, straining.

Hal's face blossomed about as red as the bloody mucus which trickled down his arms. "Gotta get this critter's feet cinched in here…"

Hal had curled a rope around his free arm; the other fed the rope into the backend of the cow. He sunk farther in, and the pregnant, laboring cow groaned pitifully.

Robin couldn't help the involuntary groan which escaped her lips.

Susan stooped by Hal, holding the cow's tail back. She turned to Robin with a severe slant of her brows. Robin couldn't tell if Sue was concerned or angry.

"Maybe you should go in the house." Susan spoke sharply. "You're no help here."

It rankled Robin—how blunt Susan could be. Robin stiffened her backbone and stepped toward the laboring mother and man, determined to prove her wrong.

"Anything I can do, Hal?" she asked with a steadiness she did not feel. Her stomach rolled, and her legs shook.

"Get a forkful of clean straw. We'll rub the calf down with straw when it comes out," Hal told Robin.

Susan threw her sour attitude into the mix. "That's if the calf comes out."

Really, I don't know what's got her goat today. For the life of her, Robin could not figure Susan out. Most days she was fine, with a fairly pleasant demeanor, but on other days, you'd better watch your step. Today was one of those days.

"Now, girl. Have a little faith." Hal grunted again, and the cow mooed mournfully. With a jerk and a pull, a pair of hooves—wound with rope—broke out of the cocoon of the cow's womb. "There we are." Hal grinned, showing a gold-capped incisor on his top row of teeth. He patted the cow's side with encouragement. "Just one more, old gal."

A few seconds later the calf slid out into the world, slick and wet. Sue dropped the tail, and Robin burst into action to get the straw.

After fetching the clean bedding, Robin dropped the pile

next to Hal, who in the meantime had loosed the calf from the rope. Turning toward her calf, the cow proceeded to lick him clean. Hal let the mother lick for a bit and then took to rubbing handfuls of straw over the calf's body.

He looked up and smiled at both Robin and Susan. "There we are. We can be thankful on this day of thanks for another little fella to add to our herd."

"Yes," Susan replied with about as much enthusiasm as a rock.

"I'm glad he was delivered safely," Robin said.

She stepped closer to touch the spotted side of the calf, who had already figured out how to suckle and eagerly guzzled away at his mother's teat. The birthing had brought some life into the day, which had been overshadowed by Willis and Thomas's absence. The Thanksgiving meal had been quiet and subdued, especially since Derek, Lynette, Cassie, and baby Reggie had gone to spend the day with Derek's folks southwest of Menomonie, near Spring Valley.

"Well, I'm gonna get washed up and go see of Ma has some of that pecan pie left." Hal wiped his hands on some of the straw. "See you girls in there."

Robin followed Susan out of the barn. Susan kicked a rock, which skidded across the yard and clanged off the galvanized tub propped up by the water pump. Obviously, she was upset. She grumbled under her breath. Robin wanted to comfort her, but she didn't know what to say.

"Would you like to play a game of checkers when we get in?"

A game of whatever usually got Robin's mind off worrying.

"I don't want to play a game!" Susan turned and bellowed at Robin, who stepped back. "My husband is away at war. It's not time for games."

Susan huffed and turned her head away. She stood still and smashed her hands into the pockets of her wool coat.

Robin took a deep breath and steeled herself to be courageous. She stepped in front of Susan. "As is mine, but dwelling on the fact doesn't help."

Susan looked up, her eyes pinpricks of gray. "You've only been married a few months. Tom and I have been together for…years." A wobble and a sob shook her voice with the last word.

Robin reached out a tentative hand. "I know you must miss Tom terribly."

She hoped this would be an opportunity to share something with Susan and become more than housemates and distant family.

Susan slowly took a hand out of her pocket and stretched it toward Robin's, but when their fingertips touched, Susan dropped her hand like she'd touched something hot and tipped her chin up. She gave Robin a look which almost spoke of an apology before walking briskly past her and into the house.

Robin stood where she was. She couldn't figure out why Susan always maintained such a hard front, like nothing could ever break her. Everyone had their breaking points. *At least that's what Dad used to say.*

Robin took her time in getting to the house. As she did, she thought about her father, who had a temper. He had called it his breaking point, the thing which always reminded him of his humanity.

Her father's words floated to Robin as if on the wind. *"It's how the Lord's Light can enter, so having breaking points and cracks can be a good thing. You just have to know how to surrender those faults to the One who can bring a purpose to them."*

"Thanks, Dad," she uttered out loud, before opening the screen door to go into the house. She missed her folks, but the expensive train fare across the state and her condition didn't make a visit possible.

Robin hung up her coat and hat on the hooks in the entryway and took her boots off. She heard Marge talking to Susan; their words were unclear. *Maybe what Susan needs right now is her mother.* Robin would give Susan time and space, but she hoped that one day she and Susan could respect each other, even if they couldn't understand one another.

Robin decided to allow mother and daughter some time alone. She went upstairs to her and Willis's bedroom, where now a bassinet and a small chest of drawers awaited another occupant. Robin softly closed the door behind her and rubbed the side of her stomach. She lay down on the colorful, cross-stitch quilt covering the bed—patterned in red roses and blue ribbons. She prayed and cried for her little one's health and Willis and Thomas and so many other men headed into battle.

Robin opened her eyes to a darkened room. *I must have fallen asleep.*

She rose up on her elbow on her side and stretched her neck. Sitting up all the way, she reached over to light the black, pottery, kerosene lamp on the bedside table. The base of it fit in her hands like a globe. She removed the glass, cranked up the wick, and struck a match. A flame surged against the coated-sulfur end of the stick.

Robin focused on the tiny blaze a little too long and almost burnt the tip of her finger before she had the webbed wick lit. She waved out the match and returned the glass to the globe. The light burned warm and lent a pleasant glow to the room.

Robin's gaze fell on the waiting bassinet. She wondered

what her child would be like. *Will it be a girl or boy? Be more like Willis or me? Have my eyes or his?*

She looked forward to the day in February or March when she would find out.

"Robin, dear? Are you coming down to have some supper?" Marge's voice called up the stairwell.

"Yes. I'll be right down," Robin answered loudly.

She smoothed back her hair, straightened her dress, and stood up. She got up and looked around the room before she turned to head down the steps. An intense longing for Willis rose up in her chest and brought tears to her eyes. She thought that maybe one day she and Susan might talk about their shared grief over their missing husbands. But for now, Robin determined to do the best she could. She liked her life here with Marge and Hal. In many ways, the farm and the Holcombs reminded her of home. If only Willis would come home, life would be very nearly perfect.

The rumble of Robin's stomach made her feet move, descending the stairs to fill her belly, hopefully with leftover pie. *That is if Hal hasn't finished it off.* Robin could relate to Marge's grievance against him, the way he could eat anything and stay as thin as a fence post. She shook her head and hurried up with the imagined taste of pecan and pumpkin pie on her tongue.

No matter how deep the canyon of forgetfulness is that I will fall into,
He is deeper still.

CHAPTER ELEVEN

Enid

A few days before Christmas 1983

"Do you think you'll bring your Mom out for Christmas?" Cassie asks.

She sits across from me at a booth in The Pepper Mill restaurant in the Thunderbird mall in Menomonie. We're having brunch together and talking about why the farmhouse and property hasn't sold.

"I'm not sure. She's got a cold. I don't think she feels very well."

I search through the breakfast options on the menu; nothing sounds good.

Cassandra peers at me over the top of her menu, her round, orangish glasses giving her an owl-like appearance. "Gosh, I'm sure she'd want to come out. Don't you think?"

Her usual blue eyeshadow is replaced with a deep pink that matches the argyle sweater-vest she's wearing over a baby-pink, oxford shirt. In contrast, I'm dressed in a gray sweatshirt with no makeup except a little blush and lip gloss, which I applied mostly for my chapped lips. I couldn't find my usual Chapstick in my purse.

I sigh; Cassie is three years older than me but manages to look ten years younger.

"Yes, but it's not as easy as it used to be."

I try to tamp down the frustration igniting in my chest like heartburn. Cassie doesn't fully understand what Mom is like when she doesn't feel well. Usually, she's pretty placid, but when she's in pain, she's cranky, belligerent, and just plain stubborn. She will not listen to direction.

"Sheldon and I can pick her up. It'd be no trouble."

That is a helpful idea. I think about it and say, "Well…"

But I don't get to finish.

"Ohh, eggs Benedict. I'm having that," Cassie decides firmly.

She folds up her menu and places it on the table. She looks expectantly at me.

I finish my sentence. "You wouldn't mind picking her up? Are you sure?"

I examine her eyes to gauge her sincerity. Cassandra has been known to promise something and forget she did.

"Of course. No trouble at all. That way you can concentrate on cooking." She winks, and I smile. "Grandma taught you well." Her blue eyes sparkle, and Cassie whispers across the table, "I'm hoping for the usual array of Christmas cookies and treats."

Cassie has gotten her grandfather's constitution in the body type and weight department: skinny. I resemble a plump chickadee, while she's a roadrunner. Although a slight roll has started to form around her waist in recent years.

I harbor fond memories of baking with Aunt Marge. I can

picture her wrinkled, liver-spotted hands next to mine, teaching me how to roll out cookies. I think I was around ten. Cassie never liked cooking or baking, but she did take after Marge with her love of crochet and cross-stitch. And don't I know it. It seems like every year since we were teenagers she's given me something stitched or crocheted for a Christmas gift.

I can feel the teasing, crooked grin on my face. "I'll try not to disappoint anyone."

"Oh good." Cassie releases a relieved sounding breath and changes the subject. "So...why don't you think the farm is selling? Could it be the economy? Have you considered renting the house or land at least?"

I don't answer because the waitress—dressed in a white shirt, black slacks, and a green apron—comes to take our order. Her name tag reads Ilene.

"Hiya. What to drink?" she asks, bouncing her pen against her pad of paper.

I'm focused on the pink streak in her hair and the spiked earring cuff on her left ear. It reminds me of something a mean bulldog might wear. Heavy, black eyeliner rings her dark eyes. She lifts her tweezed-to-a-tee eyebrows with impatience.

"Ahem, yes. I'll have tea. Bring a variety, if you can," I get out.

"Coffee and a dish of creamers. Can't drink that stuff black," Cassie tells her with a smile. She doesn't appear to be fazed by our waitress's punk-rocker look.

"And I think we've decided what we want to eat," I say. I wait for a response, but Ilene simply flicks her gaze my way and waits with poised pen. "Umm, I'll take the pancake trio," I tell her.

"Eggs Benedict for me," Cassie cheerfully says.

She's so much like her mother. I miss Lynette, but she's been gone ten years now. Cancer.

"Got it," Ilene mumbles.

She cracks her gum, folds up her notepad, and walks back to the kitchen.

Thank God I had a boy, I can't help thinking.

"Well. What do you think?" Cassandra says, clearly waiting for an answer.

"About?" I've forgotten what we were talking about.

"What's wrong with you lately?" She tilts her head. True concern creases her face and glosses her eyes. "You're not the same Enie I've always known."

Gosh, how do I tell Cassie about the guilt I carry around, the strange secrets that I fear are buried in Mom's diaries, and the first-person perspective I am getting from Mom's entries about her recognizing her memory troubles?

I shrug my shoulders and wish for a warm drink to wrap my hands around. Instead I ball them into fists in my lap. "It's difficult. You know. With Mom's Alzheimer's."

I'm not sure that I'm ready to reveal the heart of my burdens to her.

"Listen, I know you well enough to recognize when you're holding something back." Cassie narrows her eyes, reading me.

I'm sure the lines and the spots on my face tell a story. My graying hair too.

"I feel bad. Her being there. It's like I'm committing her again," I confess.

I fiddle with my napkin; it's real cloth and not paper.

She drums the table with her lacquered fingernails—pink, of course. "It's not an insane asylum, and what in the world do you mean by 'again?'"

Shoot! I didn't realize I said that. I roll my eyes and inwardly groan. I might as well tell her.

I settle my eyes on hers. "I've been reading Mom's diaries. Some parts are really sad. I'm actually finding out a lot about her that I didn't know. Some of it is how she dealt with losing her memory in recent years, but some entries reminisce about a time long ago just after she and Dad moved out here, I believe."

Thankfully, the punk waitress brings us our drinks. I choose my tea bag, dunk it in the hot water, and continue, cradling the cup as I talk. Surprisingly, Cassie sits quiet and listens. She empties two creams into her coffee and stirs, jingling the spoon loudly against the sides.

"Did you know Marge and Hal committed Mom to the insane asylum that used to be where the Dunn County Health Care Center is now?"

"Huh?" Cassandra sends an incredulous look across the booth's table at me. Her lip curls up, and she frowns and tilts her head to the left. "What the heck for?"

"That's what I'm trying to figure out."

I take a sip of tea and burn my tongue. Figures. I'm never patient enough with hot drinks.

Cassie flicks her hand in the air. "I didn't know Aunt Robin kept a diary or journals, whatever you call them."

She calls my mom her aunt, but really, they are cousins. My dad and her mother were first cousins.

"I guess I've seen her writing in a book now and again throughout the years, but I never really paid too much attention to what they were. There is one for almost every year. Some are missing, though. I wonder if she didn't keep a diary those years or if…she destroyed them."

Cassie shakes her head and appears confused. "Wait. So, when was this committal supposed to have happened?"

"I don't know. In her entries from about six years ago, she's recounting some memories, equating that we might think her crazy like they did when she stayed at the asylum."

"Wow. Poor Robin. I had no idea."

Cassie holds her coffee cup in midair, appearing to be thinking. Finally, she brings it slowly to her mouth and takes a drink.

I sigh. "I'm guessing it had to be when I was very little and you too young to remember anything."

We lock eyes again.

I want a clue, even if it's just a little one. "You don't recall anything?"

Cassie screws up her face for a few seconds. "No. I mean, I was only three when you were born." Her face lightens. "Wait. I do remember Grandma and Aunt Sue holding you a lot. I was annoyed at you for taking up their time and attention."

None of this makes sense to me. "How old do you think I was then?"

"I don't know. Maybe…still a baby. I remember you being wrapped in a blanket. A pink one." Cassie takes another drink, and Ilene comes back with our food. "Ooh, more coffee please." Cassie smiles angelic-like and holds out her cup.

"All right. Be back in a minute," Ilene says grudgingly.

She turns and heads back to where the coffee pots are stashed by the waitress station.

I take in the fluffy stack of pancakes. They look good, and my stomach grumbles in response. I doctor them up with plenty of butter and blueberry syrup. Cassie digs into her food, and Ilene comes back to fill her cup. She leaves just as quietly as she came.

"So, where were we?" Cassie asks between bites.

"Not knowing when Mom was committed," I remind her.

"Right. This might take some old-fashioned sleuthing. I wonder if the courthouse would still have records of who was at the asylum or if they even did. I can ask Sheldon to check. He's got an old buddy in the clerk's office."

I cringe. I don't want Sheldon to know, but I guess that would be a good way to go about taking the first step in digging up some information. "Sure. That would be good, but…don't tell him too much."

My eyes plead with her to use discretion.

"I'm sure Sheldon won't mind, and he won't spread any gossip, if that's what you're worried about." She sounds like she's taken affront to my request.

"I'm sorry. I didn't mean to imply that he would," I reassure her.

She gives me a weak smile and nods. Cassandra is family and has been my best friend since childhood. I'd hate to hurt her feelings, but I've done it before. She can be rather sensitive.

She shrugs her pink-sweater-clad shoulders. "I get it. I wouldn't want word spreading of my mom being kept in the looney-bin." Her gaze flicks up at me. "Sorry. I didn't mean to put it like that."

"It's okay," I tell her.

But is it? I hate the idea too. I'm determined to find out more about the asylum. It's been on my "to do list" for months, but I've been dragging my feet. Maybe because I am scared of what I might find.

"Look, let's talk about something else for a while." She smiles warmly. A bit of egg sits in the corner of her mouth.

"Sure," I agree.

"How's Pammie and Phoebe doing? Any boyfriends on the horizon?"

"I hope not. Those girls are too flighty and giggle-prone for dating yet. Anyway, I'm sure Kelly has set that privilege at age sixteen."

Cassie winks at me. "Come on. A girl's got to have fun."

We talk of family and friends and leave the discussion about Mom behind, but when I get home, I'm going to dig through the diaries again to see if I've missed something.

Later that day

Clive is tucked in bed, snoring lightly. He was reading, but he must have fallen asleep and left his light on. No matter. I'll turn it off when I get up.

I'm snuggled in my blue chair in the corner of the bedroom reading the last entry in Mom's diary from '77. There's an oily spot on the page. It looks like she was writing and eating at the same time.

December 29th, 1977

Dear Diary,

I dreamt of the flower gardens at the asylum last night. Hollyhocks stood, staked against a trellis. The rows of gladiolus and dahlias were stunning and displayed brighter colors than I ever remember seeing in real life. Zinnias, larkspur, four o'clocks, daisies, and nasturtium filled up whole sections of the beds. I recall running my hands over them, their fragrance floating up to me softly. I don't remember everything that happened in the dream, but the images of the flowers stick with me. I awoke with a sense of peace.

Back then when I was at the asylum, I was not physically well enough to help with the dairy, so I helped tend the flower gardens instead. I know without a doubt, the act of gardening helped me get better. It's why I've always loved being in my flower garden. It reminds me that healing follows when we care for something or someone else.

The specialist I saw, called in by the acting doctor on staff—I can't recall his name now—got a lot of things wrong, at least according to me. A forced surgery and water therapy—which sounds like a soak in a hot tub, but it was not; it bordered on torture—didn't end up healing me. Talking with Molly and keeping the weeds out of the flowerbeds did. Of course, I'm sure God touched my mind and allowed me to see things more clearly. What a terrible, terrible darkness depression is.

As I look toward this new year, I'm tempted to be afraid. I am walking into another blackhole. But I know whatever comes, the Lord will be by my side just as He was back then in that dark pit of my thoughts. No matter how deep the canyon of forgetfulness is that I will fall into, He is deeper still.

"Honey?"

I sniff and look over at the bed. Clive has propped himself up on an elbow.

He squints at me. "You okay? You were crying."

I don't answer. I don't know what to say. I haven't told Clive yet what I am finding out about my mom.

He sits all the way up on the edge of the bed and stands, moving over to me. He's shirtless and in his blue-checked boxers. He comes to stand near my chair, and I lean into him. The gray hair on the crest of his rounded belly tickles and warms my cheek. I can hear his heart pumping.

He prods my shoulder. "Come to bed. We can snuggle for a while."

I tilt my head up. "That leads to something else usually, and I'm really not in the mood." I feel bad. I can't remember the last time we were intimate. It's been months. "Besides," I pinch him playfully in the side, "we're too old for that."

"Ha! Who says?"

Clive pulls me up. I drop the diary on the chair as he draws me closer and kisses my neck. He always did know where to start.

"Clive," I warn him and weakly push on his chest.

His lips do feel wonderful. A tingle runs down my spine.

"Hmm?" he mumbles back in between kisses.

"I...I need to talk to you."

He stops and looks me in the eye. "That's the worst mood-killer right there." He kisses my forehead and wraps me in a tight hug. "All right. Come on. At least we can be warm while we *talk*."

He leads the way back to the bed; we get settled under the covers. He's holding me from behind. I feel like an egg nestled in a carton: safe.

I end up blurting it out. "Mom was committed to a mental institution years ago. It's in her diaries."

"Wow. That's a bombshell." He pauses. "You never knew, did you?"

His quiet words tickle my neck.

"No. Can you believe it? She never told me."

"She might have had a good reason not to." He brings up a valid point.

"Ya, well. Maybe."

I feel deflated; I thought he would be as shocked and appalled as I was to find out.

"What does it matter now?"

"I'm trying to understand her. Maybe this will somehow...
draw us closer."

Why am I searching, anyway?

"Maybe in your heart, but you're past the point of mending
any fences with your mom. And with her mind the way it is,
she can no longer go there."

"Ya. I know."

He's right, but I have to figure out what happened to her...
to us.

"Forget about it for tonight."

He resumes his exploration of my neck, and strangely, I let
him. I need a distraction to take me away for a while from worry
about the past and future. I want to focus on the now. And the
now feels good.

No mother is perfect.

CHAPTER TWELVE

Robin
Early February 1918

Robin rocked in Marge's chair, crocheting some booties for the baby. She thought about the last few months. They had gone by with barely a bump. Christmas came and went. Letters between Robin and Willis shuffled back and forth. Susan sometimes shared a portion of hers but mostly kept them to herself. She took over more of the barn work as Robin's belly expanded.

There were moments when Susan almost let her guard down, but still she had kept her reserve up. She had been civil enough minus a few minor mishaps, but it made Robin sad. She and Susan could be friends.

Marge was wonderful, of course, but Robin missed her mother and family. She missed lying in bed and talking over the day with Mabel. Mabel would be seventeen now. Robin had missed sending her well wishes. A sore spot in her heart told her she behaved badly and let her responsibly as a sister and a friend slip. *Tonight, before I go to bed, I'm writing Mabel a letter.* Robin let go of a breath she hadn't known she still held.

Suddenly, a tight, uncomfortable feeling gripped her. Robin paused in her rocking and crocheting to rub at a bulge, which was probably a foot, poking her below her breastbone.

Marge entered the sitting room; the floorboards squeaked slightly under her slippered feet. "Oh, those are shaping up to be so sweet."

Robin didn't want to dislodge Marge from her usual seating. "Would you like your chair back?"

"No, no. I'll be fine on the couch." She sat down on the wood-framed piece of furniture upholstered in a tight-looped, russet-colored fabric with a deep texture. Marge ran her hand over the surface of the cushion next to her. "It's only a few short weeks until the baby comes. Sue, Lynn, and I planned a surprise for you. A baby shower."

Marge's hazel eyes were kind as always, but held a steady glint, as if she expected Robin to object to the idea.

"You shouldn't have."

Robin shook her head and started to say more, but Marge rushed ahead.

"Yes, we should. We all need a little fun to liven up these weary winter days, and an expectant mother and her baby are the perfect excuse." Marge nodded firmly and smiled. She leaned forward and placed her hands on her knees. "We're going to rent the church hall and invite our neighbors and friends. It'll be a regular neighborhood party."

"But none of them know me very well," Robin tried to protest. She really didn't want Marge going out of her way.

"Nonsense. They know you live and work with us, and that's all that's required for now. They'll all have the opportunity to get to know you. Other than livening our spirits and furnishing some gifts, that's what the party is for."

"Well...thank you." Robin sensed her cheeks flushing with warmth. It felt good to be fawned over a little. "When?"

"Next Saturday. Sue and I have everything set for the food, and Lynette is doing some games." Marge's eyes twinkled. "There will be quite a spread."

Robin laughed. "Of course. Hopefully your famous potato salad will be among the offerings."

Marge winked. "I could arrange that."

She and Robin talked past their bedtime about the details. Finally, they said goodnight.

Robin could hardly believe how eager to help Marge made Susan sound. Susan did not fit the image of a social party planner, so it couldn't be the joy of arranging the event that made Susan volunteer to work with Marge. Maybe Susan was bending, fully accepting Robin now. Or maybe she simply wanted a distraction from the worry like they all did. Either way it was nice. Robin nestled her head in her feather pillow and fell asleep with a smile on her face instead of a tear in her eye.

Days later

Robin couldn't keep track of all the names. Marge had introduced her to what seemed like half the county. A group of about twenty-five ladies mingled in the basement hall of St. Katherine's church. Robin looked around for Susan but didn't see her.

"Where's Sue at?" Robin questioned Marge.

Marge smiled widely and her close-to-perfect teeth showed. "Oh, she'll be along presently."

She tugged at the sleeve of her cotton, floral-print dress. It fit her tight under the bust and flared out in a gathered skirt. The style was rather old-fashioned, but it suited Marge's figure.

A drop waist would have made her look heavier than she was.

Robin studied Marge, who looked radiant. Maybe it was the new dress. Despite finances and rationing, Marge had managed to sew a new dress for herself and Robin. Marge had offered to sew one for Susan, but she'd insisted that her green poplin would do perfectly well. To one of Lynette's dresses, Marge had added some lace at the collar and sleeves, and it had taken on a whole new look.

"I think it's time to gather the chicks up." Marge bustled through the crowd and raised her voice as she came to where the food was laid out. "Ladies. Ladies! If I could have your attention, please."

She clapped her hands, and the voices in the room died down.

Marge spread her arm out to where some small tables and chairs had been set up. "Please take a seat, and we will begin."

Marge signaled to Robin to come stand by her. Robin disliked being the center of attention, but she came to Marge's side as requested.

Marge caught up Robin's hand and held it tightly. "I think all of you know that the guest of honor is my lovely niece, Robin, and her expected little one."

Robin looked out at the sea of friendly faces. She offered the warmest smile she could muster in return.

"Firstly, we have a special surprise for our woman of the hour." Marge squeezed Robin's hand again before letting it go. She held up both of her hands. "Please join me in welcoming Robin's mother, Mrs. Beryl Massart, and Robin's sister, Mabel."

The room erupted with polite clapping.

Robin's jaw dropped and instant tears rushed from her eyes

as she watched her mother and sister, directed by Susan, walk from the back of the room toward her. She couldn't believe her happiness at seeing some of her family and almost sobbed with joy, but she kept her feelings reined in. She didn't want to embarrass them or Marge. Robin, still speechless from shock, hugged her mother tightly.

Robin's mother spoke into her ear and kissed her on the cheek. "It feels so good to have my spring Robin back in my arms again."

The sound of Mom's nickname for her made Robin cry in earnest. Mabel squeezed Robin in a tight embrace next.

"I missed you, Sissy," Mabel told her as they hugged cheek to cheek.

Mabel has grown! When Robin had left in April, Mabel had still been an inch or two shorter than her. *Not anymore.* The sisters leaned back and smiled widely at each other.

After a few seconds, Marge quieted the group. Robin, her mother, and Mabel stood holding hands.

Marge spoke up. "Lynette will come and direct us in our first game. The winner will take home a lovely, embroidered dishcloth set handmade and donated by Dorothy Shumacher."

More clapping accompanied sisters and mother as they followed Marge's lead and seated themselves at the front-most table.

Lynette moved to the front of the room. She had passed sleeping Reggie off to a neighbor. "I hope you all remember your nursery rhymes. The person who can match the most phrases with the correct rhyme wins. I'll say the phrase. The first person who responds will be recorded by Susan." Lynette pointed to Sue, who stood off to the side with her hand poised over a small chalkboard, gripping a piece of chalk. "Here's the first one..."

Lynette read her first clue off a paper in her hand and started. A hilariously entertaining fifteen minutes resulted.

Lily Kline ended up winning with nineteen out of twenty answers correct. In the rhyme *Polly Put the Kettle On,* she had mixed up the name and said Molly.

Next, they played "pin the diaper on the doll" while blindfolded. Each table of ladies was instructed by Lynette to select a player and was given a doll, a diaper, and a set of pins. The winner had to get the diaper pinned around the correct anatomical parts first.

When Lynette yelled, "Time!" the ladies all cheered their respective players on. Robin had elected Mabel to be the pinner at their table. Mabel did a good job, but Henrietta Luddington, Marge's best friend, won.

Marge turned to Robin and nudged her, speaking loud enough so that both Robin and her mother could hear. "Henrietta has borne twelve children, so if anyone can pin a diaper on a baby blindfolded, it's her."

Mom laughed. "Well, I would hope so."

"Thanks everyone for playing!" Lynette announced with enthusiasm to the group. "Why don't you all take your seats? We will have our refreshments shortly, but first Marge has told me that Mrs. Massart will lead us in a short devotional and prayer."

Robin's mother smiled warmly at her and walked to the front. She spoke with an ease in public that Robin hadn't known her mother possessed.

"Thank you all for the warm welcome and coming out to help us celebrate Robin and the new life she shelters." Mom cleared her throat. "The Bible calls the fruit of the womb a gift from God. Robin has certainly been a gift to her father and me.

She has blessed our life in countless ways and is a joy to our whole family." Mom turned to bestow a wobbly smile on Marge. "She has flown far from home, but Edward and I are so glad that she and Willis have found a surrogate family here in Dunn County."

Robin noticed Marge brush the corner of her eye with a white handkerchief.

"Thank you all for making my daughter feel a part of your community." The group clapped lightly at Mom's words. "Let us pray." She opened up a palm-sized book and read a short prayer of thanks. Closing the book, she added, "Lord, we commit this new life to you. Restore Willis to his family, so he may be the father this child needs. We pray for all the men of the community that are abroad and fighting. May your grace cover them, your Spirit comfort, and your angels protect our sons, husbands, and brothers. Amen."

A few sniffles could be heard around the room as Mom came back to sit next to Robin.

Robin reached out and clasped her mother's hand in hers. "Thanks, Mom. I love you."

"I love you too and always will."

Robin's gaze lingered on her mother. They connected in a way that they hadn't before, for now they would share motherhood. Questions rose to the surface of Robin's thoughts about being a mother.

It felt the right time to ask, so she did. "Were you scared...to give birth?"

Mom shrugged her shoulders. "I suppose every woman is." She shook her head. "I was more scared after you were born. I watched you closely at every opportunity, terrified that you would slip away...like Lyle did."

Mom hadn't mentioned Robin's dead brother—born before Robin—in some time. Robin remembered visiting his grave with her mother and siblings. A small, rounded headstone marked the spot. Mom had told them about their brother—how he sucked in his bottom lip when he slept, smelled of spring flowers and talcum, and looked just like their father. They had always gone in the spring to the Catholic cemetery in Oconto to visit and lay pastel mayflowers and white trillium on his grave.

Robin wanted to ask the other questions rattling around in her brain, but Marge gave the invitation to partake of the buffet-style food. An array of light sandwiches, salads, and white cake for dessert with both blue and pink decorations covered a table at the head of the room.

The most pressing question Robin had was: *Will I be a good mother?*

Robin's mother squeezed her hand. "We can talk more later."

Robin nodded. "Sure. I'd like that."

Robin's table got the privilege of getting their food first, so Robin, Mom, Mabel, Lynette, Sue, Henrietta, and Marge started the line at the serving table. After the meal, Marge led Robin around the room, introducing her to people she had not met yet. Mom and Mabel followed along, but soon weariness started to wash over Robin.

"You're looking rather peaked. We better get you to a chair," Marge insisted, and she planted Robin in a seat with a glass of water.

"Thanks," Robin uttered and took a sip.

"We'll let you rest for a bit and then you can open gifts. Mabel, would you write down who gave what for your sister?" Marge turned to Mabel. "I'll get a pen and paper for you."

"Yes, ma'am. I'd be happy to," Mabel responded with sweetness, her cheeks flushing pink.

Robin decided her sister looked much more like a young lady now with her hair twisted in a becoming knot. Her lace-trimmed dress curved over her bosom snuggly, and her thick lashes and charming, full smile spoke femininity.

"Wonderful," Marge responded. "I'm going to check and see how Lynette and Susan are doing with the cleanup from the meal."

Marge hurried off to the kitchen.

Robin leaned back in her chair. "I owe Lynette and Susan a big thank you for all of their help with this lovely day. Even though I'm tired, this has been so fun. And having you both here is miraculous." She smiled at her mother and sister. "I didn't even ask yet…how did you manage the cost?"

Mom dipped her head and looked at her hands. "Oh, it didn't amount to much."

Robin knew that to be a tell-tale sign of her mother stretching the truth.

"The better question is how Dad's going to manage without Mom," Mabel offered.

"Oh? Miss you, will he?" Robin turned to her mother, whom she thought was still a pretty woman even though she approached forty.

Mom shook her head. "I suppose he will, but I think Mabel is referring to your brothers. They've been getting into one spat after another recently, and if your father can handle them without his anger rising, it will be a miracle."

Mom's always been able to calm Dad's temper. Robin wanted

to hear more about her family, but Marge clustered the gifts at their table, and the unwrapping began.

Hours later

Marge lifted herself up from her chair in the sitting room and tucked her crocheting in a small carpet bag with wooden handles. "Hal already went up. I should follow. Will you turn down the lamps when you are done?"

She looked over to where Robin and her mother occupied the couch.

"Of course, don't worry," Robin reassured her. "We won't leave anything burning."

"Thank you. Well, goodnight."

Marge set her gaze first on Mom then Robin. It was as if Marge knew Robin desired to talk alone with her mother. Susan had gone to her room after supper complaining of a headache. Mabel had happily followed soon after with a book tucked under her arm from Marge and Hal's modest but well-stocked library. Now Robin and her mother would be alone.

"Goodnight," Robin and Mom chimed in together, wishing Marge a good rest.

They looked at each other and grinned.

After Marge had gone, Robin asked the question which had been burning in her heart all afternoon. She faced her mother. "How do I know I'll be a good mom?"

"Oh honey, no mother is perfect. You shouldn't worry so. Remember you have five younger siblings. You always did an exemplary job of watching them when I asked you. You have an awareness of how to keep children safe and give them love. That's all that's required for now." While she was speaking, Mom took Robin's hand and folded it gently in her own. "The rest will come. You will learn as they grow. Your father and I did."

"Thanks, Mom. Maybe I'm worried over nothing, I know I'd be more confident if Willis was here with me," Robin admitted.

"That may be, but you have Marge and Lynette, both experienced mothers, and a whole community of neighbors and friends. Surely everything will be fine."

Robin nodded and tried to take the words her mother shared with her as truth, but something in her repelled Mom's reassurances when it came to Robin's aptitude for motherhood. She doubted herself greatly.

"God says that 'every good and perfect gift comes down from the Father of lights.' This child is a good and perfect gift. Trust God; He will equip you for this role of motherhood, which He has called you to." Mom leaned back and released Robin's hand.

Mom looks so tired. It's selfish of me to keep her up to bolster my faith.

"We should turn in. It's been a long day," Robin told her mother.

Mom covered a yawn with the back of her hand. "I am sorry. The travel and the long day are catching up with me it seems."

"Yes." Robin rose from the couch and helped Mom up. "Let's get some rest. I'll get this lamp, if you turn down the other."

Robin pointed out the bright lamp next to Marge's chair.

"Certainly," Mom replied.

Soon they were left in relative dark, except for what light came from the candle in a holder on the kitchen table. They walked to the kitchen, and Robin picked up the brass holder.

She carried the lit candle, and they made their way up the narrow stairwell. When they reached the landing, Robin gave the candle to her mother.

"I am accustomed to finding my way in the dark upstairs now." She pointed out the way for Mom. "The guest room is across the way."

Mom turned to her. "Thank you, dear. Sleep well."

Robin noticed how the candlelight deepened the dark smudges under her mother's eyes and made her look haggard.

"Goodnight, Mom." Robin held her gaze a moment. "Thanks for coming."

Mom nodded and turned her lips up in a slow, tired smile. "I knew you needed me."

She turned and walked toward the guest room. Robin stood still for a few seconds and watched her mother's back before turning and walking the few steps to her room. Robin prayed she would have the confidence that her mother had in knowing what her child needed. *Maybe that's an ingrained trait,* Robin told herself as she entered her room. She turned and looked once more at the guest room door before shutting her own bedroom door quietly behind her.

I marked the worst year of my mother's life, apparently.

CHAPTER THIRTEEN

Enid
January 1984
"Are you sure there's nothing?" I stand on one leg and lean over the counter, hoping to get a view of the file that the secretary in the county clerk's office is looking through.

She shakes her head and looks up at me. "I don't see any asylum records. You could check with the historical society. I could give you a number."

She blinks big, brown eyes at me. Her Farrah Fowcett hairstyle in deep brown feathers her hair away from her face. She appears to be in her thirties, which means she's over thirty-five years younger than me. A mere baby.

I lean back and stand up straight. "You're certain?"

I don't want to leave here without any answers or at least a clue. Sheldon told Cassie, who told me, that he thought the clerk's office might have old records, so I came to find out.

"I'm sorry." She shakes her head again and glances up at the clock on the wall, ticking out the minutes.

I sigh heavily. "All right. Well, I appreciate you checking."

I back up a little and hike the shoulder strap of my purse

higher up. The young woman nods and shuffles the papers back together in the file.

"Have a good day. Stay warm out there," she says as I turn to leave.

"Thanks. You too," I say back.

That's what people say to each other in Wisconsin in January when it's fifteen below zero: wishes for warmth. I zip my down jacket and pull my gloves on. My crocheted hat is still on my head. I clomp down the hall in my boots, go down a flight of stairs, and exit the building.

"Where to now?" I ask myself aloud.

Thankfully no one is around. The streets are pretty quiet for the middle of the day, but then Stout is still on its Christmas break. I get in the Dodge, which I didn't bother to lock, and go to start it, but the engine chokes and turns over a few times with no spark of life. I pump the pedal a mite…one more time. I turn the key again…

Great. I must have flooded the engine. I pound the steering wheel and end up blowing the horn. A woman walking by on the sidewalk gives me a dirty look.

I yank open the truck door, slide out, slam the door behind me, and walk back up to the courthouse to see if there's a payphone. Or maybe I can ask the thirty-something woman if I can borrow her phone and make a call. The weather should grant me some sympathy.

Hours later
Clive holds the Dodge's door open for me. "It probably just got too cold. You didn't do anything wrong."

Thankfully I was able to call Clive's shop, and he sent one of the guys with a tow truck. They pulled it inside, tinkered with it, and got it going again. That was after I sat and read through every *People*, *Good Housekeeping*, and *Family Circle* in the waiting room.

"Thanks for rescuing me." I give my hubby a peck on the cheek.

"But it's the last time," he says sternly. He frowns but then laughs. I know he's kidding. "Hey." He switches to a lighter tone. "We going over to Kelly and Doris's for the girls' birthdays tonight? Fourteen. Man! A couple more years and they'll be graduating. That makes me feel old." Clive shakes his head.

"I hear ya. The woman at the clerk's office who looked for information for me was less than half my age and gorgeous," I get in.

Clive kisses me on the cheek. "You'll always be that sweet young thing I shared a cone with at the DQ."

I roll my eyes. "I was fifteen, freckle-faced, and flat-chested."

He grins. "I never noticed."

"Close the door. I'm ready to get out of this cold."

He nods. "See you at home."

Clive closes the truck door and gives it a slap, as if it were a horse. I pop it into gear and wave. He gives me a brief salute and heads back inside.

I rumble on toward home, taking Broadway to Highway 25 and hanging a right on Cty Road D. About a half a mile in, I pull into our driveway, park the truck, get out, and walk to the house. The large, white, wooden goose standing by the door greets me. Apparently, geese are chic in the country decor theme. At least that's what Doris told me when she gave me the goose at Christmas.

I chuckle. "A Christmas goose."

I open the door, which I hadn't locked. We trust our neighbors out here. An involuntary shiver runs through me. The warmth of the house welcomes me. I shed my coat, boots, hat, and mittens, and feel ten pounds lighter.

I have about an hour and a half before Clive gets home and we need to get ready to go to Kelly's. A lounge before the fire with a cup of tea sounds great to me. After I heat some water and get my tea, I make a fire in the fireplace, and draw up my cozy, plush chair. The flames dance before me and make me think.

Since nothing resulted from the search at the courthouse, where do I turn to next? The historical society? Maybe. But I could keep digging through Mom's diaries. I am bound to come across something. I get up, switch on a light, and rifle through the stack of them next to my desk. I finished with '77. Now I'm on to '78. I carry the book back to my chair, cover up with an Afghan, and get settled. I sip my tea and open the diary.

January 20th, 1978
Dear Diary,
Today is the anniversary of my mother's death. She's been gone twenty-two years now, and I still miss her. Those last ten years or so, we got to see each other more than we had before. The modern highways connecting the east and west sides of Wisconsin helped. Although Mom never drove out alone. Dad drove mostly, and they took the train. I went back to Maple Grove once every year at least for a visit.

I saw Delvin the most out of the boys. He remained single for quite some time and traveled around. He stayed here at the farm for months during one stint of his adventures. He finally settled down with a nurse he met in Albert Lee, Minnesota. Albert and

Earl came out a time or two, but their visits tapered off in the thirties and forties as their families grew.

My oldest brother...I...can't recall his name. N...it starts with an N. I can picture his face. Well, he never came. After I moved out here to the Holcombs' I saw him only two or three times when I went back home to visit. After that he joined some civil service parks program out west. He ended up dying out there and is buried in...I can't think of what town or state.

Muriel married a man from Oconto. What is his name? Man, this frustrates me. I can't remember my own brother's name, much less my brother-in-law's! Well, anyway, he was a marine engineer. They moved to Marinette when he got a job at the ship builders there. I don't remember them ever coming out here to visit, but I usually saw them every year.

Gosh, I don't know why I am recounting my family. Maybe it's because I feel stuck in the past. I can recall the past more than the present these days.

Mabel came out to see us the most. She grew very fond of Enid. It was Mabel who first called her Enie. The name stuck. I miss my sister. Out of all my siblings Mabel and I were the closest, but she's been gone for some years now. Breast cancer. She was only forty-one when she died. I was forty-three. She stayed one whole summer here with us once, but that was so long ago, the year after...that terrible time. That summer she met Lincoln at the Dunn County fair, and when she left, they wrote letters back and forth until he finally proposed. They lived and raised their family on a farm in...hmm, I can't seem to think of the name of the town. It's not too far from here. An hour east, I think.

Thinking of that summer makes me remember the one before. I don't recall what I had for lunch or what I watched on TV this afternoon, but I remember the day I tried to free myself from my sorrows under the weeping willow and the following summer among the flowers. Why is this so fresh and real of late? I don't know. Maybe something I learned during that time will help prepare me for this journey into forgetfulness—the path I'm forced to walk on. Time is stealing my memories.

That reminds me, I have to talk to Enid. I'm sure the woman she hired to come clean for me is stealing my jewelry. Two of my favorite pins are gone, and all of my clip-on earrings. I don't know how she thinks she can get away with stealing that many at a time, but I plan to watch her closely the next time she's here. That is, if I remember to.

I lower the diary to my lap and finish my tea. Not too long ago when cleaning the kitchen in the farmhouse, I found all of Mom's clip-on earrings buried beneath ground coffee in a Folger's can, as if they were treasure. Poor Mom.

I think of Aunt Mabel. Which summer is Mom talking about? I know I have seen an old photo of Mabel and Lincoln at their wedding somewhere. Maybe it would have the date on the back. That would help me narrow down when Mom must have been at the asylum. *Hmm, where have I seen that?* Oh yes, I think in the basket of old family photos Mom kept. I don't know why she didn't put them in a photo album. Many times over the years, I remember digging through the basket. It was always a good way to weather a rainy day.

I get up from my cozy spot, determined to find the basket of photos. I start with the boxes of Mom's things stashed in the closet in the guest room.

After a good search I find the basket. I dump the photos on the floor and sort through them. Among others, I find photos of: Mom and Dad posing for a shot with the new tractor; me as a toddler in an Easter dress and riding a tricycle; Cassie and her mom and dad smiling at me from a park somewhere; Dad in his uniform…

Here it is. Mabel and Lincoln are exiting a church. She looks alive in the snapshot. Mabel has her arm up, warding off the rice that people are throwing. Dark, wavy hair frames her face. Her eyes are closed, but I remember them as dark and lovely, two perfect ovals. Her face is shaped like Grandpa Edward's with a strong jaw. In the photo it's the only feature that mars her almost perfect feminine image. She was a beautiful woman.

I remember Mabel fondly and the way she would brush and braid my hair, the silly games we would play, but mostly the stories she could tell. Mom said her stories were the best because she had so many in her head. Mabel was a voracious reader, consuming books as if they were food. If I remember right, she worked at a library for a while. I brush my finger over her image and flip the photo over. The words "Mabel's wedding August 1919" are scrolled in Mom's handwriting on the back.

So, if Mom wrote in her diary that the year before Mabel's marriage was "the terrible time," that would make it 1918—the year I was born. An ache forms in my chest. I marked the worst year of my mother's life, apparently.

"Hey. Whatcha up to? Looks like a tornado hit."

I look up. Clive stands in the doorway of the guest room. I didn't hear him come in.

"Oh, just looking through old photos."

I work at collecting the pictures and put them back in the basket.

Clive walks in and kneels down to help me. I spy a large grease stain on his pants, but I don't say anything. At the moment I don't care if the guest room carpet gets grease on it.

"Find what you were looking for?" he asks as he collects some photos.

I don't want to talk about how hurt I feel, and it would lead to that if I told Clive about what I read in Mom's diary and the photo of Mabel's wedding.

I change the subject. "Yes, but we better hurry. Thanks for helping me pick these up. I didn't realize it was so late."

"You think the girls will like their gifts?" he asks as he deposits the last bunch of photographs into the basket.

I made them matching aprons with fabric from some of Mom's vintage dresses, and we splurged and bought them a Kitchen Aid mixer in a coral color. They are both in Home Economics at school, and they have both taken to baking. Clive teasingly calls Pam "Betty Crocker" and Phoebe "Bopsy Crocker." They don't seem to mind.

"I think they'll be thrilled. They will probably want to start baking right away."

Clive grins lopsidedly. "I'd be okay with that."

I laugh and realize how much I love this man. "I bet you would."

I swat his arm playfully as I walk by him and out of the room.

He follows. "I'm gonna jump in the shower. Care to join me?"

Good grief! What is he thinking?

I look back at him. "No. We'll be running late as it is. What has gotten into you lately?"

I turn and keep walking to our bedroom. I need to put on a party frock.

"Nothin'," he says to my back. "It's not a crime to love my wife."

I shake my head and ignore him. I enter our bedroom and peel off the baggy sweater I have on. I slide back the mirrored closet door and file through my dresses. *No. Definitely not. Too small. Too big...*

"This one may fit the bill," I express out loud and pull out a little, black number in a sheath style made from a stretchy, polyester fabric. It has simple but elegant lines. The dress's one frivolity is the scalloped, white lace at the hem. I think I'll wear my pearl necklace too.

After I change, I brush through my hair, adding a pearl-coated barrette on one side of my head when I'm done. The mirror tells me that I don't look too bad for an old lady. But maybe some blush and lipstick will add a little more sparkle. I pull the cosmetics off the vanity one by one and apply them. Clive walks in, his lower half wrapped in a towel, just as I smack my lips.

"Don't you look fine." He scans me up and down. His face falls a tad. "Does this mean I have to wear a suit?"

I chuckle. "No." I know how much he hates wearing formalwear. "A nice shirt and slacks will do. Put on your black pair. Then we'll match."

I kiss him on the cheek and move to get my black, leather boots. He slips on his briefs, socks, and pants while I pull on my boots and zip them.

"I don't have to wear a tie, do I?" Clive asks as he puts his arms in a gray-striped shirt.

"No, you'll be fine as you are."

He finishes dressing, and I walk to the entry to put on my gray, wool coat and collect my purse. Clive meets me at the front door, dressed and smelling of aftershave. He grabs a jacket, and we leave for Kelly's house in town.

In about fifteen minutes, we arrive and park in the drive. Kelly and Doris have a nice home. The one-level house is spacious with a fully furnished basement, a nice backyard, and a two-door garage. The one drawback is the tiny entryway, which has nowhere to hang coats, much less stow any shoes.

We get out of the gray, two-door Pontiac—Clive's car—and walk several yards to the house. Clive carries the wrapped box with the heavy mixer, and I carry the aprons, wrapped in matching paper. Pam waits at the door; I see her face smiling at us through the glass. *Well, at least I think it's Pam.*

She opens the door and shouts, "Grammie Enie and Papa C!"

Her face is split wide in a smile, and her braces shine in the light. When I get closer, I can tell for sure that she's Pam. Of the twins, Pam has bluish-hazel eyes; Phoebe's are light blue, almost icy.

Her face reflects some concern and sadness. "Grammie isn't coming?"

"No. I'm sorry. Grammie doesn't do too well in the evening."

"Oh. I miss her."

Pam and Phoebe, even at a very young age, gravitated toward Mom, which surprised me. Mom had never been one to snuggle a baby. In fact, she seemed to have an aversion to infants, but from the get-go, she coddled the twins and poured out love on them with kisses, endearments, and snuggles. If I am honest, it made me rather jealous. She had never lavished love on me in such ways—not that I know of.

There was at least one thing which connected us: a love for reading. I stow away my memories for another day and agree with Pam.

"Me too," I say as I step into the house and hug Pam, grateful to love and be loved in return by my granddaughter.

Sometimes I feel I compensate for the lack of closeness between my mother and me by showering my granddaughters with affection. I let Pam go and her sister bounces forward.

"That looks heavy," Phoebe greets us, grinning from ear to ear at the package Clive holds.

We walk in. I give Phoebe a hug too.

"Mom. Dad." Kelly approaches us. "Doris is finishing up supper. Come on in."

Clive hands the gift to Kelly, who comments, "Whatcha got in here, gold bricks?"

"Almost," Clive teases.

I pass the package I carry to Pam. "This goes with it."

"Thanks!" Pam says. "I'll put this with the others."

She steps quickly through the door-less threshold and into the kitchen, where I can see a small card table set up with a cake and birthday gifts on it. Kelly has already placed our other present there.

Doris flashes me an easy smile and glances up from dicing tomatoes. "Hello, Enid."

It looks like the party menu is Mexican. The fixings for tacos litter the countertop of the kitchen peninsula.

"Hi. Looks and smells good." I smile back. "Anything I can do?"

"I think everything is complete except for these tomatoes. The girls wanted tacos, and I was fine with that. Hope that's okay with you and Clive."

Clive comes to stand by the counter and comments in his usual goofy way, "I love me a good taco."

"Good." Doris finishes with the tomatoes and transfers

them to a round dish. She has a set of Pfaltzgraff in a creamy-white. "All set, I think."

She rinses her hands at the sink. I notice Mom's white hobnail glass displayed in her china hutch. Doris must like it. I'm glad Kelly packed it up for her.

"Is it just us? Your folks not coming?" I ask Doris.

"No. They couldn't make it. Dad's not feeling well."

"Oh? Not anything serious I hope."

I know Doris is close to her dad. Her folks live not far away in Hudson, Wisconsin. He's a retired lawyer and her mother a housekeeper.

Doris wipes up the counter where she's been cutting the tomatoes. "Mom said his heart is racing and giving him some difficulty. They are seeing a cardiologist tomorrow."

"I'm sorry. I hope it's nothing too serious."

"Thanks. I think he's been overdoing it lately. Too much consulting, and I thought he had retired." She rolls her eyes, places the rag over the kitchen faucet, and raises her voice. "Everything's ready. Gather by the counter, and we'll say a quick blessing."

The girls stand next to each other in matching salmon-pink dresses. A white piping runs diagonally across the chest, accenting the edge of a large, white, fold-down collar.

Kelly offers a prayer for his daughters, which brings tears to my eyes. He is a tender man like his father. My hand finds Clive's, and he squeezes back. We give each other a look of understanding. I can hear what he's thinking—we didn't do too bad. We are proud of our son and his daughters.

Neither of us had bad childhoods, but neither were we fed a steady meal of love. Clive's mom died when he was nine; his dad never remarried and turned rather bitter. Clive has a sister he's close to, but she lives in Colorado now. She was his saving grace in the love department until I came along.

Clive and I met when we were teens. He's always said that he fell in love with me the first time he saw me. He just didn't know what the feeling was then, but neither did I. I do now. We have grown together, part of the same heart, and I don't think anything could ever split us apart.

Her own daughter was like a stranger's child to her.

CHAPTER FOURTEEN

Robin
Late March 1918

Robin looked out her bedroom window, which faced south. She put her nose close to the windowpane, looking to her left. The horizon blushed pink to the east, but the sky had the beginnings of a baby-blue color. The snowy landscape lay before her covered in an early morning hoarfrost. The weeping branches of the willow tree looked like it had been coated in an egg wash and dipped in raw sugar. The sleeping, frozen pond rested underneath the large tree, looking like a large, silvery mirror in the morning light. The lawn and pasture shone as if a glittered Christmas card. All together it painted a stunning winter scene, but Robin had hoped for signs of spring in March, not another frosting of snow and ice.

She let the lined, floral curtain drop from her hand, and it fell into place, covering the window again. The baby cried, and Robin's heart plummeted. She would have to feed her again. *Shouldn't I look forward to nursing my child?* Robin felt the answer should be yes, but since her delivery she had experienced a strange urge to withdraw from the little person she had carried in her womb for nine months. Honestly, Robin had sensed a deeper connection between her and her child when they had been physically bonded together, but now she had to drum up an affection for her daughter and pretend. Surely, something was wrong.

Robin wished her mother and Mabel had stayed long enough to have been here for Enid's birth, but they had left just a week ago. One day before Robin had gone into labor. She had been attended by Henrietta, Marge's friend with the large family. Marge said that Henrietta had given birth to most of her children by herself. The mere idea made Robin want to faint. Despite Robin's sheer exhaustion from her hours in labor, according to Henrietta, Enid's birth had gone "swimmingly."

Enid's cries were pitching from mewing to wailing. Robin forced her feet to move to the bassinet. She reached in carefully and picked up Enid. Robin jiggled her and patted her back. Enid's cries calmed to whimpers.

Robin carried her to the rocking chair, which Hal and Marge had bought her as a shower gift, and sat down. She manipulated her nursing nightgown so Enid could have access to her breast. Enid suckled, but instead of feeling the contentment Henrietta had told her would come when nursing, a sadness washed over Robin. While her baby nourished herself, Robin cried slow, silent tears. She thought of what a bad mother she must be to host such a lack of affection for her own child. It was not that she wished Enid harm, but Robin experienced no joy when holding her. And there should be joy. *There should be!*

A knock on the door startled her. "Yes?"

Robin stopped rocking, feeling shame flame her face with heat over the thoughts in her head.

The sound of Marge's sweet voice drifted through the door. "Breakfast is ready. Do you want to come down, or should I bring some up on a tray for you?"

"I'll come down, but I have to finish nursing Enid first. I'll be just a few more minutes."

Robin thought that if she went downstairs, then Susan or Marge could hold Enid, and Robin would be able to eat in peace.

"Fine. Susan and I will wait for you. Hal had his breakfast early and is out doing chores." Marge's footsteps retreated.

Robin switched Enid to her other breast. After a few minutes, the baby's sucking slowed. Moving Enid up to her shoulder, Robin burped her daughter. She got up from her seat and checked Enid's diaper out of duty, but she disliked the job greatly. *None of this is how I imagined it would be!*

Enid's gray-blue eyes looked up at Robin. The child lay quiet under Robin's touch as she switched out the wet diaper for a clean one. When she was finished, Robin pulled Enid's gown back down and cinched her legs and feet in the drawstring closure at the bottom. Robin wrapped Enid back up in her blanket, laid her on the bed, and fetched a robe from the hook on the door to wrap herself in. After she used the chamberpot, Robin poured some water into the wash basin on the stand and scrubbed her hands and face with a cake of lavender soap. She dried off and quickly ran a brush through her hair.

Snatching her daughter from the bed, Robin hurried down the steps. The smell of coffee and cinnamon met her nose.

"Well, here's our little sweet pea." Marge set down a plate of cinnamon rolls on the kitchen table and moved toward Robin and the baby with her arms held out. "Come to Great Auntie Marge."

Robin passed off Enid and sat at her usual place at the table. The food looked and smelled delicious, but Robin hardly felt hungry.

Susan took the cover off a pot on the table and scooped some oatmeal out and into a cereal bowl. She placed the serving in front of Robin. Raisins and cinnamon dotted the surface with a slurry of melted butter on top.

Susan pointed to the tiny, brown pottery jug in the middle of the table. "Honey's in the pot, if you want some."

"Thanks." Robin stirred her cereal, adding a dollop of honey from the pot and a splash of milk from the glass pitcher.

Susan sat down across from Robin and pulled apart a cinnamon roll, eating small chunks one at a time. "Baby sleeping better?"

For how efficient Susan could be, she ate slowly. She certainly looked to be savoring the sweet roll.

"Yes. She only woke up once last night," Robin answered.

She poured herself some coffee.

"It took months for Susan to figure out a schedule when she was a baby. She kept us awake till all hours of the night." Marge joined the conversation and sat down, snuggling Enid against her ample bosom. She peered at Enid's sleeping face with love and turned large, love-struck eyes on Robin. "She looks so angelic, doesn't she?"

A pain jabbed at Robin's heart. She wished she could say the same. Yes, Robin supposed her daughter was beautiful as babies went, but nothing in her made her look or feel like Marge so obviously did—smitten.

"Yes," Robin agreed.

She mustered a happy smile, but she knew in her heart that she pretended. Lied would be the better word.

"I thought after breakfast you might want to take a bath. I had Hal set the tub up by the stove, and he has strict instructions not to come into the kitchen."

Robin looked over to the side of the range. *Sure enough.* She didn't know how she had missed noticing the large, galvanized tub.

All Robin wanted to do was go back to bed, but she forced herself to say yes. "That sounds fine. Thank you."

Robin took a bit of oatmeal and swallowed. It warmed her, and she found she was hungrier than she thought.

"I can watch Enid while you have your bath." Susan slipped the words out before nonchalantly taking a large drink of coffee from her cup.

Her voice held an excited tone, though Robin could tell Sue tried to disguise it by covering up her kindness with an ordinary action. *Even fussy Susan is more excited about watching Enid than I am.*

"That would be nice. Thanks."

Robin looked across at Susan, who actually smiled at her. Robin dropped her gaze back to her food. She really didn't deserve anybody's kindness, much less Susan's.

Marge cuddled Enid and ate her breakfast with one hand, while she talked of Susan and Lynette's first weeks as infants. Robin listened and commented as needed between bites but didn't rejoice with Marge over the small victories Enid made each day. *It's as if Enid belongs to Marge and not me.* It grated on Robin's nerves to hear all the sweet stories of Marge's daughters' early days compared to Enid's.

Robin finished her coffee, while Susan cleaned up and took Enid to the sitting room. Marge heated water for the bath, and soon Robin disrobed behind the screen Marge had pulled from the corner. Robin stuck a couple of fingers in to test the temperature. *Just right.* She stepped in and sunk down into the tub. The water rose up to her chin.

Robin leaned back and relaxed. The sound of Susan singing a lullaby to Enid made her jealous. She recalled some of the songs her mother had sung to her and that, in turn, she had sung to her siblings. But none of them rose up in Robin's heart when she looked at Enid. Her own daughter was like a stranger's child to her.

How would Willis think of you? Poorly. The accusation drummed in her mind. She hated herself for her lack of love and for her sadness, but she didn't know what to do or how to change her thoughts. In a spontaneous action, Robin dunked her head under the water. The action blissfully drowned out Susan's song. It seemed Robin floated free and unburdened for a moment, but then the need to breathe made her surface.

When out of the water, she pulled her wet hair back from her face and grabbed the soap. *Wash and get out,* she told herself. She suddenly hated the sensation of the water surrounding her and longed to be out of its clutches.

Maybe I don't know my mother as well as I thought I did.

CHAPTER FIFTEEN

Enid
April 1984

"Ahhhh! Stoooop! No!!!"

I cringe, hearing Mom's screams and cries from down the hall. I don't know if I should go help or wait in her room. I forgot Saturday morning was bath time, otherwise I would have come a different day. Mom has always disliked taking a bath, and she never used to go swimming. *"I was not made to bob around in water like an olive in a glass of gin,"* she always said about baths. She took sponge baths or showers.

"Robin!" a CNA shouts at her. "Settle down! We have you. It will be okay."

Mom replies with much splashing and a few curse words. "Aaaaah! Hhh…elp!"

Mom's screams reach a higher pitch. My feet are glued to the floor. I have never heard my mother so utterly petrified before. It frightens me.

An exasperated statement from the nurse accompanies a gurgling sound and more splashing. "That's it. We're done."

I decide to wait for a while until they get her dressed.

Hopefully, she'll be calmer when she's out of the water.

I walk back toward the entryway and perch on a bench, watching the bustle of nursing assistants hauling tail from one room to another. It appears they need more staff, probably the curse of every nursing home. A woman who looks to be in her seventies, with thin, white-blonde hair, wheels slowly past me. She's using the handrail on the wall to pull herself along with one arm. One foot helps on the floor as well. Her other arm rests immobile in her lap with some sort of brace on. I wonder whether I should help, but then decide not to, as she turns into a room, the name Penny Holt marked on a nameplate on the wall. I glance at my watch to see if enough time has passed: seventeen minutes. I get up and head back toward Mom's room.

I rap my knuckles on the partially closed door before entering.

"Mom?" I call out as I walk in.

She sits in her chair by the window dressed in a pink sweatsuit and slippers. A rolling tray-table stands nearby with a half-eaten container of red Jello and a small glass of orange juice sitting on top. Her hair is damp. Her eyes, droopy and large, meet mine. She smells of cheap, fruity shampoo and baby powder.

"All spic and span, huh?" I ask rhetorically.

I plant myself on the end of her bed. She doesn't say anything. She looks down at her lap where her hands fold together. We sit in silence for a few seconds before I figure out what to chat about. It will most likely be a visit where I do all of the talking. We seem to be having more of those lately. Mom retreats into herself at those times and doesn't appear to care what I say or do.

"Pam and Phoebe had a birthday recently. Clive and I bought them a mixer. They love to bake. Remember making cookies with the girls?"

Mom lifts her gaze to the corner of the wall, like she's inwardly searching for an answer. After a few seconds, she says, "Ging-er-bread," in a slow, rusty voice that sounds like it needs oil.

I feel a smile lift my lips. "Yes. That was always your favorite cookie to make, even in the summer. Except then you cut them into other shapes than men."

Mom's lips stay together but one side slants up. She looks like a little kid and reminds me of how the twins used to smile when they were up to mischief. The faint grin fades, and she turns to gaze out the window where several robins peck at the ground. A flat-topped bird feeder on a post with a shingle roof hosts a blue jay pecking at sunflower seeds. I'm glad she has the birds to watch from her room.

"Looks like it's warming up outside." I hate it when I revert to talking about the weather with Mom, like we're strangers and have nothing better to discuss. I change the topic. "How about eating the rest of your Jello?"

I move and pick up the plastic cup of gelatin and a spoon. It smells like cherry. I fill up the spoon and hold it out to her. She opens her mouth like a baby bird, and I spoon in the rubbery sweetness.

"Mmm," she responds as her lips slide the Jello off the spoon.

Mom always did like cherry. That gives me an idea.

"Next time I come, I'll stop and pick up a cherry dilly bar from the DQ for you. Would you like that?" I study her face, hoping for a remembrance of her favorite fast-food treat to light up her expression, but none comes. "Well, I'm sure you will," I answer for her.

With my help, she finishes her mid-morning snack. I turn the TV on, and together we watch Bonanza. Mom falls asleep part of the way through. I shut off the TV, toss the empty Jello cup in the trash, tuck an Afghan around her, and leave.

"Time to head to the store," I tell myself.

I hate grocery shopping. If it were up to me, Clive would do it all the time. He enjoys it; I have no clue why. It's such a chore: picking out the food, packing it in the car, driving it home, unloading it, putting it away. Clive's working today, and it falls to me to bring home the bacon.

I'm almost to the main entrance when a voice calls me back. "Mrs. Fenton. I'd like to speak with you a moment."

The director of the nursing home briskly walks my way, her clogs clomping with each step. I stop and wait for her. When she reaches me, she huffs, like she's out of breath, as if she ran down the hall after me.

"Yes? How can I help you?" She can't have anything good to say; I'm sure.

"It's about your mother."

Of course it is. What else would it be about?

"I'm listening," I tell her with a stiff smile.

"I had to file an incident report this morning. While helping your mother wash, one of the CNAs received a nasty scratch." The director's face holds some sympathy. Mrs. Simpson is an attractive woman with dark hair and eyes. I'd guess her to be in her forties. "Now, I know your mother is confused, and clearly something must have frightened her, but we can't have our staff getting hurt. We might want to think about some medication to calm Robin at these times."

"Medication?" Is she thinking of doping Mom with tranquilizers?

Her face and voice are kind but unmoving. "Nothing too strong, just to help her with whatever anxiety she seems to be experiencing. I really recommend it…and if this happens again, I will have to insist."

"I see." I pin her with a direct gaze. "Just so you know, my mother hates baths. She didn't take them. Ever. Maybe you could try another way of helping her wash before you ply her with pills." My voice has taken on a sharp edge.

"Oh, my," she gasps. "I was unaware. We could consider that."

"Do you have a shower?"

"We have movable wands on the bath heads. We could put a stool in an empty tub for her to sit on while she's rinsed with the wand." She looks at me sideways, testing my reaction.

"That sounds like a good idea." I am sincere, and I hope she can hear it. "Please try this before medication."

She nods and seems satisfied. "I will implement that change. We want what is best for our residents."

Her expression holds sincerity.

"Thank you." I nod and move to go.

She stops me by placing a hand on my forearm. Her eyes soften. "Robin is really a very lovely woman. I know how difficult it is to see a parent slide into the cloud of memory loss."

"Thanks. I appreciate that. Good day."

"The same to you."

She smiles again and turns, walking back the way she came. Her shoes clomp quieter this time. I exit the building and think about what she recognized in Mom. "*A very lovely woman,*" she said. Yes, Mom always has been congenial, never one to be difficult. It saddens me yet again that she has to walk down this path of behavior which is so unlike her. But is it? Maybe I don't know my mother as well as I thought I did. Her diaries are telling me that fact.

I sigh and hop in the Dodge, reluctant to do battle with groceries. Think I'll take a detour first. I stop at the Cennex gas station, get a coffee and a package of mini powdered donuts, then head down to the park off 21st Street by Lake Menomin. Not many people are around. A woman in a green sweater pushes a small girl with her long, brown hair in pigtails on one of the swings. A couple—around my age—walk together. In one hand the man holds a red leash attached to a large, yellow Labrador.

I pull into a parking space, shut off the engine, roll the window down, and bite open the clear, cellophane package of my mini donuts, spraying out a puff of powdered sugar with the effort. *Nice.* I brush off my shirt and pants, before eating a donut whole in retaliation. My gaze roves over the lake, which is mostly clear of ice, but a few stubborn spots remain. It's strange not to see anyone fishing. In a few weeks, after the fishing opener, this park will be crowded with boats and fishing-folk.

I take a swallow of coffee—thankfully it's not too hot—and I rehash the scene from this morning, Mom screaming about her bath. I wonder why she hates water so. She never prevented me from taking a bath, and I remember going swimming with Sue, Lynette, and Cassie many times. Mom never came with us on those occasions. Maybe further digging in her diaries will unearth some reason for her abstinence from being in water. I guess here is as good a place as any to try and find out. I wipe traces of powdered sugar off on my pants, rifle through my bag, and pull out a diary. The year reads 1978. Yesterday, when I met Cassie for tea, I took it with me to show her. Mom had written something sweet about Cassie, and I wanted her to read it. Dusting off my hands, I open up the diary to the next entry.

April 21st, 1978
Dear Diary,
It's a beautiful spring day. I decided to walk out to the willow today and sit on the bench Willis made me before he left for war all those years ago in 1918. I'm surprised the wood hasn't rotted completely away, but it holds my slight frame sturdily enough.

I am thinking clearly today. I thought about the locket Willis gave me, so I came to look in the willow to see if it is still there. It is. So many times over the years I wanted to free it. However, the necklace marks the day I almost threw it all away, and here it will remain. Hidden.

I wish I could forget that time. Why is it that I can recall certain memories and not others? Why can't I pick the best and remember those? Instead I am stuck with my worst mistake.

The pond is serene now and free of ice. A family of ducks tour around the edge. The swampy grass is just starting to sprout up. Really, it is a lovely spot. I feel close to Willis here. I miss him. I wish he was here to help me navigate these days of forgetfulness. I can only pray Enid will be patient with me.

For the millionth time, I regret the space I've kept between my daughter and me. I know it stems from guilt. Enid has always been a good girl and a dutiful daughter. She deserves better than me, but me is what she got. I hope I won't be too much of a burden. Nobody wants that.

With my heart heavy, I close my mother's diary. What guilt kept space between us? Why would I deserve better? What is Mom talking about?

I understand what guilt is. It burns in my chest yet over admitting her to the nursing home. I hope she doesn't hate me for making that decision, but then she wouldn't. Mom was not a hater. *Isn't!* I'm doing it again—placing her in the past.

I finish my coffee and eat the rest of the donuts, making sure to check my face in the mirror for evidence of my indulgence before I head to the grocery store. I start the Dodge, pull out of my parking spot, and drive to the store, all the while trying to figure out the puzzle of my mother, but I am missing some pieces. There is no one left alive to shed light on the mysteries she writes about. She certainly can't tell me, and I've hit a dead end in the records department, looking for documents about the asylum. I do something I should have done months ago. I pray.

I whisper aloud, "Lord, there are no secrets from you. Would you help me figure out the pieces of Mom that I never understood? Please. I feel the need to uncover what she's kept from me. I pray it gives me freedom from the need to try to win her love."

There it is. The core of the issue with Mom: a need to win her love. My eyesight blurs. It takes me a few seconds to realize that I'm crying. I wipe my eyes with the back of my hand and keep driving, determined to keep digging and praying.

God, how do I stop this runaway train in my mind,
which is loaded with all the awful things I expect that I am?

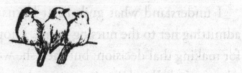

CHAPTER SIXTEEN

Robin
Early April 1918

The sky hung heavy and gray like Robin's thoughts. She sat alone on the couch in the sitting room where so many warm Holcomb family gatherings had taken place, but Robin did not sense the cozy feeling of love in the room now. She sensed a hollowness in the space, which matched her heart.

Thinking of something hollow made Robin suddenly remember a tree she'd seen once at home in Maple Grove. She had been helping her father cut lumber, and they had been spying out the dead and rotting trees to fell first and haul away.

"This one's rotten to the core," her father, Edward, had told her.

He'd stood pointing to a tall, old maple.

Robin had questioned him. "But, Dad, it looks perfectly healthy. I don't see any rot."

Robin had tipped her head at him.

He'd motioned to her. "Come 'round to this side."

Robin had walked around the tree, coming to where her

father stood, and he had been right. A hole in the tree—twice as big as a man's head—had revealed a hollow, rotten center. She remembered thinking how strange it was that the tree appeared to be healthy when in fact it wasn't.

She was that tree now, looking normal and put-together on the outside, while her inside had disintegrated into a rotten bleakness.

I'm a terrible excuse for a mother. Willis will not want to come home to the likes of me. He deserves someone better to be his wife and raise his child.

Robin clenched her hands into tight fists, while thoughts bombarded her mind. With each onslaught of terrible truths and accusations, Robin's frustration lessened and gave way to a hopeless, empty hole through which her life was being sucked. In the back of her mind, Robin could recognize the mountain she careened down, but that part of her stood by, watching like a helpless bystander witnessing a tragic accident.

She stared down at her hands in her lap, her fingers relaxed. Four red half-moons were etched in the palm of each hand, where her fingernails had pressed into her flesh.

Oh, Willis. Oh, God, Robin prayed. A sob caught in her throat, and her fingers found the locket around her neck with her and Willis's pictures in. "*Two halves of the same heart,*" Willis had told her. Robin tried to hold onto his words, but they drifted from her. She sat in a quiet daze, senselessly staring out the window at the dreary spring day.

"Robin. Robin!" With her hand on her hip and a frown on her face, Susan stood a few feet away from Robin. "What is the matter with you? I've been calling you. Can't you hear Enid crying? She's awake and wants to be fed. Marge is changing her diaper. Do you want to nurse her in here or upstairs?"

Susan waited for an answer.

Robin shrugged. "Wherever."

She tried to curve her lips into a smile for the sake of appearances, but she couldn't.

"Dad will be coming in from chores soon, but he'll most likely sit in the kitchen and read the paper while we fix supper. I'll bring Enid in here. That'll be best," Susan told Robin.

Robin nodded and turned her eyes slowly up to Susan.

Susan's face softened, and she sat on the edge of the couch next to Robin. "Listen, I don't know what has happened, but you don't seem yourself. Is there anything Mom or I can do to help?"

"I'm just missing Willis. I'm worried about him."

Her words held truth but lacked the whole. Robin knew whatever plagued her originated from more than missing her husband, but worry for his safety did eat at her. His last letter had confirmed that his unit now fought in France.

Susan reached for one of Robin's hands and folded her fingers around Robin's. "I know. Tom wrote they had arrived and are fighting. Oh, he makes jokes, like usual, in his letters, but in between the lines, I can tell he's scared." Susan turned Robin's hand palm-side up. "What's this? Did you hurt yourself?"

Robin looked at the fingernail marks. One had begun bleeding.

She pulled her hand from Susan's grasp. "It's nothing."

Susan stared, her forehead in a wrinkle. "Oh? It doesn't…"

She got cut off by Marge entering the room with Enid, who whimpered.

Marge stepped close to the couch and passed Enid into Robin's hands. "Someone wants her mommy."

"Thanks. Sorry about before. I...I was daydreaming." Robin attempted a weak smile, hoping she could pull off her fib.

"No harm done except for a few tears," Marge graciously replied. She nodded and wiped her hands on her apron. "Yes, well, you give little Enid her supper, and Sue and I will go make ours. I am thinking perhaps a chicken pot pie with our leftovers from our roasted bird yesterday. Sound good?"

Marge spoke to Robin in such a way that one might tempt a child to eat. Robin didn't blame her. She knew she'd been acting strange and childlike in a way.

"Sure. Lovely," Robin told Marge.

"Fine." Marge smiled widely and turned, walking back to the kitchen.

Susan got up and followed, casting one long, narrowed backward glance Robin's way.

Robin positioned Enid with the help of a couch cushion, and the baby started to feed. She ran her hand over Enid's downy head.

"I'm sorry," Robin whispered to her daughter.

The real pain she experienced at the moment made her close her eyes. *God, how do I stop this runaway train in my mind, which is loaded with all the awful things I expect that I am?* She sighed and worked on relaxing, but Robin didn't know how much longer she could expect to keep fooling the Holcombs. *One of these days, they will all find out who I truly am and what I am capable of.*

Days later

Robin tested one boot on the ice at the edge of the pond. It easily gave way, cracking and breaking into sharp splinters like a hammered pane of glass. She watched the water gush up through the cracks, swallowing the surface of the ice. In a few more days there would be no ice. The sun had done its job of ridding the landscape of snow. Signs of spring were beginning to emerge. Birds twittered, and a warm breeze blew and tickled the hairs on Robin's neck.

She stared at that watery splotch on the ice, and it sent a shiver down her spine, making her crave the numbness the cold water would bring. On a sudden impulse, she reached down and plunged her fingers into the chill water. She kept her fingers submerged until they bit with the pain of the cold temperature. She couldn't help but think what it would feel like to have her whole body engulfed in the pond's icy water.

She pulled her hand out in one swift motion when she could no longer stand the pain. After shaking her hand, Robin dried it on her coat and shoved her poor, red hand back into her mitten. She fondled the naked branches of the willow with her other mittened hand and dared herself to step out onto the cracked surface of the pond. Surely the cold would ease the barrage of accusations in her mind. She needed peace and couldn't figure out how to find it. She held onto the branches with one hand and made to step out onto the water.

"Whoa! You don't want to do that."

A thick hand grasped her by the elbow. *Hal? Where did he come from?*

Embarrassment heated Robin's face. "Oh, I was just testing it."

She turned to him but didn't look him in the eye, for surely he would see the lie hidden in hers.

"It's deep here, and the ice is nary but a thin coat. It'll be gone soon, I reckon, though." Hal pulled her back, establishing her feet firmly on the ground a foot away from the edge. He gazed around and let out a deep breath. "Nice day for a walk. Care to take a stroll down the road with an old farmer?"

He smiled, and the silver-capped tooth on his row of top teeth glinted in the sun. Although the sun felt warm, Hal had his hat with flannel earflaps pulled down tightly over his head. His face was grizzled with the faintest tinge of gray whiskers, which clustered darker in the grooves of his smile.

"No. I should get back to relieve Marge."

Robin looked back toward the farmhouse where the daughter she couldn't bring herself to love fully was being taken care of by a woman who could. *Enid belongs with Marge or even Susan. Not me.*

"Oh, Marge eats up every chance she gets to be with your little darling. That's for sure. It's no hardship for her." Hal released Robin's arm. "But if you want to head back in, I'll go with you. Time for a mid-morning snack, I'd say." Hal smacked his lean midriff and grinned. "I bet Marge has some cookies hidden away somewhere."

Robin would have laughed with amusement months ago at Hal's mischief, but not today. Not now. Nothing held amusement for her anymore. Her laughter had been swallowed by too many tears, and she didn't think it would ever come back.

She forced herself to respond. "Sure. That'd be fine."

She fell in step with Hal's bow-legged gait and listened as he talked of the new kittens which had been born in the haymow, but the whole way back to the house she could not get the vision of herself breaking through the icy water of the pond out of her mind. For some odd reason it didn't frighten her. What frightened her were the empty days before her, trying to be a better mother. And she was tired of trying.

Tending living things heals the spirit.

CHAPTER SEVENTEEN

Enid
May 1984

"I was wondering if you might help me?"

"I can try," the tall, middle-aged man responds with a smile on his tanned face and in his deep brown eyes, set behind studious, black glasses. His eyes hold attention, peering down at me from across the counter.

I stand in a stone church building in Menomonie, which now serves as The Dunn County Historical Society museum. The air in the small room hangs sticky yet dusty with the smell of old things.

I clear my throat and continue. "I'm looking for information about the asylum which used to be here in town. Would you happen to have any sort of register or documentation of those admitted there?"

I wait with bated breath. The last lead in my trail of inquiry lies here.

"We do have several registers but not every year. Which were you looking for?"

He moves a few paces and pulls out a crate with several old, black books in it.

Hope settles in my heart. I don't know why it's so important to me to see my mother's name etched in the asylum's records. Maybe I need some solidity to the secrets which have been kept from me.

"Wonderful. Nineteen-eighteen, specifically."

"All right. Let me take a look." The man searches through the books. "Ah, here we are." He sets a faded, black, leather-bound book before me.

"Thank you."

I flip it open. Starting in January, I file through the names. *Nothing.* I look through February and the following few months. This is probably a wasted effort too. Then my eye stops unbelievably at *Mrs. Robin Holcomb, admitted May 16th, 1918 - Female hysteria.* Hysteria? What in the world does that mean? I look for more information and a check-out date, but there is nothing else written about Mom. My heart sinks with disappointment. I push the book back toward the man across the wooden counter.

"Find what you're looking for?" he asks in a concerned voice.

"Yes and no." I sigh and try to smile. "I appreciate your help. Would...would you have anything else about the asylum?"

"I have a general history book of Dunn County, which I know includes information about the asylum." He pauses and waits, looking as if he's gauging my interest.

"I should take a look while I'm here."

I nod, and he steps around the counter to a small, wooden podium, on which a thick book rests.

He motions for me to follow him. "This is the best book on Dunn County that I know of. It gets its own stand." He opens the book to the table of contents, running his finger down the headings. "Ah-ha." Creases on either side of his smile furrow his face. "Here we are." He turns the pages of the book in sections until he's about a third of the way in. "A couple of pages about the asylum." He backs up, giving me space to come look, which I do. "I'll leave you to it."

He walks back behind the counter, puts on a pair of glasses, which he perches halfway down his nose, and sits down on a stool. He un-creases *The Dunn County News* and spreads it open, holding it up in both hands.

I turn to the old but well-cared-for book and read through the pages detailing information about The Dunn County Asylum for the Chronic Insane. I hate that Mom was at such a facility with such a name, but the more I read, the better I feel. From what it says here, some people actually got better at the asylum. When I picture county or state asylums at the turn of the century, I see jail-like institutions, but this doesn't seem to be how the Dunn County asylum was run. Residents of the asylum who were mentally and physically able worked at the dairy that the asylum operated. Apparently, from what I can read, it even made money for the county.

No wonder some people recovered. *"Tending living things heals the spirit."* A sudden memory of Mom saying those very words jogs my mind. As if it were yesterday, I can see Mom in her flowerbed, wearing a straw sunhat with a pruner gripped in one hand. It's spring, and she snips at the hydrangea bushes. *"Pruning is a necessary part of life; just you remember that."* Mom shook the pruners at me, and I nodded. It's funny how I recall that memory. Mom didn't spew wisdom at me on a regular basis, but now and then she came out with something worth remembering. And I guess I did.

I focus back on the page and read the rest of the section

about the asylum. It doesn't tell me much about what Mom's experience may have been like there, but the sick feeling I've carried in the pit of my stomach since discovering Mom was in the asylum has lessened.

I gaze at the picture of the institution once more before I close the book. The building is almost in the exact location as the nursing home. I wonder if Mom knows that. She must have at some point. My hand gives a little wave and my head a nod as I thank the museum attendant and walk out into the bright sunshine.

It's beginning to heat up. Maybe I'll go grab an ice cream cone and sit down by the lake.

A while later

I have my vanilla cone almost gone, well, at least the dome of melting ice cream on the top. My teeth crunch into the cone. It doesn't take me long to finish it off. I lick my sticky fingers and wipe the slobber on my fingertips on the thick mat of green grass underneath me. A fisherman in a boat cruises by on his way in from fishing in the cemetery slough. I decided to drive to Butch's Bay and sit here instead of by the library or the park in North Menomonie. I like it better here.

Thoughts of Mom squiggle through my mind. In a way I feel closer to her now than I did before her diagnosis. Reading her diary and having the simple interactions with her that I do now has alleviated the unnamed strain which always stretched between us, like a guitar string about to snap. I want to read more of Mom's words.

I sift through my bag and find one of the diaries that I tucked inside before I left home. I pull it out and open to a new section.

June 5th, 1978

Dear Diary,

I have less and less interest to write in here. The days are blending together, and I can't define them. Enid stops out to check on me every day, or so she says. I don't remember her being here every day. I don't think she came today, but she must have…

I'm tired of trying to remember. Perhaps it will be easier to be blissfully ignorant. I'm less worried about the whole thing. Whatever comes, comes.

One thing that helps me: The Lord promises to be with me no matter what my journey looks like. No matter if I can't remember where I am or who I am. He'll know, and that will have to be enough.

I pray Enie won't be too hard on herself, if she has to take care of me or pay someone else to. I have so many regrets in life, but there's one that I've never let go of—keeping my distance from my own daughter. I hope she can forgive me one day. She'll likely never understand why I held her at arm's length. I thought it was for her own protection, and I suppose because I didn't feel worthy of her. She should have been someone else's daughter. Again, why can I remember all this and recount my feelings when I can't recount the day today?

I think of Molly and me all those years ago, working side by side at the asylum. She's the reason I love flowers so much. Whenever I see a hollyhock, I think of her. She was a friend to me at a time when I had none. She's long gone now, but I'll be seeing her again one of these days.

Time to go. My head pains me, writing all this out. I have to concentrate so hard. My temples are pounding. The days of my diary records are numbered, I think.

Stopping there, I thumb through the rest of the year's entries. They are hit and miss. Mom must have found it increasingly difficult to keep up with recording her thoughts. I sigh heavily and try not to think about what's around the corner for Mom, but I can't help it. How many years will Mom go on like this, living in a world she doesn't know? How long before the other world comes calling?

I shake my head, tuck the book back in my bag, and stand up. I swat off a few bits of debris from my tan chinos, hoist my bag, and walk to the Dodge. Time to go home and fix supper. What do I make tonight? I took some hamburger out of the freezer to thaw this morning. Maybe lasagna. I haven't made that in ages, and it's Clive's favorite hot dish. Well, one of the two he'll eat anyway. Tater tot hotdish is the other. Clive likes his food separated for the most part.

The Dodge's door creaks as I open it. I hop in, start the truck up, and hightail it for home. I left my watch at home, but the traffic and the sky signal to me that it nears the dinner hour. Clive might beat me home. I press on the gas, happy to be thinking about something else besides my mother.

She'd been so consumed with her own ineptitude.
And those same damning thoughts still rested in her chest.

CHAPTER EIGHTEEN

Robin
May 1918

Even though Marge and Hal were gone to town and Susan was doing chores in the barn, Robin hadn't planned it, but now that she stood at the end of the pond, an inner voice drew her in.

Be free. This is your only way out. Everyone, especially your daughter, will be better off without you.

Robin didn't bother taking off her shoes. She slowly walked into the pond, the water resisting the forward motion of her legs. The chilly temperature of the water shocked her and made her suck in a deep breath. She paused but after a few seconds forged ahead. Her shoe got momentarily caught in something at the bottom. Robin wiggled her leg and pulled it out. She dragged her hands along the surface of the pond, as if preparing the little body of water to receive her.

When the water reached her chin, Robin stopped, for she had heard a voice tell her to. Where it came from, she didn't know, but she couldn't listen. *This is my only way out of the guilt*, she told herself. Robin closed her eyes and stepped off the bottom ledge of the pond, where the deepest portion beckoned.

The pond engulfed her like one big, hungry fish and she its prey. An involuntary response forced her to hold her breath. Her lungs burned. She sank like a lead sinker. Robin had no idea how long she held her burning lungs restricted…seconds…minutes. She knew she should let go of her captured breath and let the water do its job, but she couldn't. Instead, her hands started scooping back water, and she pedaled her arms. Robin pushed off the muddy bottom with her feet, her eyes flashed open, and she ascended to the circle of lighter blue above her head. She broke through the surface with a gasp. Sucking in air, she splashed her arms and tried to swim, but her heavy dress and shoes weighed her down. She fought to keep her head above the water. A voice echoed in her ears. This time it was audible.

"Robin! Grab the branch! Come on! You can do it! Reach out, for God's sake. Reach out!"

In between splashes, Robin saw that Susan stood in water up to her knees, holding out a broken limb from the willow tree. For a split-second, Robin contemplated resisting and falling back down into the water, but something compelled her forward. She paddled as best she could toward the branch.

"A little farther, you can do it!" Susan urged.

Robin listened, and her fingers brushed the limb then grabbed ahold of the wet, slippery branch—an anchor amidst the tiny sea. Susan pulled on the other end. Just as Robin started moving to safety, a chunk of the branch that she held broke off, and she started to sink again. She took in a mouthful of water, flailing her arms to try to rise.

Panic rose in her chest and rang in her ears. Robin could see the ledge of the murky drop-off ahead. If she could only make it there and get on higher ground, but she tired of struggling. *Surrender, and it will be over soon.* She needed to, but an innate desire in her kept urging her to resist. When she thought she wouldn't have a choice, she felt a hand grip hers and tug. Soon arms were around her chest. Her head broke the surface of the pond, and she wheezed in another breath, sputtering out pond water in the process. Robin lay against Susan, who swam backward a few strokes.

"You can stand here," Susan told her, coughing. In her clinging shift, Susan stood and pulled Robin up with her, the water level with her chest. Robin coughed and spewed out more water. "Use your legs now," Susan demanded, and she pulled Robin forward toward the edge of the pond.

Robin and her rescuer sloshed out of the water. It had begun to rain. Robin didn't know how she could get any wetter, for she felt as if she'd been soaking in a bathtub for a week.

Susan let Robin's arm go. Reaching for her dress, lying in the muck at the edge of the pond, Susan pulled it over her head, mud and all. She plucked her shoes and socks up in one dripping hand. Her hair was matted to her head, and Robin could see her shivering, which she was doing too.

Susan reached out a hand and helped Robin up the slippery bank. "Come on. We need to get to the house and make a fire in the stove."

The rain dropped down in a steady rhythm. When they were on level ground, Susan pinned Robin with a hard look. Sue's eyes narrowed. She swiped her damp hair back from her cheek with an arm and studied Robin. Her mouth opened, and she seemed on the verge of questioning Robin, but she didn't. Instead, Susan turned and walked barefoot back to the house. Robin followed, eaten up with the shame of what she had almost done.

When in the house, Sue gathered kindling and a few small chunks of wood and started a fire in the stove in the sitting room. Robin hung back and pulled off her shoes, feeling numb and stupid. Susan walked to the dining table, picked up a chair, and carried it toward the fire. She plopped it down with a *thunk* close to the front of the rectangular, black stove.

"Sit," she demanded of Robin.

Robin lowered her gaze to the floor and fumbled for a good excuse to escape Susan's presence. "I...I should go check on Enid."

"I'll do that and fetch us some dry things. Stay put." Susan's tone could have sliced through a block of ice.

Robin nodded and eased herself down on the seat, duly reprimanded, but she soon found out she couldn't sit still. Beyond her control, Robin's arms and legs shook. Holding her hands out toward the stove to warm them, she noticed her hands shook like she played a tambourine. She moved her hands to her head, combing her wet hair back with her fingers. Images of her walk into the pond kept flashing before her mind. She closed her eyes and tried to block out the visuals, but they kept coming until she felt like she was drowning again. By the time Susan came back, Robin gasped for air and clawed at her neck.

"Hey!" Susan dropped to her knees and held Robin's hands. She wore dry clothes and had braided her hair. "You're safe." Her tone softened, as their eyes connected for the first time since the rescue. Robin was afraid she would see judgment in Sue's eyes, but they remained wide, open, and understanding. "Breathe. Just breathe." Susan spoke slowly, with care.

Robin listened. She concentrated on her breathing and kept her eyes focused on Susan.

"Good." Susan stood up and picked up a towel that she had dropped on the floor next to them. Handing it to Robin, she said, "Dry off. Here, stand and I'll help you peel off your wet things. Enie is still sleeping."

Robin nodded and obeyed. She was like a child under Susan's care as she peeled off her clothes. After dry underclothes and a dress were on her frame, Robin sat back down on the chair. Susan wrapped her in a blanket. She finally stopped shaking, but her limbs still registered a kind of numbness.

"I'll be right back."

Robin heard Susan walk toward the kitchen. The gush of water from the indoor pump and the clink of cups told Robin that she was making tea. Robin sat quietly and waited. A few minutes later, Susan brought a tray and set it near them on a tea table. She poured tea from a brownstone teapot into two ivory cups with gold rims. She handed one cup to Robin.

"Thank you," Robin muttered.

She took the cup. The tea smelled like oil of bergamot— Earl Grey. She closed her eyes and took in the comforting scent.

The scrape of a chair sounded nearby. Robin opened her eyes to see that Susan had pulled up another chair next to Robin's. Susan held the other cup in her hands and placed her bottom on the chair; together they sat at a cozy distance in front of the stove. The warmth started to work its way through Robin's tense muscles.

Susan took a sip of tea before she asked, "Care to tell me what that was all about?"

She jerked her head toward the south window, through which the pond could be seen.

Robin didn't know what to say. *How can I possibly tell Susan that I intended to drown myself?*

She swallowed. "Well…I…don't know."

Robin lowered her head and took a sip of tea in an effort to hide her lie.

"Did you…slip?"

Robin could tell out the corner of her eye that Susan studied her, but Robin didn't want to look back. Couldn't. Or Susan would see the truth.

"I wanted to see how cold the water was, and before I knew it…" Robin left off her explanation.

Susan's fingers reached out and tipped Robin's chin up, which forced Robin to meet Susan's steady gaze.

"Tell me the truth," Susan demanded in her no-nonsense voice.

Robin closed her eyes and took a deep breath. "You won't understand."

"Try me."

Robin opened her eyes, and Susan removed her hold on her.

Robin let go of the truth. "I felt compelled to end my life. I'm a terrible mother." She burst into tears. "Enid deserves a mother like you or Marge who can love her fully." She raised her voice to a yell. "Something's wrong with me!"

She raised up her hands to emphasize her words, but forgot she held a cup of tea, which rolled off her lap and broke on the floor with a crash. She cried harder.

Susan wrapped her arms around Robin again, ignoring the spilt tea and broken cup. Robin clung to her and sobbed for the longest time. Suddenly Susan stiffened, and Robin raised her head off Susan's bony shoulder.

"I called…but no one answered." Marge stood a few feet away from them with her mouth agape and her eyes large. She looked from Susan to Robin and placed her sturdy hand over her bosom. "What has happened? What's wrong?"

No one spoke.

Marge's gaze roved to the wet towels and clothes in an enamel basin on the floor and flicked back to the roaring blaze in the stove. "You must have gotten a chill?"

Robin could tell Marge was fishing for answers, but she didn't want to tell her the truth. She turned begging eyes to Susan, pleading with her silently to keep her secret.

"We've had an…" Susan's gaze flicked to Robin's face before focusing on Marge, "accidental swim."

"Well, good thing you made a fire. The pond has to be pretty cold yet." Marge narrowed her usually soft eyes. "How exactly did your 'swim' happen?"

Seconds passed before Robin spoke up. "It was my fault. I…I…" Robin swallowed and felt like she had a giant dumpling lodged in the back of her throat.

"No, I distracted Robin, and she…well, she slipped into the pond, lost her footing, and I had to go after her," Susan explained.

Robin closed her eyes. *Thank you, God, for Susan.* Robin wouldn't have guessed she'd ever say those words. She couldn't offer a straight-up confession to Marge. She would die of embarrassment and remorse if she did.

"Yes. Without Susan…" Robin left off; she didn't know what else to say. A deep truth settled into her: *Susan saved my life.*

"Oh my, how frightening. I'm so glad you're both…" Marge didn't finish. She tapped her fingers on her chest and sucked in a deep breath, before letting out a gurgling sigh. She stepped closer and reached out a hand to both of them. "I don't know what I'd do…what Hal and I would do, I should say, if anything happened to either of you."

Her voice caught, and Marge lowered herself slowly into her stuffed chair. She blinked several times and sniffed.

"We should get these things cleared up before Dad comes in." Susan glanced over at the clock on the wall. "It's past milking time. I better go help." Susan turned to Robin. "Don't worry about coming. Dad and I'll be fine on our own."

Robin nodded. She hoped Susan could see the thankfulness in her eyes.

"Yes. You rest here, dear. I'll wrangle up some supper for us," Marge agreed. She visibly swallowed and rose from her chair. She motioned for Robin to take her spot. "It's comfier over here."

Robin didn't want to move. She experienced a rare calm and worried that any shift would disrupt it, but she did as Marge directed.

Marge tucked the blanket wrapped around Robin's body more tightly around her. "There, snug as a bug in a rug."

A wobbly smile cracked her face, but her wide blueberry eyes held questions. Robin didn't peg Marge as the gullible type. She likely guessed something more than a "slip in the pond" had happened.

"Thanks," Robin uttered.

Marge lumbered off to the kitchen with a heavy gait, favoring her left side. *Her hip must be bothering her.* A tinge of worried tugged at Robin's heart. It was the first time she'd thought of anyone else's welfare for days. She'd been so consumed with her own ineptitude. And those same damning thoughts still rested in her chest. Her almost drowning hadn't washed them away, but perhaps it had loosened the dark thoughts enough to let concern for others creep in. *A good sign,*

Robin guessed. She sighed and snuggled deeper into the blanket and Marge's chair. Her eyelids drooped.

Some time later

The rattle of a pan jerked Robin awake. *Must have drifted off.* She yawned. The room had darkened, for the sun had set. *I must have been asleep for hours. It must be well past supper time.* Marge and Susan must have let her sleep. A conversation between the two of them drifted to her from the kitchen.

"What are we going to do with her?" Marge asked.

The sound of clinking teacups accompanied her question.

Robin smacked her lips together. She was parched, but she didn't want to get up and get a drink. She stretched in the chair and listened.

"What is there to do? We love and take care of her the best we can," Susan's steady voice responded. A baby squeak followed. "There, there," Susan said in a cooing tone.

Robin supposed Susan held Enid.

"Well, yes, but something is terribly wrong with her, if she's gone to such lengths as to…" Marge tapered off then picked back up. "And what about Enie? She needs her mother. I mean, you and I love her, Sue, but a baby needs her mother. And it's almost as if Robin doesn't…well, I know she loves her, but she seems to have some aversion to her." A sad, low cant to Marge's voice made Robin strain to hear her next words. "We should perhaps…consider the asylum."

"Surely not," Susan responded. "Let's give her some time."

Their voices quieted, and the sound of water and dishes being sloshed around in it covered Sue and Marge's stilted words.

Marge thinks I'm mad. A sob caught in Robin's throat. But

wasn't that exactly what she was, if she had tried to kill herself? Robin knew she needed help, but The Dunn County Asylum for the Chronic Insane? *Am I chronically insane? Is that why I can't seem to feel normal? Have I somehow been irrevocably damaged?*

Robin's worst fear and nightmare crept into reality with Marge and Susan's conversation—*I really am crazy.*

This woman is not my mother, and yet she is.

CHAPTER NINETEEN

Enid
   June 1984

This is the last one. The last diary that holds Mom's words. She can no longer speak well, but her words speak to me here. They tell me who my mother was...is.

I turn to one of the last entries, which is legible and still compiled of sentences, rather than random gibberish.

I'm on the back porch at home. This lazy June day has finally cooled down with a breeze from the northeast. A cold drink rests on the white, wooden side table next to my wicker rocker, which I sit in, rocking gently. I'm comfortable. I fold open the diary further and begin to read.

July 8th, 1978
Dear Diary,
I am sitting under the weeping willow today. I know their—no, that's not the right word—thare...they...I give up. Anyway, I know the time approaches when I will no longer be able to sit out here, by the pond that I once hated and the tree that saved my life. Well, it was Susan who saved me. No. It was God who saved me,

covering my mental weakness with His grace. Thank you, thank you, thank you, Lord. I could have very well died the day I tried to drown myself here in this quiet, tranquil place.

Maybe I should have told Enid at some point. But how? I couldn't have said, "Oh, by the way, I was committed to a mental asylum for almost drowning myself after you were born." I feel that would have opened a reason for her to blame herself. It's probably better that she doesn't know. Some secrets should remain buried.

That makes me think—I should get rid of these diaries. I will. When I get in the house, I'll write it down, so I don't forget. That terrible time can go to the grave with me.

I'm tired. I'm always tired. Too tired to get ready for the day sometimes. I stayed in my bathrobe all day today. When I decided to come sit out here after supper, I put some clothes on. Lord knows what the neighbors would think, if they went by.

Thinking makes me tired. I'm going to put my pen to rest now...

I clench the diary to my chest and take a deep breath. Now I know. Mom tried to commit suicide. She tried to shield me all these years from the truth. I don't ever recall Mom dealing with any sort of depression. Could it have been an isolated incidence of postpartum depression severe enough to threaten her life? I'll likely never know.

I sniff and wipe a tear from the corner of my eye. I let the diary lie open in my lap and watch the motion of the water. There's some current here in this portion of the lake from the river. Some ducks bob on the surface like rubber ducks in a tub—a perfect line of five.

I need to go see Mom. It's been a few days. The last time was so disheartening. She didn't speak to me, which isn't unusual, but she didn't even look at me. Not directly. I basically visited with myself. Maybe Mom understood I had come to see her in some portion of her heart or mind. Seeing her sit there limp and quiet saddened me. She used to be so active and attentive. This woman is not my mother, and yet she is.

I sigh and check my watch, 4:45. I should get supper started or Clive will get home and be hungry. Maybe BLTs. Those are light. Heavy food on a hot day weighs one down.

I get up from my chair, tuck the diary under my arm, pick up my almost empty glass, and go to start frying the bacon.

The next day
Clive points to the finch on the bird feeder outside of Mom's room. "Look at that little fella. He's a greedy one."

Clive and I sit on a bench in the small flower and shrub garden at the nursing home. Mom is parked in her wheelchair next to us. Her eyes follow where Clive points. A slight smile registers on her face. Her cheery grin does my heart good. Most days Mom is devoid of expression, a placid cloud blocking the sun.

"Isn't that finch a bright yellow, Robin? Reminds me of those tulips that grew around the farmhouse. They sure were pretty. But you always had a way with flowers." Clive chats with Mom in a one-sided conversation. I love him even more for the way he visits with her, as if she will reply back to him any second. "I'm trying to recall the name of your favorite flowers. Tall and lanky they were." He extends his arm to shoulder height. Mom's gaze doesn't follow his motion. He doesn't seem to notice. "Some still grow on the east side of the house. Red and pink blooms," Clive reminds her.

I think he hopes for her to react. To remember. He lowers

his arm slowly back down to his side. I reach out for Clive's hand. He folds his fingers around mine.

"Hollyhocks," I remind him.

"That's right."

He smiles at me, but it's a slow, slight curve of his lips. I can tell he's sad, too, over Mom's lack of response. I drop my head to his shoulder, and we sit in silence for a few seconds.

Mom turns and looks at us. A flash of recognition glimmers in her eyes briefly but passes without any change in the droopy line of her lips. She has developed little jowls on either side of her chin, despite the fact that she is thin. The nurses have given up dressing her in her nice slacks and blouses. Mom wears a gray sweatsuit today. Her hair suffers from a lack of washing and clings together in greasy strands. Mom would have hated looking like this. She was always very fastidious about her appearance, and she always wore lipstick. Not a flashy red, something more subdued in a shade of pink, but no lipstick brightens her lips now. Guilt pricks at my heart yet again.

My gaze is captured and follows motion. The finch has flown, full enough for the time being, it seems. Perhaps we should wheel Mom back in as well.

I pat her right hand, which rests on the arm of her wheelchair. "Time to go in, Mom."

She doesn't respond. Clive and I stand, and he pushes Mom. We walk and roll toward the nursing home door. As I open it, a tiny, old woman rushes through with a black, vinyl purse clutched to her chest. It looks like she's wearing a wig because her hair is crooked. The parting lines up too far to the right, and a shock of curly, gray hair dangles in her eye.

"Ma'am," I call after her.

The woman looks over her shoulder with eyes wild and wide.

"I have to go home. I've been gone too long. George'll wonder where I've been," she tells me in a strained, shaky, high-pitched voice.

She looks rather like I would imagine the white rabbit to look in *Alice in Wonderland*, startled and determined. Clive and I glance at one another.

"Think I should—?" he begins, but he's cut off by a nurse crashing through the doors.

"Irma! Irma!" the nurse in a white uniform shouts. She speeds past us, hurrying after the older woman. The nurse catches the woman's elbow. Her tone is sugar-coated sweet. "Come on now, Irma. George is inside and wants you."

The woman holds her ground and turns puzzled eyes up to the nurse. "Is he? I thought he'd be at home."

Her wrinkled face wrinkles deeper. That poor woman.

The nurse speaks slowly, as if she's speaking to a two-year-old. "Oh, no. He's inside. Come with me, and we'll go find him."

The little, old woman nods and allows herself to be conducted back inside. Her bag hangs limply from her arm. I hold the door open for them.

"Thanks," the nurse says. She looks relieved. "It's the second time she's escaped this week," she whispers in my direction as she passes.

I nod and offer a reserved smile, a healthy dose of bile and guilt coating the back of my throat. *What is this—a prison?* I check on Mom. She sits, oblivious to the excitement that just happened.

"Let's head in," I tell Clive and Mom.

Clive wheels Mom past me. I let the door fall closed behind us. The next set of doors we manage the same way. When we get to Mom's room, Clive parks her chair near the window.

"In case our little friend comes back," he says. He pecks Mom on the cheek. "Bye, Robin."

I move forward to give Mom a loose hug.

"See you in a few days," I tell her.

She sits stiff and quiet as before.

Clive grabs my hand, and we amble back the way we came at a slow pace. Our rubber soles squeak on the waxed, linoleum floors. I think we are both reluctant to leave Mom. I hate that this is her life now. Alzheimer's has taken so much from her and will likely soon take whatever is left of her body. Tears start to slide from my eyes. I use my free hand to wipe them away.

"Oh, come on now." Clive releases my hand and slings his arm around my shoulders, drawing me closer to him. We stop and stand in the doorway of the front entrance. "Don't work yourself up. There's nothing you can change. It is what it is." He embraces me fully, and I fall into him, his belly bulge snug against my chest. He kisses me along the jawline. "I hate to see your mom like this, too, but we can't change anything."

What he says is true, but in my heart I want it to be different.

I nod and lean back. "Take me home."

His eyes reflect my pain. His gaze softens, and he caresses my cheek. "Sure."

We walk back to the Dodge and get in. Clive drives. We don't talk. As the miles pass, I pray.

Dear God, I am holding You to Your promise that You won't leave Mom. You are all she has left. Well, and us. But You can get through this cloud of Alzheimer's to her. I know You can, well...because You're God, and You have no limitations. Help me to trust that she's in good hands.

That's all I can muster. God knows my heart. He sees my fear, and I have to trust that He's with Mom. He has to be.

Robin watched the events happening around her
as if they happened to someone else.

CHAPTER TWENTY

Robin
May 1918

In the end, Robin went with them, like a sheep to the slaughter. The last few days had been difficult at the farm with a strained tension webbed between them all. Now she sat quiet and stiff in Hal's car while he and Marge drove her to be committed to the asylum. Robin didn't blame them. She didn't know what to do with herself either or how to get better. Or if that was even possible.

If I can't get well, then I do deserve to die.

The thought came from the pit of her stomach as they rattled down the road toward Menomonie. Robin didn't know why she felt numb and had no desire to hold or nurse Enid. She had done it because Marge and Susan had expected her to, but the lack of feeling Robin showed and her dunk in the pond had loosened Marge's tongue.

Marge's blue eyes had burned bright. "Can you tell me that you will love this child and not attempt to hurt yourself again?"

She had held Enid in her arms and stood over Robin while

Robin lay on the bed she and Willis had shared.

Robin hadn't known what to say. She couldn't muster up something that wasn't there. She didn't care about anything or anyone. She had buried her face in her pillow and sensed the shift of the mattress as Marge had sat down. Enid had whimpered, and Robin had felt a stab of guilt. But not deep enough.

"You're leaving us with no choice," Marge had stated, her tone hard and sad at the same time. Enid had fussed louder. "Do you understand?"

Robin had kept her face turned to the pillow. She hadn't been able speak. Wouldn't.

She had felt the bed moving up and down as Marge had comforted Enid with pats.

"Shush, now," she'd soothed. Seconds had slipped by. The mattress had sprung back up as Marge had stood. "I wired your mother, but she can't come. One of your siblings is ill. I don't...I don't know how to help you, Robin. Maybe if Willis were here..." She had left the thought, paused, and cleared her throat. "My friend Henrietta assures me that they have the best of care at the asylum. Her daughter is a nurse there. Henrietta says that people go home well sometimes. We'll pray that you recover, and you'll be returned to us in no time. You'll see."

They do think me crazy. Robin had sensed Marge's warm hand taking her shoulder in a tight grip, but Robin hadn't looked at the woman she had thought of as a second mother. She'd kept her face turned away and her voice silent. A few seconds later, Robin had heard the door open and shut.

That had been a few days ago. This morning Hal had helped Robin out to the car with her small suitcase in tow. Robin hadn't protested. Susan had stood in the doorway of the back porch, holding Enid, wrapped in a pink shawl. She'd watched, a grim, sad look on her face. Susan had offered her a brief wave, but Robin had kept her hands down and ducked into the car.

The miles rolled by and soon they were parked in front of the massive, brick building that Robin had seen on occasion from afar. It sprawled out long and wide with rounded corners almost like turrets on a castle. The lighter brick accents above the rows of windows gave Robin the feeling the building watched her. Farm buildings sat behind the structure. Fields of growing corn, clover, and alfalfa surrounded the site. Cows dotted a pasture—"the poor farm" as Marge and Hal had called it.

Hal parked and walked around and opened the car door. It protested with a creak. He reached out a hand to Robin; she took it and stepped out, her shoes crunching on the pebbly drive. Hal's lips, usually curved up in some sort of grin, were a straight, thin line, his blue eyes cloudy and dim. He opened his mouth as if to say something but shut it tight again. A windmill creaked in the wind over by the barn, filling up the blank space of Hal's unsaid words.

Marge got out and stood by them, her face pale. "Let's go in."

Hal nodded. Robin flicked her gaze to Marge. Robin should hate Marge for this committal, but she didn't. In fact, she didn't feel much of anything. She walked with them to the entrance. Hal opened and held the heavy-looking, wooden door for Robin and Marge as they walked through.

An attendant met them inside. She looked over a sheet of paper before saying, "The Holcombs, I presume?"

"Yes," Hal confirmed.

"Good. I am Nurse Sandry," the woman in the cap and blue

and white uniform told them.

Robin looked over this person who in part would be in charge of her. Nurse Sandry's dark hair was tucked up under a white cap. Her gray-blue eyes met Robin's with what looked like disdain.

"This way. Dr. Howington expects you." The nurse turned abruptly, and they followed her out of the spacious entry into a narrow hallway. Nurse Sandry's heels clipped on the wooden floorboards, which were stained a medium oak color. She stopped at the first wooden door on the right with a pane of frosted glass, gave a terse knock, and opened the door. "After you."

Nurse Sandry directed them with her arm as she stood out of the way, signaling Marge, Hal, and Robin through the doorway. They stepped in. Robin hugged the wall with her back. The air smelled of pipe smoke, which helped her relax. The odor reminded her of her father. *What would Dad say if he knew I was here and that I've stooped to being admitted to such a place?* Robin couldn't imagine.

A middle-aged man with a receding hairline, broad forehead, and prominent, brown eyes pointed to the three upholstered chairs in front of his desk. "Please. Have a seat."

He held his salt-and-pepper, goateed chin up and peered at them as they sat down. His expression was not unkind but rather like he was studying a bug in a jar.

"Mr. and Mrs. Halifax Holcomb, Doctor, and their niece, Mrs. Robin Holcomb," Nurse Sandry told Dr. Howington in a professional, crisp tone, gesturing to the family group.

"Yes." He drew the word out. "Thank you, Nurse Sandry. That'll be all."

Dr. Howington nodded in the nurse's direction. She

bobbed her head in return, turned, and left, closing the door behind her without hardly a sound.

The doctor looked at Marge. "Now, we discussed everything in person last week, Mrs. Holcomb."

"Yes." Marge's face blanched. "And you will care for Robin well? Won't you? You'll help her get better?"

Marge fumbled for Robin's hand. Robin let Marge squeeze her hand but didn't squeeze back. Marge let go. Robin didn't care if Marge felt bad for her or guilty for bringing Robin to this place. In truth, Robin felt in her heart that she deserved to be here.

"Yes. We will do all we can, of course, but a great deal depends upon this young woman." Dr. Howington lowered his chin, puckered his lips, and looked intently at Robin, who wanted to avoid his gaze but couldn't. He turned to Hal and Marge. "If you wouldn't mind stepping out for a few moments. I would like to speak with Mrs. Robin Holcomb privately."

"Anything you have to say to Robin you can say in front of us. It might be best that we stay. She isn't…" Marge stumbled through her words. "That is to say, she hasn't said much these last days. And we've only just come."

Marge twiddled her fingers around and around in her lap.

"Not to worry, Mrs. Holcomb." The doctor stood. "I must insist." He motioned to the door. "If you would step out and sit on the bench outside. I'll call you in when we are finished. It won't take long."

The doctor remained standing until Marge and Hal got up. They hesitated and walked to the door. Marge looked over her shoulder once before Hal smiled shyly and closed the door with a click of the handle.

Robin turned her gaze to her lap. The seconds ticked by

with each swing of the pendulum in the small clock on the doctor's desk.

"Robin," Dr. Howington said after some seconds. "I would like to hear in your own words what troubles you."

Robin didn't answer but met his gaze.

"I understand you have recently become a mother. Congratulations." His slight smile reflected gladness.

The words meant little to her, which she knew was wrong. They should mean everything. Robin lowered her eyes again and picked at her thumbnail.

"Mrs. Holcomb has also informed me that you…almost drowned in the pond on the Holcombs' residence. Will you tell me how this came to be?"

His voice held no urgency or demand, which Robin was glad of. She would have completely disregarded him if such had been the case. She gave a small shake of her head. *I won't use my words, for I have none. How can I explain? How can this man possibly understand?*

"I see." He sounded disappointed. "But you do recognize what you did?"

Robin nodded then bravely looked up at the doctor.

"Is there anything you want to tell me?" he asked.

Robin remained quiet and motionless.

"Hmm," the doctor responded as he stroked the hair on his chin. "Do you understand why you are here?"

Because I'm insane, Robin thought, but she revealed nothing.

"Since you will not tell me your wishes, your decision to be here or not must now be passed on to me. As a doctor I have the right to commit you to the care of this facility, if I deem you are psychologically unstable. From what Mrs. Holcomb has told me and your lack of action, I do declare that you are in a state of mental fatigue and hysteria, if what I've been told of your drowning attempt is accurate." He paused, perhaps waiting for some response from her before continuing. "You will be admitted to my care and the staff's forthwith until such a time as I am confident that you are able to conduct yourself appropriately and no longer wish to do yourself damage."

The doctor paused again, most likely waiting for Robin to say something, but she held her tongue. He sighed, walked to the door, opened it, and called for Hal and Marge to come back into his office.

After they all sat down again, the doctor spoke. "Now." He placed both of his large hands flat on his desk before shuffling through some papers. "Let's get some paperwork out of the way, then I will pass Mrs. Robin Holcomb off into Nurse Sandry's very capable hands." Dr. Howington turned several papers Marge and Hal's way. "If you would answer these questions to the best of your ability and sign at the bottom."

He pushed a pen toward them.

Robin watched the events happening around her as if they happened to someone else. She was observant but unaffected.

Hal and Marge went through the papers.

Dr. Howington handed them a paper he had signed. "So you see my signature." Hal and Marge nodded. "I'll keep these documents here at my office. I'll let you say your goodbyes. You may come visit Robin on Saturdays. Ten to two in the afternoon are visiting hours."

Dr. Howington nodded and left the room.

Marge started to cry. "Oh, Robin. I'm so sorry. I wish there was another way."

She turned into Hal's shoulders as he comforted her. "There, there, Marge. They will take good care of our Robin."

Robin met Hal's eyes, and she almost cried. He looked like a scared child. She hated to be the cause of pain to them, and a part of her wanted to say so. But her lips remained clamped shut.

"We will be back on Saturday to check on you." Hal spoke with conviction as he patted Marge on the back. "Come. We should go."

Marge blew her nose and sat up straight. She stood, bent down, and embraced Robin, who kept her arms at her side. Robin closed her eyes and breathed in. *Sugar and cinnamon.* Marge always wore the scent of baked goods about her. Marge released Robin. Hal squeezed Robin's shoulder on the way out, and then they were gone.

Robin sat in the strange chair in the strange building. She thought it odd that she wasn't afraid. She felt too numb for fright. It was as if the cold water of the pond had attached itself to her and it coursed through her body instead of blood.

But her body rebelled, and despite her controlled emotion, her physical body had taken too much for the day. The nurse came in to get her, and when Robin stood, she swayed, and the room twirled. The last thing she saw was Nurse Sandry's cold, gray eyes peering down at her.

She calms under my touch, and that makes me feel guilty too—
the fact that I don't touch her enough.

CHAPTER TWENTY-ONE

Enid
Late June 1984

"Come on. One more time around," Clive begs with his puppy-dog eyes.

He holds me in his arms in the midst of the crowd in our backyard. We sway to the crooning sound of Bing Crosby as a record on the player spins out *"I'll Be Seeing You."* Chinese lanterns and a strand of Christmas bulbs light the patio area. A "Happy Anniversary" banner is hung from the green electrical cord.

"Don't you think we've been the center of attention long enough?" I ask Clive.

He grins mischievously and tips me back in a little dip. He flips me back up with a strong arm for a man who's in his mid-sixties.

His breath tickles my ear as pulls me close. "Not nearly long enough."

His arm hugs me tighter, and our motion stills as the record spins out and the needle on the player slips. He tips my chin up and kisses me with a well-known tenderness. I love this man.

The sound of clapping makes me pull back, and I sheepishly look at friends and family gathered around. The familiar faces are dear to me. Aunt Mabel's daughter has even come for our little family reunion. We should be celebrating our anniversary next year, since that would make it forty years of marriage, but I wanted Mom to be here with us. Next year is not guaranteed for her, well, for any of us for that matter.

Doris stops the record player, and Kelly holds up a glass of punch. "Let's raise a glass to almost forty years."

He smiles our way. Pamela walks toward us with a glass of orangish-pink punch in each hand.

She hands them to Clive and me. "Grammie and Pop."

She smiles, showing a top row of braces-clad teeth. We pick our drinks out of her hands.

Kelly finishes his toast. "To Mom and Dad and many more years together."

His hair glows red in this golden hour before sunset. His tall, lean physique reminds me of Grandpa Edward, Mom's dad. Kelly's temperament, however, is Clive and I split down the middle. He's solid and reliable like his father, and bookish and nerdy like me.

Clive nods and utters, "Thanks, Son."

We take a drink at the same time and end up sharing a laugh. We've shared so much together, Clive and me. I hate to think of the day in the future when our sharing will be done. I put aside my depressing thoughts, however, and string my arm through Clive's, turning to our guests. Folks begin visiting again, and Doris puts on another record—Rosemary Clooney this time, one of my favorites.

Clive points his glass to the right side of the gathering. "Say,

I see Richard. Mind if I go say hi?"

Clive's old bowling buddy, Richard, waves at us. He's wearing a white, tunic-type bowing shirt with three royal-blue, vertical stripes running up to a breast placket with the crest of an "M" on it. The bowling league calls themselves "The Mechanics." Fitting, since Rich owns his own garage out near Elk Mound, where Rich and Clive went to school together.

"Sure. No problem," I tell Clive. "Go visit with Rich. Say hi and that I'm sorry 'bout Mary Ann."

Richard's wife died of cancer last fall.

Clive smooches me on the cheek and frees his arm from my grasp. "Thanks, but don't you want to come tell him yourself?"

I shake my head. "Na. I see Mabel's daughter, Lydia, over by the eats. I'd like to go visit with her."

"Okay, but ah…" Clive turns his look into a leer. "Don't get worn out. We might have a little more celebrating to do later." He lifts his eyebrows in a "come-hither" manner.

I roll my eyes. "Ya, ya. We'll see. I'm not promising anything."

I try to be serious but end up giggling. He winks before he turns to wade through the throng toward Richard.

I make my way to where Lydia stands, accepting a piece of cake from Phoebe. The twins baked the cake themselves. I'm so proud of the excellent job they did. It's a straight, three-layer, descending, tiered, white cake with pink roses and white piping. Really, it looks like a bakery could have decorated it. I need to sample a slice of cake to see if the taste holds up its appearance. I inch closer.

"Lydia." I smile at my cousin. "So glad you could make it."

I take in her lavender, floral-print dress, styled in the latest fashion of a tight skirt and blouson top. Lydia is fifty-five but looks thirty-five. She and Cassie have the same genes, ones that must have skipped me, I guess.

Her meticulously made-up face lights up. "Enie. So good to see you. I was delighted to get the invite, of course. Ralph couldn't come, but he said to tell you and Clive 'Happy Anniversary.' He's got some game he's got to travel to, I guess."

She shrugs and fluffs up her short, blonde, highlighted hair with one hand in a nonchalant manner.

"Isn't this the off-season?"

Ralph is a sports reporter, who usually follows the pro football leagues around.

"Training camp at Lambeau field. Some upset he has to go get the scoop on, apparently."

She shrugs again in a move that says she doesn't care, but her voice says otherwise. I decide to steer the subject to something else. I select two pieces of cake—one for Mom and one for me—from the table and whisper, "Thanks," to Phoebe, who stands watch over the cake table. She smiles, echoing Pammie's wiry grin.

"Have you seen Mom yet?" I ask Lydia.

I look around, worry nibbling at me. I left Mom in Cassie's care. Hopefully that was wise.

"Oh, over there. I think." She points across the patio to the lawn by the garage.

Several card tables are set up there, and Cassie and Mom are seated at one, along with our neighbors, the Knights.

I lead the way and soon Lydia and I are pulling up vacant chairs to join the group.

"Well, say." Cassie winks at me. "The star of the evening graces us with her presence."

I play along in a superior tone. "Yes, I've decided to float down to the world of mere mortals for a while."

I bat my eyelashes, and Cassie snorts out a laugh. Mom looks up at her. Leave it to Cassandra to get a reaction out of Mom.

I motion to Lydia. "You remember my cousin, Lydia."

Lydia smiles and Cassie says, "Sure thing. Nice to see you again."

Lydia nods her model-like head. "Likewise."

"Oh, and these are my neighbors, the Knights. George and Brenda." I tell George, who is a sports fanatic, "Lydia's husband is a sports reporter. He's covering the Packers at the moment."

The Knights and Lydia visit. I try not to feel bad about bringing up the touchy subject of Ralph's career. I busy myself with forking a bit of cake into Mom's mouth. She's been mostly on a liquid diet since she has some trouble swallowing, but a little cake should dissolve well enough. She gums the cake as if she's forgotten how to chew.

"It's cake," I remind her.

"It's good, huh?" Cassie asks, and she takes a pinch from Mom's generous slice.

I pick a chunk off my piece. *Mmm, red velvet.* Doris must have told the girls my favorite cake flavor. I give Mom another hunk and say goodbye and thank you to the Knights.

Brenda smiles. "Sorry. We need to get to at least half of our grandson's baseball game. Thanks for the invite."

She waves and George does the same. I wave back. I'm thankful we have such genuinely nice neighbors.

Cassie has a one-sided conversation with Mom, and Lydia quietly tells me, "I have something for you." She pulls her purse—lavender to match her dress, of course—off the back of her chair. She bends open the flap and pulls out a small bundle of something tied in a ribbon. "I found these the other day in a box in the back of my catch-all closet. A box of memorabilia that Mom kept. I was cleaning. Mom kept a lot of her correspondence over the years. I need to weed out some things, but I didn't want to throw these away."

She hands me the bundle. I finger through them. They are letters. Old ones. The address on the top envelope reads: Mabel Massart, Maple Grove, and the return address says: Robin Holcomb, Colfax.

"Mom's letters to Mabel?" I ask.

What a find. Why is it that when Mom's words have been taken from us, I am getting them back, in a manner of speaking? It's a sort of blessing, and I feel tears gathering in my eyes.

That's when I notice the postmark date of the letter my thumb is stuck on: *June 20th, 1918*. One month after Mom was admitted to the asylum. I undo the faded, pink ribbon. The letter has Mom's name and the asylum's address in the upper left corner. Mom wrote Aunt Mabel while she stayed at the asylum. This is the clue I was looking for.

"I didn't go through them. I figured you should see them first," Lydia says.

That means she doesn't know about the asylum. That's probably best.

"Thanks," I tell her. I tuck the letters on my lap. "Really, thank you so much. I'll enjoy reading them." I sniff and hold back the tears.

"I thought you might." Lydia smiles and takes a dainty bite of cake.

The sound of deep coughing interrupts my almost euphoric mood. I look toward the noise and see that it's Mom who is hacking. Cassie pounds her on the back. The coughing deepens, and she gasps for air with a loud wheeze.

"Oh my!" I shout, and I scurry around the table. "Mom? Mom, are you okay?"

How stupid. Of course she's not okay. She's choking. Must have been the cake. I shouldn't have tried to give her any. I raise up one of her arms.

"Fetch a glass of water," I half yell at Cassie.

Lydia pushes her cup toward us across the table, her face peaked and white. "Here, take mine."

I pick it up and try to get Mom to take a sip of water, but it's no good. She can't breathe. *God help her!* I pray.

Suddenly she sucks in a gasp of air. *Thank you, God.* I can't lose her like this, choking on our anniversary cake. I hug her and pet her hair, which is nicely styled for the party. She calms under my touch, and that makes me feel guilty too—the fact that I don't touch her enough.

"Phew, that was close." Cassie elongates the words and waves her napkin in front of her face, which has taken on a rosy sheen. She's splayed back in her chair as if she's been the one struggling to breathe.

Clive is by my side. "What happened?"

His look of concern causes me grief.

"She choked on the cake." I start to cry, quietly. At least I'm not sobbing. "It's my fault. I shouldn't have fed her any."

Clive pulls my head to his chest. "Shush now. How could you have known this would happen?"

I shake my head and back up. "I told you she's been on a liquid diet. They have to grind all her food up. She's been having trouble…"

Cassie signals to the cup. "Here, let's give her something to drink now."

I look at Mom. She's slouching in her chair, hunched over and breathing raggedly. I pick up the cup and try to get her to drink again, but she moves her head to the side, away from the cup.

I turn to Clive, giving the cup back to Cassie. "We need to get her back."

"Agreed. You should stay for our guests' sake. Cassie and I can take her back."

Cassie stands. "Sure. You bet."

I hug Mom and whisper in her ear that I'm sorry. I stand back, letting Cassie help Clive wheel Mom to the handicap van we rented to easily transport her to the house. She's not great on her feet anymore, so we thought that would be the safest option. I didn't think we'd have to consider a whole separate danger. I turn back to the gaping guests. Thankfully, Doris starts up a new record. Strains of a mellow James Taylor song flow over the atmosphere and people turn back to what they were doing. I move to head into the house and start some cleanup.

Lydia holds out the stack of letters with a sympathetic gaze. "Don't forget these."

"Thanks."

I meet her eyes. Understanding rests there—some shared guilt of being a remiss daughter. Maybe one day we can share our shortcomings. I turn toward the house, smiling at my guests as I go, pretending that all is fine. But it's not fine. It's far from it.

Later that night

After I hear Clive's waffling snore, I roll out of bed. I can't sleep and a cup of tea calls to me. I pad out to the kitchen in my bare feet and make myself a cup of chamomile. Last summer I grew chamomile in a clump in the garden near the veggie patch. Even though I appreciate harvesting and using my own herbs for tea, putting the plants too near the veggies was a mistake. I've been pulling out chamomile every time I go to weed the beds. It has come up in most every available patch of dirt at that end of the garden.

Regrets aside, I collect my tea in a stoneware mug, turn on a lamp, and sit in my comfy chair. My gaze rests on the stack of letters I've tossed on the end table, and I reach for them. I select the envelope with the June 1918 postmark from the asylum and pull the letter out. It reads:

Dear Mabel,

You are my only confidante. I cannot put into words what I'm feeling, or what I've done for fear it will be too dark for you. I want you to remember me happy and content, but in reality, I am neither.

Everything has changed since I gave birth to Enid. I've changed. My once carefree outlook on life has been dampened by a heavy curtain of sorrow, but I don't know why. My thinking has been turned upside down and every aspect of my life is acquainted well with an element of grief.

I grieve for my separation from Willis and my daughter, my actions, and their consequences. Sorrow has overtaken me, and I don't know how to be rid of it. I have lost control of my life and my decisions. Maybe that's why I've chosen not to speak. My spoken words are something that I can control, and it gives me some bit of power when all else has been washed away with my dunk in the pond.

Do not hate me for this, for I could not bear it. Love me as you can and write soon.

Your sister,

Robin

Tears roll from my eyes as I imagine how Mom must have suffered during this time. I wipe my face with the edge of my nightgown. Why am I finding out all of this now when I can't talk to her about it? It's ironic and stupid and unfair. I pound my fist on the arm of my chair in frustration.

Why, God? Why? I inwardly scream. But there is no answer.

Gradually my tears fade, my hands unclench, and I think of a verse in Ecclesiastes, referencing time and how there is a time for everything under heaven. Maybe I am reading these at the time I am supposed to. With that thought, a great layer of peace rests on me like a soft blanket, and I fold the letter and put it back in the aged envelope, which smells faintly of roses.

I let my head fall back against the cushion of the chair and try to trust God with what I can't understand.

Everything was new here at this home for the insane,
of whom she was apparently a member.

CHAPTER TWENTY-TWO

Robin
June 1918

Robin imagined something more beautiful than the confinement of her room. No picture, mirror, or decoration of any kind hung on the four white walls. Only lots of white, empty space met her.

I might hate the color white from now on. Robin spent hours in her room at the asylum. She looked around at her surroundings, wishing some color would leak into the bland space lighted by one window and a lantern hung from the ceiling. White walls. White, metal bedstead. White sheets. White water basin and pitcher on a white-washed, wooden stand. Even the gown she had been assigned was white. The only color in the room was the gray, wool blanket on her bed and the faded, fabric covers of the small stack of books she had been allowed to borrow from the asylum's library.

Reaching her hand up to the hollow of her neck, Robin felt for her locket from Willis, but she met an empty space. The locket was gone, taken by Nurse Sandry. *"No jewelry allowed. Doctor's orders,"* she had said in a superior sounding voice.

Willis. They were separated by more than a war now. Robin's state of mind divided them. She hadn't replied to his last two letters. How could she? What could she say? Could she tell him of her crazed thoughts of ending her own life and of her lack of motherly regard for their daughter? No, she could not.

Robin sighed and let her hand slide from her throat. She ran her fingers over the pleats in her nightgown-like dress. She wore a shift, bloomers, and stockings underneath but no corset. The nurse had taken that as well, claiming it to be a hazard. *What does she think I'm going to do? Pick the whale bones out and stab myself?* Most likely.

The sound of a key in the lock of the door made Robin turn to look. Nurse Sandry entered, pocketing the ring of keys in one of the plentiful patch pockets on her white apron.

"I have good news for you." She eyed Robin as if she were a queen bestowing a favor on a servant. "The doctor has assigned you some duties in the garden. He deems you capable enough to help Molly, our chief gardener."

Robin breathed a sigh of relief. She had hoped she wouldn't have to go through a second "treatment" this week. The electric shock hurt and made her feel like jelly afterward.

Nurse Sandry waved her hand at Robin with impatience. "Well, don't dilly-dally. Come on."

Robin stood up and put on a simple pair of slip-on shoes that sat by her bed. She hadn't been allowed to keep her own shoes in her room. Where her things were that she'd brought from the farm, Robin didn't know. She followed Nurse Sandry out of her room and down the hall of patient rooms. One door stood open. Shouting drifted into the hall as they neared the open room. A woman's scream made Robin's heart skip a beat and fear prick her heart. She looked into the room. Two nurses tussled with a woman with frizzy, mousey hair.

"Irene! Calm yourself!" one of the nurses shouted.

The woman shook her head and uttered a wailing screech like a banshee. The hairs on Robin's forearms stood up.

Nurse Sandry gave Robin a light shove on the shoulder. "Don't gawk. Irene is probably refusing to take her medicine again."

Robin walked away from the upsetting scene. It made her wonder why she herself had not protested when Doctor Howington had insisted upon the shock therapy to try to cure her melancholy. Now Robin wished she had screamed with the freedom this Irene had. She could at least have voiced her concern, but Robin still hadn't spoken. Her speech was something she could control, and it felt good to be in control of something.

Robin shuffled her feet along after the nurse's quick steps, until they reached the back of the building. A screened door let in some light and the smell of the outdoors: mown hay, manure, and blossoms of some sort. Nurse Sandry led the way to a vegetable patch. Robin recognized pea shoots sprouting from one of the rows in the rich-looking dirt. Several other rows showed signs of life, with seedlings bursting forth and plants flourishing. A woman in a light brown dress with a muslin apron over the top bent over and plucked at some of the sprouts, which Robin took to be weeds.

Nurse Sandry spoke as they stopped near the woman weeding. "Molly."

The woman named Molly stood up, straightened the pale blue bonnet hung around her neck, and turned their way.

"This is Robin. She's to help you with the gardens. You may

keep her until supper time." Nurse Sandry nodded her head, turned, and walked back the way they had come without waiting for a response from Molly.

Molly kept her face turned to the side and pulled her sunbonnet up over her head.

She asked Robin in a quiet, raspy voice, "Have you done much gardening?"

Robin didn't answer. She dropped her gaze to the earth. She knew she should reply, but she wasn't ready to yet.

"Well, I can show you which are the plants we want to keep in this row." She pointed to the row next to the one she worked. Skinny, grass-line stems of bright green poked through the dirt, thick like hair on a dog. "This is the carrot row. The plants need to be weeded and thinned."

She stepped closer to the row and bent over, yanking out some plants Robin recognized as weeds and some of the carrot sprouts as well. Robin's father had taught her how to thin carrots. There needed to be enough room between the plants for them to grow long, straight roots. Molly stood up and wiped the dirt off her fingers with her apron.

Her gaze flicked up and down Robin's dress. "Didn't they give you an apron?"

Robin shook her head.

Sighing, Molly said, "I'll find one for you for next time. A bonnet too. Sandry will tan your hide if you get your gown dirty with soil." She motioned to the row. "It's all yours."

Robin moved forward, bent down, and fingered the clean, new green of the carrot seedlings. The warm, fresh sensation of the plants comforted her and reminded her of working with her father in the garden at home, back in Maple Grove. While she pulled weeds and thinned seedlings, Robin wondered, if she could talk to her parents about her troubles, what she would say. The truth she supposed. *But what is the truth?* That she tried to kill herself. That was the God-awful truth. Maybe she would write Mabel. She needed to tell someone. She sighed and focused her eyes and hands on her task, gradually putting her guilty thoughts from her mind. It soothed her soul, this simple work. She and Molly worked silently side by side.

After Robin finished, she stood up, a massive sore band spreading along the base of her spine. It had been many months since she'd bent over that long, tending a garden.

Molly stood at the end of her row. "It does put a crick in one's back."

A smile lit one side of her face. The other was covered in the shadow of her bonnet. Robin nodded.

"That's enough for now. Let's get a drink."

Molly moved toward a water pump a few feet away. A cup hung from the handle. She pumped the metal handle several times before a spout of water gushed forth. She held the cup under the stream then gave it to Robin without comment.

Robin took it and drank deeply, thankful for the cold water refreshing her parched throat. She returned the empty cup to Molly's hand. Molly pumped up more water and took a drink too. After she hung the cup back up, she motioned to a bench in the shade of one of the only trees around the property.

Molly sat down with a sigh. "Let's sit for a spell before ol' Sandry comes to wrestle us in."

Robin perched on the bench, not completely comfortable but not frightened, simply cautious. Everything was new here at this home for the insane, of whom she was apparently a member. She peered to the side, studying Molly, whose profile was mostly hidden by her bonnet. Robin wondered why Molly hadn't taken the bonnet off, now that they were in the shade. Her gaze fell to Molly's lap where her hands rested. The sleeve of her dress on her left arm had worked its way up. Red, corded skin showed underneath. To Robin it looked like a burn, a severe one. Molly turned her head Robin's way, as if she knew she was being inspected. The same corded, red, scarred skin covered the left side of Molly's face. Her eye was halfway hooded with scar tissue as well. Robin breathed in sharply, mouthing a quiet gasp.

"Frightening, I know." A resigned tone accompanied Molly's rough-sounding words. She turned her head back and pulled the edge of her bonnet forward to cover her face. "Most here have gotten used to me."

Molly's voice rasped drier the more that she talked. Robin placed a tentative arm lightly on Molly's unaffected arm and shook her head. She couldn't bear to have Molly think that she was repulsed by her appearance. No, it was the pain behind the scars that had made Robin gasp. In a way, Robin wished she had a visual mark of the pain she had borne for the last few months, but it was only a phantom. No one could see it but her.

"Don't fret. I'm used to it." Molly patted Robin's hand. She pointed with her other arm. "Yonder sails the S.S. Sandry."

Molly said the words with such satire, it almost made Robin laugh. Sure enough, Nurse Sandry walked with purpose in her step and a prim line to her lips. Her white cap flopped in the breeze like the sail of a ship.

Molly stood up. Robin followed. Nurse Sandry arrived to face them.

"All done? There's time before supper. The doctor wishes to speak with Mrs. Holcomb before he leaves for the day." She looked at Molly, nodded in a kind of dismissal, and turned to Robin. "Come with me." She walked briskly back.

Robin hesitated before following. It seemed to her that she should acknowledge Molly's help, but she didn't want to talk. Not yet. She settled for a slight smile. Molly smiled back, crookedly, the scarred side of her face not lifting as high as the other.

"The doctor's not a bad man," Molly told Robin before Robin stepped forward to follow the nurse.

What does she mean by that? Do some people consider Dr. Howington bad? And what would he have done to make people think so? The questions rattled around in her head as Robin caught up with Nurse Sandry. Robin was taller than her, but Nurse Sandry had the quicker stride.

When they were inside the building, Robin followed the nurse to a room she hadn't been in before. The room held shelves of books, various medical instruments, what looked pharmaceutical tools, and green, blue, and clear, glass bottles of liquids and compounds. A counter with a stool took up one half of the room. Several chairs, a low table, and a floor lamp took up the rest of the space.

Dr. Howington sat in one of the chairs, waiting, it seemed, for Robin.

"Ah, Mrs. Holcomb. Have a seat." He gestured to the vacant chair in a welcoming voice. Robin did as he said. After Nurse Sandry closed the door, he spoke again. "We've been through one round of treatment. I wanted to see how you are. If your melancholy is less. Do you think you could talk to me about how you are feeling? I know it's difficult for you, but I can assist you much better if we can discuss your health." Dr. Howington bristled his eyebrows together and steepled his fingers together across his chest. He appeared to be waiting for Robin's response.

Part of her wanted to talk and tell this man everything. Every hateful word she heard in her head about herself and every way in which she failed as a mother, but she couldn't. Her tongue felt pasted to the roof of her mouth. Robin couldn't be certain what power in her kept her from speaking, using her words. She met the doctor's firm gaze with a blank stare.

"You are not ready to tell me anything?" He paused, waiting. He sighed softly. "You are safe here. No one will harm you for anything you say. I will not judge you. Have you not heard the words, 'The truth shall set you free?' If you speak, some of what holds you may be released. Often the secrets we keep only serve to damage and enslave us."

Robin looked him in the eye. She supposed he told the truth, but she couldn't say it, for if she did, she would name the truth and how insane she feared she was. Only an insane person would attempt to kill themselves. It strove against the grain of what it meant to live. *Truth be told, if I had a bottle of poison now, I would drink it. I don't deserve to be at the farm, here, or anywhere. Everyone's life would be better if I vanished into nothingness.*

An image of Enid's sweet baby face flashed in her memory. The vision burned bright and made her gulp down a lump in her throat. Next came Willis's smile, Hal's teasing wink, and Marge's comforting hand. Then her parents and siblings.

There are so many that love and need you. The thought came stronger than the ones before. Robin shook her head and groaned. She closed her eyes. Her whole body seemed to shake. The opposing factions of self-hatred and self-importance fought with one another.

"Mrs. Holcomb." Dr. Howington had risen from his seat and placed his hands on Robin's forearms. "Look at me." He paused while Robin tried to focus her dancing eyes on his wide, brown ones. "Breathe in…and out. Relax. In and out," he instructed her slowly. "That's right."

Robin did sense a calm coming with the sound of his voice and each breath and release. A stillness settled on her.

"Good." He straightened. "I think we must try another session tomorrow, after you've rested." He turned and picked up a small, waxed, paper packet off the counter by the black-veined, marble mortar and pestle. "I will give this to Nurse Sandry to administer to you before bed. A restful sleep will help prepare you for treatment."

He pulled a cord on the wall and a bell rang. Seconds later, the nurse came into the room. The doctor gave the nurse the packet and his instructions in a quiet but firm voice.

He tipped his head to Robin in a gentlemanly manner. "Until tomorrow then, Mrs. Holcomb. Sleep well."

She nodded and followed Nurse Sandry from the room. *Will another treatment help me?* She couldn't fathom how an electric current sent through her body would help her rid herself of damaging thoughts, but she was not a doctor nor a scientist. With each step back to her room, she prayed for help, whatever form it took.

Instead of being happy Mom can remember the woman for a glimmer of time, I'm hurt because Mom doesn't remember me.

CHAPTER TWENTY-THREE

Enid
July 1984

The sun scorches down on my head. An itchy spot begs to be taken care of under my sunhat, and I can't resist any longer. I reach underneath my hat and scratch liberally, afterward realizing that I didn't wipe the worm guts off my fingers from the last redworm I impaled on my hook. I rub my fingers on my jeans and a revulsive shiver runs through me.

"Getting hot?" Clive asks as he casts his fishing line from his seat up front in the boat.

We've decided to travel upriver and fish the beds in a little backwater slough.

"I'm warm."

I repress a giggle. A memory of Mom rises up. *"You should never say, 'I'm hot.' A lady is never hot. Say you're warm instead."* Mom chided me one hot day in July as we stood under the clothesline unpinning sun-dried laundry. I was twelve and begging for some lemonade. I remember Mom wore a red hollyhock blossom in her hair, tucked above her ear.

"Well…we could try to find some shade." Clive inches his line up and suddenly gives a jerk. "Drat. Missed 'im."

"I'd go for that." I reel up and catch my hook with its drowned worm through one of the line guides on my fishing pole.

"Maybe we should just head in. Not much biting now anyway. Should have waited to come till later in the day." Clive reels up, secures his hook, and places his pole in the storage slot on the inside of the boat.

"Okay," I agree. I'm feeling antsy and the heat is starting to make me cranky, along with the fact—I forgot to pack drinks. "What have we caught so far?"

Clive shrugs and moves to the engine to pull the starter. "Couple o' Crappie and Sunfish."

"Enough for supper?"

"Maybe," he says before the engine chugs to life.

He sits and gets our Alumacraft moving, turning the tiller as need be. We don't have a fancy fishing boat like some with stripes, cushy seats, and sparkly paint on the bow, but it suits us fine.

We're silent as Clive tours us through the twists and turns of the waterway. I love how the air pushes against my face in a continuous caress. I yank my hat off and let the wind cool my sweaty scalp. My jaw-length hair whips around my face, feeling like wings. When we get back to our dock, Clive angles in and kills the motor. The boat bumps against the old tires lining the dock for a cushion, and I reach over and grab a post. I anchor a rope around it. Clive collects our catch and steps out of the boat onto the dock.

After, he reaches down to help me get out. "I'll clean these if you want to start whatever side fixings you want to have."

"Sure," I say as he saunters over to the back of the house where he keeps an old picnic table for fish cleaning.

I love these kind of lazy Sunday afternoons with just me and Clive. I walk to the house trying to think of what I can scrape together to go with the fish for supper. That image of Mom folding fresh laundry with a reprimanding voice and the red hollyhock in her hair sticks with me. Not for the first time, I wonder why hollyhocks are her favorite. I've never cared much for them—leggy, droopy, and messy as they are.

After I enter the house, I wash my hands in the kitchen and take stock of what's in the fridge. I hope for something to jump out at me, but the condiments, cheese, eggs, milk, and random containers of leftovers don't give me many possibilities. I close the white door. I head to the pantry hoping we at least have some chips and beans. We're in luck. I grab the box of Old Dutch chips off the floor and pluck a can of Van De Camps baked beans off the shelf. I snag the last apple from a bowl on the counter, so we'll have something to eat that's healthy.

Clive missed grocery shopping yesterday. He and Kelly went car shopping instead. Kelly needs a new one, I guess. His Ford Escort does have its share of rust, and Clive said the transmission's going.

After I collect the food items and set out some plates and silverware, I get the oil in the pan ready and mix up a simple cornmeal and flour coating with seasoned salt and lemon pepper. I add a pinch of dried dill.

The door bangs, and Clive carries in a stainless-steel bowl. He sets it on the counter near the sink and washes off the fillets. He puts the washed fillets in a bowl that I've filled with milk. He rinses his hands and dries them on a towel printed with a fruit motif of oranges.

I lean against the counter, watching him work. "What do you want to drink?"

"I don't know."

Most folks in Wisconsin drink beer with their fish, but Clive is not a beer drinker; neither am I.

"How about lemonade?" I ask.

I think I remember seeing a container of powdered lemonade mix in the pantry.

"Sure." He turns my way and smiles before coating the fish by tossing the strained fish in the bowl of coating. The pan of oil sizzles as some milk splashes in it. "Looks like she's ready."

He places half the fillets in the pan. The oil snaps and crackles in protest. His back is to me as I mix up our drink.

"Oh, by the way," he shouts over the sound of the water coming from the faucet I've turned on to fill the drink pitcher.

He says something that I can't make out.

I flick the handle down. "Huh?"

"I found an old picture. Looks like your mom and some lady I don't recognize. Must have fell out of one of the diaries."

He turns and jerks his head toward the table, and I turn and look. There is a sepia-toned picture next to the truck keys on the blue, gingham tablecloth. I dry my hands on a towel and move to pick it up. Mom's eyes look back at me from the photo, steady and strong. As Clive said, she stands next to a woman I don't know, who is in shadow, half her face hidden by a striped bonnet, her revealed eye looking down instead of at the camera. She holds something loosely in one hand. Mom wears a simple dress with an apron over the top. Her hair fringes around her face in a bobbed style. They stand, holding hands against a backdrop of flowers in a garden. I can pick out glads, larkspur, and hollyhocks. I see now that mom has a hollyhock blossom tucked in her hair, and the woman holds one. The color of the blooms is dark, so I imagine they were red. *Red hollyhocks.*

I flip the photo over. The letters AFCI are written in ink on the back, along with the inscription: *Molly and I.* Mom appears young, and the style of her dress hails from somewhere around the 20s.

"Babe. Robin?" Clive gets my attention with his raised voice. "Hey, I'm almost done frying. You got everything else ready?"

I put the photo back. "Sorry. I'll get right on that."

I step over to the sink and quickly finish mixing up our drink. I open the canned beans and heat those in a small saucepan.

Clive puts the last fried fillet on a plate covered in paper towel. "Weird photo, huh?"

"Ya. I don't recognize the woman nor where they're at."

The beans bubble in the pan, so I give them a stir with a wooden spoon and turn off the heat.

"Robin had more than a few secrets it seems."

"So it appears," I concur. I pivot back to the counter to open the chip bag. *Drat! I haven't cut the apple yet.* I finger the fruit. "Want some apple?" I ask Clive.

"Na. Don't bother. This is good enough." He digs in the refrigerator and pulls out some tartar sauce and dill pickles. "Now we have everything."

He grins. My husband is a pickle hound. I've even caught him drinking the brine after we've emptied out a jar. Of course, I scolded him. There's enough salt in the brine to raise his blood pressure sky-high.

I can't keep myself from an eye roll. "I see."

We fill our plates and go to the patio to sit and eat. The

heavy, still air has shifted, and a breeze blows now with the smell of rain.

"Think I'll go to Mom's tomorrow. Maybe I'll bring the photo." I bite into a crisp piece of delicious fish.

"I think you need to try to stop asking for your mom to remember things. You need to face the fact that she can't anymore."

Clive speaks his directions matter-of-factly. It rankles me.

"How do you know what's best for Mom?" I bite out. "And don't tell me what to do." I shovel in a big mouthful of food and chomp it up.

"Hey. Relax. I'm giving you a suggestion." He shakes his head and holds his hands up for a moment in a kind of surrender. "It bothers me to see you get your hopes up with your mom. That's all. I just want you to face reality."

And there's the trouble. Clive is a realist; I'm a dreamer.

"Sorry."

I cool down. He flicks his gaze my direction in a way that says he forgives me before taking another bite of fish.

Clive has put up with a lot from me and Mom through the years, all the misunderstandings, innuendos, and secret agendas—our general rocky relationship. At least that's what it has felt like to me. He doesn't have as many flaws as me. Overall, he's an easy-going guy.

We finish our meal and talk of other things, but my mind can't get off that photo and the hollyhocks. I'm like a dog with a bone: obsessed. I *will* go to Mom's tomorrow and bring the picture. She might have a moment of lucidity and mention something. Just maybe.

The next day

"Would you like to go outside, Mom?"

She doesn't respond but stares off to the left, looking unconcerned or unaware of anything. I sigh. I should be used to this, but I'm not.

Her room has the feel of confinement today, so I wheel Mom—dressed in a blue sweatsuit this time—to the vacant commons room and park her at a table. I pull up a chair next to her wheelchair. The air smells of burnt coffee and the faint sulfur of eggs.

Clive and I skipped church this morning; he went fishing, and I came to see Mom. I picked her Bible up before we left her room, thinking I could read a few chapters to her. I pluck the book out of her lap where I placed it.

"Where should we start?" I ask, leafing through the vellum-like pages. A faint scent of dusty rose escapes into the air. She looks at me, but her face is placid and unchanging. I open to Psalms and start reading at the 31st Psalm. "*In You, O Lord, I put my trust; let me never be ashamed; deliver me in Your righteousness. Bow down Your ear to me. Deliver me speedily; be my rock of refuge, a fortress of defense to save me.*"

I continue on through Kind David's plea for help from God. David's prayer speaks of knowing how God will answer, how He blesses the faithful, and the result of those who do not look to God for help. It's a beautiful chapter.

I want to trust that God is here with us on this Sunday morning and every minute of every day. I think Mom knows this deep down in a spot in her spirit, which is deeper than the Alzheimer's. A rare peace hangs between us. God's promises connect us for the moment.

I finish reading and set her Bible aside and take the photo I have of Mom and the woman named Molly out of my crossbody bag. I hold the photo in front of me. Mom's eyes behind her smudged glasses focus on it.

Pointing out her image, I say, "That's you and a woman named Molly."

I watch her face for any recognition. Her brow twitches a fraction of an inch.

"Who's Molly, and where are you in the photo?" I ask.

Mom's brows lower more. She reaches a shaky hand up to her ear to the exact spot where the hollyhock blossom nestles in her hair in the photo. Her lips twitch and form a sound.

"Mmm…Mo…lly."

She draws out the "O," as if it's stuck in her throat. Mom reaches for the photo with one hand. One corner of her mouth rises in a sort of smile. Her fingertip brushes first her face and then the woman's. Her lucid attention passes as quickly as it came, however, and her hand falls back to her lap. That placid look once more covers her face.

Instead of being happy Mom can remember the woman for a glimmer of time, I'm hurt because Mom doesn't remember me. She hasn't caressed my face like she did the woman in the photo. This Molly must have had some significant link to Mom, but I can't recall a mention of any Molly. I wonder how many more secrets Mom has harbored from me. The peaceful feeling has flown, and once more the proverbial elephant in the room heaves a seat down between us—her distance and my wounding.

I tuck the photo back in my purse. It's useless now to try to get any information from her about where Mom posed with this woman for the shot. Mom has returned to her quiet world. It makes me sad and angry. Just when I think I have dealt with my emotional issues over Mom having Alzheimer's and all that has always lain between us, I realize that I have a ways to go yet. The peacefulness from reading the Psalms has slipped away.

I stand and walk behind Mom's wheelchair, gripping the handles with unnecessary force. I transport us back to her room. I chat a few more minutes about nothing in particular and kiss her on the cheek before I leave. Slow tears press out of the corners of my eyes as I head down the hall. Will I cry every time I leave this place?

"Visiting your mom?" a CNA in white asks.

She's not the usual one I've seen, but her face looks familiar. I sniff.

I pause in my hurried clip. "Yes."

I check out her top, looking for a name tag, but I find none.

"Miss Robin is a dear," she rolls out with a faint southern drawl behind her vowels, and she smiles, showing healthy rows of teeth.

I'm jealous. I'd look like a horse whose lips had rotted away if I simulated her grin. I nod.

"Yes," I agree, because it's the thing to do.

"Have a nice day. We'll see you again, I'm sure." She gives a little wave and flips her head around; her long, blonde ponytail goes with it. She heads into the adjoining room.

I continue on with the exit sign in sight. All the staff seem to think well of Mom. Why can't I? Why do I punish her in my heart for keeping secrets, for making me wait so long to begin to understand who she is?

The tears come in full now, and I speed-walk out the exit down the cement walkway to the Buick. I get in and close the door behind me with a slam. After wiping my eyes on an old tissue crammed between the coin catch-all and the emergency brake, I look around the parking lot, hoping no one caught my display of emotion. The lot is empty of people. Ten or so cars fill some parking spots in various positions in the lot.

I exhale heavily and take a deep breath. Why do I care what others think? I shake my head and start up the Buick, whose whine has long been fixed by Clive. Clicking it in drive, I move forward out of my spot since no car is parked in front of me. I drive and don't want to think about Mom, her secrets, or my emotional baggage. I should pray and pour my heart out to God like David did. I will, but not now. Chocolate calls to me. After over sixty-some-years, I've come to the unabashed reality that I am an emotional eater. I own who I am and pull into the nearest gas station to claim my drug of choice.

Willis deserves better than me. Robin didn't want to believe those words, but the thought kept beating at her.

CHAPTER TWENTY-FOUR

Robin
July 1918

"You're nothing but skin and bones." Marge fussed over Robin, concern evident in her voice. "What do they feed you here?"

Robin didn't speak, but she reached out her hand to Marge. Marge took it and squeezed. Tears sprouted from the corners of Marge's blueberry-colored eyes, and her small, bulbous nose turned pink. Robin hated to see Marge cry.

"You shouldn't be here. We made a mistake bringing you here. I…" Marge gulped back whatever else she had wanted to say as Dr. Howington approached them.

Marge, Hal, and Robin sat at a round table in the large gathering area in the middle of the asylum.

Doctor Howington, looking as well-groomed as always, pulled out a chair and sat opposite Marge. "Ah, Mr. and Mrs. Holcomb. How good of you to come. Thank you for answering my summons so promptly."

"Yes. Of course." Marge let go of Robin's hand and pulled a faded handkerchief out of her sleeve. She dabbed at her nose.

"What is this regarding?" Hal growled out, his usual cheerful countenance absent.

"Robin has not been making the progress I've hoped for." Dr. Howington quieted for a few seconds and appeared to be considering how to explain. He gazed up at the ceiling as if hoping to find his words there.

Robin counted the times she had endured the shock therapy. *Five. No, six times.* It had done nothing but cause her pain and make her jittery. She wondered if his new suggestion would help.

"With your permission, since Robin's husband is still away with the war, I'd like to take another measure in hand." The doctor cleared his throat and paused. "A surgery to remove Robin's reproductive organs."

Hal's tanned cheeks blushed a deep pink.

Marge gasped. "What in the world for?"

"This has been known to calm women who are prone to hysteria and a melancholic tendency," Dr. Howington answered matter-of-factly in a smooth, practiced tone. "It's not as frequently used these days, but with her latest episode…" He let his words taper away.

Marge turned to Robin. "But…"

Robin met her worried gaze. The doctor had already discussed the surgery with her. He had termed it a hysterectomy. It worried her, of course. He'd told her about the risk of infection but assured her they would take every possible precaution and it would be performed by a surgeon at the hospital. If the surgery helped her out of this valley of guilt and self-hatred and onto the level ground of being her normal self, she wouldn't protest.

"You won't be able to have any more children," Marge told

Robin. She started crying in earnest.

"There, there, Marge. Don't work yourself up," Hal soothed Marge. He patted her on the shoulder of her flower-print dress.

I don't deserve more children. The thought of having more children scared Robin. *What if this happened again?* The possibility terrified her.

Marge's voice took on a low, watery whine. "But what about Willis? What will he think?"

Before they had left the farm to bring her to the asylum, Robin had made Marge and Hal promise that they would not write Willis to tell him of her "accident." That's what they had called her attempted suicide then.

"I really think this is in everyone's best interest," Dr. Howington relayed with calm resignation.

"I don't see how it can be," Marge spit out. She looked at Hal. "Say something. Surely, you can't think this wise."

Hal sighed and yanked at his collar. "I'd hate to see Robin…cut into." Hal met Robin's gaze. "But if this surgery brings back our old Robin, then it might be best."

Hal leaned back in his chair with slumped shoulders, looking as if he'd unburdened himself of a heavy weight.

"Oh, Hal." Marge sniffed and wiped her eyes with the hankie she had pulled out of her sleeve.

Robin had to make her feelings known, but not in words yet. She pointed to her chest and nodded with what she hoped was a serious look on her face.

"You…you want to have this done?" Marge asked.

Robin nodded again.

Marge sighed and shook her head. She shrugged. "Well, that's that then." She looked at a Dr. Howington. "Please tell us more about the surgery, what Robin can expect, and recovery time."

Dr. Howington obliged. Robin zoned out. She'd heard all this days prior, after she had calmed from her last incident. She didn't remember everything, but the image of Nurse Sandry pulling the bloody letter opener away from her grasp was burned in Robin's mind. She had tried and failed to exit life again. How she had gotten into the doctor's office, Robin didn't know. Dr. Howington always kept the door locked. She didn't remember planning it, or anything about that day. It was as if she then woke from some sort of twisted dream.

When Robin had seen the blood, she'd panicked and screamed. The nurse had found her kneeling on the oriental rug in the doctor's office with her left wrist gouged open and the silver letter opener in her right hand, blood dripping off the tip.

"Robin. Robin?" Marge waved a hand in front of Robin's eyes. "Hal and I are heading home."

Robin looked around. She hadn't realized the doctor had left. She turned her eyes up to Marge and Hal, who stood near her.

"I hope and pray we are not making a mistake in allowing this, but since you agree…well, there's nothing much I can do." Marge leaned down and placed a warm kiss on Robin's cheek. "You are loved. Hal will bring me back after your surgery." She stood up straight. "We will pray all goes well."

She nodded and turned. Hal smiled sadly at Robin and followed Marge.

Robin watched them walk away, fear and hope both present in her heart.

Days later

Robin held the letter from Mabel in her shaking hands. Her surgery was scheduled for tomorrow morning. Robin regretted giving her permission now, for her fear increased as the day neared. She set her worry aside for the moment, opened Mabel's letter to her, and leaned back on the bench by the garden behind the asylum.

July 20th, 1918
Dear Robin,
How could you think I could hate you? I love you, dear sister, and always will. Nothing you could do or say could change that. Mom and Dad miss you and ask about you. Why have you not written to them and told them the real nature of your "illness," as Marge put it in the telegram she sent? Mom is arranging a way for us to come and see you. It's hard with the garden producing now and the farm work, but we'll manage.

Have you written to Willis yet? I know you were hesitant to share your trouble with him, but he is your husband and loves you. Maybe he could even take leave and come home. Please write to him. He deserves to know.

I hope to see you soon. All my love and prayers,
Mabel

Robin folded up the letter and tucked it back in the envelope. She hadn't written to Willis in months, although she had received several letters from him since her arrival at the asylum. The post hadn't been mailed directly to the facility. Marge and Hal had brought it. But how could she tell him? Where would she start? She couldn't lie, and she wouldn't write about the everyday events of life like how their daughter grew, the farm, or the weather. To Robin, the life she and Willis had shared had flown far away and might never come home. *Willis deserves better than me.* Robin didn't want to believe those words, but the thought kept beating at her. She crumbled under the abuse of these kinds of destructive thoughts. Robin knew she shouldn't have them. It wasn't normal or right.

"Letter from home?" Molly asked.

She sauntered over, her bonnet hiding the side of her scarred face like usual. She sat next to Robin and leaned the hoe she had been using against the bench.

Robin nodded. Something stirred in her—a whirlwind of worry and the need to tell someone about it.

She spoke for the first time since her arrival at the asylum. Her voice operated like a rusty hinge. "I…I'm sc-ar-ed,"

Molly turned her face to Robin. "You found your tongue." A one-sided smile tilted her lips. "What are you scared of?"

She gazed into Robin's eyes so hard that Robin leaned back.

"What if…I don't get better?" Robin lifted her hands in frustration and shook her head. "I don't want to live like this."

She could sense a heavy cry on the horizon and practiced the breathing Dr. Howington had taught her. Robin bowed her head and sucked air into her lungs slowly.

Molly's hand came to rest on Robin's tightly clenched hands in her lap. "You must hold on to hope. I've heard you praying when you thought no one was listening. Surely God will hear your plea. We do our best, and we must trust Him with the rest."

Molly's scratchy voice soothed Robin's anxiety, and her words rang true in Robin's heart. *Now if only I can believe them.*

Robin nodded. "Yes. Thank you."

Molly rose off the bench and picked up the hoe. "Come." She jerked her head toward the garden plots. "I know just the thing for a worried mind: hard work." She grinned crookedly. "Tending to our food supply and the flowers will be helpful to your soul." She tapped the side of her bonnet at the temple. "I know."

Robin put the letter in her apron pocket and stood to follow Molly. As they walked the few feet to the garden and began to work, Robin asked, "How did you come to be here? How do you know what you said is true?"

What Robin really wanted to ask was how Molly had gotten the scars.

Molly handed Robin a hoe. She began weeding, and Robin followed suit.

"That's a long story. Why don't we save the telling of it until your recovery? I'll visit you every day after your surgery, that is, if Sandry permits me." She gave Robin a wink. "It might help make your pain seem less." Molly tipped her head down and turned her back on Robin.

Robin sensed their conversation was over. She sliced into the dirt with her hoe, satisfied with the weeds she cut out of the soil, allowing the plants to grow unencumbered. That's what she wanted to do in her life—cut the weeds out. Each time she uprooted a section of weeds in the dirt, Robin thought about a rotten thought that plagued her. The physical act of tending growing plants made her want to strive to tend the good parts of her and let the rest go. But more than that, she desired to cut herself free from what burdened her. For the first time since arriving, she felt that might be possible. She had Molly to thank for reminding her of that hope.

That night

Robin tossed and turned. Ghoulish images of Dr. Howington and Nurse Sandry lurked in the corridors of Robin's mind. For the moment, she lay away on her bed, the bedsheet and blanket twisted around her legs. Sweat pooled underneath her breasts. She peeled back the covers and exposed her legs to the warm

July air. *Why did I put a blanket on in the first place?* When Robin had gone to bed several hours ago, she'd wanted something to snuggle with. The blanket had been her only option.

Robin grabbed the portion of her nightgown covering her chest and lifted it back and forth to get some air flowing underneath it. After a few seconds she started to cool. Her thoughts drifted to her husband. *What if I die tomorrow, and Willis never heard me explain what I did?* Robin's heart pounded faster, and her gut twisted with the idea of describing her actions in a letter. She wished she could get up and simply write him, but she had no pen or pencil nor any sharp object in her room. *I'll beg Nurse Sandry to let me write one before we go to the hospital.* Satisfied with that, Robin closed her eyes and imagined what she would say.

Dear Willis,
I am sorry it has been so long since I've written. I haven't known how to put into words what I must tell you. Everything has changed. I've changed. I am not the same person who kissed you goodbye in August, but then maybe you aren't either. I am sure you have endured and seen many harsh things. That makes what I tell you now even worse. While you have been fighting, trying to stay alive, I have attempted to drown myself in the pond under the weeping willow.
There. I said it. Hate me or love me, it is the truth. I can't give you an exact reason why. In general, I feel you and Enid deserve better than me. I battle a steady stream of self-damning thoughts. It's pathetic, and I hate it. I want it to stop.
Since the end of May, I have resided in The Dunn County Asylum for the Chronic Insane. Those are words I would have

*never imagined writing, but here I am. Dr. Howington, the doctor
in charge here, has talked to me about my severe melancholy and
administered some treatment, however, he feels it is not helping
enough. I will be undergoing an operation to rid me of my female
organs in the hopes that this will restore some balance to my life.*

*Again, I'm sorry. This will mean, of course, that I will never be
able to have another child. You will be coming home to a barren
wife. I'd understand if you didn't want to come home at all.*

Forgive me,
Robin

A release rolled over Robin as she finished writing the letter to
Willis in her head. Letting that secret free lifted a physical
weight off her. Robin's chest felt lighter; her breath came easier.
The compression in her forehead lessened. She took a couple
of deep breaths and listened to the rain pinging on the window.
The rhythm soon relaxed her, and she melted into a deep sleep.

CHAPTER TWENTY-FIVE

Enid
August 1984

"Thought we'd go to a movie tonight. Red from work told me that the drive-in has *Supergirl* now. We could take the girls. A last hurrah before school starts."

"That starring Faye Dunaway?" I ask.

The young actress demanded my attention in an article in one of the magazines I read at the beauty shop recently, otherwise I probably wouldn't have known. Clive and I relax on the patio, the afternoon lazy and uneventful. I'm stationed in my favorite chair with the puffy, daisy-covered cushion and an Agatha Christie novel, *Then There Were None*, in my hands. Clive stretches out in the hammock. He rolls toward me.

"Think so," he answers.

"Well, sure." I close my book and change out my reading glasses for my regular vision pair. I should wear bifocals, but I tried them, and they made me dizzy. "What time does it start?"

I lean forward and stretch. I've been sitting too long; my back hurts under my ribs.

"Nine o'clock, I think."

Clive rolls out of his cocoon with a bit of ungracious floundering. I can't help myself and laugh.

"What's so funny? Never seen Super Spider emerge from his nest?"

He half crouches and lurches toward me with huge, giant steps. He pounces and play-bites my neck. I swat at him with my book.

"Are you a vampire spider?" I giggle.

"Hardly." He wiggles his eyebrows and kisses me firmly.

I do love this crazy fool.

"We should probably call Kelly and Doris to see if we can steal the girls. It will be past their curfew."

Clive pushes off my chair and stands up straight. He makes a face and swats his hand in a downward motion. "Curfew, shmurfew. Grandparents are outside of the rules."

"Well, we'll see."

I stand and kiss him on the cheek before walking into the house to call Kelly. Picking up the receiver on the blue phone on the wall, I dial my son's number. After three rings, he picks up.

"Kelly speaking." He always answers the phone like he's at the office.

"Hey, Kelly. How are you?"

"Oh, you know…fair to middling." He tries to make light, but I can tell something's troubling him.

"That bad, huh," I tease, hoping to flush him out.

We rarely have a direct conversation. Sadly, I inherited this from Mom—avoidance. But I'm done with doing things because of ingrained patterns. I don't want to keep secrets from my child the way my mother kept them from me. This is my son, and I love him and want him to know.

"I'm here if you want to talk, Kel." I use his shortened name from childhood.

"Another time maybe. Thanks, Mom."

In his voice, I can hear that he loves me too. I also know my son likes to truly think things over before talking about them.

"Why'd ya call?" he asks.

"Your dad and I would like to take the girls to a drive-in movie tonight." I talk quickly, giving him reasons why he should say yes. "We know it'd be late, but they could sleep over here. Dad and I will bring them back after breakfast tomorrow. It'd give you and Doris a free night."

A few seconds of silence. "Sure. They would like that. I'm not sure if Doris will mind, but at the moment, I don't care."

Clearly something is wrong between Kelly and his wife. I'm not positive I should ask more, but I do. "Something happen?"

"Ya...No. Well, I don't know." He lowers his voice. "Sometimes I can't read her. She's been odd lately, like she's a different person."

Tell me about it, I can't help thinking. I've seen Mom change literally before my eyes.

"How so?" I ask.

"Well, you see..." He pauses. I hear some muffled noises like he's holding the phone next to his shirt. "I got to go, Mom." He sounds stressed. "What time will you be by to get the girls?"

I calculate the time. "Oh, about 8:15."

"Okay. They'll be ready. Bye."

"Wait. Can't you tell me what's going on?"

I'm worried about him and Doris. To me it seemed like they had a rock-solid relationship. But you never can tell. People change.

"Not now, Mom. We'll talk another time. Got to go."

He hangs up before I can say anything else. I instantly pray for him and Doris, whom I've always thought well of. I can't imagine what she could have done to ruffle Kelly's feathers, which is not an easy task, being as he's like Clive that way.

I hang up the phone with a sigh and head to the guest room to put fresh sheets on the bed.

Hours later

"This is super cool, Grammie!" Pammie bounces in the back seat of the Buick, holding her soda in a striped, red and white cup in one hand.

Phoebe flashes her braces at Clive and I, peeking her head in between us from the back. "Yes! Thanks so much. Both of you."

Clive winks at me and asks in mock horror, "What? Do we have some movie crashers in the back seat?"

I smile. "We are happy to have you. You two young things give us a good excuse to go to a movie like this."

I pass back a box of popcorn to Phoebe, who flaps her eyelashes and grins. My ring catches on the row of jelly bracelets adorning her arm in rainbow colors—some fad, apparently.

Clive tunes into the right channel on the radio, and we begin to hear the previews. The girls comment excitedly through everything. This is the first time they have been to the drive-in, which looks like it's located in someone's farm field. Not much else is around. We drove through Elk Mound to get here. The theater borders the outskirts of Eau Claire.

"Did you ever go to a movie with your grandparents?" Pammie asks me, crunching on popcorn. A small bit of butter-yellow kernel sticks in the corner of her lips.

"No. They lived too far away," I tell her.

"What was the first movie you saw?" Phoebe asks, clearly not wanting to be outdone by her sister in doing the questioning.

"I went with your great grammie and granddad to a Shirley Temple movie. *The Little Princess*, I think."

"What? Nothing before that?" Clive questions me, appalled.

"My Uncle Earl took me when I was a kid in knee-pants."

"Knee-pants?" Pammie laughs. "What's that?"

"Shh, here comes the good part." Clive points to the screen as Supergirl flies in to save the day.

We all watch, crunching on our snacks. A big slurp from the back indicates one of the girls is nearing the end of their soda. I turn to see who's the culprit.

Pammie smiles sheepishly at me. "I'm so thirsty."

I eye her in what I hope is a disapproving way. "Keep in mind before you guzzle your whole drink that you'll probably have to use the outdoor toilet before we go, as 'thirsty' as you are."

Pammie makes a terrible face. Her eyes widen, and she rolls her bottom lip down. "Oh. Those places usually have spiders."

"And they stink," Phoebe adds. "But I'll go with you, if you have to go."

Phoebe clearly presents the more fearsome spirit. It's nice to see that the girls have characters which are slightly different from each other. They are not completely identical in every way.

I remind the twins how blessed they are. "It's good you have such a sweet sister."

Phoebe tilts her head and scrunches up her brow. "Was it strange growing up an only child?"

She is the serious one of the two.

"I had Cassie. She and I were almost as close as siblings."

"Was Great Grammie not able to have more children?" Phoebe asks.

"Shhh. Look." Pammie points to the screen.

A dramatic fight scene plays out between the good guys and bad.

Phoebe's question remains unanswered. I wonder myself if some other factor stood behind Mom and Dad having only me. I always figured Mom thought one was enough, but how would my folks have decided that back then? Sex usually led to pregnancy. There were little available contraceptive means in the 1920s. I recall Mom hinted at something in her diaries. I'll have to go back and see if I can find where she talked about that.

I watch the movie, but in my mind, I'm thinking of what reasons prevented my folks from having more children. I never asked Mom. Sex was something I never talked with her about. Aunt Sue filled me in when my curiosity got the better of me.

Why was I an only child? I would have chosen to have more children, if I could have, but I had such problems after pregnancy. Continual bleeding and cramps. I had a hysterectomy to solve the issues. The idea hits me. *Could Mom have had one?* Did they do that back then? And if so, what for? I'm determined to find out.

It felt good to Robin to think of things she would never do,
for that meant she thought in terms of being there to not do them.

CHAPTER TWENTY-SIX

Robin
August 1918

Molly smiled down at Robin. "I promised I'd come."

"Thank you," Robin whispered.

Tiredness washed over her, but she was better than yesterday. She'd felt like she'd been horse-whipped, coming off the morphine they'd given her for pain. It gladdened Robin's spirit to be rid of the drug. It clouded her mind and made her weep. Today marked a full week since her surgery. She endured some pain but would take that over the muddled feeling the drug induced.

The bouquet of flowers Molly had brought for Robin sat in a vase by her bed. The bright colors cheered her. She particularly liked the red flowers—hollyhocks, Molly had told her.

Molly smiled her strange, half-frozen grin. "When you're feeling a bit stronger. I'll wheel you out to the garden. Everything's grown so much. You can be proud that you helped make that happen."

Her bonnet hung from her neck behind her head. It did

Robin's heart good to know that Molly trusted her and felt comfortable enough in her presence to expose the scars.

"You promised a story," Robin croaked out, and she shakily reached for the glass of water next to the bed on the stand.

Molly picked up the glass and held it to Robin's lips. "Here, let me."

Robin picked up her head as much as she could and took a deep drink. "Thank you."

Robin finished and leaned back on the pillows; Nurse Sandry had begrudgingly allowed her an extra one.

Molly put the glass back and cleared her throat. She looked down at the blanket on the bed and picked at the wool fuzz. "I used to sing."

The simple words came out heavy. They shocked Robin, for she couldn't equate Molly's rough voice with a singer's.

"What happened?" Robin asked. "Why don't you anymore?"

Molly touched the scarred hollow of her neck. Deep, pink grooves etched the uneven surface of her skin. "Smoke inhalation and the burns went deep. Damaged my vocal cords."

Molly choked out a cough and looked directly at Robin, who recognized a deep sorrow in her friend.

Robin pushed herself higher up on the pillows, so she could see Molly better. "A fire?"

"Something else." Molly sighed deeply. She coughed again, sniffed, and wiped the end of her nose with the back of her sleeve in a quick motion. "I was employed young and stockpiled my earnings. I used the money for vocal lessons with an opera teacher. She said I had talent." Molly smiled in a wounded way. "Singing is one of my first memories." Molly's one good eye took on a faraway look. "My pa had made a board swing for me and hung it from the biggest tree in our front yard. I'd swing and sing for hours."

She fell silent, and the gap in conversation draped Molly's face in despair. The tight scars pulled back her lips in a sort of grimace, while the other side curved up. Molly's hooded eye tightened as if she squinted at the sun on a bright day. Robin thought it was the saddest look she'd ever seen on a person's face.

"Go on," Robin gently prompted. "Tell me more, if you want."

Molly breathed in deeply and sighed. "It's a hard story to tell, and I haven't spoken of it in years. But suffice to say: I lost something more valuable the day that I received these burns, worth much more than my voice."

"What?" Robin stretched out her hand to her friend, cupping her fingers under Molly's, but before Molly could answer, Nurse Sandry sauntered into Robin's room.

Nurse Sandry checked a watch pinned to her apron before eyeing Robin with an authoritative look. "All right now. Time for you to rest."

"But we were talking," Robin protested. "And it's only mid-morning."

"You can talk later. Doctor's orders are for you to take a morning rest." The nurse tucked the covers tighter around Robin's legs and made a shooing motion with one hand. "Off with you, Molly. You can come back and visit Robin another time."

Molly nodded submissively, pulled her bonnet back up over her head, rose, and stepped lightly toward the doorway.

"Thanks for the flowers, Molly. See you tomorrow."

Robin wanted to hear the rest of Molly's story, but she did feel tired. Her eyes were hard to keep open and a weight seemed to press down on her body.

Molly paused and gave a slight wave before leaving. After Nurse Sandry stopped her fussing, she left with her usual proficiency and closed the door behind her.

Robin relaxed and found herself phasing in and out of sleep until she saw herself in the midst of a dark wood, stirring boiling contents in a huge, black kettle over an open fire. Her body tensed as pairs of eyes from the shadows watched her. Dark and grim characters and settings took Robin through a series of scenes, none of which made sense to her. She awoke with a jolt like someone had swatted her upside the head. She stared around her white room until her gaze landed on the colorful bouquet left by Molly.

Robin's heart ached for her friend. The physical and mental pain she had endured must have been great. *What did she mean she lost something more valuable?* She wanted to hear the rest of Molly's story, but for the moment Robin rested content in the fact that she did not tend a burning witch's cauldron in the middle of a dark wood. For the first time, she was grateful to find herself in her own bed in the asylum.

A tightness along her lower abdomen made Robin run her fingers over the place where her incision ran—from her navel to her pubic area. Bandages still covered the spot, winding around her lower torso like graveclothes.

Robin's head turned as a key rattled in the lock of her door. Nurse Phelps walked into Robin's room. Robin liked Nurse Phelps better than Sandry. Phelps treated Robin more like a hotel guest and less like a naughty child.

A sunny smile lightened the dark features of the nurse's face. "Ah, you're awake."

She had a swarthy look about her, as if she hailed from across the ocean from some ancient Persian country. Thick, dark brows arched over chocolate, almond-shaped eyes; a medium-sized nose drew the smooth halves of her face together, but her small chin disappeared against the prominence of her soulful eyes.

"Yes." Robin pulled herself up as best she could into a sitting position, but a sudden pain made her cringe and cry out.

"Oh, my. Let me help." Nurse Phelps steadied Robin and fluffed the pillows behind her back, helping her slide farther back toward the headboard. "There now. Is that better?" Although Phelps appeared foreign, her speech contained the vowel sounds of the Midwest.

"Much," Robin answered. "Thank you."

Nurse Phelps stood up straight and smoothed down her apron, which had hiked up while helping Robin. "I came to tell you that you have some visitors."

"Oh?" Robin supposed Hal and Marge had come to see her.

"Yes." Phelps broke into a crooked smile, which kept her teeth firmly behind her lips. "Should I show them in?"

Robin nodded, and the nurse walked to the door, beckoning with her hand as she peeked around the frame into the hall. Robin hoped she looked well enough. Guilt made her stomach plummet at all that she'd put the Holcombs through. *What will Hal and Marge think of me talking?* The last time Robin had seen them, she still hadn't chosen to speak.

"Robin?"

Robin looked up and saw not the Holcombs but her mother and sister. A tightening gripped her throat and tears rushed to the corners of her eyes.

"Mom?" Robin asked unbelievingly. "Mabel?"

Mabel hurried forward to grasp Robin's hand, all smiles and tears.

"But what about the farm?" Robin didn't want her family to be inconvenienced over her issues.

"Your pa and brothers will manage while we stay for a few days. We booked a room in town." Mom reached out a shaky hand and smoothed her fingers over Robin's cheek. "And here I was thinking you'd be pale, but I find you tanned as a ripened plum." She gave a modest grin, but Robin saw the worry in her mother's hazel eyes.

Robin swallowed down her tears. "I was helping outside in the gardens before…"

Her gaze flicked down to her belly, where she had once sheltered Enid.

"Yes. Mabel told me."

Robin noticed the droop of her mother's face. *There I am, reflecting disappointment.*

"I'm sorry, Robin, but Ma had to know. We had to come see you. Oh…" Mabel buried her head into Robin's shoulder and cried.

"Now, now," Mom soothed. She rubbed Mabel's back. "We didn't come all this way to cry on Robin's shoulder. We came to tell her that…"

Robin met her mother's gaze and could see the love there. It made the pain of what she'd almost done ache again.

"We love her very much." Mom spoke the words in a fierce, soft voice. "And that will never change."

Robin nodded and swallowed.

Mabel raised her head and asked in a soft, strained voice, "But why? Why did you do it? How could you ever think life would be better without you in it?"

Slow tears leaked from Mabel's eyes. Her perfect nose took on a rosy color, and she sniffed loudly in an unladylike manner.

Mom pointed at the white handkerchief peeking out from under Mabel's pale blue shirtwaist at the wrist. "Heavens, Mabel. Use your hankie."

"Oh, who cares?" Mabel sniffed again and leaned back from hovering over Robin. She crossed her arms and huffed.

Robin had never heard Mabel speak contrary to their mother nor seen her in such a sour mood. She had every right to be. Robin supposed she would feel angry if Mabel had tried to end her life.

"The kind nurse told us we could use a wheelchair to take you out to the garden, if you like. And you could wear this." Reaching into the carpet bag she held, Mom pulled out a robe made of blue, printed, silk fabric in a rose design.

"Oh my. That looks expensive." Robin shook her head. "You shouldn't have, Mom."

With a shake, Mom opened the robe and held it up. "I figured something special might help speed your recovery."

"Help your sister," Mom directed Mabel.

Mabel sniffed loudly and helped Robin stand. As Mabel pulled Robin up, she spit out words into her ear. "Never, ever do this again."

Robin ventured a look at her sister. Equal parts venom and despair met her in the depths of Mabel's dark eyes. Robin didn't reply but turned her lips up in the slightest of smiles as if to offer Mabel some hope. After steading herself, Robin slipped her arms into the sleeves of the robe and turned around.

"There. I'll tie it loosely." Mom secured the tie around Robin's waist. "Go fetch that nurse, Mabel."

Mabel tucked in her lips for a moment in hesitation but turned and did as Mom requested. Soon Nurse Phelps and Mabel returned with a wheelchair. Nurse Phelps helped Robin sit down in the chair, and off they went. They were almost to the back door when a woman entered the hall.

The elderly woman in a tattered dressing gown hobbled along the edge of the hall, almost hugging the wall. Her long, braided, gray hair hung over her shoulder. She carried something small wrapped in a shawl.

"A good day to you," Mom said, when they drew close to the old woman.

"An' to you. Care to meet my baby? He's a bright little thing." The woman crooned into the blanket. "Ain't you now?"

Robin had seen the woman several times, and she always carried her bundle. This was the first time Robin had heard her refer to it being a baby.

A mixture of shock and kindness widened Mom's eyes and lips. "Ah…yes, I'm sure he is."

Nurse Phelps paused and tapped the woman on the shoulder. "Best tuck him in for a nap, Maidie. He'll be tired."

"Yes…I s'pect." Maidie turned cold, blue eyes on Robin.

It gave Robin a shiver, for she recognized some lack of understanding in the old woman, like the woman grappled with a memory she couldn't quite hold on to.

Nurse Phelps turned to Mom. "You three head on out. The door's just yonder." She pointed to the back door. "I'll help Maidie with Timmy." The nurse whispered to them as she walked past and hooked her arm through Maidie's, "That's her dead son."

Robin looked at her mother and then at Mabel, whose eyes took up most of her face.

"Come. Let's continue," Mom said.

She pushed the wheelchair, and Mabel held the door open. There was a wooden ramp for the chair to roll down to the lawn's level. A warm breeze stirred the air.

Mom parked Robin near a wooden table under a tree. "Ah, that's so much better."

Robin pointed at the rows of corn, peas, carrots, beans, and lettuce and mounds of wondering squash and melons. "That's the garden I worked in."

On the edge of the plot stood the flower beds full of blossoms of every color and shape. Her gaze rested on the red hollyhocks in the center, staked against a trestle.

"You did all this yourself?" Mom asked.

She sat on a bench by the table. Mabel plopped down on the grass.

"Oh, no. Molly is the chief gardener. She was a patient here at one time, but now I'm not sure. She works here anyhow."

Mabel picked absentmindedly at some blades of grass. "That's odd."

Robin wanted to defend Molly. "She's kind. She's…been a friend to me."

Mom patted Robin on the knee. "And we are glad of it."

Robin felt she should talk with her mother and sister about what happened in May, but she couldn't make the words come out. It had been hard enough writing to Mabel about it.

She thought of one thing she wanted to know. "Does Pa know?"

"I've told him you're in an institution for nervous issues and that you had an operation. Any further than that, you will need to explain," Mom told Robin.

"Thank you."

Robin hung her head. She would never tell her father the truth, nor anyone else, if she could help it. And Enid. *I will never tell Enid.*

It felt good to Robin to think of things she would never do, for that meant she thought in terms of being there to not do them. She thought of the future, and for the first time in months, it didn't appear like a black hole. Though not quite herself, Robin could say she had improved. If that could be attributed to the surgery, the prior treatments, praying, talking with Molly about her issues, or just the passage of time, she didn't know. But one thing she did know for sure: she wanted to see and hold Enid again.

"Look at that lovely, orange lily." Mom pointed at a cluster of tiger lilies near the hollyhocks.

Robin nudged her sister with her foot. "Go pick some for Ma."

"Oh, no…" Mom started to protest.

"Molly won't mind. We can add them to the vase of flowers in my room."

"If you say so." Mabel obliged and walked toward the garden.

A few seconds after Mabel left, Mom asked, "What brought you to this, Robin?"

Her mother looked tired to Robin. Older. *And that's partially my fault, no doubt.*

"Honestly, I don't know." Robin shrugged, tipped her head back, and stared at the sky through the leafy branches of the elm overhead. "It started after Enid was born. The terrible bleakness." Robin rested her head on the back of the chair and closed her eyes. "My world became gray, and then it became black. Nothing mattered to me." She righted her head and looked her mother in the eye. "I am ashamed to say even my own daughter. I would not have ever hurt Enid intentionally, but my lack of regard for her frightened me. Marge and Hal did the right thing in bringing me here. I was not a fit mother."

Robin could say those words and not feel devastated by them now. Now they were simply a fact from the past, but the past didn't have to become the future.

Neither of them spoke further, and Mabel came back with several lily stems with a few blossoms each. She held one out to Robin and one out to their mother. Robin took hers and studied the shape of the flowers. Several buds hung, long and skinny like a pointed boat, on the stem. Some open blossoms were spread like a hand, but the mature blooms were turned back on themselves, like a kind of hat. In fact, Robin recalled Molly saying these kinds of flowers were called Turk's Cap Lilies.

The different stages of the blooms were all present on the stem, and it presented a picture to Robin of her life. She realized herself to be in that peeled-back stage where everything seemed to turn in on itself, but it also became the place of full bloom and maturity. The bending back had been painful, and God only knew if she was out of the woods with her female hysteria. Time would tell. Robin didn't want to be afraid of the future, but in the back of her mind and at the end of every day lurked the possibility of her succumbing to the darkness again.

How will I face that fear and move into the future I long to have with Willis and Enid? The question sat like a slab of granite on her heart.

It's just with my mom and her secrets,
the stuff she bore by herself—it gets to me.
I might have helped lighten her load. We might have been closer.

CHAPTER TWENTY-SEVEN

Enid
Late August 1984

"I don't know what to do." Kelly sits before me, dejected. His shoulders slump, and the contours of his face deepen. The green of his eyes glows paler than usual behind his glasses. He looks unkempt: stubble sprouts from his chin and jaw, creases line his shirt as if he's slept in it, and the slight tang of unwashed underarm reaches my nose.

I rub my hand over the arm of my deck chair and wonder what advice I can give my son, who appears to be suffering greatly. I want to gather him in my arms, kiss him, and make it better like when he was a kid. But those days are long gone.

"Are you sure?" I ask.

He raises his elbows off the chair next to me and holds up his hands. "Well, what else would Doris be doing at that time of night? And the new clothes and hair." He lets out a steady stream of breath and leans back against the chair, spent. "I would never in a million years have imagined that she'd cheat on me."

Nor I. Doris is sweet, kind, well-put-together, and she's always been affectionate with Kelly. Of late, maybe not so much, but they've been busy with the girls and work.

"Maybe she's doing all this for you, and she's just keeping it a secret." I try to raise the hope of that possibility, but the words sound fake to my own ears.

He shakes his head and sighs. "Na. I don't think so."

I sit up straighter and lean toward him. "Where does she go every Thursday night? She hasn't told you?"

"Oh," Kelly draws out the word and tells me with sarcasm, "She *says* she's going to community art class at the college, but I called and checked the class roster, and the name Doris Fenton is not on the list."

"Hmm, maybe there's an explanation and this is all a big misunderstanding." I hope my words are true. I love Doris, and she's a great mom, and I always thought a good wife. "Have you talked to her?"

Kelly scratches the side of his head near his shaggy, red sideburns; he needs a trim. "Well...I tried, but in the end, I couldn't come right out and ask her, 'Are you cheating on me?'"

"No. I suppose not." I look up at the cloudless sky and wonder how I can fix this. "Have you seen any other strange things? I mean, the last time I saw Doris she seemed normal to me."

"That's just it, Mom. She puts on a front. Perfectly normal, but when we're alone, she's quiet. Frosty. Strange."

"Huh."

I'm stumped. I want to offer help, but I'm not sure what would be helpful.

We sit in silence for a few seconds.

Thank the Lord. I hear the Dodge pulling into the drive;

Clive's home. I pray he can direct Kelly to what he should do. I'm at a loss sometimes when problems like this arise. I'm like Mom that way. I don't know how to handle emotional difficulties well. Mom never knew how to manage my outbursts as a young woman. And when I moved out of that phase, we mainly kept our thoughts to ourselves.

The truck stops, the door slams shut, and then I hear Clive's feet crunching on the path.

Clive saunters into the backyard, where Kelly and I have pulled deck chairs closer to the lake and dock. "I see you started the party without me."

Grease smudges darken his full cheeks.

I motion to where his smudges are. "Didn't bother to look in a mirror before you left, I see."

Clive shrugs and sets his lunch box down. He pulls a hankie out of his back pocket and wipes at his face, but it only gets worse.

"I think you'll need soap on that," I comment.

"Probably." He takes the vacant seat on the other side of me. He looks at both of us with a questioning gaze, his eyebrows puzzled down. "Who died?"

Clive gets to the point in his usual straightforward, hyperbolic manner.

I shake my head and roll my eyes at him. "No one."

He shrugs, sheepish. "What?"

I struggle to find the right words. "Kelly's come to…talk about a…difficulty."

"I think Doris is having an affair," Kelly throws out. He looks over at his father.

"What?" Clive widens his eyes, pushing his head back and his neck forward in a joking way. He waits for Kelly to say something. "You're kidding, right?"

I pin him with a stare and use my no-nonsense voice. "Clive, this is serious."

He sets his gaze intently on our son and leans forward; the chair creaks in protest.

His expression straightens. "You…you know for certain?"

Kelly waffles his head back and forth. "I've not caught her at it, if that's what you mean."

He sounds bitter and heartbroken.

Clive leans back and lets out a sigh. "Phew…" His lips flap as he does. "Doris doesn't seem like the type."

"Sorry. I…I shouldn't have come and bothered you both. There's nothing you can do about it." Kelly makes to get up, but I stop him.

"I'm glad you came." I reach my hand out to him. "Burdens like this are too heavy to bear alone. We're family, and we're meant to share these things."

A sudden sob catches in my throat, and I start to cry.

"Oh, Mom. Don't cry," Kelly moans.

"Sorry." I sniff and wipe at my eyes. "It's just with my mom and her secrets, the stuff she bore by herself—it gets to me. I might have helped lighten her load." I'm outright sobbing now. "We might have been closer." I sniff loudly and gulp. "I don't want that to be us, Kelly." I grasp his hand tightly in mine. "Please," I beg.

He moves closer and puts his arm around me. "I'm not sure what you're talking about with Grandma. I knew you two were never very close, but that's not us, Mom." He tips my head back and looks into my watery eyes. "Okay?"

I nod and sniff again. "I'm sorry. These last few months have been emotional, and now this…"

I feel another cry coming on.

"Listen. We're here for you. Whatever you want, Son." Even Clive sounds emotional, his usual kidding set aside.

I blot my eyes on my sleeve and lean back in my chair. Kelly gives me space.

"Just make sure you know the facts." I turn my eyes directly to his. "You're going to have to confront her. Dad and I can take the girls for an evening again, so you can be alone."

"Ya. That'd probably be best." Kelly swipes his hand through his hair. "I'll give you a call." He stands. "I have to go pick up the girls from school now. They stayed after for some project."

"Okay. Make sure to let us know, and, Kelly...we'll be praying for you."

I hold my breath. Kelly has walked away some from the faith we raised him with. I wait for his protest, but it doesn't come.

He simply says, "Thanks, Mom."

He nods at Clive and walks back to the driveway.

Clive holds my hand, and we sit in silence for a while. I watch a fishing boat putter by. *Most likely heading in for supper.* The light slants low over the lake, casting the shadows of the trees longer.

I should go in and get supper going, but I ask Clive, "Mind if we pray for Doris and Kelly now?"

He shakes his head and removes his cap. His hair lies scrunched down on his head. A definite ring shows where his cap sat.

"Dear, Lord," he starts...

Hours later

Clive sleeps, and I read by the light of my little desk lamp. I'm tired, but I can't rest. So, I read another letter from Mabel to Mom.

August 30th, 1918
Dear Robin,
It was so very good to see you. I love you, dear sister, and wish we could have stayed longer. I hope you forgive me for my burst of anger. The thought of life going on without you made me angry. At you and at God. I'm holding you to your promise. I'm glad you are feeling better and, with care, I'm sure you'll be back home soon.

On our train ride home, I begged Ma to let me come stay with you as we talked about. She said yes! I might even be able to attend college out there. I'll write to Mr. and Mrs. Holcomb right away and ask if they would have room for a boarder.

I hope to see you again soon. Until then, love and prayers,
Mabel

I never knew how close Mom and Mabel were. Yet another thing she didn't tell me, but then, why would she? I hardly remember Aunt Mabel. I remember Mom telling me that Mabel moved to Minnesota after school with a fella she met there. His family were Norwegian wheat farmers. I remember seeing Mabel, Del, and Lydia during holidays, but after Mabel passed, the visits grew fewer.

I fold up the letter and tuck it back in the box. Getting up from my chair, I turn out the light and set the box on the table.

The warm body of my husband calls to me. My feet are cold on the tile floor. This is the first chilly night we've had. I get into bed and snuggle next to Clive. He grunts as I place my ice-cold feet on his toasty ones. Next to him, I start to relax but also cry. I think about the years Clive and I have had together. Kelly's marriage may not make it past the fifteen-year mark. How sad that would be.

And if I may say, you're the
two most beautiful blooms in the garden.

CHAPTER TWENTY-EIGHT

Robin
Late August
"Look at these! The blooms are gorgeous."

Robin tucked a red hollyhock in her hair and did a slow swirl in her drab, off-white dress, pretending it was red silk instead. She almost wished for the blue-rose robe her mother had made her, but she'd liked the act of putting on her regular dress that morning. It represented another step back to her life.

Molly plucked a cherry-red, cup-shaped blossom off the leggy plant. "Yes."

Robin stilled at the dip in Molly's tone. She faced her friend. "Tell me more of your story, please."

"I can't remember where we left off before Nurse Sandry came." Molly fingered the petals of the flower in her hand. She seemed reluctant to speak.

Robin walked to the grass near the edge of the garden and sat down. The day was mild in temperature. A slight breeze ruffled Robin's hair, and the late-afternoon sun hid behind some puffy, white clouds.

"Come sit with me, but if you'd rather not say, I understand."

Robin had her secrets, and she wouldn't begrudge Molly hers.

"Sure." Molly followed and sat sideways next to Robin. She still cupped the bloom in her hand. "What's the last thing you recall me mentioning?"

Robin picked at the grass. A distant cow's bellow made her turn her head to look toward the barn, but she didn't see anything out of the ordinary.

She looked back at Molly and snapped her fingers. "Oh, a great loss…"

She left off, hoping Molly would fill in the gaps.

"Ah, yes. That's right." Molly nodded. She didn't smile, and continued to smooth the tips of her fingers over the silky petals of the flower she held. "The burns were bad enough for me, but…" She turned her soulful, good eye on Robin. "I don't know if I am ready to talk about it with anyone in specifics, but I also lost someone I loved."

Molly's hand fluttered to her throat.

"I'm so sorry." Robin didn't know what else to say. She ventured another question. "How did you come to be here?"

Molly took a deep breath. She shook her head and gazed down at her lap. "Everything went dark after that. There are days which I have no memory of, and then one day…"

"There you two are." Nurse Sandry tramped down the path toward them with a young man carrying a large case and wooden poles, her mouth set in her usual grim line.

Molly and Robin exchanged a questioning look.

"This young man from the newspaper would like to take some pictures of the farm and gardens. He wanted some folks in the picture." Nurse Sandry gave them a quick inspection with her sweeping gaze. "I suppose you'll do." She snapped her fingers. "Spit spot. Up on your feet." She turned to the man. "Where do you want them?"

Molly stood and shook her head.

"No," she rasped out. "Not me."

Nurse Sandry flipped her hand in an annoyed manner. "Oh, tut, tut. You may leave your bonnet on, I'm sure."

The man pointed toward the staked hollyhocks. "I think over by that trellis."

Robin noticed his slightly disheveled state. His tie slanted to the right. One arm of his suit gaped at the wrist. *No doubt a missing button,* Robin surmised. The cap on his head teetered to the left, and a smudge of dirt on his face highlighted his pointed cheekbone. He appeared thin and rather waif-like, but with warm, brown eyes.

He smiled at them kindly. "Would that suit you ladies?"

Robin nodded. "Surely."

She stood, smiled, and linked her arm through Molly's.

Molly protested in an adamant whisper. "I can't have my picture taken."

She shook her head, but Robin propelled her forward.

"Don't worry. You can turn your face away if you like," she whispered back.

"It will take me a few minutes to get set up. In the meantime, please position yourself by the trellis. You," he pointed at Robin, "over there, on the right."

Robin stepped over some plants and waded through the asters to stand at the spot he indicated.

"Now you."

He motioned Molly to stand opposite Robin on the other side of the hollyhocks. Molly moved to the spot but kept her head down. He stepped back and held his arms out, holding his fingers up like a frame. He peered through the space and moved it here and there, tilting his head with each shift.

"Yes. Perfect," he announced, and he smiled.

He turned his back on them and proceeded to arrange his photography equipment.

Robin reached her hand out to Molly. "It'll be okay. You'll see." She smiled warmly at her friend, hoping Molly would tilt her head up. But Molly didn't look up.

After a few minutes, the man stepped toward them.

"May I?" he asked Robin with his hands hovering near her. She nodded her consent, and he touched her shoulders, moving them to the angle he desired. "Perfect." He briefly touched the red bloom in her hair. "Now, you'll look directly at the camera."

He motioned to where the camera stood on a tripod with its lens pointing at them.

"Yes, of course, but my friend doesn't want to. She's…shy."

Robin withheld the truth from him, as she was certain that would bring embarrassment to Molly.

He hesitated a moment. "Yes, I can see that." He set his jaw in a determined way. "No matter. Sometimes the best photographs have a bit of mystery to them." He reached out his hands to Molly, but she backed away. "Ah." He let his hands slip back to his sides. "If you could step back. Yes." He tilted his head and eyed her position. "A bit more to the left." A few seconds of silent deliberation. "Now look down at your hand." He paused and studied her, then leaned forward and plucked off another hollyhock bloom. He placed it in her hand with the other one, which had become a bit scrunched. "There. Something for your gaze to be focused on." Molly nodded. "I think we're ready."

He turned and walked back to his camera.

To Robin's surprise, Nurse Sandry had remained quiet throughout the posing, but she stood in the grass near the camera like a policeman on watch.

"Ladies, I'll count down from three, then I'll take the shot. I want you to hold as still as possible, until I re-emerge from under the cover." He pointed to the heavy, black fabric draping the backside of the camera. "Understand?"

Both Robin and Molly replied, "Yes."

"Good."

He grinned, looking less rat-like, and ducked underneath the fabric. He counted down and took the shot. After a few seconds, he uncovered himself and stood up.

"Beautiful," he uttered as he rubbed his hands together. "Now, if you like, you can buy a photograph." He pulled several small, folded sheets out of his jacket pocket. He walked back to them, extending the papers. "Fill this out and drop it by The Dunn County News, and we'll be happy to oblige."

Robin shook her head. "But I don't know when we'd be able to…"

She hoped to return to the farm within the month, but Doctor Howington had the final say.

"Sorry. How stupid of me." His cheeks blossomed pink. "You may mail the request in as well, with the payment stipulated at the bottom of the paper." He gave a final nod. "Thank you, ladies, for allowing me to photograph you. And if I may say, you're the two most beautiful blooms in the garden."

He turned, walked back, and began collecting his things.

"Nurse, will you accompany me to the barn?" he asked Sandry.

"I believe you can manage on your own, sir. I have duties to attend to," Nurse Sandry stated in her commanding tone. "If you need assistance in the barn, Miles Henry should be around. Tall fellow with blond hair—you can't miss him."

She dismissed the photographer with a nod and marched back into the building through the open back doorway.

Robin watched the man hike off toward the barn.

"That was fun," she told Molly.

Molly met her gaze. "It wasn't as bad as I feared."

"Could I hear the rest of your story sometime?"

Robin didn't want to press her friend, but her curiosity had gotten the better of her. She walked out of the garden and stood at the spot where they had sat together before.

Molly stood near and shook her head. "I'm tired. I would like to rest, but perhaps one day I'll tell you the rest. I promise."

Molly looked up at Robin. One corner of her hooded eye could be seen behind the scarring. For a brief moment, it reminded Robin of how a reptile closed its eyelids over its eyeballs. She shook the thought from her mind. She didn't want the image equating to how she perceived Molly, whom she saw as a beautiful bloom despite her scars, just as the man had said.

"Another day," Robin consented.

"Thank you," Molly uttered as she followed the path back to the asylum building.

Robin noticed that the hollyhock blooms fell from her hand halfway to the door. It registered as a picture of sadness—life spent and crumbled. Forgotten. She wondered if Molly felt that way, or if she held hope for her future.

As Robin walked back, she found herself praying for Molly, asking that God would grant her a future and a hope. Robin had heard those words from the visiting minister's lips last

Sunday as he read from the Old Testament book of Jeremiah.

A future and a hope. Those words echoed in her heart as she entered the insane asylum and closed the door behind her.

The most valuable things in life always require effort.

CHAPTER TWENTY-NINE

Enid
September 1984

I can hardly believe it, but Mom just sang a song. I've accompanied her to the church service today at the nursing home. It's become my habit to visit her on Sunday mornings. I don't feel badly about missing church to be with her. Often, I read to her from her Bible; we sit together, and I talk to her about everything I can think of until either I run out of things to say or she falls asleep. But today I decided to wheel Mom down to the common room, where a service is scheduled. Usually it's in the afternoon, but for some reason they are having it in the morning today.

We've just finished singing *What a Friend We Have in Jesus.* She sang through the whole first verse. I haven't heard Mom speak in months, so, needless to say, she's shocked me. Music must have a special memory link that defies even Alzheimer's.

I'm settled back next to her now on a folding chair, listening to the message. My mind wanders; I can't get over her singing. I turn to study her to see if more life registers in her eyes, but I can see nothing more than a cloudy calm. Her head droops, and her eyes close and open a few times, heavy with tiredness.

The middle-aged minister wraps up his message of hope with a verse from Hebrews. His smooth voice rolls out the words in a practiced manner, and I grasp onto the words: "This hope we have as an anchor of the soul, both sure and steadfast…" I lose track of what he continues to read, as I mull over the hope, which is Jesus, the anchor of our souls. Because of His sacrifice we are tethered in a stable link to God. Jesus broke the division between God and man. He is the missing link we ultimately all seek.

Mom's eyes are shut now, and the service is over. I greet a few residents as I wheel Mom back to her room. My faith has been bolstered this morning. I continue to believe that the Lord knows Mom's predicament. He is the hope we can hold on to. Hope for more. For life. For being with our creator, and some purpose past the pain.

I wheel Mom in. She seems peaceful, so I don't want to wake her. I worry about her neck being in pain, though; her chin touches her chest.

I bend over and give her a quick kiss on the cheek. "I'm gonna go, Mom. I'll be back mid-week. I…love you."

I hesitated over the last few words. We've not often said that to each other, but I want her to hear me. I want her to know. I'm hoping she does.

I walk out lighter in spirit than I came, but then I think about Kelly.

Oh, Lord. Spare him the pain of divorce. As a parent, I want to keep him from hurt, but I can't. To live is to feel pain. Pain is often wrapped up as the consequence of our or another's actions. In this case Doris's. But if they're having trouble, it can't only be her fault. Can it? I hate to admit that Kelly might have a part to play in their upheaval.

I open the car door and step into the Buick. I fit the key into the ignition, and it hits me. *Maybe it goes all the way back to Mom and me.* Could it? Is my strained relationship with my mother somehow in part responsible for Kelly's marital difficulties? Have I patterned poor relationship behaviors to him?

"But Clive and I have had a strong marriage," I argue out loud to myself.

We have, but he's Clive, patient, kind, and funny and more than willing to tolerate the way I keep everything and everyone at arm's length, which includes him, on occasion. I'm better than I used to be, but when Clive and I first married…well, let's just say, looking back, I can see what a stubborn, little brat I was at times.

My hand still holds the key. I shake my head, turn the ignition, and pull out of the parking slot. On a whim, I take a right onto Stout Road in the direction of Kelly's home. I need to talk to him. I need to ask.

Ten minutes later

I stand on Kelly's doorstep. "I thought we might grab a cup of coffee together. What do you say?"

He's in a sweatshirt, jeans, and stockinged feet. The hair on top of his head tufts up and reminds me of when he was small. The stubble on his face and a few wrinkles around his eyes reflect his age, though. I hear the girls talking in the background. Doris doesn't appear to be around.

"Sure." He takes a quick look over his shoulder before asking, "You want to come in or should we go somewhere?"

"Whatever you think would be best."

He shrugs and looks noncommittal. "The girls are busy in the kitchen baking. I've got coffee on. We could grab some and sit in the atrium."

"Sounds good," I say, and I follow Kelly into his slate-blue, ranch-style house.

We move down the hall, laden with pictures of the girls at various ages, and into the kitchen.

"Hey, Grammie." Phoebe grins at me as I lean over the counter. She's at the opposite counter adding ingredients to the twins' new mixer. "Pop with you?"

"No, left him at home. I was just visiting your great grammie."

She nods and pulls one corner of her lips back in a kind of sad smile. "I miss Great Grammie."

"I got the raisins," Pamela cuts in. She emerges from the basement with a plastic container in her hands. She turns to me. "Morning, Grammie."

"Morning," I respond with a big smile. "You on a treasure hunt?"

She walks toward Phoebe and sets the small tub down on the counter where various baking utensils, ingredients, and bowls are splayed out. "Sort of. Mom keeps a bulk supply of some things we like to bake with in the basement. We ran out of raisins in the pantry."

"I see." I wonder where Doris is. "Your mom helping too?"

Kelly gives me a strange look and hands me a filled mug of coffee with a spoon sticking out of it and the creamer bottle. I set the mug down on the counter and stir in the cream until the coffee reaches the right caramel color. I snap the lid shut, take a sip of my coffee, and hand Kelly back the cream. He stashes it in the fridge.

Pammie opens the container and scoops out some golden

raisins. "Mom went to visit Aunt Linda. She'll be back tonight."

Phoebe adds baking soda to the bowl of the mixer. Her middle is encased in a pink, gingham apron. "We're making oatmeal raisin cookies."

I grin. "One of my favorites."

"We'll send some home for you and Pop," Pammie says.

"I'm gonna make some noise," Phoebe warns before switching on the mixer.

Kelly signals me with a jerk of his head and walks through the dining room. I wave at the girls and follow my son into the little atrium where a cafe-type table sits on top of an earth-toned, braided rug amidst the greenery. I take a seat, and so does he. It feels ten degrees warmer in this area of the house. I unbutton my sweater with one hand.

He looks at me with questions in his eyes, but he doesn't ask. He sips his coffee instead and points out a large orchid laden with fist-sized, olive and lime-green blooms and long, tapered leaves. Kelly takes after Mom with his love for plants. He grows orchids, of all things, and has a veritable jungle of houseplants in every size and shape.

"My mini cymbidium finally bloomed again. I almost lost hope." He reaches out and snaps one of the ten or so blooms off the stem. "Take it home." He sets it gently by my cup.

"How lovely. Thank you." I touch the flower's waxy petals. "You know the minister talked about hope at the nursing home this morning."

I eye him to see if I should go on.

"Oh, ya," Kelly replies nonchalantly. He takes another drink.

"Mom and I listened to the visiting minister this morning instead of me reading to her. It was nice." I study the contents of my coffee mug, trying to drum up the courage to ask Kelly what I came to ask him. I toy with the handle. "I'm sorry for the mistakes I've made."

I venture a look into his eyes.

He shakes his head, a confused furrow on his brow. "What in the world do you mean?"

"Well..." I raise my left shoulder and grimace. "It was rough between your grandmother and I sometimes. I kept too much distance between us. She never knew how to deal with my stubborn streak, and I never knew how to deal with her quiet, secret streak." I laugh. "Your father tricked and loved it out of me."

"What are you getting at, Mom?" He seems confused at my confession.

I take a deep breath. "I'm not sure what's been going on between you and Doris, but I hope my poor example hasn't influenced your troubles."

Our hazel eyes meet.

"I never saw you like that. You were a good mother. Are. Always there." He touches my hand briefly. "And you're here now, trying to take the blame, which isn't yours to take." He sighs. "I don't really understand what our 'trouble' is or where we went wrong."

"Have you spoken with her?" I take one last swig of my coffee and then wish I hadn't; a dose of grounds came with it.

"Ya." He scratches the back of his head and stretches his arms back. "That was probably the most awkward conversation I've ever had in my life." He gives a snide grin. "Except Dad's talk with me about sex."

I laugh, imagining Clive tackling that subject, and he sobers.

"She's been seeing someone, like I thought, but she swears

it isn't physical." He laughs bitterly and pauses between statements. "A professor at the college. In the English department. They write poetry together." Kelly lowers his arms and slumps forward over the table. "She says I've neglected her. Honestly, Mom, I don't know what she wants."

"Have you asked her?"

"Friday night, as she tossed some clothes in her suitcase, she said that I should know. It's all a mixed-up mess that appeared out of nowhere, if you ask me. I don't get it."

"Is she coming back?"

"She's says she is." Kelly looks at his watch. "She said she'd be back by supper." He levels his gaze at me. "The girls don't know anything."

I nod but think it unlikely that they are entirely in the dark. Pammie and Phoebe are smart and perceptive. But I don't say so.

"What about counseling? I mean, you want to work it out, right?"

Please, Lord.

He pushes his mug away and leans back in his chair again. "We haven't decided."

"The most valuable things in life always require effort. I hope you'll both be willing to try." I reach out to him. He grabs my hand. "You have a good life here with your daughters, and you want them to see that their parents tried to fix things and didn't give up without a fight."

He lets go, nods, and mutters, "Ya, I guess."

"Maybe you need to rekindle what brought you together in the first place. What drew you to Doris?"

Kelly's eyes glaze slightly and every feature on his face stills; he looks lost in a memory. "Her bright, sunny confidence." He tilts his head to the right and closes his eyes. "She had a way about her, a sparkle in her eye, that captivated me."

"When did you last tell her that?"

He opened his eyes. "It's been a while."

We are silent for some seconds.

"Well, I should get home. Your father will be looking for some lunch soon." I look directly at my son. "Your dad and I want what's best for you and your family, and we'll be here in whatever way you need our support."

"I know. Thanks."

We smile at each other. He stands; so do I.

He hugs me and whispers into my ear, "I love you, Mom."

My heart melts a little. Those few words move my world.

"I love you too," I whisper back.

Will I be the mother she deserves?
Robin didn't know, but she had to find out.

CHAPTER THIRTY

Robin
September 1918

The blooms were spent. No flowers clung to the leggy stalks; instead, seed pods, like bulbous buttons, dotted the stems. Robin ran her fingers over one of the pods, which was soft to the touch, as most were. A few had begun to dry out and were brittle.

"The hollyhocks are done." Molly stepped near Robin. "I'll snap off some of the dry pods, and you can take those with you when you go home." Molly's voice rang both happy and sad to Robin's ears. "That way you'll have something to remember me by."

Her tone of voice rasped, and she coughed into her hand.

"I'll never forget you, Molly. You have been the biggest help to me here in this place. More than the doctor, treatments, or surgery. Talking with you helped the most, and gardening, of course." Robin looked out over the patch of earth which had been a place of therapy and healing for her. "I have become fond of it." Robin moved toward Molly and embraced her. "It became more than work. Thank you for that."

"I didn't do much; I only listened."

"You understood and worked beside me."

Robin released her friend. Molly stepped back and pulled up her sunbonnet again.

Molly tilted her head and questioned Robin with her good eye. "When do you leave?"

"I have yet to discuss my final treatment plan with Doctor Howington, but he hinted at this month."

A tinge of fear tickled at the back of Robin's thoughts. It had been almost four months since she had been at home. She looked forward to being back on the farm with a rainbow of cherished items around her. Her hesitation involved her family. She still held some shame over her past actions, and the unknown factor of how she would be with Enid worried her. *Will I be the mother she deserves?* Robin didn't know, but she had to find out.

"You'll be missed." Molly tipped her head down and walked along the rows of flowers, fingering a leaf or seed pod here and there. "I understand more than you know."

Robin walked parallel to Molly in another row of flowers. The asters, cosmos, and marigolds were some of the only flowers yet producing. "What do you mean?"

"I know what it's like to want your life to end. I've walked that path. After I lost the person I loved the most, I didn't want to keep living. Later, seeing my face every day...so hideous." Molly shook her head. "I could barely stand to look at myself. I wanted to die."

Robin kept quiet. She knew how ugly she'd thought her inward self to be. They had both thought along the same lines, except her torment had been unseen, Molly's seen.

"I'm sorry. That must have been difficult." Robin stopped. "But you are more than a face, Molly. You are a beautiful person."

Robin cried. Even though her spirits had felt better of late, she teared up more frequently. Dr. Howington had told her displays of emotion might be a consequence of the surgery for a time afterward.

Molly stopped, too, and peeked at her through the bent-over sunflower stalks. "I recall one night, weeks after I came here. I went to bed in deep despair, but a man spoke to me in a dream. I think he was an angel. He said, 'Just live for God's beauty.' That was a revelation to me. Really, I had been thinking only of myself and my own needs, but if I turned my life's energy to pointing other people to God's beauty then I wouldn't need to worry about my own."

"Oh, my. That's so true." Robin sniffed. "I will try to remember that. You have certainly exemplified this to me." Robin reached through the flowers and grasped Molly's hand. "Thank you, dear friend."

Molly looked her full in the face, a rare show of unashamedly being herself. "You're welcome."

Robin let go of Molly's hand. "Let's go in and see if Cook will let us have some tea. I'm craving a cup. While we're having tea, I'll read you another letter I received from Mabel."

"Your sister is so sweet. I wish I had a sister," Molly commented.

"Mabel likes you as well. She mentions you in her letter. She can be a sister to us both."

Robin and Molly walked briskly to the end of the garden and went into the asylum together.

That evening

After supper, there was singing in the common room. A musician from the local theater guild had offered to come and play the piano and lead the residents in popular songs once a month. A blonde-haired, middle-aged woman played with gusto and talent. Many voices rose in a strange, off-key harmony in one song after another, but Robin didn't mind. Those that sang did so whole-heartedly. It cheered Robin's heart. They ended with *You Are My Sunshine*.

When the music hour was done. Robin greeted a few folks, said thank you to the kind woman who had volunteered her time and talent, and headed back to her room. As she entered, she spied a letter on her nightstand. With the foreign stamps and postmark, Robin could tell it was from Willis. She carefully tore open the thin envelope. His flowing script inside made her smile.

Dear Robin,
My heart aches that you have endured so much. You have been fighting battles, as I have been. We are soldiers in arms together, and that's how we will always face life—together.

I need you to be brave. I know you have a lot of love to give. You don't have to be perfect, but I can assure you that Enid could never have a better mother than you, nor I a better wife.

I won't bore you with the details of my daily soldier's life. Needless to say, it's not all it's cracked up to be.

I love you with all my heart and look forward to being with you and giving both of my girls a kiss.
Until then,
Willis

Tears streamed down Robin's face. She lay back on her bed with the letter clutched to her chest and breathed a deep prayer of thanks and relief. *He does love me.* Willis hadn't upbraided her for her weakness and faults. He had encouraged her instead. How could she be so blessed to have married such a man?

Robin revisited as many memories as she could of her and Willis, but soon she relaxed enough to welcome sleep.

Days later

"Doctor will be waiting for you." Nurse Phelps stood at the door to Robin's room with a smile on her handsome face.

This was it—her day of reckoning. *Am I really well?* Robin thought Doctor Howington would say so, but could she be fully recovered? She felt almost like her old self. The spontaneous and carefree aspects of her person were still absent, however.

Robin smoothed down her pink and green, chintz, dress with the all-over pattern of tiny rosebuds. It had been odd to put her regular clothes on this morning instead of her usual plain resident dress of off-white muslin. Her fingers found her locket where it lay against her chest. At last, Nurse Sandry had returned all of Robin's personal articles to her.

Willis. Robin could barely picture her husband's face, and when she did, he wore a frown. A memory of their race to the farmhouse after kissing by the pond flashed in her mind. The remembered time last spring seemed so long ago. *Will we ever be that happy again?*

Nurse Sandry butted into Robin's thoughts. "Mrs. Holcomb. Times-a-wastin'. Get on with you, now." Nurse Sandry pinned poor Nurse Phelps with an icy gaze. "Nurse Phelps, in future, please carry out the doctor's requests promptly."

Phelps visibility cringed.

Robin piped up, "It's entirely my fault, Nurse Sandry. I do apologize."

She turned her head to take one last look at the colorless room which had been her abode for the last few months. In a strange way, she would miss it. The space had been her prison but also a safe harbor for her when her thoughts had all but drowned her.

Nurse Sandry tempered her tone. "Yes, well. Come along."

As Robin walked out the doorway and past Nurse Phelps, she gave the woman a parting smile and whispered, "Thank you for your kind, excellent care."

Robin would miss the interesting, young woman.

"You'll be missed, ma'am, but I am glad you're returning home," the nurse replied in a low voice, one dark eye cautiously peering at the stiff back of Nurse Sandry.

Robin walked the well-known path to Dr. Howington's office. Her heels clicked on the floor with each step.

Nurse Sandry stood at the door waiting for her, like a soldier at attention. She nodded at Robin. "Well wishes to you, Mrs. Holcomb."

For the first time, Nurse Sandry looked at Robin like an equal instead of a naughty child to be reprimanded.

"Thank you."

Robin nodded and walked past her, not sad to see the last of Sandry. Marge and Susan waited in chairs in front of Mr. Howington's desk. He stood fingering through some files in a cabinet.

He smiled fondly at Robin. "Ah, the woman of the hour."

Despite her misgivings, Robin had been treated with nothing but kindness by the man. His sympathy had been clear to her throughout the strange and often painful treatments she'd endured. She didn't think ill of him.

"Quite," she agreed with a smile.

She sat next to Susan. Robin was glad the ladies hadn't brought Enid with them. She wanted their reunion as mother and daughter to happen at home.

Susan greeted her. "Robin, it's so good to see you looking so well."

Gone were Susan's past pinched look and voice. A friendly smile curved up her full, pink-stained lips, and a welcoming glint in her eyes accompanied her warm words. Her face reflected a beauty that Robin had not seen before.

"Thanks, Sue." Robin bobbed her head at Marge. "Marge. Thank you both for coming to bring me home."

Marge leaned forward; her bosom bulged up to her neck with the effort. "Hal wanted to come, but a cow was calving. Susan was brave enough to drive us in with her and Tom's car."

Concern clouded her blue eyes, but a welcoming smile set Robin more at ease.

"Now. I have some final papers for both the Mrs. Holcombs to sign, and then you can be on your way." The doctor passed paper copies of release forms to Robin and Marge. They shared a fountain pen between them. "Keep in mind those things we discussed in our meeting a few days again, Robin."

Dr. Howington peered at her over the top of his tortoiseshell reading glasses.

"Yes," Robin said.

Dr. Howington had gone over her whole history with her since she'd been at the asylum: attempted wrist splitting, not speaking, shock therapy, water therapy, psychiatric talk therapy, and of course the results of the hysterectomy. He'd felt all four treatments had assisted her in keeping the melancholy at bay. But what he had not factored in was the time that she had spent in the garden helping Molly. In Robin's mind, that had been her biggest help, but she couldn't be sure. He had highlighted the importance of a healthy diet, exercise, and fresh air and sunshine; she had agreed.

"Well, I am glad to send you home to your family. You have my most sincere wishes for continued health and happiness."

Dr. Howington extended his hand to Robin. She rose, took it, and he clasped her hand in a firm handshake.

Robin acknowledged his care. "Thank you."

Susan and Marge stood up as well, and they walked the few feet to the front door of the asylum. Once out the door, Robin turned her head and took in the large building, which had seemed a prison to her when she'd first come. *It doesn't seem quite as assuming now.*

"I'll take your bag." Susan grabbed Robin's carpet bag and tucked it in the back of her roadster.

They all got in. Robin sat in the back since Marge tended to get carsick.

"All set?" Susan asked. She gave a quick look to Robin, who nodded and smiled. "Off we go then."

Susan put the car in gear and drove out of the driveway. Robin turned and looked out the back window. The building grew small until the trees hid it from sight. She faced forward and tried to calm the butterflies in her stomach, but with each mile closer to home, Robin's worry grew over how she would handle her reunion with Enid. *Will I be a stranger to her, or will she be happy to see me?* The questions kept nagging her. She took some deep breaths and worked at relaxing as Dr. Howington had taught her. That helped, and when the farm came into view, Robin felt a smile on her lips. *I'm home.*

I am as much to blame for my strained relationship
with my mother as she is.
The road goes both ways.

CHAPTER THIRTY-ONE

Enid
Late September

Pamela flounces up to Clive and me. "Did you like it, Grammie?"

Clive grins and pinches her cheek. "A star is born."

"Pops." She gives him a sideways look. "Quit teasing."

She smiles; a shimmer of silver braces shine under the fluorescent light in the school gym. Her long, pretty, blonde hair looks like it has been curled with orange juice cans, the kind frozen juice comes in. Big, luscious curls frame her face.

Kelly, Doris, Clive, and I are at the twins' piano recital. Pammie played Beethoven's *Moonlight Sonata,* and Phoebe played *Fur Elise.* They both did an excellent job: smooth rhythm, feeling, and no wrong notes—that I could tell. Most of the students did well. Only one girl floundered through her piece. From the red of her face and her shaky hands, I think nerves may have been her problem rather than a lack of practice.

Clive chucks Phoebe under her chin as she steps into our

circle. "Loved yours, too, young lady."

She smiles widely, her hair arranged in a similar style to her sister's. They each wear a gathered-waist, velvet dress. The color of Phoebe's dress is green and Pammie's is dark pink. *They look so grown up.*

"I'm proud of you both," Kelly comments in his dry manner.

His light brown suit and green tie look well on him and bring out the green in his hazel eyes.

Doris reaches out and strokes them each quickly on a pink cheek with her manicured fingers. "Yes. Well done, girls."

A smart, navy blazer, light blue blouse with dark red, floral dots, and a pencil skirt in the same shade of red give Doris her usual put-together facade. *Does her look transfer to the inside, or have her and Kelly's difficulties rattled her at all?*

She steps back from the girls, and I hug each one in turn. People file past us, but I cling to them longer than I should.

"Dad promised we could go and celebrate at The Bolo," Phoebe tells me in an eager voice.

"We haven't decided yet," Doris says in a polite, strained tone.

"What? You have an art class you didn't tell us about?" The words roll off Kelly's tongue like a skater at the roller-rink making a sharp turn. He sneers and tucks Phoebe under his arm. "Course we'll go."

Kelly smiles down at his daughter. She doesn't echo his grin but only raises the corners of her mouth and nods. Phoebe flashes her eyes at Doris.

In a seething voice, Doris levels at Kelly, "Why do you have to start this here? Come on."

She places one hand on her hip.

"Oh." Clive points. "I think I see the fella who was selling raffle tickets as we came in. I could use me a chocolate cake. Let's go check it out."

Clive motions to the twins, and they follow him, looking relieved to escape the uncomfortable atmosphere that has descended upon our family circle.

"I'm taking the girls and my folks out to The Bolo for a nice meal. Come or not. Whatever," Kelly huffs.

He turns on his heel and follows after Clive and the girls. Doris and I are left standing alone. I don't know what to say or if I should move or not.

Doris focuses her gaze on her shoes. "What has he told you?"

"That…that you've been seeing someone else," I admit.

A trickle of sweat runs down my temple. The overcrowded gym, which holds a distinct smell of gym socks and stale popcorn, has not cooled off yet. I remove my scarf and drape it over my arm.

She shakes her head, and her gold, dangly earrings tinkle. "I told Kelly that Len and I are just friends, but he won't believe me."

I check for the truth in her eyes, but she avoids eye contact with me.

"What do you spend time doing with your 'friend?'" I can't help but ask.

I shouldn't get in the middle of their dispute, but I can't seem to help myself.

Doris tilts her head and smiles; a light shines in her eyes. "We write. He writes poetry, and so do I, but right now, we're working on a story."

"You should form a writing club," I tell her, in the hopes that the inclusion of more people will keep romantic notions from starting, if they haven't already.

I smile and act like nothing is amiss. The crowd thins out, and I inch toward the exit.

She nods. "Maybe."

I can't tell if she does or doesn't favor the idea.

It comes out before I think too hard about it. "If you don't have feelings for this Len now, you may, if you continue to spend time alone with him. That tends to happen. Think carefully, Doris. You have more at stake than simply losing Kelly." I can't believe my audacity in speaking my mind. Clive would be proud. My mother would be shocked. I pin Doris with a straight stare before turning and tossing over my shoulder, "Come on. The Bolo sounds good. I've been craving one of their popovers."

I hear her heels click behind me. I pray: *Dear Lord, please let this not be too awkward. Somehow mend what has a tear in it.*

I wave at Clive. He stands near a table wearing an enormous grin and holding a chocolate cake. *Great.*

Later that night

"Did you really need to win a whole chocolate cake?" Annoyance rises in my question.

I've barely got my coat off and he's cracked into the thing.

"What? Don't tell me you don't want some," Clive says before he forks in a large piece of cake.

A smudge of chocolate frosting clings to the corner of his mouth. He sits at our kitchen table; a hearty portion of cake occupies the dessert plate in front of him.

"That's the problem." I pat the growing donut around my waist.

"Ah." He chews and shakes his head, a twinkle in his eye.

"You never let that stop you before."

He winks at me, but I'm in no mood for his humor. The family meal we shared with Kelly, Doris, and the girls at The Bolo supper club left me tense. Too many innuendos had floated around the table.

I swat his shoulder. "Are you saying I'm fat?"

He sobers. "Am I?" He takes another bite and appears to forgot my ire. "You know, a cup of decaf coffee would go great with this."

His eyes plead too.

"Ya? Well, make it yourself."

I storm off toward the bedroom, plucking off my jewelry as I go. My conscience pricks me. My kind, funny husband shouldn't be the recipient of my frustration. My angst belongs with those two numbskulls, Kelly and Doris. They acted like spoiled children tonight. By the time we got home, I had stewed long enough, peeved by their short-sightedness. They can't see past the ends of their noses and perceive only their own grievances.

That's what you do with Mom.

The thought blows me away. I turn on the light in the bedroom and set my jewelry down on the bureau. I sink into my chair in the corner. Thankfully, over the years, Clive has learned to let me cool off before attempting to forge through an outburst. I don't want his company right now, not when my spirit—or maybe it's God's—tells me the truth: I am as much to blame for my strained relationship with my mother as she is. The road goes both ways. I pray Kelly and Doris can figure this out before it's too late.

On impulse I pick up my Bible off the floor. I still have the one Mom bought me for confirmation with the maroon, leather cover and the gold lettering, which has long since faded. I repaired the cover numerous times and some pages are loose, but I still use it. I turn to the inscription. The last sentence reads: "*You are much more than I deserved. Love Mom.*" I finally understand those words now. At the time I thought they were weird. She must not have thought herself worthy. The depression ingrained a pattern of behavior toward me. She always tried too hard with me. Her sentiment, when present, smelled of falsehood. But after reading her diary entries and letters, her actions, or lack of, make more sense. I would have likely responded the same way toward my child if depression and a resulting suicide attempt had been my lot and choice.

For the first time, I can honestly say these words: I forgive my mother. Now I need to ask for her forgiveness.

Days later

"Well, how sick is she?"

My head hurts, and a dull pain knots in my gut. The nurse sounds serious.

"It started a couple of days ago as a sniffle, but it's set in deeper. I detected a rattle this morning when I listened to her lungs," the staff nurse at the Dunn County Health Care Center tells me.

I angle the phone closer to my ear, pinching the cradle against my shoulder with the side of my head. I dry my hands on a dish towel and relieve my cramped neck, picking up the phone in my hand. The call caught me in the middle of dinner cleanup.

"I'll come tomorrow and see her."

"Be warned that we've quarantined her wing. The influenza is having a good run for its money. Maybe you should wait a bit. We'll notify you if there's any change."

She waits for my reply.

I nod and realize that she can't see me. "Ah, I suppose, but if she doesn't improve by the weekend, I'm coming, influenza or not."

"That's understandable. We'll take good care of her, Mrs. Fenton."

My concern leaks out in my voice, though I've worked at holding it in. "Yes. I know you'll do your best. Thanks. Goodbye."

"Try not to worry. Goodbye."

She hangs up with a click, while I still hold the phone and stare at the greasy water in my kitchen sink. I sigh and walk the cradle back to the receiver.

Clive comes in from taking the garbage out. "Who was that?"

He burnt our paper garbage in the burning barrel; now he smells of smoke. He unzips his jacket.

I wave a finger toward the door. "Wait. You better hang that outside, away from the fire. It stinks."

Clive takes a sniff of the heavy twill. "It's not bad."

"Oh, fine. Whatever," I crank out.

Hanging his jacket on a peg, he looks at me. "Hey. I thought you were over your malcontent."

I roll my eyes, and my lips sag of their own volition. I don't say anything. My throat tightens, and the beginning of tears pricks the back of it.

He moves closer to me with caution. "You haven't said who called."

His solid presence makes me crumble; I cry. With Doris and Kelly's trouble and now Mom being sick, it's too much.

Between tears and sniffles, I say, "The nurse called. Mom's ill. It could be the start of some bad virus."

I lean into his welcoming arms. Calm washes over me being in his embrace.

"There, now. Is it really that bad? Do you want to go see her?"

He plays with the hair at the base of my neck. I rest my head against his shoulder. My nose twitches; his jean shirt even smells of ash. I raise my head and meet the comfort in his brown eyes. I notice how bushy his eyebrows are getting. They are in sore need of a trim.

"She said not to come. I told her I'd wait a few days, but that's it." I pause and look deeply into his eyes. "I need to ask Mom something."

One bushy eyebrow lowers. "Oh? How will she answer back?"

"I don't know, but I need to ask her to…forgive me." My eyes water again.

"Oh, Enie." He smooths his rough thumb over my cheek and tenderly kisses me in the same spot. "I'm sure she has. You're too hard on yourself."

"Like mother, like daughter, I guess."

"Come on. I'll stoke the fire, and you make us some tea. Peppermint, if we have it. My tummy's been complaining."

I can't help but chuckle at his droopy lip. "One too many spicy meatballs?"

I made a crockpot meatball recipe for supper that had sweet and hot chile sauce as ingredients.

"Something like that." He smiles and winks, whistling as he walks into the living room.

I gain comfort from Clive's easy manner. Although I'm not

prone to hysterics, every once in a while, I endure a crying binge. Those times have usually involved my mother, somehow.

I take a big sniff and get busy scrubbing the last pan in the sink. When I finish, I fill the teakettle and set out some mugs. Somehow, a cup of tea sets most things to rights, or at least makes them more manageable anyhow.

Later that evening

I pull out Mom's diaries again. She speaks only through the thoughts written on their lines now, and I need to hear her. I wish I knew where the ones pertaining to the years around my birth hid or if they even exist. Maybe she didn't start writing until after, but no. She mentioned destroying some. But maybe in the end she couldn't or forgot to.

I shake my head and take a drink of my cooled chamomile tea. Clive turned in an hour ago, and I sit in the kitchen—still smelling of spicy meatballs—with a stack of diaries open on the table. Where should I start? 1945—the year Clive and I married—sits at the bottom of the stack. I slide it out. The brown, waxy, paper cover has a ring on it, as if someone set their hot cup or mug on it. A stain of some sort lingers in the top right corner. I open it; the spine cracks, brittle with age. A faint whiff of Mom's Chanel No.5 greets me as I thumb through the pages. I stop when I reach a date around my wedding.

August 12th, 1945
I hope and pray Enie will be happy. It's all I ever wished for her. From what I can tell, Clive is a good man. The kind who sticks by you no matter what. The kind of man Willis was. I pray the war won't come between Clive and Enid the way it did for Willis and

me. Through the years I've often thought that if he'd never been called away, everything might have been different.

How she and I have grown to this spot of quiet contention eludes me. I've tried my best but failed to have the closeness with her I desire. She takes much of what I say, or don't say, the wrong way. We are crossed telegraph wires, each sending a message the other can't decipher.

Little did I know that my one act years ago would hang figuratively over my head, a swinging noose ever in my eyesight. Oh, I've ignored it, covered it, and imagined it gone, but at times, in the corner of my mind, I see it swinging, taunting me. Why I picture my past doom as a rope I'm uncertain. I should picture it as water, murky, icy cold, and clinging. Enough thoughts of the past. I pray for the future.

Dear Lord, You have woven each of our inward parts. You understand Enid when I do not and vice versa. I ask that at some point in life you will lead us to a place of mutual understanding, as mother and daughter. Help me to be the best mother I can. I've been broken, and broken things cannot always fulfill the task they were meant for. I pray you will smooth out my cracks and allow Enie to see I have nothing but care for her. At times she seems almost like my enemy, and I don't know how to wave the flag of truce, much less build a like-minded start with her. Help me to know.

I have given up wishing to restart the years with her. If I could go back and do things differently, I would, but life plods on linear regardless of our desires for an eraser. However, You, Lord, are outside of time and unrestrained by man's restrictions. I trust you will work it all out according to your timing.

Amen

I dry my eyes with the sleeve of my chenille robe and close the diary. I get up, flick off the light switch on the wall, and pad slowly to bed, thinking as I go—Mom's prayer may have come to fruition. I just hope it hasn't come too late for me to tell her.

But what is usual anymore?
"Usual" doesn't exist in this world after a shock like this.

CHAPTER THIRTY-TWO

Robin
Late September 1918
Robin remembered it all, the layout of the farmhouse and the homey articles it contained, and yet it held a newness, as if she saw it for the first time. She rubbed her fingers over a worn spot on the kitchen table. Her fingernail caught on a rough portion and split at the end. Robin attempted to bite the nail down, so it wouldn't rip further. A cup of coffee sat untouched in front of her.

Dropping her focus to the floor, Robin checked on Enid, who was fast asleep in a large, wicker basket. Robin noticed how her daughter's eyes moved underneath her tiny, violet-hued lids. Enid breathed heavily, squeaked, and half-smiled in her sleep.

Robin's old feelings of inadequacy were absent, but something she couldn't name held her back from fully showering Enid with love. In her heart, however, a dramatic change had occurred: Robin embraced her role as a mother. Determination to do her best rose in her spirit. She felt a smile curve up her lips and warm her heart as she gazed at Enid with the maternal care she had lacked months ago.

The screen door banged, and Robin looked up at Susan as she entered the house. She walked to the table and set a few letters on the tablecloth.

"Mail came early today." Susan unbuttoned her rust-colored, cable-knit sweater with antler buttons. She took it off and hung it on the back of the chair. "Whew. I'm glad to be rid of that. The air's nippy, but the sun warmed me through and through."

Susan dropped down into a kitchen chair across from Robin and fingered through the stack of mail. Robin watched Sue's fingers stop searching when they encountered a wrinkled envelope with a foreign stamp and "Mrs. Susan Demeter" scrolled across the front. Sue picked it up.

Robin didn't recognize the handwriting and asked, "Letter from Tom?"

"I don't think so."

Susan frowned, ripped open the seal, and pulled out what looked like a brief message. Robin waited quietly while Susan read to herself.

"Good news?" The question slipped out before she noticed that Sue's face had become the color of chalk.

The paper slipped from Susan's grasp and floated haphazardly to the table. Her full lips pursed together, and her eyes glazed over and began to water.

Robin reached a tentative hand toward Susan. "What is it?"

Their fingers met across the red-checked tablecloth, but Susan pulled away like she had touched something hot.

"Tom's...dead." Susan spoke with her usual candor, but her eyes were closed. Her facial muscles tensed in an obvious show of inner pain.

An ache stabbed Robin in the gut. *That could have been Willis.* She hated to hear of Tom's death, and she hurt for Susan, but a portion of her heart felt relieved; the letter hadn't been for her.

"I'm...I'm sorry," she stuttered.

Sue opened her eyes. A dead stare met Robin's gaze. The light had dimmed in the windows of Susan's soul, and her eyes took on the gray of a bleak winter's day. Nodding slightly, Susan lowered her head and brought her hands up, a thin, muscular palm pressed against each ear. The gold band on her right ring finger gleamed in the light of the gas chandelier over the table. The shine made Robin wince. Silent sobs shook Sue's shoulders. Robin got up and came around to Sue's side of the table and hugged her. Their left hands found each other; Sue gripped Robin's fingers as if they were a lifeline.

Robin didn't know what else to tell her. Nothing she could say would make the truth of Tom's death any easier to swallow.

"Do you want me to tell Marge and Hal?"

Susan's tear-streaked face lifted. She sniffed and wiped the hollows of her eyes with two fingers.

"No. Don't." She took a shaky, deep breath. "It's my news to tell."

"Of course." Robin offered the barest of smiles and moved to collect Enid, who had started to fuss. "I'm going to get a bottle ready for Enid. After, I'll get lunch ready. You should go rest."

Robin bounced Enid in her arms and walked to the icebox to pull out the pitcher of goat's milk Hal had gotten from a neighbor. Marge claimed Enid had turned colicky with cow's milk. Marge and Susan had transitioned Enid to a bottle, when Robin had been admitted to the asylum.

Susan rubbed the temple on one side of her head. "Maybe."

Her usually neat, tidy hair strayed and loosened from the bun she wore it in. Her messy ring of hair made her look small and vulnerable. Robin's heart ached more. Susan had always appeared so strong to her.

Robin went about getting a bottle ready and warm with one hand, while she held Enid with her other. Susan rose and inched toward the upstairs steps, climbing them like a person twice her age.

Later that day

Marge had called Lynette after their noon meal, which none of them had eaten much of, and Derek had driven Lynette and the children out.

Lynette perched on the edge of the sofa, her hands wringing together in worry on her green, wool skirt. "Did they say where…Tom fell or…how?"

Her lap was strangely empty. Marge cuddled the baby in her arms and rocked in her chair; a rhythmic creak broke up the awkward moments of silence in the living room. Cassandra had fallen asleep on Hal's shoulder. They sat in the dim corner of the room; Hal had not turned his reading lamp on like usual.

But what is usual anymore? "Usual" doesn't exist in this world after a shock like this.

Robin studied Hal. In the shadows he looked older than he had that morning, the lines on his face deeper. Darker. She wished she hadn't laid Enid to bed so early; Robin's arms ached to hold someone.

Susan visibly swallowed. She spoke in a near whisper. "The Battle of The Somme. His commanding officer wrote that Tom pulled several men to safety before he…"

Susan didn't finish. She lowered her gaze to the hankie she twisted in her lap.

"He died a hero, then," Derek stated in a matter-of-fact way, like that made Tom's death worth it.

He sat next to Lynette and wrapped his arm around her, drawing her back to rest against him.

"Yes." The bland word slid from Susan's lips, her eyes still focused on her lap.

"I cannot equate the thought of our light-hearted Thomas being…" Marge's voice caught, and she clamped her hand over her mouth, stifling a cry. Her blueberry-colored eyes bulged and watered with the effort.

Everyone kept quiet. Marge's sniffles and creaks were the only sounds except the tick of the clock and the faint crackle of logs in the stove that Hal had lit to drive the evening autumn chill from the room.

"Will he be buried there?" Lynette asked, sounding loud in the room. Her finely featured brow scrunched to the bridge of her nose.

Maybe she should give her questions a rest, Robin couldn't help but think. Surely Susan needed time to think and grieve before handling the details of funeral arrangements.

"Yes." Susan pulled an envelope out of the pocket of her dress. Robin recognized it as the awful missive. Holding it up slightly, Susan said, "This is all I'll receive."

"There must be something more they can send back to you." Lynette picked at her skirt with her forefinger. "I mean, what about his identification tags?" She reached her hand out to Susan. "Can I read it?"

Susan nodded and passed the letter to her sister. Lynette opened the letter and read silently.

"Must be mighty hard to keep personal belongings straight on a battlefield," Hal pointed out in a low drone.

"Hmm." Lynette handed the letter back to Sue. "We should hold a remembrance service for Tom here." She reached out and took up one of Susan's hands, acting slow as if she gentled a skittish horse.

Susan tipped her gaze up to Lynette's. "That might be nice, but not right away. Not...too soon."

"O' course not," Marge agreed.

The room swung into silence, lacking words again, but words weren't necessary. *Eyes, expressions, and tears speak the deeper pain and grief we all must feel.* Robin's gaze toured around the homey room and watched the faces of the family who had become hers. She placed her hand over her heart and silently prayed for Susan and them all as they forged ahead on the road of life, missing one of their fellow travelers.

The next day

"It doesn't seem real. I keep expecting to wake from a bad dream. But the reality has settled painfully here." Susan forcefully balled up a fist just under her breasts, anger in her actions.

"I'm sure it has." Robin didn't know how to tell Susan to grieve; she had not lost a loved one before. She'd mostly been listening while Susan talked.

"Why Tom? Why now? We talked about starting a family." Susan's bleary, red eyes peered at Robin over Enid, whom Sue held propped up on her lap. With one finger, Sue stroked Enid's downy cheek. A deep discomfort began to settle on Robin. Memories of not wanting Enid haunted her. A double dose of guilt threatened her; at the back of her mind, the old voice taunted her.

Enid would be better off as Susan's daughter.

No! She wouldn't go there again. Robin pushed away the thought. Instead, she tried to focus on Susan's pain.

"I don't know," Robin simply said.

Who is to blame for the violence of men?

It seemed from the very first human family, a violent seed had been present, and the innocent had suffered for it ever since.

The wind shook the loose pane of glass in the living room window to the west. Robin leaned forward on the cushion of the sofa and watched the first leaves of autumn swirl around in a small eddy on the yet green grass. She looked farther down the drive, until her focus rested on the weeping willow. The tree seemed sadder to her today, as if it fit its mood with the family's. Its branches hung lower and waved in the wind—a mournful motion. Robin shuttered and blocked from her mind the memory of the pull of the pond that day in May.

Robin turned from the window as Enid chortled, cooed, and smiled.

Susan smiled back, slow but true. "Thank the Lord for Enie, our one happy spot in this valley of sorrow."

"Yes," Robin agreed, but the bitter taste of jealousy coated her tongue at Susan's love for Enid.

It gladdened Robin's heart to finally experience the motherly emotions that she knew she should have, but she longed for them to come as easily as Susan's always had. Robin saw Sue's maternal instincts as odd because of Sue's bristly attitude in most other aspects of life, but when it came to Enid, Susan was little more than a melted dish of butter. *But now, Susan will not have a child of her own—at least not her and Tom's.* The thought made Robin's heart ache on a whole other level in empathy for Sue. Robin wouldn't begrudge Susan the evident bond between her and Enid; it would be wrong.

Enid started to fuss and squirm. She squeezed her little face into a fury of red.

Susan passed off Enid into Robin's arms. "She's needing her Ma."

Great. I'm only needed when Enid's hungry, an inner grumbling told Robin. She did her best to ignore the thought, stood, and picked up Enid, bouncing her daughter in her arms. Enid quieted and laid her head on Robin's shoulder.

"There, my sweet. There. Mama's got you."

A peacefulness settled on Robin with those spoken words. They hadn't been contrived or made up. They represented how she actually felt—a loving mother, imperfect though she might be. She prayed to God that her imperfections would get ironed out with time.

With time. How often have I said those words the last few days? Robin saw time as both an inescapable taskmaster and a shelter. Both heart-wrenching and forgiving. Cruel and kind. With time her body and emotions had healed, at least she hoped so, but Robin wondered if a hidden pattern of guilt over what she had done might be harder to shake. Again, time would tell.

Robin sighed, patted Enid on the back, and snuggled her face next to her daughter's.

"Thanks for listening." Susan looked up at Robin and shook her head. "I would never have thought that you and I…" She paused and blushed. "Well, let's just say we don't come from the same pod."

Robin smiled and almost laughed. "No. I guess treading a difficult path can bring even the most opposite of traveling companions together."

Susan stood and quickly embraced Robin and Enid. "Yes." She grinned despite her peaked face. "Let's go heat up some of the food our neighbors have brought over."

Robin's stomach grumbled at the thought of the pan of shepherd's pie that waited on the sideboard; one of Marge's friends from church had dropped it by that morning.

"Lead the way." Robin waved her arm and followed Susan.

I've put off going to the farm.
The thought of seeing someone else's belongings there hurts.

CHAPTER THIRTY-THREE

Enid
Early October 1984
"Look at those orange leaves. They make the tree look like a glowing pumpkin in the dark. Don't you think?"

I don't expect Mom to answer. I wheel her on the sidewalk in a wheelchair we borrowed from the nursing home. The day is gorgeous. Bright afternoon sunshine backlights the colored leaves on the maple, ash, and poplar trees in the park. The bright blue of the sky makes the red, yellow, and orange colors of the foliage pop. Several children play on the slide and spin-around thingy, which when I was a kid made me want to puke. Their giggles bring a smile to my face. Several women—probably the moms—sit nearby on a bench. A tall, lean woman with long, straight, wheat-colored, seventies-style hair walks by us with an equally skinny dog. Maybe it's part greyhound.

A gray squirrel up ahead scurries through the dried pine needles on the ground. The scent of evergreens, cut grass, and moldering leaves blend together in the crispness of the air. It's the kind of morning where anything seems possible. That's why

I asked Mom a question. I still hold onto hope that it's not too late for her to answer back, but I know it's only wishful thinking.

I asked Clive to help me bring Mom on an outing to take in the fine autumn weather before all the leaves fall. Pushing Mom off the path and over the grass, I make my way to a green-painted picnic table. I park Mom at the end. After rummaging through the bag on the back of the wheelchair, I pull out the thermos of hot chocolate I packed. I sit on one of the benches and open the thermos, pouring some cocoa into the thermos cup. I take a sip. *It's still hot!* I set the cup down on the table.

"It needs to cool, then I'll give you some."

Why do I feel the need to tell her these things when she might not understand? In truth, I talk for myself. Treating her as normally as possible helps me deal with the fact that Mom's normal has changed faster than expected.

Clive walks up behind me. "How's Robin doing?"

He carries the picnic basket I asked him to bring. The hem of his polo shirt dangles past his rump. It makes him look like a little kid. I would rather he tucked it into his jeans, but I'm not about to say so.

I gaze at Mom. "She seems fine."

Her gray-green eyes focus on some far-off point, her lips neither smile nor frown, and her hands rest clasped loosely together in her lap. No tension presses down her brow. I figured getting outside would be good for her.

Only one thing bothers me—at times, I hear a slight rasp when she breathes. Must be something left over from her bout of sickness.

"All right. Good." Clive sets the wicker basket on the opposite bench. "Should I unpack?" He flips open the lid.

I check my watch—11:30. "Sure. I could eat if you can. I had the nurse pack a liquid meal for Mom."

I don't want a repeat of what happened at our anniversary party, but I do feel bad that she can't chew food like Clive and me.

Clive grimaces and whispers, "Poor Robin."

He pulls out our sandwiches, chip bags, and a couple of small containers of applesauce.

"There should be some spoons in there." I wave my finger at him. "I thought the sauce might be easy enough for Mom to swallow. It's made from the last harvest of apples on the farm." My voice dips as my sadness over those days being gone leaks out of my heart.

"Those Jonathans sure did make great sauce."

Clive finds the spoons. He passes me two then hands me Mom's liquid lunch. He sits and flings one leg over the bench and takes a bite out of his turkey on rye.

I open the sauce and spoon some into Mom's mouth. She looks at me as I do, and I freeze. She usually looks past me, but this time our eyes connect. And then it passes as quickly as it came—that flash of recognition. She coughs; the rough sound worries me.

Mom eats all the sauce I give her. I offer her the drink from the nursing home, but she turns her head away, her lips puckered into a hard line.

"Okay."

I don't force or blame her. The stuff looks like ash mixed in yogurt. An involuntary shiver hits me.

"You cold?" Clive asks between crunches of chips.

"No." I shake my head and take a bite of my sandwich: pimento loaf and cucumber on white bread. It is rather cool in the shade of the trees, but I'm warm enough. I pull my crocheted scarf tighter around my neck and button the top and bottom button on my navy, wool sweater. "Just thinking about Mom's drink."

"Ah." Clive nods. "Robin looks pretty thin. That must really stink not to be able to eat regular food."

"I'm sure the nursing staff does their best to see that she gets nourished."

"Where's the fun in that?" Clive tips back his head and pours the bits of chips at the bottom of his bag into his mouth.

We finish up our food, throw the scraps in the garbage, and pack the sauce containers and spoons back in the basket.

Clive points to the thermos. "You gonna share that hot cocoa?"

"Oh, sorry, I forgot." I push the thermos his way and drink what I poured in the cup.

Cold. Regardless, I finish it off and hand him the red cup.

"Thanks." He smiles, screws the lid off, and pours himself a drink. After he gulps down some hot chocolate, he slaps his hand on the table. "Hey, I forgot to tell you the new owners of the farm called."

I sense my muscles tightening. "What did they want?"

"Let me see…" Clive scratches his chin and tips up the bill of the Milwaukee Brewers baseball cap he's wearing. "It was something about that tree."

I can't imagine what in the world he's talking about. "What tree?"

"The willow by the pond."

"What about it?" I glance toward Mom, wondering if she's comprehending our discussion.

Her eyelids droop. After lunch she always gets sleepy. Well, most of the time she's sleepy.

"Mr. Knutson said it split in a storm recently."

Irritation at getting involved with anything at the farm grates on me; I've worked so hard these last months to let it go. "What storm, and why are they telling us?"

Clive squints his eyes at me like I might be having memory problems. "It was mostly wind, I think. Remember a few weeks back?"

I shrug. "I guess."

"Well, anyway. I guess they found some things inside the tree."

"Huh? How's that possible?"

"He said there was a rotten, hollow spot packed with a couple of things. He wants you to stop by."

Clive pauses and seems to gauge my concern. I try to even out my facial expression. I can't tell if I've succeeded.

"Want me to come with you?" he asks. "It'd be no trouble."

"Maybe." I shrug again in a noncommittal way. I don't want to go at all. I pull my sleeve up and look at my watch; it reads 12:30. "Should we wheel Mom back to the car? She's looking done in."

Mom's chin lolls down to her chest.

"Sure. Do you want me to push?"

He waits for my command. How did I score such a sweet man?

"That would be nice."

I smile wide and sincerely, but without showing my teeth and grinning like a fool. I hold my husband's familiar eyes with mine, his gaze never failing to anchor me.

We get up at the same time. Clive begins to wheel Mom back to the path. I collect the basket and follow them, wondering while I walk. *What did the Knutsons find in the willow that could be important enough to call us about?*

Later that week
I've put off going to the farm. The thought of seeing someone else's belongings there hurts.

Kelly steps into the kitchen. "Hi, Mom. You got a minute?"
He scared me; I didn't hear him come in.

I place my hand over my heart and breathe. "Sure. What are you doing here?"

I glance at the wall clock in the kitchen, ticking out the seconds. It's a little after 5:00. He must be done for the day. I put down the knife I hold on the cutting board on the counter.

"I left early. Not much going on today."

I nod. Is that a good thing? I know how Kelly likes to stay busy.

"Okay." I continue to wrap in tinfoil the potatoes I've washed. I'm making an old standby meal tonight for supper: meatloaf and baked potatoes. "You can stay for supper, if you like." I glance up to see how he reacts to my question. "That is, if Doris isn't waiting for you."

"She should be home. The girls didn't have anything after school today." He shrugs and plops his briefcase down on the floor, loosening his tie. "Frankly, I don't want to go home. It's just so darn awkward."

Kelly sits down at the small table in the middle of the kitchen.

I turn the dial to bake and the oven knobs to the right temperature and pull the door open, placing the potatoes inside. I leave it open as I turn to the fridge to get the meatloaf I prepared hours ago.

"Have you talked over things yet?"

He runs his fingers through his hair on one side of his head. "We tried, but we ended up resorting to yelling at one another, which resolved nothing."

After placing the meatloaf in the oven, I get a glass from the cupboard.

I hold the glass up. "Water, milk, or something stronger?"

"I could use a shot of whiskey, but I'll take some milk. That is, if you have some cookies or something sweet around."

Kelly stands and walks to the corner stand, where I have my rooster cookie jar. He lifts its head off and looks inside.

"Right. Help yourself. Made molasses ones yesterday."

"My favorite."

He grins and pulls two out of the jar, giving the chicken back its head. I get his milk and set it on the table.

"What are you going to do?" I ask him outright.

"I don't know, Mom. What can I do?"

I pull my faded, pink sweater from the back of a chair, put it on, then sit next to him.

I tell him straight. "You're gonna have to decide if your marriage is worth fighting for or not."

"Ya." He pauses in finishing off the first cookie. He blinks and half-grimaces, before shoving the rest into his mouth. He switches subjects. "Hey, I meant to ask you a couple days ago, but how's Grandma? Is she over her cold yet?"

Kelly gulps down some milk—I refrain from wiping his milk mustache off—and starts on the second cookie.

"Better, but a little still lingers. She has a cough."

"That's too bad. I hope she kicks it completely." He takes a huge bite of cookie.

"Me too." I try to keep the worry from my tone. "I'm sure she'll be better soon."

Kelly glances at his wrist, where an expensive watch that Doris gave him for his birthday last year is banded. "I should get going and quit avoiding the inevitable."

He sighs heavily.

Kelly could be talking to me. I need to get my rear in gear and get out to the farm.

I attempt to reassure him. "Maybe it won't be too bad. Things usually turn out better than we imagine."

He rolls his eyes. I laugh. That must be how I look at Clive.

"Or not," he says as he stands and brushes the cookie crumbs from his suit jacket.

I stand and give him a goodbye hug. "Remember, Dad and I are praying for you."

He hugs me tightly back.

"Ya, I know. Thanks." He kisses me on the cheek and lets go, picking up his case. "See you this weekend, if not before."

"See you."

I nod, smile, and wave, but for some strange reason, all I want to do is cry. The door bangs behind him as he leaves. Why does Kelly have to deal with this? Why can't those two kids figure out their problems? I don't know.

I set the table and do what I told Kelly I'd do—pray.

That evening

We sit in our chairs before the fireplace. The logs snap and crackle, the only distinguishable sound in the room. Clive reads a mystery novel, his black reading glasses poised on the end of his nose. I sort through the letters Lydia gave me again. I choose one I haven't read yet and open it.

October 15th, 1918

Dear Mabel,

I hope you are well. Everything has changed so much while I've been gone, especially Enid. She has filled out; her plump, rosy cheeks beg to be kissed, which I do at every opportunity. I feel I must make up for lost time. At first, she was hesitant when I held or cared for her, but after a few days she stopped fussing under my attention. I don't blame Enid for her fear. She likely doesn't remember me very well.

Although I'm glad to be back here on the farm, I miss Molly. We talked so easily together. I plan on inviting Molly to the farm. Maybe in the spring or next summer. I wanted to ask if Susan or Hal would drive me into town to visit Molly sometime soon, but my request will have to wait.

Susan received a telegram revealing the terrible news of her husband's death. We all mourn Tom. He was such a funny, likable fellow. I'm heartbroken for her. I pray Willis makes it home to me.

Take care, dear sister, and give all the children a hug and kiss from me.

Love, Robin

I wonder again why Mom has never mentioned Molly to me. They were obviously close. I fold up the letter and tuck it back into the yellowed envelope. Time and circumstances separate friends; maybe that's what happened to them.

Clive removes his glasses and places his book on the side table. "Ready for bed?"

He reaches for the pull chain on the lamp.

I put the letter back with the others. "Sure."

He shuts the light off and gets up, extending a hand to help me out of my chair. "Kelly stop by today?"

"Yes. I must have forgotten to mention it. How did you guess?"

We walk hand in hand to our bedroom.

"Looked like his tire-tread pattern in the dirt."

I look sideways at him in the dim light of the hall. "You examined the dirt?"

Clive lets go of my hand and clicks on our bedroom light. "I happened to look down and noticed. Just put those new ones on his car. Makes a crisp print."

I guess a mechanic would notice something like that.

I walk to the bed and turn down the covers. "He stopped to get some advice."

Clive takes his wristwatch off and deposits it on his bureau. "About the whole Doris thing?"

"Ya. He needs to decide if he wants to give up or make his marriage work."

"Well, that takes two."

Clive gets in bed and pulls the covers up to his chin. I slide my pink slippers off and do the same.

"Someone has to make the first move toward reconciliation." Again, I am talking to myself.

"I suppose." Clive closes his eyes. "Goodnight."

"Ah, Clive."

He opens one eye. "What?"

I glance at the bright, glass ceiling light in the middle of the room. "You forgot to shut the light off."

"Me? You were the last in." He rolls over.

His sweetness apparently has a limit.

I groan and whip the covers off my legs. I hear him chuckling under the covers as I pad over to the light switch in my bare feet.

"So much for chivalry," I mutter.

I flick off the light and head back to bed.

"Tonight I am all for women's lib."

I hop in bed and poke him in the back.

"Oww!" He turns around—quicker than I expected—and tickles me behind my ear. "Back at you, wifey."

"Wifey?" I ask between giggles. He's tickling my side now. "Stop. Clive, stop!"

I try to curl up but can't avoid him. I resort to a pinch.

"Yow! That's it!"

He flips over on top of me and kisses me on the side of my neck. His tickles turn to caresses; I don't mind. Kelly and his marriage troubles are forgotten for the moment, as Clive and I remember a well-known, intimate dance.

I will remember this moment forever.

CHAPTER THIRTY-FOUR

Robin
Early October 1918

If I gut one more pumpkin, I'm going to vomit.

Robin looked at her slimy, orange hands. She scooped pumpkin from the carcass of its baked shell. Strings of pumpkin flesh covered her hands, making them itch. Grabbing a nearby dishtowel, she wiped them off. Robin couldn't understand why Susan had planted so many pumpkins. They had already canned two batches of pureed pumpkin and made pumpkin bread, muffins, and pie. They'd even cut some up to give to the chickens. The rest they had set on the porch for autumn decorations.

Marge tottered in, looking like her feet hurt her. "I think that's the last."

"Thank heavens," Robin blew a stream of air out of her mouth, her lips flapping slightly in the process. "By the time we eat all of this, we'll turn into pumpkins."

"You know Sue. Nothing gets her mind off her worries like work does."

"That's all well and good for her, but she could leave us out of it." Robin bit her tongue. "I'm sorry. I didn't mean that. Of course I'm happy to help with preserving food for us to eat this winter, but, well, she may have over-done the task a little."

Marge winked at Robin. "Just a little?"

"Just a little what?" Susan asked as she stepped into the kitchen, dressed in her coat and boots.

"Thought you were helping Dad with the milking?" Marge asked.

"Ya, well, he drove me out, saying I was giving him too many orders." Sue rolled her eyes. "Men."

She plonked down in a chair and stared at the pumpkin products spread out around the kitchen. Suddenly, she bent over the table and burst into tears, her arms splayed out on either side of her head.

Robin stood, glued to the floor; Susan's display of emotion unnerved her.

Marge moved forward to hover over her daughter. "Now, now." She smoothed her hand over Susan's thick hair, which reminded Robin of a horse's mane. "At times we miss those who have passed on in the most ordinary of moments, and all it takes is a thought, a word, to bring grief afresh to our hearts again."

Marge sniffed, and Susan raised her head.

She turned eyes the color of liquid smoke on her mother. "When will it stop hurting?"

"Maybe never." Marge sighed. "But it will lessen with time."

Susan sat up and wiped her eyes with the sleeve of her sweater. "How do you know?"

Caught up in the drama, Robin lowered herself into a chair at the table and ignored the bowl of mashed pumpkin.

"I never told you girls this, but before your father and I

married, I was engaged to another man."

Marge flicked her blueberry gaze to Susan. Her expression begged for understanding.

Susan pinched her eyebrows together. "Mom, how come you never said anything?"

"Well, that part of my life didn't need to be mentioned." Marge hiked up one shoulder and smiled sideways in a sheepish way. "His name was Grant Hartley."

Robin couldn't help herself and broke into the conversation. "Well, what happened?"

Marge tipped her gaze down to her fingers, toying with a set of aluminum measuring spoons. "He died."

Susan and Robin looked at each other, but they kept silent.

"We met in the spring, fishing along the bank of the river, of all things. We spent so much time together that summer I turned eighteen. In the fall he asked me to marry him, and I said yes."

Marge paused and looked up at Sue and Robin, a sadness in her eyes.

"How did he…?" Susan asked.

"He helped with the thrashing on my father's farm that fall. He got the hankie around his neck stuck in one of the bits of machinery and…was strangled." Marge took a deep breath. She smiled, but the corners of her lips didn't come as high as they usually did. She patted Susan on the hand. "It's all so long ago now, but I do know what it is to lose someone that you love."

Susan nodded. "I'm sorry, Mom."

She leaned into Marge, who wrapped Susan in her arms.

"Me too," Marge uttered.

Robin decided to get the pumpkin purée into the clean jars. She never would have guessed that Marge carried a secret loss from the past. Marge—although she tended to fuss over folks—was straightforward and as readable as a book, but then most people harbored a secret or two somewhere in their past. Robin wished to keep what happened to her after Enid's birth a secret. Too much shame and blame attached itself to that time to ever let it be common knowledge.

Robin continued to pack the pumpkin into jars while Sue and Marge talked, which Robin thought was healthy and good for Sue. Talking about her problems with Molly and Dr. Howington had really helped Robin.

Later that week
Robin was proud; Enid had taken her first steps. Despite the chill outside, Robin had bundled herself and Enid up. Lowering Enid to stand on her own legs, Robin had held her daughter by her hands and prompted her to take a few steps over the dormant, frosty grass.

Swinging Enid up in her arms, Robin praised her. "What a strong girl you are! Daddy would be so proud!"

Enid giggled as Robin kissed the soft, pudgy crook of her daughter's neck.

Hal walked toward them from the barn. He swung a bucket in one hand. "Well, would you look at that? Someone's getting big."

The wide grin on his face spread the deep folds around his high-boned cheeks. He patted Enid on her crocheted, pink hat. The pompom on top flattened a bit under Hal's big hand.

"She sure is," Robin agreed.

They smiled at each other over Enid's head.

The sound of a vehicle registered in Robin's ears; both she and Hal turned to look at a black Ford speeding down the driveway. The vehicle circled the turn-around in the drive and stopped in front of them.

Hal pushed his engineer's hat back on his head, revealing his white forehead. "Looks like the young man from the livery in town. Wonder what he's doing out this way?"

Robin watched as the man, dressed in overalls and a brown jacket, got out of the car and quickly hurried around to the passenger side. He opened the other car door and appeared to be helping the passenger out.

"That's good. I got it. Thanks."

The words drifted over to Robin. The timber of the voice set her heart pumping. She watched, stunned, as a man in an olive-colored, military uniform hobbled around the front of the car, his arms manipulating crutches. The driver carried a rucksack.

"Well, I'll be…" Hal shook his head. "Willis! Welcome home!" Hal moved forward and crunched Willis in a tight embrace. He backed up, swinging his arm toward Robin and Enid. "Your family's been waiting for you."

Robin stood rooted to the ground. Her mouth hung open, and she felt her cheeks heat in a flush. She couldn't believe Willis stood in front of her. He propped himself up straight with the help of the crutches, supporting himself on his left leg. The right hung down, a stump where his foot would have been.

"Robin."

Willis smiled at her, his deep-set, brown eyes holding much more than her name. They held a hollow of pain and a shame Robin recognized. The shame of not being whole. But it didn't matter to Robin—his foot being gone. She was happy to see him alive.

"Willis," Robin finally stuttered out.

Enid fussed in her arms.

Willis reached out a hand to touch Enid. "She's so beautiful, like her mom."

Enid shied away and laid her head on Robin's shoulder.

The driver walked forward and held out his hand. "I got a schedule to keep."

"Oh, certainly." Willis tilted one crutch toward Hal, who held it for him. Willis dug in his pocket, pulling out some money. He placed the money in the driver's hand. "Thanks again."

"Yep. You're welcome."

The young man tipped his cap and wasted no time in getting behind the wheel of the vehicle and driving away. Robin watched in a daze as the gravel spit up behind the skinny tires.

When the chug of the Ford died away, Hal looked from Willis to Robin. "I'll let you two get reacquainted. Mighty fine to have you back with us, Nephew." He shouldered Willis's pack, pulled his hat back down, and stepped lively toward the house. "Marge isn't gonna believe this."

Robin turned to Enid and then Willis. "Enie, meet your dada."

Willis touched Enid's cheek and leaned forward on his crutches to place a kiss on her cheek. "Hello, sweet girl."

He hobbled closer and did the same to Robin. The touch of Willis's lips and the scent of gun oil, tobacco, and woodsy aftershave made Robin close her eyes with the joy of his presence. She turned her face and kissed him on the lips, light and chaste. Willis dropped a crutch, circled his arm around her waist, and echoed with a deeper response.

Time seemed to stand still.

I will remember this moment forever.

Some memories were meant to last a lifetime, and this was one. Robin tucked Enid up in the clutch of one arm and stroked the whiskers darkening Willis's face with the other. He covered her hand with his, the warmth of his flesh making her heart flutter.

Robin held his gaze. "I'm so happy you've come home."

"Not all of me did." The words came out slow and apologetic, as Willis backed up and looked at the ground.

"You are more than a missing foot," Robin told him.

He had to know that she couldn't care less about what he left behind in France. It was what he brought with him that concerned her.

"And you are more than a mother; you're my wife."

Their eyes studied each other momentarily before they kissed again, the pressure of his lips feeling surreal to her.

He's here! Willis is home! Robin had to keep telling herself that over and over to keep from thinking a dream played out before her.

Enid fussed at being pressed between her parents, and Willis and Robin shared a laugh.

"Better go in before Marge wears a hole in the glass," Willis said.

Robin turned to look where Willis pointed. Sure enough, Marge polished the glass of the kitchen window with a cloth and then peered out intently, her wide nose flattening against the pane. She pulled back when she saw they had caught her watching. Willis threw his head back and laughed again, the ringing sound of it making Robin's heart almost burst with gladness. She retrieved his crutch from the ground, and he tucked it under his arm. He navigated the three steps onto the back stoop without mishap. Robin walked behind, in case he fell backward, but she needn't have worried. He appeared to manage fine.

But what about the farm work? The question sank Robin's joy a little as she followed her husband into the house.

How can three words mean so much?

CHAPTER THIRTY-FIVE

Enid
Early November 1984
"Nothing gold can stay…"

I speak the lines of one of Mom's favorite poems. I glance out her window. The leaves have fallen and the bare branches of the trees reach their arms up to the sky like brown skeletons poised and pleading for the coverage of living tissue. The heat whistles through the vent by the window, but the waffling racket of Mom's breathing turns my gaze back to her.

She's sitting partially up in her bed, her arms tucked under the blankets, oxygen tubes looped around her ears and into her nose. Her eyes are open, and we look at each other. For a few seconds the dawn of recognition lights her eyes, but it passes as quickly as it came. She moves her head and stares blankly at the white nursing home wall. Then her eyes fall closed.

Her breathing is labored, and I think about pressing the call button for the nurse to come, but I don't. She doesn't appear to be in pain.

"Howdy." Cassandra walks in, dressed in a turquoise, shaker-style sweater with silver, glitzy thread shining through the weave. A pink, oxford shirt collar peeks out at her neckline. Her hair is clipped back on either side of her head by silver barrettes. She carries a bouquet of wrapped, pink, mini roses. "These looked like something Aunt Robin might like. Thought I'd stop them by." She steps into Mom's room with a hesitant smile on her face. "I'm not interrupting, am I?"

She pokes her head forward like a turtle taking in the scenery.

I can't muster any cheer in my voice. "No. Just sitting with Mom."

The nurse called days ago, saying Mom's sickness had returned, and they were sure this time that it had morphed into pneumonia. The last nurse who checked in warned me that they would have to put a breathing tube in soon if her breathing didn't improve. And maybe move her to the hospital.

"I'll find something to put these in." Cassie pokes around the room and settles for putting the flowers in a drinking glass. She fills it with water and places the glass on the tray-table close to Mom, smiling at her. "There. That should add a little cheer."

Mom looks over at her but then away, not holding her gaze at all. Her eyes close again. Cassie's face falls, her bright expression dimmed.

She sits in the other chair in the room and asks in a quiet voice, "How bad is she?"

She turns to me, and we lock eyes.

I'm truthful and whisper, "Pretty bad. If she doesn't turn a corner soon, they will have to help with artificial breathing. The medicine doesn't seem to be doing much."

"Oh." She breathes out the one-word response on the wave of a mighty sigh. She's quiet for a minute, before asking, "Anything I can do?"

I look at Mom again. "No. I don't think so." I turn to Cassie. My voice catches as tears thicken my throat. "It's nice of you to come. Thank you for visiting and...for your support."

"Of course. You're family, Enie, and Aunt Robin was always so good to me. How could I not be here?"

Her voice starts to warble, and soon we both tear up. We sit in silence and sniff.

"I know. Let's turn on some music. Aunt Robin likes it when the local station plays big-band tunes on a Sunday afternoon." Cassie gets up and walks to where Mom's little, wooden radio sits on top of her dresser. She turns the knob and scrolls through a few stations. The static makes Mom's eyes flutter open. A deeper crease appears in her forehead. "Ah, here we go."

Cassie smiles as she finds a station playing music from the 40s and 50s. I watch Mom's brow relax as the sound of a trombone and trumpet blow out a bluesy band tune.

Cassie and I visit quietly over the music. I feel myself relaxing. This was what I needed—to think and talk about something other than Mom's declining health. After about twenty minutes, Cassie excuses herself and leaves. We exchange a hug before she goes.

"Call me if you need me," she tells me, and I nod.

I watch her amble out. I navigate back to Mom's side and resume staring at her.

Another twenty minutes passes, and I know I should get home and make supper. I turn off the radio. I finally ask what has taken me all afternoon to drum up the courage to ask.

"Can you forgive me, Mom?" I ask loudly in the now quiet room, and she opens her eyes. I lean over the bed and look down at her. Her eyes focus on mine. "I held too much between us. I didn't understand what you'd gone through, but now I do." I free one of her hands from the covers. "I…I love you, Mom."

I fold my fingers around hers. I can't remember the last time I said those words.

Her eyes open wide. A light shines from them. "I—love— you."

The words are stilted and choppy and hardly recognizable, but the tears I see collected in the corners of her eyes tell me I heard correctly.

For the second time today, I cry. Her eyes fall slowly closed again. I fold her hand back under the blanket and kiss her lightly on the cheek.

How can three words mean so much?

It's not like Mom hasn't told me "I love you" before, but the difference is—it's the first time that I truly believe her.

I walk out of her room feeling centered, settled. Loved. Finally.

Days later

The sigh of the tubes in Mom and the gurgling sound of her trying to breathe make me want to puke. It almost sounds like someone throwing up. I hate that Mom's lungs are filled with fluid. The doctor at the hospital said her kidneys are shutting down.

I glumly look at a vase on the window ledge containing yellow lilies. How dare they display such a bright color? They should be blue, brown, gray, or black—the colors in my heart right now. I'm losing Mom, just when I found her. Life is not fair.

"Really, I'll call if there's any change." A nurse in a white uniform, holding a clipboard, tells me. "You should go home."

"Ya. I suppose."

I glance at the large clock on the wall. I've been there for almost ten hours. Clive sat with me for much of the day, but he left not long ago, claiming a backache from sitting too long. I could say the same. Reluctantly, I let go of Mom's hand.

"She seems to be hanging on," I tell the nurse.

"Yes." She eyes me over the top of her round, blue glasses. "Perhaps she's waiting for someone to let her go." She speaks slowly, with compassion, and smiles apologetically. "Well, I'll leave you to it."

She nods and walks briskly out of Mom's hospital room. Her shoes squeak on the waxed, linoleum floor. I take a deep breath, wondering what to say, how to leave or if I even should.

Coming close to Mom, I whisper a prayer. "Dear Jesus, I'm thankful You are here with Mom." I pause, and I hear one of Mom's favorite gospel tunes, *I'll Fly Away,* in my head. I continue praying and surrender my selfishness. "Lord, help Mom not to linger. Help her spirit to fly away to you. We've made our peace, I believe. There's no reason for her to stay."

I don't say amen. I grip her arm and kiss her cheek, before I turn and hurry from the room with its bright flowers and gurgling noises. Tears pulse from my eyes, and I can hardly see to walk. But I keep walking and breathing, because there's nothing else to do.

To our future.

CHAPTER THIRTY-SIX

Robin
November 1918

Robin looked up at Willis. "Do you think it'll be safe?"

Willis held a small, tin container open in his hands.

"Yes. I'll wrap it in oilcloth when we're done." He opened the hinged container wider. "Come on."

He grinned, looking like the same light-hearted fool who had left Robin last year. His breath hung misty in the chilly November air.

"Well, all right."

Robin held out the locket Willis had given her when they had first started courting and released it into the tin. The metal, clinking sound hit Robin's heart in a similar way. Her neck felt bare without it. Since coming back to the farm, she'd gotten used to wearing it again. Her fingers traced the back of her neck, feeling the chain's absence.

"Now the note," Willis demanded.

Robin took a small, folded note from the depths of her coat pocket and placed it atop the necklace.

Last night, they had penned and signed a contract to move

forward, to forget the war, the wounds, the asylum, and the attempted drowning, and they had written a message for Enid. Robin hoped someday Enid would read it and forgive her. Forgive them for their flawed humanness.

Next, Willis added his dog tags with a jingle.

Robin smiled and tucked a tiny lock of Enid's hair tied with pink thread on the stack of articles. "To represent our future."

Willis closed the lozenge tin with a creak. He wrapped it in a square of greased cloth and tied it with string, Robin helping by putting her finger on the knot so it could be drawn tightly.

"And there we are." Willis handed Robin the bundle. "You should tuck it in. Your arm and hand are thinner than mine."

Robin nodded and grabbed the bundle, which was small but weighty with articles of their past. Standing on the bench she had scooted close to the willow, Robin put her arm down into the crevice of the tree, where a pocket had opened up, a secret hiding place not obvious to the casual observer. Reaching in as far as she could, Robin dropped the package into the tree. The tree which had almost witnessed her death now witnessed her rebirth, in a way. Robin needed this act of laying the past to rest. When Willis had suggested the idea, Robin had fully agreed.

Robin pulled back her arm and stepped off the bench into the waiting arms of her husband. The wooden prosthetic Willis now wore helped him manage stability and short distances with just one crutch.

Baby Enid stared at her parents from the little wagon Robin had tucked her into, padded on the sides with blankets and pillows so she wouldn't fall out.

"Wait, let me pick up Enie." Robin moved to the wagon and lifted her daughter into her arms.

"Yes. Our little girl is an essential part of this tryst," Wills said.

He welcomed Robin in the shelter of his arm. He kissed Enid's plump, pink cheek and smoothed back the hair against Robin's cheek under her navy, crocheted beret, the brush of his fingers making Robin's skin tingle.

Robin focused on the walnut-brown depths of Willis's eyes. "To our future."

"To our future," he repeated, and he sealed the statement with a lingering kiss.

Enid patted the side of Willis's jaw first and then Robin's. "Dada. Mama."

All three of them laughed as a consequence.

After a leisurely stroll back to the house, Willis pegged off to the barn to help Hal with chores. Milking was hard for him, but he could scoop feed from a rolling cart he'd rigged up. Robin took Enid to the house and helped Susan and Marge finish fixings for a family meal. Lynette, Derek, and the girls were expected by 5:30.

Robin shed her and Enid's outerwear and tucked her daughter in a wooden playpen in the corner of the large kitchen, propping a stuffed toy rabbit, some blocks, and a rattle next to Enid. Enid didn't protest at being confined. She happily played with her toys.

"Just in time." Marge bustled to the stove with a pot. "Could you peel those washed potatoes, cut them up, and get them on the stove to boil?"

"Certainly," Robin replied.

She washed her hands, tied on a blue, gingham apron, and started peeling spuds. Susan worked next to her, crumbling a brown sugar and oat topping onto a pan of sliced apples. Marge tottered off to the dining room with silverware and napkins.

After Marge left the kitchen, Susan spoke up. "I saw you at the pond." Susan turned her head, stilled her fingers, and looked full at Robin for a moment. "You've told Willis all about it, then?"

"Yes." Robin peeled as she talked. "We decided to move forward together by leaving objects in the willow tree that represent our past and…" she looked up at Sue, "our wounds."

Susan turned her curvy lips up and resumed crumbling the topping onto the apples. "Maybe there will be no more weeping under that tree. Let's hope there will only be joy now."

A sadness in her expression faded her smile. She scraped the remaining coating out of the small crockery bowl she held and pressed her palm on the mixture to even it out.

An idea hit Robin, her knife poised mid-way through a potato. She imagined her eyes lit up as she spoke. "Maybe you should leave something with the tree too."

"Huh, like a kind of remembrance?" Susan licked some sugar and butter off her fingers before wiping her hands on her green, geometric-patterned apron.

"Exactly. You know how God always called the Israelites in the Old Testament to build a monument and erect stones of remembrance to remind them of God's power and provision?"

"I suppose. What are you getting at?" Susan asked as she put the pan of apple crisp in the oven.

"Think how God provided you at the right time to help me and how that drew us closer. And when Thomas passed, well, God provided for you in moving back home to help your dad."

Robin quartered her peeled potato and plunked it in the pot of water that Marge had placed on the stove.

"I hated to give up my job at Stout, but moving back home

did help me feel not quite so alone in my grief."

Robin put her knife down, stepped over to Susan, and crushed her in a rare embrace. "You've become like a sister to me, Sue. I'm glad we could help each other."

Susan leaned back as Robin released her. "Me…too."

Sue appeared choked up and tongue-tied, unusual for her.

"What would you put in the tree?" Robin added, peeling another potato.

"Hmm." Susan wrinkled her forehead and bit a fingernail. "The letter…the notice of…you know."

"Are you sure?" Robin didn't want Susan to regret putting away the last thing about Thomas that she possessed.

Sue nodded. "Yes. I'm sure. I'll do it after supper."

"You could even tuck it in the same tin Willis and I used."

"I might just do that. Thanks."

"Now what are you two jabberin' on about?" Marge stepped into the kitchen and pointed to the range. "Those potatoes aren't going to jump in the pot themselves. Best get a move on."

She clapped her hands together, turning her back to collect some plates from the plate rack. Robin and Susan shared a smile.

"Here, I'll help. You peel, I'll cut and plop," Sue offered, and she moved to take over the cutting board.

Robin eagerly handed Susan the potato she'd finished peeling. "Thanks!"

Susan winked, the cold, gray color of her eyes replaced with the warm color of steeped tea. "You're welcome…Sis."

The word touched Robin's heart just as much as the love she saw in Susan's eyes.

They worked hard until 5:30 rolled around and Lynette and

her family arrived. Soon the Holcomb family were all seated around the dining table, all but Thomas, of course. Out the corner of her eye, Robin watched Susan while Hal prayed. Sue placed her right hand on the table next to her where Tom used to sit. She appeared at peace, at least for the moment.

Venturing a look at Willis, Robin caught his eye. She blushed when he winked. Having him home was like a dream come true with the three of them together, as it should be.

"All men!" Cassandra—erroneously but with a cuteness no one could deny—repeated Hal's closure of the grace he'd spoken.

Everyone chuckled.

"That's right, Cassie." Hal encouraged her. "You're growing into a right fine, little miss."

Cassie grinned. "Goompa funny."

"Let's eat!" Derek pitched in, reaching for the plate of ham.

"Eat!" Cassie repeated, grinning.

At the same time, Enid smacked her palms on her highchair tray and squealed out a word no one could comprehend, except for Cassandra. They commenced to talk in baby gibberish.

"Listen to those two jabberin' away. It seems they understand each other," Marge commented. She smiled at her granddaughter and great niece.

Lynette smiled widely, showing a row of pearly teeth. "I predict they're on their way to becoming best friends."

"How nice if that would come true," Robin said.

She thought the best friends were family.

Willis held up his glass of hard cider. "To friends and family."

Marge had splurged and set out a jug, which was usually reserved for Thanksgiving and Christmas.

"To friends and family," they all echoed.

"And to new beginnings," Robin added.

"Amen to that," Hal pronounced.

He'll never know just what a precious treasure he found—
my mother's love, buried in the weeping willow.

CHAPTER THIRTY-SEVEN

Enid

Late November 1984

"I'm so sorry it's been so long. I should have called, but with…"

I choke on my words. Speaking about Mom's death still tears at me. My arm tightens around Clive's.

"There's no need to explain. In your circumstances I entirely understand." Mr. Knutson takes his John Deere hat off his head and folds it in his hands. "You have our sympathies."

His blue eyes look as crisp as the morning hoarfrost, not burned off by the morning sun and covering everything in sight.

"Thanks," I say.

I look out over the spot on the farm where the willow tree once stood. It's terribly bare now. Mr. Knutson, the current owner of the farm, cut the tree up and hauled it away months ago when the storm cracked it in two.

He holds out a thickly wrapped, small bundle to me. "This is what we found when we were breaking the stump up. Must be old. They sure don't make oilcloth like that anymore."

Our gloved fingers brush, and he smiles. He's a handsome man with the look of a rugged cowboy about him; a bushy mustache, deep lines around his eyes, and a day or two of stubble on his chin offer a decisively western feel.

I smooth my finger over the cloth, stiff with age.

"Thank you," I manage to get out. I search his eyes. "Would you mind leaving my husband and me alone for a few minutes?"

"O' course. Take your time."

Nodding, Mr. Knutson ambles off to the driveway and leaves Clive and me standing by the pond. I uncurl my arm from around Clive's, pluck my gloves off, and try to untie the string around the package.

Clive fishes in his jacket and pulls out his pocket-knife, flicking it open for me. "Here."

The blade gleams in the morning light.

"Thanks." I smile at him, my always helpful man. "This cord seems to be embedded in the cloth." I dig the knife under the string, and it breaks with little effort.

Clive pulls me down beside him on the bench. "Let's sit."

I unwrap the cloth and find an old tin of what appears to be cough drops and a letter whose return address bears the war office. The post-office-stamped date reads 1918. The name on the envelope is Aunt Susan's.

"Just what I needed; I woke up with a tickle in my throat this morning." Clive winks at me, ever the jokester.

I give him my usual eye roll.

I decide to open the letter first. *"We regret to inform you…"* I read through the note quickly. It must be the letter Aunt Susan received when she was notified of her husband's death. How final and heart-wrenching that must have been. I flip the letter over and recognize her handwriting. *"To the dawn of a new day. Rest in peace, my love."*

I hand the letter to Clive.

He seems puzzled. "Your Aunt Susan? Is this about her husband? What was his name?"

"Thomas," I answer. "It looks like it. I'll give it to Cassie."

I shrug and grab the tin firmly to open it. The lid sticks when I try, but it gives way with some effort. I pull the contents out one at a time: a small lock of hair, military tags, a heart-shaped locket on a chain, and a folded paper. I put each item in Clive's waiting palm.

"What's in the locket?" Clive asks.

I open the heart; my parents look back at me, happy and smiling and young. Next, I examine the tags strung on a ball chain, reading the inscription. They're Dad's dog tags. I run my finger over the impression of the letters and numbers, wishing Dad was still here, but he passed years ago—heart failure. He was only fifty. The paper I keep, unfold, and read.

I, Willis Holcomb, do solemnly swear to walk the best that I can into the future with my dear wife, Robin, and our little one, Enid. I put behind what I lost and look to what I have: a family who loves me and whom I love.

Here the writing changes, and I recognize Mom's slanted penmanship.

I, Robin Holcomb, do solemnly swear to leave the past sunk. Never again will I speak of what happened at the pond under the weeping willow. I've wept enough. Now I look ahead and desire to be the best wife and mother that I can be. May God help me never go back to that doomed thinking again. I want Enid to know I love her and will try my best to be the mother she deserves.

Their signed names end the page. I gulp and swallow my

tears. Mom tried. She tried! I just didn't see it or accept it. What a fool I've been all these years. I wish I could go back and do things over with her, but in life there are no do-overs. There's just now. Sniffing, I hand the crumbly paper to Clive. I watch him read it. He smiles sincerely at me over the top of the paper.

"It's just like I've always said—your Mom loved you. She just had an odd way of showing it sometimes." He chucks me affectionately under the chin and folds the paper back up, cocking his head sideways. "Granted, she wasn't perfect, but..." We say these words together. "She tried."

Clive gathers me in a hug, and I cry on his shoulder. There's been a lot of that lately, but sometimes that's what it takes to move on.

This must have been their way of letting go of the past and looking to the future. I need to do the same.

Clive and I give each other some space, and he tucks the package into the large pocket in his jacket. "Time to go?"

His kind brown eyes study my hazel ones. He's always so considerate when it really counts.

"Ya," I agree, and we walk hand in hand to the farmhouse where Mr. Knutson waits.

I want to thank him again for saving what he uncovered. He'll never know just what a precious treasure he found—my mother's love, buried in the weeping willow.

Weeks later

"You didn't come together?" I ask Kelly, and I move to look behind him, hoping Doris and the girls will appear, coming through the door.

"I said I'd come from work, Mom. Remember?"

Kelly sounds tired. He shrugs off his suit jacket, hangs it on a hook by the door, and rolls up the sleeves of his green-gray dress shirt.

"Oh, right."

I move back to my spot at the kitchen counter and work on chopping up vegetables for a green salad. Lately I can't remember details. The grief over Mom's passing hit harder than I thought it would.

I invited Kelly, Doris, and the twins over for supper. In retrospect, I wonder if that was wise. Sitting down to a family meal together may not be comfortable with the issues that have come between my son and his wife, and with the funeral, paperwork, bills, and taking care of loose ends, I haven't had the time to talk with Kelly about how things are going.

Regardless, I wanted us to be together without the weight of Mom's passing over us. The need to be with family presses on me. I don't want to waste any time being with those I love and making sure they know that I love them.

Kelly leans against the counter and rakes his fingers through his hair on the left side. "Smells good. What's for supper?"

He's let his hair grow in a feathered-back style that looks more like something a musician or movie star might wear. It looks good on him, though.

I smile up at him. "Spaghetti. I thought the twins would like that. And chocolate cake for dessert."

Kelly smiles back but appears to study me. "You doing okay, Mom?" He shrugs and settles his gaze on the sliced cucumbers on the cutting board. "I know Grandma's passing shook you up quite a bit."

His greenish eyes meet my gaze again.

"Ya." I nod. "I am. It was rough, though." I set the knife down and wipe my hands on a tea towel. "Your grandma and I were never very close, but I think I've mourned what could have been, if that makes sense. Most of that was my fault."

I roll in my lips, ashamed, again, to be admitting my faults to my son. I want him to think well of me, but what I want more is for us to be close. And that means no secrets from the past.

He speaks kindly. "I don't see it that way."

I jerk my head sideways. "Nevertheless, that's how it was."

"Why?"

His one-word question unsettles me; my gut drops with my bottom lip.

Should I tell him Mom's secrets? Will they make him think less of her?

I decide to leave my answer simple. "I didn't understand her."

"Sometimes that's just how it is with family." Kelly picks up a cucumber slice and pops the whole thing in his mouth.

"Maybe, but it's not how it has to be. We have to work at accepting, loving, and trying to understand each other." My voice strains and I grip his arm, so he knows I'm serious.

He wraps me in a steady hug. "Hey, you don't need to worry."

I peek around his shoulder and see two identical faces through the kitchen door's glass.

"I see the girls are here."

I back up; he lets me go. Phoebe and Pamela come in with big smiles on their faces, the largest I've seen in a while. Doris follows them, her demeanor reserved but open.

"What? No matching outfits today?" I ask my granddaughters.

"No." Pamela rolls her eyes, looking like me as she does. "We're sooo over that."

She flaps her hand in the air, another trait of mine.

"A jerk in school kept calling us the 'Bopsey Twins.'"

The girls exchange a look of revulsion, their upper lips curling back. My eyes roam over Pammie's pink leggings and sweatshirt and Phoebe's blue sweater and dark blue jeans.

"Well, you look beautiful as always." I kiss each girl on the cheek.

They move into the living room, calling for their "Pops." I gauge Doris's emotional temperature; her features are smooth and unperturbed, a good sign.

"Hi, Doris." I reach for her and give her a brief hug, thinking that perhaps I could work on being closer to my daughter-in-law.

Mom's death has made me reevaluate a number of things.

"Enie," she says, smiling, and she hugs me back.

"Ah." Kelly stands up straight and steps toward Doris. "While the girls are busy," he looks at his wife then at me, "I wanted to let you know, Mom, that we've decided to go to counseling." Kelly folds Doris's hand in his. "We've gone to several sessions already with a fellow who works at the church Doris and the girls go to."

Doris and Kelly exchange a warm look and smile; it does my heart good.

"I'm...I'm so glad," I stutter, sniffing.

"Thanks for pointing us in the right direction, Mom," Kelly tells me before he kisses Doris on the cheek with a *smack*.

She blushes, looking fetching, matching her pink lipstick and shirt.

Clive ambles into the kitchen and winks at me. "When is this meal gonna be ready? You've been tempting me for the last hour with all the good smells. A man can stand only so much."

I swipe away a tear of joy. "It's not all about your stomach, Mr. Fenton."

I wink back at Clive, and everyone laughs.

"I'll get this to the table." Kelly picks up the salad, adding the cucumbers on top.

"I'll take the bread." Doris plucks the breadbasket with sliced, toasted, and buttered garlic bread off the counter and follows Kelly.

"Ohhh, cake!" Phoebe and Pamela chime in together.

They giggle and move to the sideboard where I have the frosted cake on a stand. That leaves Clive and me.

"Can I carry the main course?" he asks, grinning like the sweet fool that he is.

"Help yourself," I tell him. "Just let me dump the spaghetti in first."

I drain the noodles and pour them in a large serving bowl, topping them off with a lake of red meat sauce. I push the dish Clive's way.

My husband wraps me in his arms. "First, a kiss."

I kiss him back, my fingers gripping the back of his polo shirt to anchor myself. My eyes close, and I swirl in an eddy of happiness edged by grief. How those feelings can go hand in hand with each other puzzles me, but that's life—one big puzzle with pieces that fit together in the strangest and most unexpected of ways.

Thank you, Lord, for being the one to snap the pieces together.

Clive and I break apart. He whistles as he carries the main dish to the dining table. I hold back and listen to the happy sounds of my family before I take my apron off and step into the next moment of life.

Deep places can bring you to a richer life.

EPILOGUE

Enid
Memorial Day 1985
Mom's gravesite sprouts new grass, looking like a Chia Pet: dense with new, bright green growth. Clive inserted a shepherd's hook in the ground near the headstone. A feminine, silk, flower wreath—delivered by a local florist—in tones of pink, red, and orange hangs from the hook. My special request, hollyhocks, cluster as the main focal point of the wreath around pink ribbon loops, whose tails flutter in the breeze.

I'm the only one here at the Red Cedar Cemetery, odd for Memorial Day, but then it is late in the day. I check my watch, 6:30pm. I glance at Clive waiting in the Dodge for me. His head lolls against the headrest. He's probably sleeping, waiting patiently for me. I wanted to be alone for these last few minutes.

Evening sun slants through the arborvitae and cedar trees to the west. A citrus, woodsy smell hovers in the air. One half of Mom's headstone is in the shadow, the other in the light—kind of like I imagine her to be. Her body rests in this quiet, peaceful place, but her spirit resides elsewhere.

I pull the oldest journal I have of Mom's from my purse. The year 1919 is embossed on the front in what I imagine was once gold foil relief, but it has since worn off. I flip open to the entry I marked earlier in the day. I read silently to get to the section that caught my eye.

319

June 1919
Dear Diary,

Molly has come to stay! How ecstatic I am to have both my sister and dearest friend together. Molly doesn't readily trust many people, but she and Mabel have formed an attachment. They've written to each other since meeting at the asylum. Mabel has been staying with us since last fall and attending UW Stout. There she met a nice young man from Minnesota. I can hear wedding bells in the air, if my suspicions are correct. All Mabel can talk about is Lincoln.

My heart warms when I think of Molly. She helped me more than she could ever know with the simple ways she taught me of life and growing things. Red hollyhocks will forever be my favorite flower because of her. They remind me that deep places can bring you to a richer life, one filled with the wealth not of man but of God—wisdom.

I must go. I hear Susan coming back with her car.

I asked her to go pick up Molly. I feel life may be leading Molly onto a different path. She doesn't seem as settled as usual in her job at the asylum. I see a longing in her eyes when she sees Willis, Enid, and me together. She's been through so much pain. She deserves some happiness.

I hear Susan calling my name…

My eyes rest on Mom's words in the middle of the entry, and I read them aloud. "Red hollyhocks will forever be my favorite flower. They remind me that deep places can bring you to a richer life, one filled with the wealth not of man but of God—wisdom."

I look up at the sky, blooming pink. "Sorry I didn't recognize or treasure the true wealth you had, Mom. I'm sorry for it all."

The breeze picks up, and the ribbons flap against the wreath. A red, silk hollyhock loosens and falls to the green carpet of Mom's grave, like a sign, an answer. I can imagine Mom telling me, "I forgive you." I breathe a sigh of relief.

I wipe away a tear, close the diary, and walk slowly back to the Dodge, a strange spring in my step.

I suddenly think about Molly's story. What happened to her? Did she find happiness? I'd like to know. I'll have to do some research. Maybe I can find out. There must be someone who remembers her.

Molly.

I roll her name around in my mind, imagining what could have brought her to the asylum and on a similar path to Mom.

The End

Acknowledgments

I am grateful for the many eyes that saw and read this work before it found its way to you. My early readers and those in my Facebook group, Journeying with Jenny, have given me much support, advice, and encouragement along the way.

My family is supportive, as always, in my endeavors in authorship, and I would not be on this path of authorship without the continual strength I receive from above.

I am thankful for the help of professionals: Sara Litchfield, my editor; Jenny Q. at Historical Fiction Book Covers, my book cover designer; photographer Craig Jentink at Creative Visions Photographics, for the beautiful book cover image; and Jason, my formatter at Polgarus Studio. You have all helped this book become a work of art. I am very grateful for each of you.

Special thanks to Herb Maves for the loan of his copy of *The History of Dunn County*, Karis Jentink for being the lovely model for the book cover, and to Craig and Kristin Johnson for allowing us to use the backdrop of their willow trees and pond for the photoshoot.

Thank you, Dear Reader, for choosing to spend your valuable time reading my words. I would deem it an honor if you could take a few minutes and leave a review for *Under the*

Weeping Willow. Your kindness would be much appreciated.

Finally, I thank God for giving me the inspiration and strength to keep writing.

Many blessings,
Jenny

Author's Notes

I set *Under the Weeping Willow* in the familiar county of Wisconsin. All the characters are fictitious, but much of the description of place and setting is as accurate as I could make it.

There was an insane asylum in Menomonie, Wisconsin, by the same name and located in the place I describe, which years later became the location of the Dunn County Nursing Home. Robin's treatments while at the asylum are accurate to the time but likely may have been harsher. The asylum did have a farm and those that were able worked on the farm until labor laws changed. Some of the old buildings can still be seen on the site today.

I understand all too well the depths depression can take one to. Although I have never experienced "the baby blues" to the extent Robin did, I know it is a real concern for some mothers. I read first-hand accounts of women who went through this kind of depression, and I felt I could believably recreate their experiences through Robin.

Depression is a serious illness and should never be taken lightly. If you or someone you know may be suffering from it, please reach out, tell someone, or call a local hotline, or the National Suicide Prevention Hotline at **1-800-273-TALK**.

My father passed away from Alzheimer's in 2010. He

suffered for many years with the disease. I patterned some of Robin's experiences with Alzheimer's as an older woman after his. I read numerous books outlining the stages of the disease and abilities of people at each of those stages. Most cases of Alzheimer's last many years, but I accelerated Robin's experience to fit the timeframe of the story.

As an adult, I have wondered what a tension-filled mother/daughter relationship would be like. I have friends and acquaintances who are or were in such circumstances, but I did not experience a poor relationship with my mother. We were always very close. Sadly, I didn't have as much time with her as I would have liked. She died of myelodysplastic leukemia when I was twenty-seven. I used a major part of my imagination considering what division lay between Robin and Enid. All the psychology classes I had in college helped too.

Although there are other characters and subplots in the story, the crux of the plot revolves around Robin and Enid's relationship and if they can find true forgiveness and understanding for one another before it's too late.

I hope you enjoyed this multi-layered family drama and came away from it with a determination to seek out understanding and forgiveness in whatever relationships might be strained in your life.

Blessings,
Jenny

For further reading

Living with Grief: Alzheimer's Disease
Hospice Foundation of America 2004

A Pocket Guide to Understanding Alzheimer's Disease and Other Dementias
Dr. James Warner and Dr. Nori Graham
Jessica Kingsley Publications 2009, 2018

Alzheimer's Disease: The Complete Introduction
Dr. Judes Poirier, Dr. Serge Gauthier
Dundurn, Toronto 2011

Beyond the Blues: A Guide to Understanding and treating Prenatal and Postpartum Depression
Shoshana S. Bennett, Ph.D.
Pec Indman, Ed.D., MFT
Moodswing Press 2003

About Jenny

Jenny lives in Wisconsin with her husband, Ken, and their pet Yorkie, Ruby. She is also a mom and loves being a grandma. She enjoys many creative pursuits but finds writing the most fulfilling.

Spending many years as a librarian in a local public library, Jenny recently switched to using her skills as a floral designer in a retail flower shop. She is now retired from work due to disability. Her education background stems from psychology, music, and cultural missions.

All of Jenny's books have earned five-star reviews from Readers' Favorite, a book review and award contest company. She holds membership in the: Midwest Independent Booksellers Association, Wisconsin Writers Association, Christian Indie Publishing Association, and Independent Book Publishers Association.

Jenny's favorite place to relax is by the western shore of Lake Superior, where her novel series *By The Light of the Moon* is set.

Her new, historical-fiction, four-part series entitled *Sheltering Trees* is set in the area Jenny grew up in, where she currently lives, and places along Minnesota's Northern Shore, where she loves to visit.

She deems a cup of tea and a good book an essential part of every day. When not writing, Jenny can be found reading, tending to her many houseplants, or piecing quilt blocks at her sewing machine.

Keep current with Jenny by visiting her website at www.jennyknipfer.com. Ways to connect with Jenny via social media, newsletter, and various book sites can be found on her website.

Coming next in the *Sheltering Trees* series:

On Bur Oak Ridge

EXCERPT:

Molly
September 1919

We're better at looking back than forward. Since such is the case, our eyes would be better placed at the back of our head. I see nothing when I gaze into the future. It appears like the purple haze of the distant hills—without definition, lacking firm, clean, and distinctive lines. In a word—smudged.

The ironic truth is that "smudged" could explain my appearance. Life has taken an eraser to the right side of my face. Melted, waxy patches of pink skin shine in the lamplight from my temple to my neck. The skin around my right eye hides the small world of greenish-blue color—the window to my soul.

I know what people see through this broken window—a monster.

I tilt my head and run the tips of my fingers over the corded texture of my skin. From this viewpoint, I could play the part of Dr. Frankenstein's creation. My fingers explore lower until they reach the hollow of my neck, where the music once lived. But no longer. The notes have died. I sigh, reliving a memory of grief for what I've lost.

My hand falls. With the stare of the dead, I look back at myself in the cracked bureau mirror. A crack in the glass runs diagonal across my face from temple to jaw, bringing a visual division to my deformity. I puff out air from my nostrils with a resignation I am getting used to. Bit by bit I've buried who I used to be. That grave leaves me uncertain of who I will become.

What is left for me? Next to nothing. I have the flowers and little else.

You've made friends, my conscience tells me. Yes, I have. I should be grateful instead of mourning the past.

For the first time in years, I will leave behind the walls of my strange shelter: the asylum. Tomorrow I board a train to visit Mabel, my friend. I'll wear a mourning veil in public, so people won't gawk or reel back in revulsion at the naked sight of my face. I grieve the worst when the children cry, when I become a nightmare to some poor little soul. I hate that: adding to another's fear. We all bear enough.

My lungs command a deep breath, and I reach to turn down the lamp. The future comes tomorrow whether I am ready or not.

"Ready or not!" The words stab me in the throat, and I feel as if I'm being basted with a sharp needle. Those were Lonny's last words. My eyes roll shut, and I see the flash of white, the brown, curly head, the grin before he turned, the crash of the poles, like the blast of a mighty horn. I wanted to scream, but my voice caught in my throat, choking me. My mouth hung open, but all that came out was silence.

I breathe in and out slowly, like the doctor taught me. The visions recede.

My eyes open. The room has been thrown under a dark caul, and I realize I must have turned down the wick of the kerosene lamp. Now my face looks ghostly in the slightly spotted, silver-backed glass. I move to the bed, jump in, and tuck the covers up to my chin, praying I won't dream of Lonny.

Please, God. Not tonight.

CPSIA information can be obtained
at www.ICGtesting.com
Printed in the USA
BVHW070853160122
625954BV00004B/11